From Horseshoe to Gumshoe
The D. B. Murphy Omnibus

Richard J. Thomas

The Ginger Press

Cover photo by J. James and Daryl Phillips
Cover design by Daryl Phillips

The cover photo on Gas Head Willy, circa 1921, comes from the Grey/Bruce Image Archives (photographer John James). The cover photo on The Lost Tire Gang, circa 1922, comes from the collection of the Bruce County Museum. The Pacific Hotel in Wiarton looks much the same today, though it now serves roast spring raccoon with spiced crabapple only rarely. The cover photos for The Thimblerig, circa 1923, were provided by Dorothy Bauman of Owen Sound. Both photos show members of the Davis Smith-Malone ice-cutting crew off Squaw Point. The D.B. Murphy Omnibus cover photo, Owen Sound at night circa 1924, comes from the Grey-Bruce Image Archives (photographer John James). The mysterious man and guns are courtesy of designer Daryl Phillips. All photographs are used with permission.

National Library of Canada Cataloguing in Publication Data

Thomas, Richard J., 1959-
From horseshoe to gumshoe: the D.B. Murphy omnibus

ISBN 0-921773-58-7
I. Title

PS8589.H4633F75 2001 C813'.54 C2001-901479-1
PS9199.3.T457F75 2001

Published by
The Ginger Press, Inc
848 Second Avenue East
Owen Sound, Ontario
Canada N4K 2H3
www.gingerpress.com

Printed in Canada

PREFACE

It's hard to believe five years have passed since the publication of *Gas Head Willy*. A lot has happened in that time. Morag and I now have three beautiful children, Finn, Niamh and Renny. In 1998 I lost my mother. In 1999 I turned forty and lost my job on the same day. Hard to believe people ask me where I get my inspiration. It's all around me. It's what happens every day. During the same time period, the D.B. Murphy story has grown to three novels, with a fourth in the works. I often tell people I like his world better than mine, because in it I control everything that happens.

If you've never read any of my previous efforts at "front matter" (that's what this blurb is called in the biz) then there are a few things I should tell you about D.B. Murphy and his cronies.

Each of the novels was first written as a part of the Novel Marathon for Literacy, a fundraiser for the Adult Learning Centre of the Owen Sound and North Grey Union Public Library. Held during a long summer weekend, the event pits the author against the blank page; working from just a one-page outline, a complete novel must be written in seventy-two hours. Pledges are involved: this is, after all, a fundraiser, not a weekend in the country. Prior to writing *Gas Head Willy* (1996) I came up with the idea of selling characters so I could raise lots of money and have fewer pledges to collect. Three brave souls agreed to my rules: I would use their names and some characteristics, but beyond that they would have no say in what I did with them. Thank you Bill Van Wyck (Van), Marc Scott (Oddball) and Scott Vining (Scotty) for supporting literacy and thank you for supporting me.

When it came time to write *The Lost Tire Gang* (1997) Van, Oddball and Scotty all signed on for another adventure. Further support came from Catherine Caple, who bought the character Kate McDermid for her grandmother. By the time I started working on *The Thimblerig* (1999) the word had gotten around. The original three were joined by Everett Hall, Ken Carr, Nadine Carr, Rose

Morley (Eng), Catherine Budgeon (Ballantyne), Judy Armstrong, Valerie Sutherland and Drew Ferguson (as Lucky the dog).

There are lots of other sponsors who have contributed to the success of these books and I thank you all. As well, there are the readers. These are the brave souls who read the books prior to publication. They tear them apart and, after I've finished crying, I rewrite based on some of their comments and suggestions. Thanks over the series to Andrew Armitage, Brian Barrie, Catherine Budgeon, Melba Croft, Des Donavan, Phil Gandon, John Harrison, Tim Nicholls Harrison, Mike Holden, Cathy Huntley, Mike Kirkland, Kerry Kitchenham, Gayle Maclaughlin, Tom McKay, Brad Morley, Rose Morley, Terri Munn, Gordon Peters, Karen Petley, Norah Phillips, Harold Silk, Donna Stewart, Mariella Vigneux, Mark Vigneux, Elizabeth Warren and Gary Williams. Each of these people has contributed time and energy to make these books what they are.

I have had many teachers over the years. In addition to being my grade 12 English teacher, Charlie Minns was one of the first people to give me the sense that I could do something; Bill Goldfinch taught me Shakespeare and a love of literature in college; Martin Avery showed me how to write; Mary Lynn Williamson (Susanna Kearsley) taught me organisation; and Dan Needles taught me there is always a place for humour. I thank you all for helping me achieve my dreams.

Finally, thanks to my publisher Maryann Thomas (no relation) of The Ginger Press. Without her support there wouldn't be a D.B. Murphy.

HORSESHOE to GUMSHOE

Richard J. Thomas

Chapter One
The Wake of the Noronic

It was him alright. Floating on his back. Doughy, bloated face, unseeing eyes. Bobbing in the current like one of the trout the Sydenham routinely disgorged at spawning time.

An early evening crowd had gathered on the westside dock, just up from 10th Street. The smell of diesel and rotting fish hung in the humid June air, clinging like a second skin. The water beat rhythmically against the dock, lulling the mob into complacent voyeurism, the murmur of their voices like the buzzing of cicadas. Beefy uniforms blocked the view.

I used my size to push through towards a copper I knew. O'Malley. Ruddy complexion. Nose like a new potato. Almost a dozen kids to his credit. On a police salary. I wondered how he managed it. His face split into a grin. Square yellow teeth greeted me.

"Hey, Murph."

"Sean."

"What brings you here?"

"That stiff," I gestured.

A quizzical look crossed the big cop's face. "He yours?"

"Yeah. Who found him?"

"It's my beat." O'Malley moved aside. As I passed, he leaned close. "The Chief's right down front there." A hand the size of a tennis racket grabbed my arm. "For god's sake don't get into it with him tonight."

"Sure." I shook him off. "Like he'll return the favour and leave me alone?"

O'Malley rolled his eyes, doing his best to look the martyr. I started down the creaking wooden gangplank to the floating dock. The cops were thick as flies on a three-day carcass.

"Well, well," came a voice from the cluster of uniforms. "If it ain't little Danny-Boy Murphy."

Anger rose in my gut thick and fast. The chief had that effect on me. Jaw tight, voice emotionless, I answered, "Hello Johnny."

Smaller by a head, he blocked my way. The sharp odour of sweat stung my nose, with the smell of cheap booze and his dinner a one-two follow-up.

"Still eating herring?" I asked.

He drew a breath in sharp. Instead of yelling, his voice got silky and dangerous. "What do ya want, Danny-Boy?" My fists were still clenched. I didn't move. "Come to pick up the floater?" he gestured with his head.

"Yes."

"Still doing your brother's dirty work, eh?"

"Least I've got an honest job. Chief." I made the last word sound like a curse.

"Now look you..." He grabbed the front of my suit jacket. "I oughta..."

"What?" I stared him down.

"Get lost." He pushed me in the direction of the gangplank.

"I'd like to have a look."

"Forget it."

In 1921, Owen Sound was a city on the edge. The mid-point of east-west shipping and rail traffic on the Great Lakes, some said it had been the busiest port in the country before the war. Now there was unemployment, too much of it. Veterans were on the streets, in a city that didn't seem to want them anymore.

For me, it wasn't the war that had changed things. It was the automobile. A blacksmith by trade, I'd returned in 1919 to find fewer horses and more cars. Downtown streets were being paved and watering troughs were gone, except the ones at the Farmers' Market and the Pottawatomi bridge. The horse was dead. And I was out of a job.

Still, Owen Sound seemed prosperous. The new street lights downtown made it seem like a real city. Boardwalks were slowly being replaced with granite stone. There was going to be a new City Hall clock tower. And more and more homes were getting electricity.

I hung around for almost a year after the war. There were some jobs on township farms. Too many men had come back damaged. Or not come back at all. But I didn't know a thing about farming. So when my brother Kevin offered me work in town, I said I'd try.

He and his partner, Horace P. Wallinger, had started Sound Mutual Insurance. Insurance had been expensive in Owen Sound, provided by big out-of-town companies represented by local agents. Kevin and Horace were the first local insurers; their rates were lower and they did very well. But prosperity had its price. There had been threats. My job was to find out who and why.

The job had been complicated by the arrival of the *Noronic* and five hundred passengers from Detroit. The city declared "Detroit Day," and threw a big dance on the main street. In all the excitement Horace had disappeared.

Now the party was over. The *Noronic* was gone. And Horace was dead.

"It was him alright." My brother fell back into his chair.

"Horace? Dead? Are you sure?"

"Positive. He was in the harbour. By the railroad bridge."

"Oh no." Kevin covered his face with his hands. We were in the library of the big house he had bought on 2nd Avenue West. He sat behind his desk, work spread out in front of him.

I stood and looked down at him. "Want me to keep working?"

Kevin dropped his hands. His eyes, rimmed with red, made his handsome face look sallow. "What happened?"

"Don't know."

The jangle of a telephone bell broke the silence. Kevin left me alone while he went into the hall to answer it. He was back inside a minute. "That was Johnny Baker," he said.

"I'm impressed. I didn't know our police chief had the skills necessary to use a phone."

Kevin glared at me. I smiled thinly.

"I don't know why the two of you don't drop it, D.B. It's been too many years."

"What'd he want?"

"He said there was a woman. Seen leaving the scene."

"Well, there's a place to start."

Next morning after breakfast at The City Cafe, I went around to Oak Hall Men's and Boys' Wear. Manager William "Billy" Johnson and I had known each other just about as long as two people could. I bought most of my clothes there. At a discount since the war.

"Morning, Sil." His name had been shortened from Silly. I'd called him that since we were ten, when he boasted he could walk the length of the rail on the 10th Street bridge. The fire brigade had pulled him out of the river.

"Hello, Murph," Sil called from deep inside a rack of fifteen dollar suits. "How's the game?"

"I'm sure you know," I replied. Next to Razor Eddie, Sil knew everything that went on in town.

"Fifteen dollars for these rags? I could go over to Graftons and get a real suit for $13.95."

His head popped out of the rack. "You wouldn't!"

"Of course not," I laughed. After a second he joined in. I took my hat off and leaned against a rack of boys' pants.

Sil resumed pricing the suits, his narrow fingers deftly removing one set of tags, re-applying another. Tall and skinny, gangling almost, his bad eyesight had kept him out of the war.

"How's Kevin?"

"About like you'd expect. Know much?"

"Knickers are out this year."

"Hardy, har har." Sil loved a joke. And he expected a response, no matter how corny.

"C'mon back," he said. A good sign. We only went to the back room when he knew something.

"Y'know Horace was in the company of a woman?"

"I heard. So?"

"Wasn't Mrs. Horace."

Now I already knew that. But Sil was going somewhere. He just liked to make a game of it.

"Really. Not Mrs. Horace?" I said. "I'll be."

"Alright, alright," Sil leaned closer. "Did you know he was found with a flask of whisky in his pocket?"

"Prescription?"

"Bootleg."

Now that was interesting. Owen Sound was a temperance town. Dry. Sort of. But people like Horace didn't need the bootleggers. Doctors were happy to write prescriptions for the drinks they needed.

"Thanks, Sil."

"S'okay Murph. Comin' to dinner tonight? Marth and the kids'd love to see ya."

"Sure. Okay."

★★★

I went out through the shipping door, and walked up 1st Avenue towards the harbour. I stopped at 10th Street to let some cars pass. They made a great clatter as they went over the railroad tracks. Cars were noisy and left a trail of blue stink everywhere. Couple thousand of them in town, I'd heard. Couldn't see the need myself. You could walk everywhere. And there was still the train, if you had to leave Owen Sound.

A big Chevrolet passed and then the way was clear. I stayed on 1st as I walked up the east side of the harbour. The cool edge of early morning was gone and the heat of what would be a stifling day was coming on. The harbour was still a busy place. I could see dozens of ships, smallest at the railroad bridge, biggest out towards the railroad stations and grain elevators.

Crews were working on a new harbour wall. I talked to a few of the men but the noise of the big pile drivers made it nearly impossible to hear their responses. No one had known Wallinger. A couple didn't even know a body had been found. I took my jacket off along the way, but was still in a sweat by the time I got to the Gas Works. Standing on the road for a moment, I looked across at the train station. It seemed deserted. So I cut around the Gas Works and back down to 2nd, then back to The City for lunch.

"Eddie wants to see ya." A skinny ragged boy I recognized as Razor Eddie's stood in front of me. Out of breath. My pie and ice cream had just arrived.

"Sit down," I said, signalling the waitress for another order. The kid was shaking badly. I thought maybe he was sick, but then decided it was more likely hunger. The waitress came back and I said, "Dig in."

The kid didn't need to say a word. The look of gratitude on his face said it all. He took his time, savouring every bite. When we both finished, I pushed my plate away.

"Did he say it was important?"

"Yessir, and I'm s'posed to fetch ya back right quick." His eyes went wide and all the colour left his face. "Omigosh! I'm gonna get it fer takin' so long."

He jumped up and would have run if I hadn't grabbed his arm. "What's your name, son?"

"Peter. Peter McFee."

"Well Peter, hold on. I have to pay my bill. Then you just come back with me. I'll smooth it with Eddie. Don't worry."

Peter smiled brightly. It seemed out of place on his grimy face. "Gee, thanks Mr. Murphy."

"Call me Murph," I said, tossing two bits on the table. "Everybody does."

CHAPTER TWO
THE SECOND STOREY

Razor Eddie was at The Manjuris, on the main street next to the ladies wear store. Billiards. Tobacco. A drink, if you were connected. A couple of pool tables slouched against one wall. On the other side, a bar sold cigars, cigarettes and chew. The room was dim, lit only by sunlight slanting through the front window. A pall of smoke hung low, giving an August afternoon haze to the place.

Eddie was playing a game of stick, his muscular body thrust low across the table. A deep scar slashed across his face, starting where the left ear should have been and ending at his mouth. It glowed an angry purple as he strained to make a shot.

"Hello Eddie." He didn't even look up. Just reached back to aim a cuff at Peter, the kid who had come to fetch me.

"Lay off." I stepped between them.

That bought me a look that would have scared anyone else. But I'd known the Razor too long. He'd been with Sil and me that day on the 10th Street bridge. He was just Eddie then.

"In the back," he muttered at the kid, through lips pursed over a full mouth. Turning, Eddie spat into the nearest juice bucket. Wiping his chin, he gave a wry smile.

"Drink?"

"Why not?" I responded. It was past noon.

We crossed to the bar where Eddie gave a burly redhead a nod. A bottle and two glasses appeared.

"Smoke?"

"No."

"Chaw?" Shrugging, he poured two fingers into each glass.

"Yours?" I asked, lifting my glass. He nodded, then lifted his glass.

"To the Reverend Orr."

"And temperance," I added. The bootleg burned like hell on the way down.

"What was in Horace's pocket?"

Eddie poured again. "Horace had a problem."

"He's got none now."

"Nothing to do with me."

"Oh?"

"Look, Murph. I don't know nothin' about it. Your dead man. He come to me the other night, lookin' for booze."

"Like for a celebration?"

"Don't know." Eddie was lying. I decided not to push it.

"What've you heard?" I asked.

"I hear it was his insurance racket."

"There were some threats."

"Heard that too."

"Know why?"

"Yeah."

"Well?"

"You know that your brother and Horace were undercutting all the other insurance company agents with their fancy big-city companies?"

"That's just business. Not worth a killing."

"Lots of money, I hear."

"Thanks, Eddie." As I turned to leave, he grabbed my arm.

"Watch out for the second storey," Eddie whispered in my ear. He walked away before I could ask him why.

In 1921, there were 23 insurance agents in Owen Sound, representing a total of 56 companies. Two agencies carried most of the business. Jonas Taker & Son was the biggest. Their office was closed when I got there, but the home address was only five blocks away on 10th West, so I started walking.

It was strange. The city had recently replaced the old boardwalk with granite stone. Footsteps now sounded flat and dead. The stone slabs reminded me of headstones, lined up end-to-end.

The Taker place was big and surrounded by an ornate fence. The gate screeched. Like someone wanted to know when visitors dropped by. I'd barely got it shut before the front door opened. A pale youth came out. The closer I got, the older he got. Climbing the front steps I saw he wasn't a youth at all. He was just pale. White hair. Pinkish eyes, hard to make out in the dim porch. His hands were opaque, the blue web of veins clearly visible.

"Can I help you?" His lisp made him sound young.

"Looking for Jonas Taker."

"Not here." His tone was dismissive and he headed back inside.

"And Son."

"I'm a son," he said. "But not the one you're looking for. Who are you?"

"Sound Mutual," I responded, invoking the name of my brother's insurance company.

A clever look crossed his face. "Oh, that," he muttered.

"Anything to say?"

"They're at the Sons."

The Sons of the New Optimism. One of a spate of clubs formed in the lee of the war. Horace had been a member. Quiet. Secret. Not much was said about it. That alone made it worth checking out.

The gate creaked behind me and something like dismay crossed young Taker's face. I turned to look. An old woman in a faded print dress tottered up the walk on square-toed black shoes, too high for her age. She didn't see me until she was nearly wearing my suit. Her specs glared.

"Where's my money?"

"Ma'am?"

"Right up the steps here, Mrs Johannsen." His tone was considerably sweeter.

She looked past me, then back again. Confused. "Aren't you one of them?" Before I could get a word out, Taker was at her elbow leading her up the walk. He glanced over his shoulder once and I gave him a look. There was something about his face I didn't like.

It was just two blocks from Taker's to the home of the second busiest insurance agent in town. I decided to walk over. I'd never met Dori Storey, but I'd heard talk. She'd taken over the agency when her brother went to war. He hadn't come back. She stayed on. Ambitious. Smart. Fast looking.

4th Avenue West was still dirt and smelled like horses. It was nostalgic for me. There had been a blacksmith in my family for six generations. That was over now. Maybe it was time for my brother Kevin to breed a new line of insurance Murphys.

I stopped in front of the house. Twelve-oh-eight. It was a well-kept place. Brick, three floors. I started up the walk and could hear piano music. On the stoop I listened for a second and decided it had to be a student playing.

It was not Dori Storey who answered the door. This one was in her early twenties. Wholesome brunette, glasses, a bright smile. I liked her immediately.

"Yes?"

I fell in love with her voice right then.

"Is Miss Storey here?"

"I'm her," she said, then, noting my puzzled look, "one of them anyway."

"I'm looking for Dori Storey."

"Well, I'm not her. I'm Lori." She offered her hand. Lori Storey. I took it.

"Murphy. D.B."

"Hello," she said, taking her hand back too soon.

"Dori and Lori?"

"And our sister Glori."

"Dori, Lori and Glori?"

"You even got the order right."

"Importance or age?"

"Age of course. My father had a sense of humour." She smiled like she knew me. "What does D.B. mean?" I found myself smiling, a rare occurrence when my name was in question. "Well?"

"Danny-Boy. My father loved the song."

"We've only just met and already we have something in common."

"What's that?"

"Parents with a sense of humour."

★★★

Inside there was a child of about ten at the piano. "Keep playing your scales, Eustace," Lori said. "I'm listening." She led me into the parlour.

"Dori never gets home before six, sometimes later, Mr Murphy." Lori perched herself on the edge of a velvet chair. I sat on a lumpy sofa.

"Why so late?"

"She says she works."

"Her office was closed."

"Really." Lori was unsurprised.

"Where is she?"

"Could be a man." Lori smiled. I liked her for that. She had quite a smile.

"You here every night at this time?"

"I teach piano."

"And the rest of the time?"

"Oh, I have nowhere special to go."

"So I could stop back," I asked, "if I have more questions?"

"Yes," she said, smiling that smile.

The Sons of the New Optimism was hard to find in the early dusk of the alley that ran between 2nd and 3rd East in the downtown. A man appeared at the narrow recessed door in answer to my knock. "What?" he spat.

"Taker."

"Who's calling?"

"Sound Mutual."

"Wait," the gorilla said, shutting the door in my face.

Two minutes later he was back. "C'mon," he grunted, gesturing for me to follow, "and shut that door behind you."

We climbed a narrow flight of stairs, dimly lit. At the top, a hallway stretched in both directions, with a line of closed doors to the right and an open lounge to the left. We headed for the lounge. I wondered about all those closed doors.

There were easy chairs and deep couches. On the far wall, an ornate bar was decorated with a fancy barman. Somewhere a phonograph was playing *A Pretty Girl Is Like A Melody*. On the floor, the buckets were spit polished.

I knew the first person I saw. The Razor was hunched in a chair, pretending not to see me. The goon led me across the room in the opposite direction to a group of three men who were smoking cigars. The table in front of them was littered with empty glasses.

I looked them over while they looked me over. Finally one of them stood and introduced himself as Jonas Taker. Junior. He looked a lot like his pale brother. Only not so pale. He had no lisp and when he spoke it was with open hostility.

"What the hell do you want?"

"I want to know who killed Horace Wallinger."

"Why ask me?"

"Insurance got him killed. That's why."

"You've made a mistake. I know nothing."

He sat and I felt a large hand grab my arm. The goon had been joined by what looked to be his thug brother. Each grabbed an arm. They walked me from the room and down the hallway of closed doors. From several there came the unmistakable sounds of lust.

At the end of the hall we went through a different door and down another flight of stairs. At the bottom we stopped. The first goon turned to me. "You got insurance, ain't you?"

I kept my mouth shut and tensed. A fist like a pile driver pounded into my gut. As I doubled over, I felt a steel forearm slam down on my neck. The world exploded into stars.

I was dealt more punches and kicks than I gave. After awhile they shoved me out the door, laughing.

"You ever come back," the goon yelled, "you should have a better policy."

The door slammed and I was alone, face down in the alley.

CHAPTER THREE
THE MYSTERY WOMAN

"Murphy! Hey Murph?" I felt someone tugging at my sleeve. I hurt. But I could have ended up dead like Horace. I rolled onto my back. Razor Eddie's boy stood over me, hand outstretched. I took it and got to my feet.

"Thanks."

"I was waitin' for Eddie and I seen them two push you out the door of the Sons."

"Next time I won't be so nice," I said, rubbing the back of my neck. It still throbbed where the forearm had landed.

"Yeah well, you better get outta here before they come back for more."

"You're probably right. What's Eddie got to do with this place?" The kid glanced quickly up and down the alley, grabbed my arm and led me to an empty doorway.

"He gives 'em bootleg. Free."

"Just a little late for din..." The gibe died on Sil's lips when light spilled from the foyer onto my battered face. "Holy cow, Murph." He pulled me into the safety of the house. "What happened?"

"Danced with a couple of boys down at the Sons," I said, letting him help me with my coat. The warm smell of cooking was in the house and from the upstairs came the sound of the boys tumbling around. I envied Sil. Thought briefly of a bright smile.

"Learn anything?"

"Sure," I said. "Never go to the Sons without an invite."

"They could have just told you."

"It's more than that."

"You need some painkiller?"

"You keep some around?"

"Just for emergencies. Is this one?"

"Of the worst sort," I said dryly, following him into his study.

"When you didn't come back we went ahead. With dinner, that is. The kids, y'know. But there's a plate on the stove for you."

I sat on the sofa. He poured two fingers of whisky into a tumbler and handed it over.

"You can eat later. First we've got to get you cleaned up."

In the few minutes it took to drink the whisky, he was back. A basin of warm water, bandages and a change of clothing from my upstairs room were in his arms.

"Thanks, Sil." He and Marth had taken me in when I came back from the war disoriented and broke. I owed them for that.

I was cleaned up by the time Sil came in and poured two more whiskies.

"Anything good today?"

"Razor Eddie says insurance killed Horace."

"Be careful," he said, turning and walking off to Oak Hall.

★★★

There was a beautiful cruelty about Dori Storey. Closer to six than five feet, dark ringlets framed her face. Ice blue eyes were offset by full, re-painted lips. The sharp lines of her hose threatened the severe business suit she wore.

"Yes?" she answered my knock at once.

"Hello Dori," I said, strolling past her into the office.

"Do I know you?" she followed, confident.

"I know you."

"Do you?" Her eyes narrowed.

"Sure. Why don't you tell me about Horace?"

She paled.

"What about Horace?"

"You know. The night he died. What were you doing there?"

"You're Murphy. Lori told me you were at the house. I'd kindly thank you not to do that again."

"Might have some more questions for your sister."

"My business is my business. I take care of it here. Understand?"

"I didn't say they were questions about you." How could the two of them be so different? I answered my own question by thinking of my brother, Kevin. "Anyhow, what were you doing down there?"

"I wasn't there and I'll thank you to leave this office before I call the police."

★★★

I waited across the street and up aways, under the canopy at Woolworths. It didn't take long. Dori dashed out the door and up the street towards me. I ducked inside the store for a second, then crossed and followed her when she went by.

I followed her all the way up the main street. I didn't know where she was going, but she was far enough away to give me time. I turned and quickly went back to her office. Time to check the web while the spider was away. My pocketknife made short work of the doorlatch. I closed it quietly behind me. There would only be a few minutes. I wasn't even sure what I was looking for until I found it. In the bottom drawer at the back. A note: *I've found out what's going on. Meet me at the harbour 10 pm. -H*

"I'll take that," Dori said from the doorway, her gun pointed at me.

"That big gun makes your hands look little."

"Never send a boy to do a man's job." Closing the door, she started across the room.

Dori stopped in front of the desk. I passed the note with my left hand, forcing her to use her left. Across her gun arm. I grabbed the advancing hand and forced it and her gun hand down towards the floor.

"There," I said, the gun in my hand. "This makes a better accessory to my outfit, don't you think? Sit down." She ground her teeth together and for a second I thought she might cry.

"Assault with a weapon, that's a pretty serious charge."

"You broke in."

"Yup. I thought you had something to hide. Looks like I was right."

"What do you want?"

"I want to know who killed Horace."

"You think I know that?" She flushed, her voice rising.

"I just assumed you did. You were at the dock that night." This time her lower lip trembled.

"What do you want to know?"

"Tell me everything."

"There's nothing to tell. I got the note. I went to meet Horace. He didn't show."

"If that's all, why the gun just now?"

"I saw his body."

"What?"

"On the way back in from the I dock. I saw him. In the water. I got scared."

CHAPTER FOUR
A SHOT IN THE DARK

Eddie wasn't at The Manjuris. Neither was his boy. I left word that I was looking for him. It was near eleven, so I decided to go over to The City for lunch.

Sean O'Malley was there, the top few buttons of his blue uniform undone. In front of him sat a huge plate of food.

"Sean." I nodded a greeting. "Mind if I sit?"

"Murph! Sure, sure." He gestured with a beefy paw.

I ordered coffee and a hot hamburg sandwich, then asked how things were going. Sean looked up from his plate. "They're sayin' maybe Horace just got himself drunk and fell into the harbour."

"What? They who?"

"The Chief."

That explained a lot. I'd been wondering why I hadn't run across many uniforms in my investigation of Horace's death.

"What's his game?"

"Don't know." O'Malley shoved a huge forkful into his mouth, then talked around it. "He just called us off."

"Strange," I said, "because Dori Storey says Horace was murdered."

"Oh?"

"What do you know about the Sons of the New Optimism?" I asked.

Sean suddenly became really interested in something on his plate. "Nuthin'," he mumbled.

"Jonas Taker?"

At this O'Malley paused. "There's a fellow you'd best stay clear of."

"Oh?"

"Jonas is tight with the Chief."

I smelled a rat. "And I suppose the Chief is a member of the Sons?"

"Don't know," Sean said, but his eyes gave him away.

"Say Sean," I asked, "how do you manage to support that family of yours on a cop's salary?"

★★★

"What was Horace up to?" I'd gone looking for Eddie again when I left The City. Not finding him, I went on to Sound Mutual.

"What do you mean?" My brother Kevin looked up from his desk as I closed the office door behind me.

"What does Jonas Taker have to do with this murder?"

Surprise flicked across Kevin's face. "Jonas Taker? Nothing. At least I don't think so. Why?"

I told him about my attempts to see Taker. The fact that every time I mentioned Sound Mutual someone got it in their head to take a bite out of me.

"We compete with Taker."

"You take a lot of business away from him?"

"I suppose. A lot of people were unhappy with him. They switched when we opened. That's just business though."

"What do you know about Jonas Taker?"

"It's a family business. Jonas and Jr. Oh, and then there's Larry."

"What's his story?"

There was a commotion in the outer office. Kevin went to the door. I followed. Kevin's secretary was being addressed in a very loud voice. It was the old lady I'd seen at Taker's earlier.

"I don't care where he is," she shouted. "I want to see him now!"

"Mrs Johannsen, please," Miss Wilkins was saying. "Horace Wallinger died two nights ago."

"I want my money."

"I'm sorry, Ma'am, but I don't recall seeing you on our client list."

"I'm not. But the other man said he'd help me."

"Other man? Do you mean Mr Wallinger?"

"That's right. He said he'd get my money."

"Ma'am, perhaps if you would just tell us what happened?" I asked.

"Nothing to tell," she responded. "I paid my premiums. Had a fire and Taker's pretended they never heard of me. Horace Wallinger said he'd help me."

We found what we needed in the secret drawer in Horace's desk. Fraud. The Takers were writing fake policies and collecting the premiums. Thousands of dollars worth by the look of the documents Horace had gathered.

"Why wouldn't Horace tell me about this?" I asked Kevin.

"I don't know. He didn't tell me either."

"Anyone who does know could be in real danger. They'd have…" I stopped mid sentence and clapped a hand to my head.

"What is it?" Kevin asked.

"Dori Storey!" I shouted, running from the office.

I'd told Sean O'Malley about Dori. The Chief had called off the investigation. Both he and Taker were members of the Sons of the New Optimism.

The glass-fronted door of her building was open, so I went in. Halfway up the stairs all hell broke loose. The sound of shattering glass was accompanied by a scream. I took the remaining steps two at a time.

The door to her office hung open, the glass panel in front smashed out. I paused for a second. It was quiet. Carefully I went through the door. Dori was on the floor, her legs just visible behind the desk. There was a movement behind me. The last thing I remember was a pair of shiny black shoes.

"Well Danny-Boy," the Chief gave me a benevolent smile and spoke to the room. "I knew it wouldn't be long before you ran afoul of the law." His grin hardened and he leaned close, so just the two of us could hear. "I've waited a long time for this."

Someone had moved me onto the chair behind Dori's desk. I looked for her.

"Is Dori alive?"

"Looks like you might be up on a murder charge."

"What?"

"Sure. Murder. Oh, she's not dead yet. But it doesn't look good."

"And?"

"Seems pretty clear to me what happened. You found out she was the one who killed Horace. The mystery woman at the dock. You came here to kill her."

"Knocking myself out in the process?"

"There's any number of ways that could have happened. Count on me."

"Alright, Johnny," I said quietly. "That's enough."

His face went dead serious. "A long time I've been waiting," he said before barking at the nearest bluecoat. "Get this bum out of here."

A rough hand dragged me up and Sean O'Malley looked at me, then back to the Chief, who nodded.

"Let's go, Danny-Boy."

I thought I might be in for a stay at the crowbar hotel, but much to my surprise all I had to do was sign a paper for the Justice of the Peace. I hadn't planned on leaving town anyway. Still, it was well after dark before I left the police office and headed back downtown.

At The Manjuris they still hadn't seen Eddie. A couple of drinks helped to dull the pain in my head. By then Eddie's boy had arrived.

"Peter," I called to him.

He came right over, eyeing the bump on my head.

"There's trouble. Where's Eddie?"

"At the harbour. There's a shipment coming in."

I ran across the railway bridge at 10th, over to the west side. Avoiding the electric lights on 1st Avenue West, I cut between two buildings to the waterfront, where an occasional gas lamp burned. The hubbub of motor cars and people gave way to the steady cadence of water slapping against hulls. The harbour was as busy as ever. People joked that you could walk across without ever hitting water, the ships were crowded in so tightly. I noticed lights burning on many as I walked up the dock. The occasional clink of bottles was often followed with muted laughter. The air smelled fishy and the slight evening breeze did little to improve it.

I walked past boxes, crates and bales as I headed towards the far end of the wharf. Peter had refused to tell me exactly where Eddie was. But I knew the Razor well enough. It would be way out, where the ships were fewer and farther between. But there would be enough to cover what was going on. The trick would be letting him know who I was without getting hurt. I imagined his boys could be pretty rough if they thought trouble was coming. I got around the problem with the secret whistle we'd used as boys. Eddie's head went up and he smiled.

"Okay, I hear you," he said in a hoarse whisper. "C'mon out." I stepped from behind a pile of crates. Eddie saw me and came straight over.

"What happened to you?" His concern seemed genuine.

"The Chief."

"Murphy," he smiled. "Looks like you are gonna have to teach that boy another lesson. Where'd he catch you?"

"Dori Storey was hit. So was I."

The concern that crossed his face was genuine. But it didn't surprise me nearly as much as the gunshot that followed.

CHAPTER FIVE
GRUDGE MATCH

I saw one of his men fall, as Eddie and I scrambled for cover. A second shot was followed by the sound of a heavy lead slug slamming into one of the whisky cases we hid behind.

"See anything?" The hoarse sound of Eddie's voice carried on the night air. I shoved him hard, then dropped flat myself. A third shot slammed through the space we had just occupied. I signalled him to keep his mouth shut and pulled Dori's gun from my coat pocket. Eddie's eyes widened as I checked the load.

"How'd you get Dori's gun?"

"It's a long story." I handed the weapon to him. "I'm going to get behind that gunman. Try not to shoot me."

"Do my best."

I crawled around the stack of crates. It took a second for my eyes to adjust to the sudden dark. Behind me, Eddie fired. I inched behind a row of boxes, crates and barrels, towards the gunman. I waited for the next muzzle flash and moved closer. The acrid smell of gunpowder burned my nose. I heaved a stack of crates and heard a cry of surprise as they came down.

"Murph? Hey Murph, you okay?" I could hear Eddie calling from the dock.

"Yeah. Come on up here and bring a light."

A pair of shiny black shoes stuck out from the bottom of the pile of boxes. We moved a few. Sean O'Malley was underneath, alive but out cold.

Eddie pried the top off one of his cases and uncorked a bottle. It was good whisky.

"How long?" I asked.

"Huh?"

"How long? For you and Dori."

Eddie took a long swallow. "Coupla years." I took another drink. "I wouldn't let her tell no one. She's high class. Not a bootlegger's moll."

"That how the Sons got you on the hook? Someone find out and threaten you?"

"The Chief."

I nodded, unsurprised.

"He said he'd take me down. And make sure Dori got caught in it too. Looks like he kept his promise."

"This isn't about your business." I passed him the bottle again. "It's hers."

"What?"

"Remember you told me Horace got hit because of his racket?"

"Sure."

"He found out Taker was selling fake insurance policies. I think he told Dori. Or was about to. She saw him killed. That's why they had to whack her. It was her good luck and my bad that I showed up before the job got finished."

"Taker behind it all?"

"The Chief's in it too. I'm not sure how."

On the dock in front of us, O'Malley groaned softly.

"I love her."

"Don't tell me. Tell everybody. No secret, no blackmail. Everyone knows what you do. No one minds much."

O'Malley let out a deep whistling breath and his eyes fluttered open. He lay still for a second, then turned to look at us.

"This how you support that family of yours, Sean? Murder?"

"Ach. I didn't murder anyone, Danny-Boy. I was only to scare ya."

I pointed at Eddie's dead henchman. "You scared him dead."

"I didna kill anyone."

"First on the scene the night Horace died. That's what you told me. Sounds pretty convenient."

"It wasn't me!" O'Malley sat up fast and fell back to the dock as quickly, his hand clapped to his head.

I leaned forward and spoke in a low voice. "Someone's played you for a patsy, Sean. If you didn't kill anyone, I might be able to keep you out of it. But you have to help me."

"It was the Chief," he said with a deep sigh. "It was all the Chief."

★★★

Half an hour later I was at the back door of the Sons of the New Optimism to help deliver the shipment of bootleg. Razor Eddie was on his way to the hospital, to be sure Dori was okay. Sean was getting help.

He'd laid it all out for us, there on the dock. As much as he knew anyway. Enough people had complained and the Chief had found out about the insurance scam. It was worth thousands. Instead of ending it, he forced his way in and used his position to stop the public complaints. When Horace threatened to blow the whistle, Sean was hired to convince him not to. The plan worked, but then Horace turned up dead. It would have looked like Sean did it. Except for Dori. I walked in the door with the Razor's men and piled a case. Instead of returning for another, I slipped up the back stairs. The Chief and Jonas Taker were supposed to be there. When I got to the bar, I saw Jonas Junior and Larry, but no Chief. I cut straight across the room and was at their table before they saw me.

"Hello boys," I said to two very startled faces. "How's the phony insurance business?" Neither of them said a word, so I sat down. "Where's your partner?"

"Pa…partner?" Larry was so pale he was almost see-through.

"Look boys," I leaned forward. "A little bird has been singing. It's all over." They looked at one another. Larry scared, Junior angry.

"Now look…" Junior started.

"No, you look." I leaned forward again. "It's murder now, not just fraud."

"You can't prove a thing Murphy," Junior hissed through clenched teeth. He didn't look very nice when he spoke like that and I decided to tell him so.

"Junior," I said, "you're a waste of skin."

He jumped at me and I had to slap him down. Pacifism only worked if both sides played. So there he was on the table, tears in his eyes and me holding him in a hammerlock. Larry was nearly invisible with fright.

"Tell me," I said.

"Alright," he whispered as the pain contorted his face. "It was him. He made me do it."

"Him who?"

"Him," he said, gesturing with a twist of his head. I looked down and saw a shiny pair of police shoes. Like Sean's. Just like the ones at Dori's office.

"Hello Chief," I spat, letting Junior go and turning at the same time.

Flanked by the strong arms who had worked me over before, he smiled a threat. "C'mon Danny-Boy." The Chief's voice was flat, emotionless.

"You only use that voice at killings, Chief?"

The smile faltered and the strong arms looked uncertain. Moving fast I grabbed my chair and overhanded it at the three of them. It knocked one of the goons down and slowed the other. The Chief stepped aside, apparently content to let them do the work. I looked for something else to throw and settled on Larry. He squealed at the high end of the scale as he soared toward the second thug. The Chief headed for the door. Off to regroup. I picked the chair up one more time and hit the first thug over the head. He went down for the count. The second guy was still under Larry, so I lit out after the Chief.

I caught up to him near the end of the alley. He'd always been slower. It was one of the things he hated. Ever since school. He'd been a bully then too. No one would stand up to him. Except me. I was already strong from working in the forge. One day I'd had enough of his picking on smallers, so I had given him the beating of a lifetime in front of a cheering, jeering playground. He hated me for it. And he'd tried me again and again over the years. He'd never come out the winner. Not yet anyway.

The Chief turned as I caught up to him and charged headlong into me. We both hit the ground, him on top. He set the stakes right at the start, wrapping his hands around my neck and squeezing. A man on top of another is vulnerable though and I wasted no time using my knee. It worked, but by the time I was up, the Chief was on his feet with a knife in his hand.

I tore my jacket off and wrapped it around my hand to deflect the blade. Neither of us had spoken. There was just the rasp of our breathing, magnified by the alley walls. The Chief lunged and I turned the blade. It caught me in the forearm, slicing a long gash. The pleasure on his face turned to pain as I shoved him away, then kicked hard. Ribs broke. I heard it and saw it on his face. Pain and rage transformed him. With a scream, the Chief raised the knife over his head and charged. In that moment I was glad I'd been to war. I knew exactly what to do. I caught his upraised arm by the wrist and pivoted so my back was facing him, then locked his arm under mine. Using his forward momentum, I went down on one knee, neatly broke the extended limb, then threw him off to the side.

The Chief landed hard and screamed more in pain than rage this time. When he started struggling for the gun, I shoved him on his face, put a knee in the middle of his back and waited for help to arrive.

"He says it's not over between the two of you, you know." We were sitting on the front porch in the dappled evening light, drinking coffee after dinner.

"Sil," I said, "I'd like to know how he plans on continuing it from jail." I stood and stretched, then rolled my sleeves down, one of them over the freshly healed scar.

"I guess he'll be there a long time and the Taker boys too, with the evidence Sean O'Malley gave against them," Razor Eddie said from where he sat. He'd been coming around more since the trial ended. Took my advice and stepped out with Dori now.

"He's lucky he only got life," I said, putting my jacket on, "and not a hanging."

"Goin' somewhere?" Sil asked, winking in Eddie's general direction.

"Sure," I said. "I've got some unfinished business."

"Wouldn't happen to be on 4th Avenue West, would it?" Eddie taunted.

"What makes you think that?" I asked, thinking of a pretty face and a voice filled with promise.

"A little bird told me," Eddie called, as he and Sil laughed.

I laughed too, strolling down the front walk and through the gate. There was a second Storey in my future. And I couldn't wait.

THE END

A brilliant, thrilling, ingenious detective story set in Owen Sound, 1921

GAS HEAD WILLY

Introducing
D.B. Murphy
Private Detective

Richard J Thomas

Chapter One
My First Job

"Willy has disappeared." The dark haired woman pulled my office door shut behind her, then leaned against it, uncertain of her next move.

"Come in. Sit down." I gestured at the two chairs in front of my desk. She chose the wrong one, the rickety job with the split leg. I didn't say anything. Just hoped it would hold. Perched on the chair she paused, taking in the office at a glance. It was a brief glance. There wasn't much to see. A desk. Battered three drawer oak file cabinet. And two windows, one cracked, that looked over a bustling 2nd Avenue East.

"I just moved in." I startled her, as if she'd forgotten there was someone else in the room.

"Forgive me." Her composure was returning. "I've never been in a detective's office before."

"Me either," I said.

"I'm sorry. I thought you...?" Genuinely confused, her unfinished sentence hung in the air between us.

"I am, but like I said, I just opened the office. Earlier this week. You're my first client. If you are one. Who is Willy?"

She snapped open her black patent bag. A gloved hand disappeared nearly to the elbow, returning with some newspaper clippings. I pushed aside the pile of papers on my desk, back issues of *The Sun Times* and *The Owen Sound Advertiser*. She dropped her clippings in the newly vacated space in front of me. I opened the top drawer of my desk and pulled out a writing tablet, grabbed a pen and, in my best handwriting, wrote "Willy" at the top of the page. Another handful of clippings and assorted papers landed on the desk in front of me. "What is Willy's full name?"

"Robertson. William James Robertson."

I tried not to look surprised. Willy Robertson. First son of an old money family. He'd been in the war too. We'd been on the same transport home. A survivor of the gas at Ypres, he'd also been front and centre at Vimy Ridge. When I met him he'd barely known who or where he was. I hadn't seen him since.

"And your name?" I asked the woman in front of me.

"Oh yes, I'm sorry." She stood and offered her hand across the desk. "I'm Pearl. Pearl Robertson."

"Wife?"

"Sister."

I wrote her name down then sorted through the stuff she'd pulled out of her bag. The newspaper clippings were all about me. At the start of the summer I'd been working for my brother Kevin, an insurance agent. I'd solved an insurance fraud turned murder. My first investigation had been so successful, I'd decided to go into business for myself. Pearl's newspaper clippings celebrated the arrest and conviction of the Owen Sound police chief, the brains behind the scheme.

"You can see why I came to you," Pearl said, smiling nervously.

"No. Why?"

"The clippings. I found them in Willy's room. He's in trouble. And he meant me to come here."

I couldn't think of anything to say, so I shuffled through the rest of the pile. There were two items of interest. Tickets. One for a Chinese laundry. The other for the *Michipicoten*, which sailed weekly from Owen Sound to Meaford, Collingwood and points beyond. The ticket was for next week's sailing.

"I found it all in his top dresser drawer, Mr. Murphy," she said when I looked up. "And there's a show card there too."

"Call me Murph." I picked up the show card. The handsome face gazing back at me announced itself as William S. Robertson Esq. "This from before the war?"

"Oh, yes, yes of course. We could never…I mean it just wouldn't be appropriate now."

"Why don't you start from the beginning?"

She took a deep breath, and started.

"It's been bad since Willy came back from the war. He just isn't the same. He hardly seems to know who he is, much less the rest of the family. At first, he'd wake up in the night. Screaming. It was horrible." Her hands trembled until she caught one with the other, steadying both.

"What was it all about?"

"The war. What else?"

"Can you be more specific?"

She shook her head. "I covered my head with a pillow when it happened. I couldn't stand to listen."

"Go on."

"Things got worse. He started drinking. At first, we couldn't tell. We were all just so happy that he wasn't screaming. But then he was drunk all the time."

"Where'd he get his stuff?"

"I don't know. All I do know is he started spending a lot of time down in Mudtown." She shuddered at the thought of her brother in that place.

"When did you see him last?"

"Tuesday night. When I got up Wednesday morning, he was gone. And he hasn't been back since. Can you help me?"

"I'll need a twenty dollar advance. Then it's ten dollars a day, plus expenses."

"When can you start?"

"Now."

"You'll work over the weekend?"

"All except Monday. It's Labour Day you know. "

A twenty materialized. I took the case.

Owen Sound was a city on the move. Progress was the word of the day. The centre of commerce for Bruce and Grey counties, it had been, before the war, the busiest port on the Great Lakes. As the northern terminus for the Grand Trunk and Canadian Pacific railways, it was the transfer point for western migration. Many immigrant families, some speaking little English, passed through Owen Sound. A few stayed, tempted by either the fertile farmlands of the surrounding townships or perhaps the promise of harvest from Georgian Bay. Slowly, the little county town had grown into a city.

It was divided straight through the middle by the Sydenham River, with the downtown on the east side. Shoulder to shoulder, buildings crowded 2nd Avenue East. Most days, the start of business was signalled by the unfurling of storefront canopies up and down the street. Clustered thick as leaves, it was possible on a hot summer's day to walk from one end of the main street to the other in cool shade. The boardwalks had long since been replaced with cement, the main street paved. Hitching rails and watering troughs had disappeared, replaced by angle parked automobiles. No matter. Few horse and buggy owners would risk the city, due to the increasing frequency of accidents involving fast cars. Even the silent policemen—concrete barriers in each intersection—failed to slow many drivers, especially the young ones. I didn't have a car myself. I suppose in some way, I held cars responsible for ruining my life. At least temporarily.

Now I had a case. I'd have to mark September 2 on my 1922 calendar. My first anniversary.

Booze seemed to be the starting point. Owen Sound was a prohibition town and the vote in April against importation of alcohol had strengthened the hold of the dry forces. It seemed to me the only real change since the vote was an increase in illegal activity. People still drank as much as ever. If you had money you could get the stuff on prescription from your doctor. Otherwise, every Tom, Dick and Harry had swamp whisky going in the laundry tub.

There was any number of booze cans in the city, but you had to keep up. They moved often, to stay ahead of the Temperance Enforcement Officers. Dry cops. The other option was to find a bootlegger and my boyhood friend Razor Eddie happened to be just about the busiest. He spent a lot of his time at The Manjuris, a local pool hall. That's where I decided to start my search for Willy.

A set of stairs rose from the main street up to The Manjuris. I had to turn slightly to fit the stairwell, which was about the width of a normal set of shoulders. At the top I paused in the twilight of the unlit hallway and took my hat off. I tapped twice on the door, then waited. A moment later, Red, the counterman, slid open a panel high in the door and peered out. Cigar smoke poured from the room behind him like a chimney.

His eyes grew accustomed to the dark and a smile crossed his face when he saw my eyes level with his. I was one of the few visitors to The Manjuris who could look him right in the eye.

"Hey, Murph!" The panel slid shut and the door opened. A cascade of smoke crossed the landing as I stepped inside. If anyone had been watching from below, I might have looked like one of the conjurers they sometimes got on stage down at Griffins Theatre. Disappearing in a puff of smoke.

"Thanks Red."

"Eddie's playin'." He sauntered across the room to a long row of display counters. Glass fronted, each cabinet displayed a different brand of tobacco. Snuff, chaw, cigarettes and cigars of every size and shape lined the wall. Across the room, mid-morning sunlight slanted through three grime covered windows. In front of me, Eddie leaned low over a table, ready to shoot. I flung my hat just as he drew the cue stick back. The hat fell directly on top of the cue ball.

"What the hell…!" he exploded, leaping up from the table. When Eddie was angry, his face went beet red. The scar running from where his left ear had been to his chin glared an angry purple.

I laughed aloud. "You look like old man McGroarie's bull! Remember?"

Eddie relaxed, then grinned. "Danny-Boy you sonofabitch!"

"Eddie." I retrieved my hat from the table. "You are as eloquent as ever. Remember that bull?"

"El...what? You musta paid attention, all them years at Ryerson School. Sure I remember the bull. Never did get an apple."

"Sil did. Wouldn't share it either."

"Good ol' four eyes. Drink?"

"Sure." Before the war I'd had a strict no-drinks-before-noon policy. Not any more. I was easily swayed, especially at ten in the morning. Eddie led the way to the counter. He was shorter than me by a head, but lean and muscular. He dressed well, in close-fitting suits. Grey pinstripe was his favourite. I rarely saw him in anything else. He'd taken to carrying a gun since we'd nearly been killed on the waterfront one night last June. I didn't mind. We were friends. Might be brothers-in-law someday too, since we were dating a pair of sisters.

At the counter, Red had two glasses out. Eddie nodded and reached down for a bottle. Two fingers in each glass and Eddie handed the bottle back.

"To temperance," Eddie laughed, tossing his back.

I took mine in one burning gulp and nearly heaved it up.

"Jeez," I spluttered. "That's worse than war rum. How old is it?"

Eddie grabbed the bottle from Red and poured again. "Aged nearly twelve hours," he said.

"Takes longer than that to get here from Montreal. This local?"

"Takes longer is right. I'm still waitin' for this month's load. Hadta get this from a coupla local boys. Moonshine, from up Balaclava way. It ain't too good. Costs more every time I get it too." He took a sip from the second glassful. "What brings you in here?"

I drank too, then asked, "Know much about Willy Robertson?"

"Crazy as a shithouse rat."

"What?"

"He's a crazy man. He don't know who or where he is half the time. Why?"

"He's missing. I've got a case."

"Tough."

"Sister says he drank. He get it here?"

"At first maybe, right after he came back. But not lately. I hadta cut him off. He was gettin' bad for business, runnin' around all the time talkin' crazy."

"Anything else?"

"Nope." I finished my drink and thanked him.

"You still livin' with Silly?" he asked.

"Yes."

"How're those boys of his?"

"Wild."

"You give 'em a wrassle for me. And say hi to Sil. And Marth."

"Sure Eddie." I picked up my hat and gulped the last of the moonshine. "See ya."

From The Manjuris I strolled round the corner to The City Cafe. It was one of my daily rituals, dinner at The City. A small diner with about a dozen tables and a lunch counter, it featured home cooking and a cozy atmosphere. You could eat for a quarter, sometimes less if there was a special.

It was crowded when I walked in. From across the room I saw a hand waving and heard someone call. "Murph! Over here!" It was Sean O'Malley. There was a vacant chair at his table. I went over. Sean had been a city cop; that's how we met. He'd been one of the players in the insurance fraud. I genuinely liked Sean, so I'd kept him out of it. He left the force, but didn't go to jail.

"Hey Murph." He shook my hand when I got to the table.

"Hello Sean." I took my hat off, and hung it on a peg on the wall behind him. O'Malley was a big man. A nose like a new potato dominated the homely face, which was crowned with black hair, greased. His suit of clothes was cheap—even I could tell—but it was clean. His voice carried a light Irish accent. He was eating a hamburg sandwich. I sat at the gingham-clad table and grabbed a menu. Dolores came over with coffee.

"'Lo, you look better to me every time I come in here," I said. "How come you're not on the menu?"

"D.B. Murphy! If Marth knew how fresh you were, why she'd throw you out of her house on your ear!" She said it with a smile. We'd known each other a long time.

"I'd like a hot hamburg sandwich."

"Coffee?"

"Of course. And for dessert..." I reached a playful hand towards her.

"Oh you..." She slipped out of my reach and headed around the counter toward the kitchen.

"You always talk to her like that?" Sean asked.

I nodded. "Since grade school."

Sean took a bite of his sandwich. A dribble of gravy slid down his chin. "I heard ya went out on yer own?" he asked, mopping his face with a napkin.

"Yes. Even got my first case. Just this morning."

He raised his eyebrows. "That was quick."

"Uh huh. How about you Sean? What are you doing now?"

"Got myself a job. I'm workin' for the High Constable, on patrol."

"What's that?"

"Heard of The Lost Tire Gang?"

"They come out of Shelburne?"

"That's right," Sean said, talking around another mouthful of sandwich. "They drop a spare tire right in the middle of the road, usually on a curve. When a car comes 'round and runs over it, they're waitin'. Usually a couple of men with guns. They rob the car owner, pick up their tire, and get away."

Dolores brought my lunch. "What's that got to do with Grey County?"

"Well, either they're comin' up this far now. Or someone else thinks it's a pretty good way to make a livin'. In any case, the High Constable thinks we gotta do somethin' about it."

"You hear about the hit and run Wednesday?" I asked. The hamburg sandwich was delicious.

"You mean Mr. McColl?"

"Yeah. What happened?"

"Car tried to pass him on the Meaford Road. Hit his horse by mistake and kept goin'. Turned over the whole rig. McColl made it. He was lucky."

"His horse?"

"Not so lucky."

"You doing anything about it?"

"No. There aren't enough of us on the roads."

"Too bad." I finished my sandwich. "Too many horses getting hurt. How do you know where to find these gangs?"

"We don't. Just drive around in a big Packard, trying to look like we got money. They find us."

Dolores took my plate and an order for pie. The City had the best pie in Owen Sound, bar none.

"You ever hear of a guy called Willy Robertson?"

"Nope. He yer case?" Sean sipped his triple-creamed coffee.

"Yeah. He disappeared. Keep an eye out. Let me know if you find him."

A sly look crossed his face and he said, "I guess you'll have to find him before Monday."

My pie arrived at the table and Dolores waited for a minute, having overheard O'Malley's comment. "Why is that Sean?" I asked.

"'Cause the west side is going to pull the east side to hell and back!"

"Hah!" Dolores shouted. "You west side lilies better get ready for a whippin', cause the east side boys are better'n you!"

I laughed, as a murmur of voices rose from every table in the room. A lot of people were looking forward to the big east side versus west side tug-of-war on Monday. It would be the last event of our festive Labour Day celebration.

"See what you started?" I asked. The rivalry between Owen Sound's east and west sides was long standing. No one really knew what started it. But it was the reason for a continuing series of athletic challenges. Tug-of-war aside, the real highlight of the celebration in Victoria Park would be a parade from the downtown, followed by the Guelph versus Owen Sound football match. It was the playoff game for the Western Football Association, and Guelph was heavily favoured. Except in Owen Sound. "Scotty and I are leading the parade," I said, shovelling in a mouthful of pie.

"How come?"

"They wanted a veteran in uniform, because of the big meeting they're having Monday night. You know, to talk about forming that club for veterans. They're calling it the Legion."

Lunch cost a quarter. I paid Fran Caple, the cashier, out of the twenty Pearl Robertson had advanced me. I was feeling pretty good, so I tipped Dolores a dime. I said goodbye to Sean, that maybe I'd see him around. Told him to be careful with that family of his. With a laugh he assured me he was simply doing the Pope's will.

It was pleasant in the afternoon sun, so I walked the long way around to the office. Up 3rd to 8th Street, then back down to 2nd and through the downtown. There were lots of people about, it being Friday afternoon, and a holiday weekend to boot. I could almost feel the excitement in the air, as they bustled here and there.

In an alley near the main street, boys pitched pennies. The last holiday of the summer. High school would start back on Tuesday, a week later than the elementaries. It seemed a long time since I'd attended Owen Sound Collegiate. But every September, Labour Day still felt like the start of the year.

I stopped in front of MacLean's Marketeria. A sign in the window informed me it was York canned goods week. Buy one tin, get one free. In the other window, fruit and vegetables were piled below a sign proclaiming the store HEADQUARTERS FOR FISH. Above the front door a sign in the shape of a fish advertised fresh lake trout. The canopy promised good things to eat. I went in.

A bell attached to the back of the door jangled my arrival. Inside, displays of Aylmers tinned goods and Lyons Tea invited me to buy and try. Across the back of the store was the dry goods counter. Behind it, a round man with dark hair stood near the scales. James MacLean. He was squinting through tiny round spectacles which may have fit his face once. His white apron fairly splitting at the seams, he was the picture of mercantile prosperity.

"Ahhhh, D.B.!" he fairly squealed. "How is the business of detection?" It was an honest question, but I knew he really wondered if I'd be able to pay my rent. I took what was left of the twenty out of my trouser pocket and dropped ten on the counter. His eyes lit up, a sly grin of satisfaction crossing his face.

"That's for the month?"

"Business is good."

"So far."

"Right." Since I'd first rented the tiny office above his store, I'd wondered how such a pessimist ever made it in business. He was sure no one would hire me. That I'd fail and he'd be out the rent money. I was determined to prove him wrong.

"Have you got any McLauchlin's cream soda?"

"Sweet tooth. Sure, just here in the back. How many you want?"

"Two," I said, "and leave the caps on. They're for the boys."

"Ahhh," he said again, in the all-knowing way he had. I passed him ten cents, which promptly disappeared into the big front pocket on his apron.

"Don't forget to bring the bottles back. Two cents deposit."

Our transaction complete, he turned back to the woman he'd been helping when I came in. He had my money. I had, at least until rent was due next, ceased to exist. I carried the two sodas in my left hand, while I fumbled my keys into the right. Pushing the street door open, I went upstairs to finish unpacking.

When I opened the door just after four o'clock, the big house on 5th Street was warm with the rich smell of cooking. The boys greeted me with punches, yells and general rough-housing. Once they had me reasonably subdued, the search of my pockets began. Seven year old Finn did the dirty work, while five year old Aidan held me down.

"Help! Help!" I shouted to no one in particular, struggling all the while. "I'm beset. It's the Lost Tire Gang! Highwaymen! Help!"

"I got 'em!" Finn screamed, triumphantly holding the cream sodas, one in each hand. "C'mon Aid, let's go!" Aidan released me and the two retreated a safe distance. When I jumped up and made like I might chase them, they sprinted out through the kitchen. I heard the back door slam, and laughter in the backyard.

The Johnson home was large. Built of local brick, it was three stories. On the main floor, off the foyer, there were four options. The stairs, a door to the left leading into Sil's study, a door to the right leading into the parlour and dining room, or straight ahead into the kitchen. Upstairs, there were four bedrooms, enough for all and then some. The attic was large but unfinished. In the basement, the coal cellar and furnace took up much of the space.

Sil and Marth had been among the first on the street to install electric lights. In the dining room, a chandelier ordered from Eaton's in Toronto delighted and amazed everyone.

I doffed my coat and hat. The smell which had greeted me grew more delicious as I went until, arriving in the kitchen, I thought I might be overcome. "Hi Marth. What's for dinner?"

Marth turned from a pot she'd been furiously stirring on the stove. As good humoured as she was attractive, Martha Johnson was a kind and gentle wife and mother. A good and caring friend too. Tall and blond, she had a straight nose, blue eyes and full lips. She smiled often and her teeth were perfect. She had an excellent figure that I tried not to think about. She and Sil loved one another dearly. I couldn't think of two people who went together more perfectly. Sil was the snips and snails and puppy dogs tails to her sugar and spice.

"Danny-Boy Murphy! That's the first thing you ask every night when you walk through that door."

"I like to know. In case I don't like it. Then I've got time to look for better offers."

She smiled sweetly. "You wouldn't be referring to someplace like the Storey household?" Marth had taken an intense interest in my relationship with Lori Storey, the woman I'd met on my insurance case. Lori hadn't been involved. Then.

"I have no comment. You haven't answered my question."

"It's the same answer I always give you. You'll see when it's on the plate in front of you." She was thoughtful for a second. "Come to think of it, it's the same answer I give all you boys every day."

"And every day you manage to surpass the one preceding it."

"Why Murph," she said good humouredly. "Thank you. Now get out of my kitchen. I'm busy."

"How long have I got?"

"Until five, like always. Are you going out to play?"

"Of course. You think they'd let me get away with staying inside and reading *The Sun Times*?"

"No, I suppose not. But you should look at it. You're in there."

"Oh?"

"It's got the whole program for Labour Day printed. It mentions you and Scotty leading the parade, the speeches, the tug-of-war and everything."

"Hey Murph!" I heard one of the boys scream from the backyard.

"You can read it later," Marth said, turning back to the stove. "You know, if you got married and had kids of your own, you'd always have someone to play with."

"Easier to play with yours," I said. "When I get tired I can go home and leave them behind."

"This is your home."

I slapped a hand to my forehead in mock dismay. "Well I'll be. You're right. That must be why I spend so much time with those ruffians."

I walked around the table in the centre of the room, pushed through the screen door to the back yard. It was warm yet, but not too much so. Just comfortable. One of those perfect September afternoons that won't let you forget you're on the wrong side of summer.

The boys had finished their cream sodas and were kicking a ball around the yard. I dashed into the centre of it and took the ball away. We played a vicious game of keep-away until we all collapsed breathless.

"How was school today boys?"

"I'm gonna be on the football team," Finn said.

"Did you know your dad used to play?"

"Really?"

"Sure, me and him together. Maybe after dinner he'll come out here and we'll show you a thing or two."

★★★

Dinner was the usual raucous affair with the two boys trying to outdo one another in the telling, or yelling, of the day's adventures. There was little room for adult talk, so it was usual for Sil and I to retire to his study afterwards to catch up on the day's events. There was generally a drink involved—Canadian rye. I don't know where he got it, but Sil always had a bottle at hand. "For medicinal purposes," he liked to say.

We sat opposite one another in comfortable chairs in an alcove near the front windows. Our drinks sat on the table between us. Sil was a big man, tall but not wide. Well over six feet, he weighed less than 170 pounds, which was a lot. When we were boys he'd been nearly the same height, but only 120 pounds. He was forever trying to compensate for his gangliness and that's what had led to the incident on the bridge. Sil was a good-looking, strong-featured man, with sandy brown hair. His eyesight had kept him out of the war, much to his chagrin and Marth's relief. But he'd done his share at home, selling war bonds, sending me regular packages and minding my horse.

"I saw the Razor today."

Sil raised his eyebrows. "You're not drinking, are you?"

"No, no. Nothing like that. I got my first case."

Sil jumped up and shook my hand, a big smile on his face. "Congratulations. Wow! Already. You got your first case." I loved it when he got enthusiastic about something. It turned him into the boy I'd grown up with. He sat back down and propped his size twelves up on the ottoman. "Tell me all about it," he said, picking up his drink.

"Know anything about the Robertson family?"

"The lumber Robertsons? The Robertson-mill Robertsons? The we-have-so-much-money-there's-nothing-in-the-world-we-can't-do Robertsons? Those Robertsons?

"Yup."

"What do they need you for?"

"The oldest boy, Willy, has disappeared."

Sil cranked his eyebrows up an extra notch and gave a low whistle. "Isn't that something," he said, then smiled. "Of course I expected it."

"What?"

"Well, it's not as if he was exactly right, after the war. A little strange in the head is what I heard. Okay, okay, a lot strange in the head. Lot of people might think this is for the best."

"Oh? And why is that?"

Sil leaned forward and dropped his voice. He really loved this kind of stuff. He kept his ear to the ground and was a neverending source of information about what really went on in Owen Sound.

"Before the war," he began, "Willy Robertson moved from one scandal to another, like a tannery fly hopping hides. He always relied on daddy's money to bail him out. Now I've heard," Sil sat back and took on an authoritative air, "that just before the war he got caught at something. It was the biggest scandal ever. The family money almost couldn't save him. But it did. And he got sent off to war. As punishment."

"Must have killed his folks, him coming back the way he did."

"I'll say. Really makes you wonder."

"What?" I asked.

"Makes you wonder what the crime must have been, to fit that punishment."

"Try to find out for me."

"Sure. It's been a few years. Maybe someone is ready to talk. What's your plan?"

"His sister Pearl told me he spent a good deal of time in Mudtown. I guess I'll start there."

CHAPTER TWO
CLABBA KILLER

3rd Avenue East led from the downtown to the busy industrial district of the Owen Sound waterfront. Beyond that lay Mudtown, my destination on the clear morning of September third. It was cool when I left the house just after nine and, though there was a nip in the morning air, the day held the promise of warmth. It would have been a good day to take Scotty for a trot. But I decided it wasn't worth the effort, when I could get to Mudtown in twenty minutes on foot.

I'm not always at my best in the morning. The walk helped and by the time I passed the Grey County Courthouse, my pace—mental and physical—was brisk.

I could only guess at the meaning of the pile of junk Pearl said Willy had collected. The boat ticket was self evident. The Chinese laundry ticket was probably incidental, just a shirt. It was obvious Willy meant to catch the *Michipicoten*. Had he known he was in trouble? That might explain the newspaper clippings as well. If he was in trouble, it could have been his way of telling his family. Why he'd chosen me I couldn't say. Unless it was the convenience of the newspaper articles and nothing else.

I had met Willy. On the transport ship. After the war, we'd all been moved from France into England and then shipped home. For those who had to wait, looking for friends and relatives who had survived became a major occupation. I'd joined up as a gunner in Toronto, so I hadn't seen many Owen Sounders. When I got word a platoon from Grey County was waiting for rotation home, I sought them out. Eddie was there, already known to the others in his unit as Razor Eddie because of the fresh scar that marked his face. It wasn't really a surprise to see him. We had kept in touch and on the rare occasion during those hellish four years when we both got leave at the same time, we met when possible.

Willy was with Eddie's platoon. His body slumped like everyone else's just in from the front. But, in the sea of drawn and exhausted faces, Willy's stood out in ghastly relief. His eyes. I'd seen shell shock and this was worse. Willy's eyes were totally vacant. There was nothing there. At all. Someone, I was told, had to lead him around. He had no will of his own. I was less surprised at that once I learned where he'd been. Gassed at Ypres. On the front lines of the infantry at Vimy. Four long years in the trenches.

I had been lucky. The big guns were far behind the lines. I was even farther back with the biggest howitzers. Along with most of the men in my unit, I'd been hand picked for size. Hell, the shells we had to manhandle were more than two hundred pounds. At Vimy we were instrumental in creating the creeping artillery barrage that subdued the Hun, helping Canada succeed where both the British and French had failed. It had been hard work, but our jobs were nothing compared with what infantrymen living with the daily horror of the trenches had to put up with. Some lived for months in water and hip-deep muck, the rotting bodies of comrades nearby, grisly reminders of the end that waited for all. It surprised me that more hadn't come home like Willy.

Owen Sound's factory district crowded the east side of the harbour. It started right at the 10th Street bridge, squeezed into a narrow strip between the water and the railroad. By the time you got to around 17th Street, it was as if the pressure on that wedge had become too much. The district expanded rapidly, until every square inch of land from the escarpment to the water's edge was put to some use.

It wasn't a pretty area to look at. The landscape was barren, stripped down to nothing by the demands of commerce. The water was obscured from view by buildings, docks and ships. Roads, dirt lanes and alleyways wove the whole district together.

It was from here that most people in the world knew Owen Sound. It wasn't a pretty little city on the shores of Georgian Bay to others. Owen Sound was the name on the seat of a chair or the door of a stove. It was the stamp in a piece of ironwork, the brand on a tanned hide, the name imprinted on a table bottom. It was a place where things were made—things of quality that found their way from that waterfront to the rest of the world.

Things were making their way to the rest of the world, even on a Saturday. As I walked through, I could see that many of the factories were in full production, probably trying to make up for the loss of the coming Monday, Labour Day.

Mudtown was part of the factory district. Most of Owen Sound pretended it didn't exist. A ragtag collection of shanties, huts and sheds, this illegal community of the indigent expanded where the factory district ended. From 3rd Avenue to the water it sprawled in all directions, as though it had been shaken and tossed like a handful of dice. Still, there was an order of sorts to the twisting alleys, paths and lanes. None was big enough for a car, or even a horse. There was no need. No one in Mudtown owned either. And for the most part, they weren't interested in anyone who did.

My destination was the one and only speakeasy in Mudtown. I knew it was somewhere near the geographical centre of the place. In my suit and hat, I stood out like a sore toe. Here and there men drank openly, even at that hour. They sat on broken chairs, old furniture. One sat in what had once been a buggy. It looked as though it had been driven to the edge of Mudtown, but before it could leave, the creeping malaise of the place had trapped it. The occupant had a pop bottle full of bootleg in one hand, a crudely wrapped cigar in the other. I nodded as I went by. An unfriendly stare was the response. My last impression was of a toothless mouth as he lifted his head and drank.

There were children everywhere, dirt-covered urchins playing in the squalor of Mudtown's alleyways. Turning one corner I came upon a game of war. Sticks were machine guns, discarded bottles were grenades and rocks doubled for bullets. An armistice was declared as I walked through the centre of no man's land. I reached the far side and heard the rat-a-tat-tat of their machine guns begin again. So much death. I wanted to turn and say something. But I kept walking.

The speakeasy stood in a clearing. It had no name that I knew of; in the midst of such squalor I guess there was no need. It was at the very centre of Mudtown. Town hall, community centre and church all wrapped up in one rambling tumbledown package. The place looked as though it had begun as a single room shack with piece after piece added on over time. From the outside it gave the impression of a patchwork quilt, a group of smaller buildings all stitched together to make one large one. The single unifying factor was the covered porch, made from old pieces of boardwalk stretched across the front.

It was a bit early, or perhaps late, for people to be inside. But I could hear music. I stepped onto the porch. The front door, crooked on its hinges, stood open. In front of it, a mutt was sleeping in a patch of sunlight. He lifted his head a fraction, and cracked one eye. A listless thump of the tail and he was asleep again. I went inside.

I found a large room with tables and chairs scattered around, some upright, others not. It stank of stale booze and old smoke. The only source of light was what filtered in through filthy windows covered with oilcloth drapes. In a back corner, a phonograph played a badly scratched copy of *A Pretty Girl Is Like A Melody*.

"Hello!" I yelled into the dim room. Nothing. I went back outside and stood on the porch looking out across the bare patch of dirt that passed for the town square.

"He'p yo?" I looked down, but the dog was asleep. Then I peered into the darkened corners of the porch. One contained a collection of nothing. In the other, a wizened old man sat deep in a sofa that had seen better days.

"Hello," I said. "D.B. Murphy."

"Old Joe," came the slow response. I moved in for a closer look. Old Joe was about as frail a human being as I'd ever seen. His arms and legs were stick thin. As a result his head looked like a pumpkin balanced on a broom handle. Nearly as stable too. He smiled when I sat on the other end of the sofa. A nearly new set of plywood teeth crowded his mouth. The top of his head was smooth as a billiard ball and the colour of burnished ebony.

"Joe, I'm looking for someone."

"Old Joe."

"Oh. Sorry. Old Joe."

"Most folks is."

"What? Sorry?"

"Lookin' for somebody."

I shifted a bit to get more comfortable and sank even deeper into the formless shape. "Nice chesterfield," I said.

"Spent pretty near every day for the past twenny years here," he said, then added, "every warm day leastaways." The accent had likely been as thick as blackstrap molasses once. Deep south.

"You lived here a long time?"

"Nah." Joe shifted the plywood teeth into a more comfortable talking position with a loud sucking noise. "Just them twenny year. 'Fore that I was down in York."

"New York?"

"Nah. What they call it now? T'ronta?"

"Oh."

"Yep. I left my home durin' the war. Come to Canada they all says. So I come."

"Where was your home then?"

"Sweet Georgia." At the mention of the name he smiled. I could almost see the flood of memories pass across his face.

"Which war was it then?"

"The American war."

"The American war?" I sat up a little straighter. "The civil war you mean? That was over fifty years ago!"

"Yes sir, I suppose it were."

"What year did you come to Canada?"

"Well, now let me see..." he sucked his teeth for a second, while he considered. "Guess it'd be about 1862."

"How old are you, Old Joe?"

"'Bout ninety two."

"How come you didn't go back? After the war I mean?"

"Nothin' to go back to. Not after I ran away. Ain't much call for any old slave boy like me to come back down there, I don't suppose. 'Sides, I got me a family here. A son an' two daughters. Even got me some grans and great grans. Didn't you say you're lookin' for someone?"

"Oh, right." I'd forgotten for a second. I was so excited by Old Joe's story. In school I'd heard of the underground railroad and slaves coming north to Owen Sound. Old Joe was the first one I'd met. "I'm looking for a fellow named William Robertson. Heard he used to hang around here."

"Hmmmmm…what he look like?"

"About my height, I guess. But not as big. Blond hair, blue eyes."

"Nope, don't sound familiar. But my memory for yesterday ain't as good as it is for fifty year ago."

"Anyone else around here I could ask?"

"They all sleepin' last night off."

"But not you?"

"Too old to drink. But I used to. Yes I did, with the best of them. Doesn't matter now though. Since the vote, there's only rotgut around. Moonshine from up north. They call it Clabba Killer, on account of it comes from Bal'clabba."

"I guess I'll take a look around," I said, "to see if I can find anyone else who might have seen Willy. Thanks, Old Joe."

I couldn't think of much else to do but walk and talk. I had been able to choose from the four points of the compass leaving the speakeasy. So I went west, toward the water. The only plan I had was to walk every alleyway in Mudtown until I found someone who could tell me about Willy. I had all day. Almost all day. I'd promised Lori that we'd go to see the ventriloquist at Griffins Theatre. And Marth expected me home for supper.

It was difficult to tell one dwelling from another. The closer I got to the water, the closer together they seemed to be. The image of a house of cards came to mind. Pull one out and the lot would come crashing down. At the water's edge I came to a rickety dock. A Watts skiff was tied to it and standing on the shore were half a dozen barrels of fresh fish. Empty drying racks stood all around. In the centre of it all, a man of medium height and build was working, standing at a table. He wore a heavy burlap fishing coat and warm woollen pants which were tucked into a pair of knee high gum boots. His head was turned down so that his greasy black hair fell across his unshaven face. I watched for a second as he expertly gutted whitefish with a wicked looking knife. It took less than a minute for him to clean a fish. The guts went into a bucket on the left side of the table and the cleaned fish were piled to the right.

Without slowing the pace of his work, he spoke, in English with a thick French-Canadian accent. "What do you want?"

"I'm looking for someone."

"So? You lookin' for a fish, I can help you. People I don't got much use for."

"His name is Willy. Willy Robertson. Blond hair, blue eyes. About my height."

"See these fish?" He stopped work and gestured with the long thin blade of his knife. "This is all I know. I work. All the time. I work for my family. I work for me. I work to get outta here. I don't know no one and no one knows me. All I want is to get outta here. And you better do the same."

"That a threat?"

"No, it's advice. This isn't a nice place. Especially for a man in a suit."

"Well thanks for the advice. But I think I can handle myself."

"*Bien,*" he said and turned back to his work.

From the waterfront I worked my way south. I thought I'd wind up back at the speakeasy. Maybe by then there'd be someone to talk to. I eventually circled back to the man sitting in the wreck of the buggy. He was younger than I'd thought, despite his toothlessness. Scarred knuckles told a tale and the hard look he gave me as I approached was a warning. He still had the bottle clenched in one hand and the soggy cigar in the other.

"You'd best get outta here," he said before I could open my mouth.

"Name's Murphy," I said. "I'm looking for someone."

"You're lookin' for trouble. This here is Mudtown. Ain't no place for you here." His approach was decidedly hostile. I pressed on.

"He's about my height. Blond hair, blue eyes. Seen him?" He looked at me with cold eyes. Then he snorted something up and hawked it onto the ground near my feet. I try to avoid fighting whenever possible and I couldn't see any point in getting into it with him. So I thanked him and walked on.

They caught up to me in the clearing by the speakeasy. I say they, because Toothless had brought a couple of buddies along, both of them bigger and uglier than he was. Within about a second a crowd started to gather. Whatever means of communication they had in Mudtown, it was good. There were plenty of people for me to talk to now, so I ignored the thugs and began to canvass the crowd. It didn't last long.

"I told you to get lost mister!" Toothless screamed from behind me. "Mudtown ain't for the likes o' you!"

"Too bad you've got no teeth," I said turning to face him. "It's going to take the fun out of this for me." It was important to go on the offensive when it became clear a fight was inevitable. And it was clear. The crowd was closing around us in a loose circle. I spotted a boy in the front. "Son, I'll pay you a nickel to watch my things. Okay?"

"Okay, mister. But you gotta pay me now," he nodded, holding his hand out. I tossed him the coin, then removed my hat, jacket and shirt. Toothless and the boys were taking turns drinking from the bottle. I turned and was pleased to see my opponents pause. It was part of the effect I was hoping for. Years of blacksmithing had left me with a hard, muscular body. I figured just looking tough would go a long way with these boys. I was right. They became more wary and even put the bottle down before they came at me. The faces in the crowd grew eager and the buzz of voices increased a notch as the thugs approached. Toothless came straight up the middle, closely flanked by his friends.

"You don't have to do this you know," I called out.

Toothless sneered. They kept coming.

"I just wanted to give you fair warning," I said. "Hope your insurance is paid up."

A flicker of doubt crossed the face of the thug on the right. My right. They stopped directly in front of me. Still bunched up. Toothless stepped up and raised an arm. I swung a hard uppercut. I had good aim. The shot lifted him straight off his feet and flung him backwards. The crowd roared. The other two looked at Toothless, who appeared to be unconscious. While they were distracted I stepped right and doubled the doubter over with a shot to the stomach. At the same time, Lefty hit me in the eye. It hurt. I snapped my head up and connected with the doubter, who went down hard. Another roar from the crowd. Then it was just me and Lefty. He was big—over six feet—and had to weigh close to three hundred. He didn't look drunk either. Lefty came at me, arms spread wide, a bear hug in mind. Now I haven't done a lot of fighting, but I know enough to keep moving. Once a guy gets hold of you, the going is tougher, especially if you're a pugilist and not a grappler. So I stepped back and over the doubter, putting him between us. It slowed Lefty for about a second. I watched as he kicked the doubter, literally lifting him off the ground and out of the way. The frenzied crowd around me was chanting, "CRU-SHER! CRU-SHER!" It made me think they'd seen this happen before.

It was time for offence, so I waited for him to lunge then twisted out of the way. As he went by I wheeled and landed a solid forearm on the back of his neck. He went down as far as his knees. Then he grabbed my leg and I was on the ground. I kicked him in the face in my haste to get back up. Twice. Didn't stop him though. He was up and straight at me and the one-two combination to his midsection did nothing. For a second I wished I'd brought a gun. But then I didn't have time to think of anything else, because he caught me up in the bearhug he'd been trying for earlier.

The crowd started chanting again, "CRU-SHER! CRU-SHER!" as he squeezed the air out of me. The way he'd grabbed me, I had a good view of his face from slightly above. His eyes were closed tight and sweat was forming on his brow. He was really trying.

"Hey!" I used the last of my air to get his attention. He opened his eyes and gave me an executioner's grin. I returned the smile and arched my back. Too late he realized what was coming. I snapped myself forward and the top of my head connected with the bridge of his nose. It really hurt. But it worked. He screamed and dropped me, bringing both hands to his shattered nose. I took in a couple of long ragged gulps of air. The blackness that had been creeping in at the edges of my vision disappeared.

The other two were still on the ground and not worth bothering. Crusher had been the only fighter. I looked at him. He stood with his head bent, blood dripping through hands which held the remains of his nose.

"Will that be enough?" I asked. He nodded emphatically and dropped his hands from his face.

"Buy you a drink?" he asked in a nasal voice.

"What?" A second ago he'd been trying to kill me.

"A drink."

"Uh…okay. Sure. I'll just get dressed."

The speakeasy was full as Crusher and I walked up the stairs together. Old Joe sat in the same place.

"See you've met the family," he drawled from his dark corner.

"What?" I asked, surprised.

"That strappin' fella next to ya there. That'd be my grandson Rufus." I turned to look at Crusher, now Rufus, who smiled and nodded. Then I held my hand out. He took it and shook.

"D.B. Murphy."

"Rufus Jones."

"You always beat people up, then buy them drinks?"

"Nuthin' personal. Sport, that's all."

"You find that fella you lookin' for?" Old Joe asked.

"Nope. Seems no one's seen him either."

"You sure he'd come around here?"

"That's what his sister told me."

"Sit down here for a second," he gestured at the sofa, "and tell me what he looks like again." The two of us sat. His weight carried Rufus deeper into the formless shape than I'd gone.

"His name is William Robertson. Blond hair, blue eyes. A veteran."

"He got any other names?"

"His sister called him Willy."

Old Joe clapped his hands to his head. "That'd be the Gas Head!"

"I'm sorry," I said. "What?"

"Gas Head Willy. That's what we call him 'round here. On account o' he crazy from the last war."

"Sounds like the right guy," I said. "Let's have a drink and you can tell me some more." Inside the speakeasy, things were lively. People were in the mood to drink and they clapped me on the back and shook my hand as we walked through to a table. It seemed I was the first to defeat the home team. One of whom I was about to drink with. "This place have a name, Rufus?"

"Maisie's. You drinkin'?"

"Yes." I could feel a mouse under my left eye. My entire body was beginning to stiffen up. I'd be sore later. A little anaesthetic, if not good for the body, would certainly be good for the soul.

Rufus came back with a bottle of hooch and some glasses. I picked up the bottle after he poured. "This what they call Clabba Killer?"

"Oh yeah," said Rufus holding his glass up for a toast. "Try not ta smell it before ya drink." So of course I did. After the burning subsided, and Rufus and Old Joe stopped laughing at the look on my face, I decided skunk must play some part in the fermentation of Clabba Killer. I made a big show of pinching my nose between my fingers before I poured it down my throat.

The burn in my nose was nothing when compared with the damage the stuff did on the way down. A Borax cocktail would have been pleasanter. It hit my stomach with a fiery explosion. I slammed the empty glass down onto the table in front of me. "Give me another!" I drank the second one more slowly. I'm not sure which was the best way.

"Why do you call him Gas Head Willy?" I asked Old Joe.

"T'aint just me," he shrugged. "Ever'one call him dat. On account o' dem fits."

"He'd get really drunk," Rufus said, "and run screamin' through town."

"Screaming about what?" I asked.

"That the gas was comin'," Old Joe finished.

"When's the last time you saw him?"

Old Joe and Rufus looked at one another. Rufus shrugged and said, "Thursday, maybe?"

"Said he was goin' up to Bal'clabba. To get himself some Killer."

"Old Joe," I said. "You're beautiful."

CHAPTER THREE
THE BODY

I wasn't feeling much pain when I left Maisie's. In fact, I felt pretty good. Even the prospect of a trip to Balaclava didn't really bother me. Such was the strength of Clabba Killer.

Balaclava was at the northernmost extreme of Sydenham Township, which was adjacent to Owen Sound. Sydenham had the reputation of being lawless. What held true for the township went double for the tiny community of Balaclava. That's what I'd heard anyway. I'd never been there myself. Few people went to Balaclava without good reason. I could only guess at Willy's reason. To get some Clabba Killer, Old Joe had said. Why? He could get it just fine at Maisie's. Why go to Balaclava?

Now I had a reason to go to Balaclava. And I needed to know more about it. I pulled out my pocket watch. Half past one. I had lots of time.

3rd Avenue East would take me right by the Grey County Courthouse, and the High Constable's office. A good place to get information, certainly on the type of people I'd be looking up when I got to Balaclava. I needed to find out who was behind Clabba Killer. If anyone knew, it'd be Oddball. Marc Scott had been the High Constable in Grey County for three years. He'd picked up the nickname Oddball before that, during his rookie years. Those were the days before the county issued proper equipment, expecting each constable to outfit himself. Unable to afford a proper gunbelt, Rookie Marc had carried his gun tucked inside the front of his pants. One night he'd chased and cornered a robber. In his haste, he cocked his gun before it was clear of his pants. It discharged prematurely and Marc went from an even to an Odd. And was forever tagged with the name Oddball Scott.

My footsteps echoed in the Saturday afternoon hallway. It was cool, the heat of the day shut out by the imposing granite exterior of the courthouse. Along each side of the main floor, glass fronted doors announced a variety of occupants, each of them tied to the administration of criminal justice in the county. I stopped at the constabulary door. A horseshoe of letters announced HIGH CONSTABLE and in smaller writing underneath, Marc Scott.

I grabbed the handle and pushed the door open. I walked smack into a walnut counter, a sort of corral to prevent the public from going further into the office. In the back right corner was a temporary cage. Empty. The other side of the office was crowded with desks, most of them empty. In the far corner a man sat tilted back in a chair, feet propped against the desk. A newspaper hid him from view. It was Oddball.

"Excuse me," I rapped my knuckles on the counter. "How does a fella get service around here?"

The paper was folded with a flourish. "Murphy! What the hell happened to ya?" Oddball stood and tossed the paper on the desk. He couldn't read and I knew it. Just used the paper for effect when he heard people coming through the door. He thought it made him look smart. He was a decent looking man, with a broad open face and ready smile. His easy manner was endearing and that was good. It helped one overlook the fact that he didn't wash quite as often as he should. Carrot topped, Oddball was 36, older than me by half a dozen years.

"Anything in the paper?" I asked.

"Lot about Labour Day. I hear you an' Scotty're leadin' the parade."

I lifted the hinged section of the counter, went back to his desk and sat on a chair in front of it. "That's right."

"Playin' football?" Oddball sat back down. He refrained from putting his feet back on the desk.

"Nope. Tug-of-war."

"Oh. Gonna kill those west-siders?"

"Without question."

Oddball leaned forward, studying my face. "You here to lay charges against whoever done that?"

"No." I laughed.

"Why not?"

"I won."

"Oh. Right. Well, what can I do fer ya?"

"I'm looking for a guy named Willy Robertson. He disappeared Tuesday night. Maybe went to Balaclava."

Oddball let out a low whistle. "From the Owen Sound Robertsons? What'd he go up to Balaclava for?"

"Booze. Clabba Killer they call it in Mudtown."

Oddball bolted upright in his chair. "Jesus Murphy!" he exclaimed. "The two Franks!" It was my turn to lean forward with interest. "They're brothers," he went on excitedly. "Big Frank and Little Frank Walker."

"They're both called Frank? Really?" Oddball nodded, sitting back down. He pulled an obviously used cigar from his top shirt pocket and stuck it in the corner of his mouth. "Nice parents," I said.

"Oh sure. You've got a lot to talk about." He took a deep breath and started to sing, "Oh Danny Boy, the pipes, the pipes are calling, from glen to glen and down the mountainside…"

"Right. I get your point," I interrupted. It was a cruel trick played on me by fate, the name my father had given me. Danny-Boy. His favourite song had become the bane of my existence.

"Ever been to Balaclava before?" Oddball turned serious.

"No. I was hoping you could give me a few pointers."

"You wanna watch out if you're dealin' with the two Franks. They're tough customers. Moonshine mostly, but they grow hemp out there too."

"And you just let 'em?"

"Have to," he said, annoyed. "They've got more men than me. I've heard the dry cops might make a move. May even have someone up there now."

The dry police enforced the Temperance Act. They generally worked border areas. I hadn't heard of them in Owen Sound before. I'd have to remember to tell Eddie to watch out. "Anything else I should know?"

"Yeah. The two Franks are pig mean. They'd as soon shoot ya as talk to ya."

"Guess I'll have to take my gun. It's a real conversation piece."

The office door behind burst open with a crash, sending Oddball and I both to our feet. "What the hell you want Sleepy? You damn near scared the life outta me." Odd's chubby, sweating deputy gave me a brief look, then turned his attention back to the boss.

"Just got a wire from Meaford. We got a body. Out the Annan Road." Odd and I exchanged a glance.

"Man or woman?" he asked.

"Man. I don't know nothin' more. It was the Reverend Klingenberg delivered the word. Says Long Tom is out there now, waitin'."

Oddball turned to me. "You could be out of a job. Wanna come?"

"I guess I'd better."

It wasn't the first ride I'd had in a car, but it was the wildest. Oddball careened out of the courthouse parking lot, tires squealing, siren blaring. He pushed the big Chevrolet up to twenty, "so we can make it up St. Mary's Hill," he shouted over the wind that forced me to hold my hat.

The car made a fearful noise as it clattered up the hill. Oddball swore under his breath and shifted down. A horse could have made it in less time and with less fuss. Or at least with less swearing. In spite of that, I didn't mind the ride.

By the time we got onto the Meaford Road, Oddball had it cranked back up. The road had just been rebuilt all the way to Meaford, according to the papers. The ride was a lot smoother and we could even talk despite the twenty-five mile an hour clip we were travelling at. Though we did have to shout to be heard.

"When you plannin' on headin' up to Balaclava?" Oddball shouted.

"Tomorrow's Sunday. Labour Day Monday. Not 'til Tuesday I guess."

"I got some men patrolling the roads out here," he hollered. "Maybe you can keep an eye out for 'em."

"In case they need some help?"

"Yeah, right. Smartass."

"Highway robbery seems to be a growing vocation."

"It's the cars. These crooks seem ta think 'cause you gotta car you got money. Ain't necessarily so. But a lot o' these guys, they ain't gonna take no for an answer. Only a matter a time 'fore someone gets killed."

"They all carry weapons?"

"Some do. Not all of 'em."

The Annan Road had started as little more than a track, rutted and potholed. Years of heavy use had turned it into a broad dirt road, well suited to horse and buggy, not a speeding car. All conversation ended as we turned onto it, primarily because Oddball refused to slow down. He kept the car at twenty where he could and swore like a trooper when he couldn't. If a county politician had been available, I'm sure he would have had an earful from the high constable about the condition of the roads.

As we clattered along, I couldn't help but think this was about to become the shortest investigation in history. If Willy was dead, I doubted there would be any need for me. His family had hired me to find him, alive. If the body we were rushing to see did belong to him, the investigation would become Oddball's. Two days at ten dollars a day would just cover the advance I'd gotten. It wouldn't go far in paying next month's rent or the cost of the telephone I'd installed in the office.

"You know what Willy looks like?" Odd shouted. The din of the car had dropped, as he slowed to go through the village of Annan. Little more than a crossroads, Annan consisted of a church with cemetery and half a dozen or so houses. At the corner was a general store and post office that a sign told me was run by the Speedie Family.

God, graves and groceries. Annan had everything it needed. "Well?" Odd asked, as he shifted up into third gear leaving the village.

"I met him. In the war. Think I remember well enough."

"Will you know if this stiff is him?"

"Depends how long he's been lying there, I guess."

Odd swivelled in the seat to look at the deputy in the backseat. "This one fresh?"

Sleepy shrugged his shoulders. "All I know is the wire came from Reverend Klingenberg, from the church out to Balaclava. He musta been goin' to Meaford for supplies and Long Tom asked him to send the wire. Otherwise it'd be a coupla hours ride for him to come in and tell us."

Odd turned his attention back to the road. The farther north of Annan we got, the worse it became. He was forced to slow down and that set up a whole new round of colourful language. It was about twenty minutes north of Annan, still a ways from Balaclava, that we saw Long Tom's horse hobbled at the side of the road, snacking, as only a horse of its size could. I could see by the swath it had cleared they had been there for a while.

Oddball pulled the car over as far as he could and the three of us piled out. Long Tom had been resting under an elm. He stood and stretched as we approached. Now I'm of average height, about six foot, but Long Tom was taller than me by a head and then some. "What the hell…" I muttered under my breath towards Oddball as the big man gave a bone crackling stretch.

"You never met Long Tom?" he asked as we came to a stop in front of the man. "Long Tom. This here's D.B. Murphy. A detective. He's lookin' for a missin' guy. So I thought we'd bring him on out here on accounta we got a found one."

Long Tom held out a hand the size of a catcher's mitt. "Pleased to meet ya."

"Likewise," I said, watching as my large hand was swallowed by his. The big fish eat the little ones, I thought.

"Well, what we got here Tommy?" Oddball pulled the used cigar from its special place in his top pocket and put it in his mouth. In all the time I had known him, I had never known Odd to actually light a cigar.

"Acrost there," Long Tom gestured towards the other side of the field he'd been sitting beside. "We got a body at the bottom of a gully. Right at the edge of the field. Farmer found it when he was workin'."

"You touch it?"

"No sir. You told me never touch a body when I find it. Just call you. So that's what I did. Course," he added, "I had to wait for the Reverend to come by on his way to Meaford. So he could send you a wire."

"How long you been here Tom?" Odd asked.

"Since last night."

"You been sleepin' under that tree the whole time?"

"No," he said with a what-do-you-take-me-for look. "I had to go to the bathroom."

"Why the hell didn't you just ride into town last night and tell me in person?"

"Had to guard the body. I was afraid someone might take it. Once they knew we found it."

"Fair enough I guess," Odd said. "But shouldn't you've stayed closer, y'know to keep a watch like?"

"I don't think so," Long Tom said. "This was as close to a body as I wanted to sleep."

"Great," was the reply. "Let's go then and get it over with."

Long Tom led us through the field, which was planted with corn. There was a clear path, where I guessed his size fourteens had tromped everything down the day before. We walked single file, so as not to disturb too much more of the crop. At the far edge of the field there was a sharp drop which led down a small ravine. From the road it had been completely invisible. On the other side of it, the farm fields continued on, sloping down to eventually end up at the shores of Georgian Bay. I could see it in the distance, vibrant blue.

The corpse of a man stood out in sharp contrast to the placid beauty of the rolling fields and sparkling water. It was directly below us, face down at the bottom of the slope. The head and body were obscured by an overcoat and hat.

"Why's his hat still on?" I asked aloud, to no one in particular.

"Hmmmph." Oddball responded, starting down the slope. "You check all around?" he called over his shoulder to Long Tom.

"Yessir. Didn't find nothing." I started down the slope after them. A cascade of dirt preceded me down the slippery incline, and I had more than a little trouble keeping to my feet. At the bottom, the air was still and heavy. The buzz of flies accompanied by the odd yellow jacket surrounded the body. Oddball combed the area and, finding nothing, he rolled the body over. It wasn't Willy. The unfortunate victim had black hair and swarthy skin. He might have been handsome once. But someone had shot his left eye out. Now he didn't look like much at all.

"I bet they pulled his hat down hard to cut down on the mess," Oddball commented, pulling the fedora off. "Want to see?" he asked. Apparently I'd been promoted to staff member. Probably for surviving the car ride out.

"I saw enough bodies at the war to last a lifetime," I replied. I had. "Most of 'em worse than this."

"You sure this ain't Willy?"

"It's not."

"That's too bad. Means I'm gonna have to investigate." Oddball rolled the cigar around his mouth a couple of times, thinking. As I watched, he absently rested a foot on top of the corpse. It was all I could do to suppress a laugh. He looked like the great white hunter. "Well," he said, "no point callin' the coroner all the way out here. He's dead, that's plain." Oddball gestured to the two deputies with his sodden cigar, then waved in the general direction of the car. "Load 'im up boys." Long Tom and Sleepy looked at one another, then back at Oddball. "Go on," he shouted. "Time's a wastin'."

Between them they picked the body up and started to hump it up the slope. The going was slow and they almost made it. Near the top Sleepy lost his footing and the body tumbled back down, end over end, the two deputies sliding and slithering behind it.

They decided not to try carrying it again. Sleepy went back to the car for rope. He tied one end around the feet and Long Tom took the other end to the top of the ravine. It didn't take long to drag the body up. Then they carried it the rest of the way to the car.

They call them stiffs for a reason. After the second attempt at folding the unwilling corpse into the trunk, the boys knew it too. "Well don't fret boys," Oddball said. "Sleepy, he can ride in back with you."

The ride home was much the same as the ride out. Except Sleepy had company in the back seat. It was late afternoon when we got back. I asked Odd to drop me in front of The Manjuris. I wanted to see what Eddie could tell me about the two Franks.

"You be careful up there in Balaclava," Oddball said.

"I can watch out for myself."

"Who knows," he said, shoving the car into reverse with a grind. "Might see you there. I 'spect I'm gonna have to investigate this." He pointed at the corpse with his cigar. "Unless the coroner calls it accidental." With a laugh and another vicious grind, Oddball sped off down the main street.

It was after five when I climbed the stairs to The Manjuris. Razor Eddie was standing at the bar. "What's the other guy look like?"

"Huh?" He couldn't know about the body already.

"That's two fights so far this summer. I hope you won."

"Oh, that. I'd forgotten." In the long mirror above the bar I caught a look at myself. It wasn't pretty. I used a hand to smooth some of my hair back. It was all over the place, thanks to Oddball and his car. The mouse under my left eye was a nice hue of purple and slightly swollen. There would be other bruises.

"Two fights?"

"Sure," Eddie said pouring me a drink. "Remember when you caught the chief? Didn't he struggle a bit?"

"He tried. Never beaten me yet, though."

"He hates you for it too. Ever since that time in the playground at Ryerson." Ryerson was the elementary school that Eddie, Silly and I had attended. Along with Johnny Baker who was the playground bully, the kind of guy kids tried to stay away from. Johnny's reign of terror had gone unchecked, until the day he humiliated my brother in front of the whole school. It had been too much for me. Outraged, I thrashed him to within an inch of his life. He'd hated me ever since. Now he had more reason to hate me. I'd had him busted out of his job and into the Kingston pen last summer.

"Yeah well, he can hate me all he likes. It'll give him something to do while he's in pokey.

Eddie laughed and poured us each a drink. "Say you know," he lowered his voice conspiratorially, "you could prob'ly get a prescription with that eye."

"What for? I can always come here for a drink."

"True enough. To the ex-chief!" He raised his glass and drank. I did too.

"What do you know about the two Franks?" I asked. Eddie paled and for a second his scar looked almost fresh. I was probably the only person in Owen Sound who knew he'd lost his ear and gained his scar in a whorehouse in France. Arguing over price.

"I know enough to stay away from them. If you're smart you'll do the same."

"Can't. Willy's trail leads straight to them."

Eddie looked at me a long moment, then poured another round. "They're killers," he said and took a drink

"Killers?"

"They like to kill almost as much as they like to drink."

"How much do they drink?"

"A lot."

I considered the danger for a moment. Then asked if it was their stuff we were drinking.

"I told you I was waitin' for Montreal to come through. When it don't come, they're the only ones around can supply me. I got a lot of loyal customers."

"What else do you know about the Franks?"

"They inherited the business from their dad."

"His name Frank?"

"How'd ya know?"

"Just a hunch."

"You detectives," Eddie laid on the sarcasm. "You amaze me."

"If you liked that you're gonna love this. I hear the dry cops have got it in for the two Franks. You better watch yourself."

"Dry cops? Up here? Shit."

"Okay, that's my good deed for today. Now you tell me something."

"They got a farm north of Balaclava. Dun Wurkin they call it. There's a whole compound. Fenced, with armed men. Lots of 'em."

"What're they into?"

"Booze mostly. Clabba Killer. Beer. And they grow hemp."

"That's different."

"Little Frank did some travellin'. Got himself a taste for the dope. So he grows it and sells to most anyone who wants it."

"Thanks Eddie. I've got to get home for dinner."

He grabbed my arm before I had a chance to move. His voice was low when he spoke. "You got a piece?"

"Sure."

He let go of my arm and slowly nodded. "Take it."

Oak Hall was just a few doors away from The Manjuris. It was near closing time and the canopy had been rolled up. The front doors stood open, drinking in the late afternoon air. With the exception of some last minute shoppers, the street was quiet.

The hardwood floor creaked as I stepped through the front door. Oak Hall was not a large store and I saw right away that Sil wasn't out front. Unless he was hiding somewhere among the racks and shelves that crowded every foot of available floor space.

"How does a guy get some service around here?" I called into the still air. There was a muffled response from the back. It was likely Sil, sunk to the gunnels in a sea of coats, suits and shirts. I walked down the centre aisle, toward the stock room doors. Along one side were suits, seven to fifteen dollars. On the other side, stockings, shirts, sweaters and varsity caps were stacked, all part of the big Labour Day sale Sil had been talking about for weeks.

I pushed through to the back and was struck by jackets. Hundreds of them, piled on every available surface. Right in the middle was Sil, grease pencil in hand, marking down prices. The air smelled of mothballs.

"How'd you make out in Mudtown?" he asked, without looking up.

"Isn't it a bit early for overcoats?"

"Isn't it a bit early for overcoats?"

"Not when there's a sale. First law of retail. When there's a sale, put everything out. Even if it is three years out of fashion. Someone will buy it. Say," he looked up, "what happened to you?"

I sat down on a chair piled with coats and told him about my day. I finished at about the same time he did.

"I'm starved. Let's get out of here," he said. We took our time walking home. Supper wasn't til six on weekends. "Any idea who the body belongs to?" Sil asked.

"Nope. It wasn't Willy though and that's my only concern."

"So what next?"

"I guess I'll head up to Balaclava. But not until Tuesday. I'll stay over and come home Wednesday."

"Oh good. I thought maybe you were trying to weasel your way out of the tug-of-war."

"Never. Gotta beat those west siders. 'Sides, Scotty and I are leading the parade. Couldn't miss that."

"I know a fellow in Balaclava. He's the shopkeeper up there. A single fellow, and a veteran too. You could probably stay the night at his place. He likes to have company."

"What's the catch?"

Sil smiled. "He's an inventor of sorts. Shampoo for horses was the last I heard."

"Who on earth would shampoo a horse?"

"Exactly. I'll write you a letter of introduction. His name is Bill Van Wyck." We were coming up the front walk and before I had a chance to respond we were ambushed by a couple of wild men with guns.

"Bang! Bang! You're dead!" Sil fell over like he'd been pole-axed. I staggered up the walk a few more feet and fell to the ground. Finn and Aidan squealed with delight. In the next second they were standing over me.

"Hey Murph, what happened to your eye?" Finn asked, a serious expression on his face.

"Happened when I fell over just now."

"No really. C'mon. What happened?"

"Not a thing you need to know about, Sonny boy," Sil said standing. "Now let's get inside and get ready for dinner."

"Will you be seeing Lori tonight?" Marth asked at dinner. It was the opening the boys had been waiting for.

"Murphy and Lori sitting in a tree, k-i-s-s-i-n-g. First comes love and then comes marriage, then comes Danny-Boy in the baby carriage!"

"Boys!" Marth didn't do much of a job suppressing a giggle. Finn was closest to me at the table. I grabbed his arm and gave it a pinch. Not too hard. Just enough to make the point.

"You better watch out for me after dinner."

"I'm really scared," he said and stuck his tongue out at me.

"Boys, you are excused," Marth said, the ill-concealed giggle threatening to become an all out laugh.

Once the boys were gone, Sil turned and raised an eyebrow. "Well?"

"I suppose I may call on Miss Storey tonight. I believe there is a performer at Griffins she'd like to see."

I was crazy about Lori Storey. Of course, I hadn't told her that yet. We'd met a few months earlier, when I investigated her sister. Dori had taken over her brother's insurance business when he went to war. He didn't come home and the business became hers. She was at the docks the night my brother's partner had been killed. I considered her a suspect, until my investigation proved her innocence. Tall, dark and stylish, there was an urban beauty about her. And, as I learned later, it was a beauty that appealed to Razor Eddie.

Lori on the other hand, was my ideal woman. A piano teacher, she too was beautiful. Of average height, she was perfectly proportioned, with brown hair and blue eyes. She smiled a lot and her voice could melt ice. Add to that a sunny disposition and quick intelligence and I fell like a ton of bricks. At 26, she still lived at home and taught her lessons there.

Standing on the step outside her front door, I could hear the sound of playing drifting from the front parlour. After listening for a moment, I decided it had to be a student. My knock was answered by a petite blond. Glori was the youngest of the Storey sisters.

"Hi Murphy," she said. "Lori said to c'mon in an' wait."

"Okay." I followed her into the foyer. Cool and dark, the late summer heat hadn't penetrated it. The sound of the piano grew louder and harder to take. I peeked my head around the door to look into the music room and saw Lori sharing the piano bench with a little girl of eight or nine. Black haired with glasses, she was having some difficulty controlling her hands as they travelled up and down the keys.

"Okay, that's fine for today," Lori said, throwing me a wink. "You be sure and practise some more before our next time."

"Yes Miss," was the polite response. I ducked back into the foyer to spare the little girl's feelings. They came out right after me and stopped.

"Hello Mr. Murphy," Lori shot me a smile hotter than the day. Gesturing to the girl beside her she said, "This is Maryann."

"Hello Maryann," I said. "Are you an Owen Sounder?"

After her student left, Lori pressed her body against me in the dark foyer. We kissed, then she touched my eye where it was swollen. "I can't wait to hear about this."

Before I could say a word, Mrs. Storey was coming down the hallway from the kitchen. "What are you two up to out here, all alone and in the dark?" she teased. We quickly peeled ourselves apart and went into the parlour. Mrs. Storey followed. "Oh, Danny-Boy," she tut-tutted when she saw me. "What on earth have you been up to? Not brawling in the streets?"

"No Ma'am. Just a little work-related injury."

"Well, I don't think I need to know anything about that. I've some lovely fresh cookies. And milk?"

I thought about the after-dinner rye Sil would be drinking in his study. "Yes ma'am. That'd be lovely." As she left the room Lori and I looked at one another. And started to laugh. Quietly. It was a ritual, the cookies and milk. Once I had told Mrs. Storey that the thing I missed most at war was cookies and milk. Now a visit never passed that she didn't offer some.

No sooner had she gone than we heard the front door open, then slam shut. "Hello!" a voice boomed. Jack Storey stuck his head around the corner. A smile broke out when he saw us. "Ah, Private Murphy!" he cried.

I jumped to my feet and snapped a smart salute. "Sergeant Major, Sir!"

"At ease, my boy," he laughed aloud, disappearing back into the hallway.

"You guys," Lori laughed and squeezed my knee.

Jack Storey and I had gotten along well from our first meeting. A big man, he had iron grey hair and the biggest moustache I'd ever seen. It was a souvenir, he said, of the Boer War and his service under Lord Kitchener. He loved the drill sergeant routine. I think it reminded him of his own military days. Now a shift supervisor at Kennedy's foundry, he'd often expressed an interest in exerting the same type of discipline on the men under his charge.

"Hmmmm," he muttered, returning with a glint in his eye. "You look different. Got a hair cut, have you?" He sat heavily in the chair opposite us.

"More of a close shave, Sergeant Major," I replied.

"And who might the barber have been?" he laughed.

"A fellow I met up in Mudtown this afternoon."

"Mudtown!" Lori exclaimed, squeezing my hand.

"Gad, man," the Sergeant Major said. "Mudtown? Worse than Vimy, I should think."

"Not by half," I replied. "It wasn't nearly as bad as people say."

"But your face…" Lori touched my eye again.

"I wore a suit. They don't like strangers in suits. But it's okay. I'm not a stranger anymore. And the next time I won't wear a suit."

Mrs. Storey returned with a plate of cookies and a tall glass of milk. "What's all this about Mudtown?" she asked.

"D.B. went out there for some dancin' lessons today," said the Sergeant Major. She gave me a quizzical look, then sat down next to her husband.

"I got my first client," I said, accepting their congratulations. "A veteran disappeared and I've been hired to look for him. He spent a lot of time in Mudtown."

"Who is it, Danny?" Lori asked.

"In Mudtown they call him Gas Head Willy. Willy Robertson."

"Hell and damnation!" The Sergeant Major cursed under his breath and jumped up. Mrs. Storey clapped a hand to the side of her face and Lori gasped. I looked from one to the other, not quite sure what I'd said.

"Uh…did I say something?"

"That no-good, two-bit, lying, cheating, thieving scoundrel!" The Sergeant Major was working himself into a froth.

Mrs. Storey jumped up. "Now Jack," she scolded, "come out of here and leave the kids alone." She shooed him ahead of her out the door. Turning, she gave me a sympathetic smile and pulled the pocket doors until they were almost, but not quite, closed. They were never closed tight. House rule.

I turned to Lori. "What on earth was that all about?"

"That's a name we don't say in this house."

"And?"

"Kiss me first." I did.

"Okay," I said after a few minutes. "It's not that I'm more interested in Willy Robertson."

"But you are," she teased. I gave her my best pout and tried to work up a tear. Fortunately she stepped in, or we may have been waiting a while. "The Robertsons were cutting trees on our property on White Cloud Island. Willy stole the money, instead of giving it to the Sergeant Major."

"When? How? How much?"

"Before the war. No one is allowed to ask and Daddy doesn't talk about it much." She undid a button on my shirt, and gently caressed my chest. It felt pretty good. Also made it hard to concentrate.

"I've gotta go to Balaclava," I said. She leaned closer. Her voice was a whisper in my ear.

"I thought we were spending Labour Day together," she purred.

I gave an involuntary shudder and glanced nervously at the open door. "I'm going to wait until Tuesday."

"How long will you be gone?"

"Couple of days. Maybe just overnight. Not sure yet."

"Don't be gone too long. We've got a wedding on Friday." I'd been hoping she'd forget. The wedding was for a friend of hers. Someone I didn't get along with at all. The bride was nosy, gossipy and judgmental. People like that drove me crazy. I tried not to be around whenever she was.

"Do we have to go?" I whined.

"Of course we have to go. Luella is my friend."

Luella. Didn't that just say it all. I decided it was a subject best dropped. "I'll be home in time for the wedding."

"You'd better be," she whispered softly in my ear. Her teasing fingers and husky voice got to be too much. With one last glance at the still vacant doorway, I turned towards her.

Leaning in close I said, "Don't worry," and kissed her on the mouth, then added, "I'll be there," before continuing the kiss.

"Hey have you guys…Eeew!"

We jumped apart at the sound of Glori's voice. "Ssshhh!" Lori hissed at her, starting to giggle. "C'mon," she grabbed my hand and jumped up. "Let's go to the theatre."

CHAPTER FOUR
A REAL LEADER

There's nothing like a parade to make the weather turn. It had been cloudy and threatening all morning and now, walking towards the City Hotel, it was starting to spit rain. It felt strange to have my uniform on again. At one time I couldn't imagine wearing anything else. Now it seemed stiff and formal, the leftover relic of a time I wanted to forget.

Sunday had been spent quietly. Church in the morning with the Johnsons. Then a family picnic at Balmy Beach, followed by an afternoon of rough-housing with the boys. I don't recall having as much energy when I was a boy. As an adult I could use it. Evening had been spent cleaning my kit and preparing for the big parade.

I kept Scotty at the City Hotel stables. A piebald gelding, I'd had him for a long time, nearly ten years. Sil had kept him in shape for me during the war and he was still a good runner, though he was prone to the occasional tendon problem in his groin area. For some reason, no one really knew why, he had started losing the hair between his ears. It gave him an oddly human look. But I tried not to mention it, so as not to hurt his feelings.

The Lugan had Scotty ready when I arrived. A small man, with red hair and a prominent hump, I had no idea of his real name. He'd been the stableman at the City Hotel for as long as anyone could remember. That wasn't quite as long as he'd been called the Lugan: no one could remember where that had come from either. He was an agreeable enough fellow and always did his best for the horses.

"Lugan," I said coming into the stable. Curried and saddled, Scotty looked about the best he had in a long time.

"Hey Murph," the Lugan said. "Skinhead's already to go."

"Sssssh!" I placed a hand in front of my mouth. "You know it upsets him when you say things like that."

"Oh, sorry." He pretended I was telling him something he didn't already know. "But Scotty's already in a pretty strange mood."

"Oh great. Just what I need on parade day." As good a horse as he was, Scotty had a mind of his own. He liked to show it, occasionally in strange ways. Racing automobiles was a favourite. I'd decided that he couldn't stand it when there was something on the road that was faster than he was. More than once I'd been led a merry chase, while he defended his horsehood by racing a Ford or a Chevrolet. I pulled half an apple out of my pocket and offered it.

"Be good today," I cautioned. "The whole county will be watching."

I could have saved my breath. Initially, things went well. We rode over to Queen's Park, at 8th Street and 1st Avenue on the west side. The parade was to start at twelve thirty, then move through the downtown and up to Victoria Park, which sat on top of the escarpment on the east side. There was nothing difficult about the route. Unless you were a horse with a mind of your own and a predilection for automobiles.

I had been told by the Labour Day Committee to lead the parade away from the downtown up to 6th Street, before circling back to travel the length of the main street. Everything went well for a block. Then a car came by. I only got a glimpse, but I think it was Colin Carr. He had the newest automobile in town, one that would go forty miles an hour. As he passed us at 8th Street, I felt Scotty stiffen under me and I knew there was trouble afoot. I leaned over to whisper, "not now," or something equally convincing in his ear when I felt him start after the car. I yanked on the reins and managed to slow him, but couldn't change his direction. Scotty was determined to follow that car and was around the corner and heading in the wrong direction in a flash.

There weren't many people gathered this far along the route yet. Most, I surmised, would be at the start, about four blocks away. So there was still a chance of correcting the mistake, without too much embarrassment. Until Scotty followed the car around another wrong turn. By this time I'd decided it was best to cut my losses, get him back to the stable and let the parade continue along its route without a marshall. I managed at last to reign Scotty in. Smugly satisfied, I was about to put my plan into effect, when the parade came wheeling around the corner—the wrong corner—and up the street towards us.

★★★

I walked from the City Hotel Stable up to Victoria Park, which was also known as the Pleasure Grounds. I hoped that by leaving Scotty behind, he'd get the idea he was being punished. It wasn't the first time he'd chased an automobile. But I was certain it would be the most humiliating. For me.

Victoria Park had a lot of uses. The Owen Sound Fall Fair was about the biggest thing that went on there, but it looked like Labour Day would run a close second this year. Dominating the park was a large grandstand. In front of it, there were several football fields where matches were being played. Behind the grandstand, there were barns belonging to the Agricultural Society and the baseball fields. Between the football fields and the grandstand, a stage had been set. A dancing exhibition from one of the local academies was to be held there, just before the politicians extolled their own virtues. I was hard pressed to decide which would have the greater entertainment value. With a federal election in the offing, I guessed the preening politicians might be more fun. But most of them would likely wait until the big meeting at town hall.

I paid my 35 cents and went in. "Hey Murph!" The first person I saw coming through the gate was Razor Eddie. Dori was with him, all smiles, happy to be out in public with her man.

"Hello Eddie. Dori." I nodded a greeting, then asked, "Have you seen Lori?"

"She's over in the grandstand waiting for you. The speeches are starting soon."

"Oh great," I said with a groan. "She wants to hear the speeches?"

"Everyone does," Dori said. "There's woman from south Grey who wants to run for the United Farmers in the election."

"A woman?"

"Yes. About time too."

"What is it with that horse of yours?" Eddie asked with a grin.

I decided to play dumb. "What about him?"

"C'mon, it's all the talk. How Scotty went chasing after an Oldsmobile or something. Led the parade all over downtown. Everywhere 'cept where it was supposed to go."

"Oh. That. Well, you know Scotty." It was all I could think of. How could you explain a horse that liked to chase cars?

"Hey c'mon have a drink with us."

"No. I'd better go find Lori."

"Your loss," Eddie said, leading Dori towards the side of the fields where cars were parked. I imagine he had some hooch stashed in his auto. Probably enough for everyone in the place. His was the kind of concession the cops would turn a blind eye to, for the sake of a good celebration. More so in the evening than the daytime. There was a dance planned after the speeches at town hall.

Eddie and Dori had been wrong, as far as I could see. The grandstand was nearly empty. On stage, a young lady was highland dancing, accompanied by a caterwauling set of bagpipes. It was, I assumed, the advertised Miss Iona Pettigrew.

Lori was five rows up and directly in the centre. She liked to be able to see. Especially since one of her students would be playing *God Save the King* before the speeches started. I excused myself to three or four couples and one family on my way to join her.

"Excuse me Miss, is this seat taken?" I gestured to the spot beside her.

"Well," she smiled coyly, "I am waiting for my boyfriend. But you can sit there until he comes."

"Thank you." I sat beside her, close, until our arms were touching.

"You'd best be careful sir. He could be here any time."

"Jealous type, is he?"

"Oh yes."

"I could take him."

"He's awfully big. And mean tempered."

"I guess I'd best keep to myself then," I said, and started to slide away. Lori grabbed my arm and pulled me closer.

"I'm glad you're here," she whispered and kissed me on the ear. The dancing over, the speakers filed onto the platform.

"I'm glad to see you," I whispered back. "You're the prettiest girl here."

Lori blushed. "Oh, you."

"What I'm not sure about is being here, to listen to this. I have to go tonight, so I'll just hear the same thing over."

"I'm not allowed to go tonight. The Sergeant Major says it's not proper for women. And I really want to hear Miss Macphail."

"She's the one who wants to be a politician?"

"That's right."

"Good luck."

"Wha…?" Her question was cut off at the first note of the piano. Grey County Warden Sing asked everyone to stand for *God Save the King*. Lori's student performed flawlessly, but I don't think she noticed. She started in as soon as we sat.

"Danny-Boy Murphy!" I knew I was in trouble when she used my full name. "Do you mean to tell me you don't think there's a place for women in politics?"

"There's probably more place for women than men. After all, men can't seem to get it right. All I meant was good luck getting elected in Grey County. Especially in the southeast."

As we talked, politicians got up, one by one, to bring greetings, comment on the weather and make jokes. My interest grew when Captain Mullowney got up to speak. He'd been the chaplain for the 147th regiment from Grey County and was the man behind the new Canadian Legion everyone was talking about. His comments were brief, aimed at drawing more people to the big meeting later at the town hall.

Miss Macphail took the stage when he finished. Her address was short and to the point. Women, returned men, farmers and labour should take control of the country. It belonged to the people, not the politicians. Her comments were treated to the same polite applause everyone got. But her speech had been the best.

Miss Macphail was followed by the longest winded of the politicians. Dr. Salem Bland went on at length as we sat there and baked in the afternoon sun. The key to a responsible government, he said, was a coalition of farmers, labour, soldiers and women. He called men like me idealists, who had come back home with a great vision of what Canada could be. Instead, "their dreams seemed to have been forgotten, for they have come back to a country which is trying only to make and spend money." By the end of his speech the crowd was enthused.

Afterwards, Lori wanted to meet Miss Macphail. On our way to the stage I was forced to drop behind when someone grabbed my arm. Pearl Robertson's look of apology turned to surprise when she saw my bruised face.

"Have you found my brother?"

"Not yet, ma'am." She began to guide me away from the stage and back towards the grandstand. Looking over my shoulder, I could see Lori waiting at the edge of a group that had surrounded Miss Macphail.

"Where are we going?"

"Papa wants to meet you." It was then I saw Silas Robertson, sitting on the lowest bench of the grandstand. His father had made a fortune in lumber. Silas had added value to the family business by building a sawmill and processing the logs he stripped from local forests. There was another man sitting with him, a face I recognized but couldn't place.

Silas Robertson stood as we approached. His body was bent and twisted by the ravages of early arthritis. Shorter than me by a head, an habitual scowl was all over his face.

"Papa," Pearl said. "This is Mr. Murphy." The hand he offered was more like a claw.

"Go away Pearl," he said without looking at her. The abruptness of the request surprised me, but it was apparently nothing new for her. She went without further comment.

"Sit down," Robertson said, doing the same. "Now I called you over here," he started, "because I like to know what I'm spending my money on. By the way, this is Jamieson Johnston."

Jamieson Johnston was in lumber too, I remembered. He sat on one side of Robertson, so I took the other. Lori was still waiting for Miss Macphail.

"Did someone rearrange your face while you were searching for my son?" He sounded educated, expressing his words in a precise and civilized way.

"In a manner of speaking," I replied, "but it would have happened no matter who I was looking for."

"What do you mean?" I told him about Mudtown and the investigation so far.

"Gas Head Willy?" He shook his head. "I always knew that boy was headed for a bad end."

"From what I hear you've spent a lot of time and money trying to prevent that."

He looked at me sharply, then a sly grin crossed his face. "Do you have any children, Mr. Murphy?"

"No."

"When you have your own, you'll understand. How will you proceed next?"

"Tomorrow I'm going to Balaclava to see if I can pick up his trail there."

"You find my boy," he said, "and bring him home. Do it by the end of the week and I'll pay you a hundred dollar bonus. By the way," he said, the grin broadening, "Will you ride your horse to Balaclava?"

"Yes." I walked right into it. "Why?"

"You'd best be careful you don't end up in Meaford." The frown disappeared as Silas Robertson broke into an all out laugh. Beside him, Johnston snickered into his hand.

★★★

Owen Sound won the big football match with a score of 3-2. Everyone agreed, it was one of the best games ever played at Victoria Park. Now that might have been because the hometown boys waxed the tails off the division champs. Whatever the case, there had to be five thousand people watching the game from the sidelines.

Exciting as the game had been, there was a real buzz when the men were called forward for the tug-of-war. Ten per side, we lined up. There was a lot of disappointment on our side when we saw the anchor for the west. Big Charlie Couture weighed at least three-fifty. The crowd broke up into two very distinct parts, one backing the west, the other the east. The chanting started before the pulling. "East is least, west is best" came from the end of the field opposite our team.

We lined up and picked up the rope. Our legislative member, D. J. Taylor, stood at the centre of the rope where a lady's scarf had been tied. It was to be the best two out of three. I had just twined my right arm in the rope when the gun went off. I dug my feet in and thrust backwards with the rest of the east side team. The rope went taut and the crowd went wild. "Go, go, go!" the chant came from all around us, as the scarf at the centre see-sawed first one way, then the other. For five minutes it went on, until with one great "Heave!" I felt my legs give way and all of us on the east team were flat on our faces.

The laughter from the west supporters helped us greatly in the next pull. From the start we steadily dragged. The men of the west were lying in front of us after less than a minute and our supporters were laughing at them.

Third pull would decide it all. The roar of the crowd dropped to a hush as we took the rope up again. I could see Big Charlie down at the west end of the rope, placidly smiling. The gun went off. They had us from the start. One long, steady pull. Thirty seconds and it was over. The west side went crazy, hoisting the winners up on to shoulders and parading them around. All except Big Charlie. He walked.

I got up early Tuesday morning. I was still packing a small bag when Sil came into my room. He was dressed and ready for work. He was carrying a bundle of oily rags. "You'd better take this," he said, tossing it onto the bed. I picked it up and knew without looking there was a gun inside. I gave Sil a questioning look, then started to unwrap it.

"Eddie wanted you to have that," he said simply, as a Smith and Wesson .45 calibre revolver surfaced. Sil reached into his pocket and pulled out a box of cartridges to go with the weapon.

"I've already got a gun. Two in fact."

I pulled my Webley & Scott .455 automatic out of my shoulder holster. Sil's eyes widened briefly as I handed him the gun.

"Brought that back from England with me. Got it from a British flyer." While he looked at it, I bent over and pulled the smaller .32 calibre automatic out of my riding boot. "Got this one over there too." Sil's look at seeing the second gun was out and out amazement.

"I guess Eddie didn't need to worry."

I reached into an inside pocket and pulled out a handful of the flat-fronted lead bullets I'd bought with the Webley & Scott.

"What on earth?" Sil took one and held it in front of his face.

"The Manstopper. They stopped making 'em a few years ago. Figured they did too much damage. Hit a guy with this, it's a sure thing."

"Are you expecting trouble?"

"If you've gotta shoot at someone any bullet will do. But there's something I learned in the war. When people start shooting to kill, life and death isn't decided in minutes or even seconds. It's tenths of seconds, hundredths of seconds. A sure thing…it's a comfort."

Sil turned the cylinder in his hands. "Ever used one?"

"No. They came with the gun." I went to my cupboard and pulled out a rifle.

"Another souvenir?" Sil asked.

"Exactly," I said handing him the British made Lee Enfield rifle. "None of the boys in the trenches used the Ross rifles the government issued. The mud jammed 'em and they froze up too easily. We all switched to British weapons as quickly as we could."

"I read about that," he said. "Our illustrious minister of defence, Sam Hughes, denied it all."

"Sure he did. And he ordered us to keep using Canadian guns even though they didn't work. A lot of our boys died 'cause of that."

"So are you expecting war when you get to Balaclava?"

"I don't know what to expect. So I'll prepare for the worst. If it doesn't happen, fine. If it does, I'll be ready."

"Say it is the worst. Are you ready to die for Gas Head Willy?"

I tucked the last few things into my saddlebag and cinched it shut.

"Are you worried about me?"

He coloured slightly, but held my gaze. "Of course I am. Marth too."

"Don't."

"But it's not worth dying for."

"What is?"

"What do you mean?"

"What I mean is, I spent four years in France, ready to die for my country. Thousands of boys did die for it. Why?"

"To stop the Kaiser."

"Exactly. We could have said no. Let him have Europe. But it wouldn't have stopped there. In five, ten years, we'd be fighting evil here, on our own streets. So we went and fought. Not just to keep him from taking Europe. To keep him from taking everything."

"What's your point?"

"My point is, if I'm going to die for something, I want it to be the right thing. Fighting the Kaiser was the right thing. I think fighting bad people at home is the right thing too. Because they want the same as the Kaiser."

"Everything."

"Right."

Scotty was saddled and ready to go when I arrived at the City Stables. "You might want to keep him movin' this morning Murph," the Lugan warned me. "He's got a bit of wind."

"Thanks for the tip," I said, leading Scotty out the stable door. I mounted up and walked him the half-block to my office.

It was still early and 2nd Avenue was quiet. In front of the Marketeria, James MacLean was sweeping the sidewalk. "Morning D.B.!" he shouted cheerily.

"Readying Fish Headquarters for another day?" He stopped sweeping and looked at me, puzzled. I pointed to the sign above the door.

"Oh that," he said. "Sometimes I forget it's even there."

There were no hitching posts left downtown, so I took a chance and left Scotty standing in front of the store. "If you see a car coming, can you grab his lead and hold on, please?"

"A car?"

"He likes cars. I don't have time to chase him."

"Sure, sure. I'll be a few more minutes yet."

I turned to Scotty, and gave him a stern look. "You stay here. I'll be right back. No chasing cars!" The look he gave me in return seemed to indicate compliance, so I turned and ran up the stairs to my office.

I sorted through the stuff Pearl had left to find the steamer ticket. I wanted to check it out at the Owen Sound Transportation office before I left town.

On the way back down I could hear the panicky sound of MacLean's voice. I took the last few stairs two by two and burst out the door onto the sidewalk.

The first thing I saw was Scotty, straining to start down the street after a passing Dodge. The only thing holding him back was the portly shopkeeper, who was lying flat on his back. He had one hand on Scotty's lead, while his other searched for something to hold on to.

The few people on the street at that hour had stopped to watch. Many were laughing openly. I rushed to help him, barely suppressing my own laughter.

Grabbing the lead, I yanked hard. Scotty didn't desist exactly, but I did get his attention long enough to help MacLean up. He sputtered and coughed as he stood and then, to my surprise, joined everyone else by laughing himself. Scotty looked longingly as the Dodge turned a corner and disappeared from sight.

"The *Michipicoten* doesn't leave until Thursday."

"Why the delay?" I was standing in the doorway of an office on the waterfront, addressing the elderly clerk of the Owen Sound Transportation Company. His thick glasses made him look owlish. Behind me, the docks were alive with activity. Unlike 2nd Avenue, work on the waterfront started early.

"It's because of the holiday, sir," he said. "Everything's back a day."

"Doesn't say that on the ticket," I said, showing it to him.

"Then this can't be your ticket, sir. Everyone who bought a ticket for this week's sailing knows it's leaving on Thursday, instead of Wednesday. I told them myself. And about the layover too."

"What layover?"

"Got an overnight layover in Meaford. A repair. Left over from when she ran aground in April up at Philip Edward Island. She'll leave Meaford Friday at noon."

"Really. Well, thanks a lot."

I closed the door behind me, and led Scotty down the dock. We crossed the bridge onto 1st Avenue East. It was a bustle of activity—trucks, carts and people coming and going. I walked partway up the street, then mounted up near the CPR station. We headed across 3rd Avenue towards Mudtown. Beyond it lay Lakeshore Road and Balaclava.

CHAPTER FIVE
THE LAWLESS TOWNSHIP

Lakeshore Road began on the edge of Mudtown and followed the shoreline north to the village of Leith. Once the only way to the tiny village had been by boat. The road went in at the same time the Canadian Pacific laid its track. A sort of bonus I guess. We took the ride at an easy pace. My plan was to stop somewhere along the way to enjoy the bag lunch Marth had packed for me. Mid-afternoon would be soon enough to arrive in Balaclava.

Georgian Bay was so blue it hurt. Just beyond Mudtown it came into full view, forcing me to squint. Near the shore, I could see a Watts skiff coming in. The two men shouted back and forth in French. I had no idea what they were saying. I took a deep breath and enjoyed the smell of the bay. It was a light, clean smell. Nothing like the ocean. I'd found the Atlantic's saltiness heavy and oppressive.

The ride was uneventful. For most of the way, there was forest on both sides of the roadway. The morning was grand and I could tell it was going to be another peach of a day. Perfect for riding. I wondered if Willy was riding. Or walking. Or dead. Like the man in that farm field. I wondered who he was. How he'd gotten there. Whether anyone was having sleepless nights, wondering where he was. I wished I'd stopped to see Oddball.

There wasn't much to the village of Leith. A Rotary Camp in the summer. An annual sports day that brought crowds from all around. A porcupine hunt. Its one famous son, an artist, had died a few years ago. Some sort of a canoeing accident. About the most excitement they'd had in Leith was the spring installation of electric street lights. Two thousand dollars, the papers had said, for a gas powered dynamo.

Most of the village lay along the water side of Lakeshore Road. It was a summer place, where well-to-do Owen Sounders brought their families. The other big summer destinations were Oliphant on the Saugeen Peninsula and the Lake Huron beaches. On the outskirts of the village, the houses were few and far between. Their numbers rapidly increased, until they stood cheek by jowl near the post office and general store.

A two storey building, the Leith General Store looked as though it had been there forever. It was built with the same cedars that surrounded it. The sunbleached shake roof had the beginnings of a moss beard. There were wooden benches on either side of the front door. The left hand bench was occupied by a man who looked even older than the store. A cob pipe was clenched in his gnarled left hand, a tin coffee cup in his right. His eyes were open, but I doubt he could see much beyond the cataracts that covered them. Nonetheless his head turned as I approached, in an attitude of open curiosity.

"Good morning," I called. He continued to look at me, but remained silent. "Nice day," I continued.

The scrape of a match broke his silence, as he tried to light the cob pipe. He began to chuckle. It was a wet, throaty, disjointed sound.

"Don't mind him," a voice called from the doorway. "He don't talk much no more. Not to strangers 'specially."

A woman stepped out of the doorway, and into the morning light. I'd guess she was 45 or so and on the heavy side. Steel grey hair was pulled back in a severe bun and an apron covered her skirts. She was not an unattractive woman, but she'd lived. I could tell by the etching of lines that crossed her face.

"I'm Callie Walter. My husband and I own this place." When she smiled, it transformed her into a young woman again.

"Murphy," I said, dismounting. "D.B. Murphy."

"This fella's my uncle." He didn't say a word. Just watched. At least the chuckling had stopped. "Things get pretty quiet after Labour Day," Callie said, "so we let him sit out front here. Durin' summer he sits 'round the back an' looks at the water."

"Back," he said quietly without moving his lips.

"Where you headed Mr. Murphy?"

"Back," the voice said again.

We both looked at him. There was a slight frown on Callie's face.

"I'm on my way out to Balaclava."

"Cup of coffee? It's almost fresh."

"Sure," I said. "I'd like that. Do you get many cars out here?"

"Nope."

"Good," I said dropping Scotty's lead on the ground. I followed Callie into the store. I stopped just inside while my eyes adjusted to the change in light. When I could see again I was glad I had stopped. Every available surface in the store was piled high with stock. It would have been easy to blunder into something in the dim light. Tipping one thing over would probably result in everything coming down, like dominoes.

"C'mon round here." I followed Callie's voice around the shelves that ran down the centre of the store. She was bent over a small pot-bellied stove on the other side, pouring coffee from a tin pot. A small window between us afforded a view. To the right was the river mouth and the wharf, now in a state of disrepair. Straight ahead, at the end of a long sandy stretch of beach, a man was knee deep in the water, shore fishing.

"That's my John," Callie said holding a cup of coffee out to me. "C'mon out back."

The back of the store was identical to the front. Except the benches were empty. I thought of the uncle out front. A memory of gargoyles I'd seen guarding a church in France came to mind.

"What brings you out this way?"

"I'm looking for someone."

"Oh?"

The coffee she gave me was good. Strong, the way I liked it.

"His name's Willy Robertson. Been gone from Owen Sound for about a week now. Don't suppose he came through here?"

She shook her head. "But that don't mean nothin'. Usually it's John does the store work. I just come down so's he can fish." She stood and walked to the edge of the wooden porch that ran the length of the store. Cupping her hands, she bellowed "John!" at the top of her lungs.

The man in the water whipped his head around and waved with his free hand. While we watched, he reeled in his line and trudged across the sand to where we sat.

"John," Callie said. "This here's Mr. Murphy."

"Murph," I shook his hand. "Just call me Murph."

"Well hello then, Murph," he said. "Welcome to paradise." He tromped up the steps and leaned his pole against the wall. A big man with a hearty grin. What was left of his hair, a fringe above his ears, was sandy brown. He wore spectacles on a crooked nose and carried a solid paunch in the region of his belt. He had an easy smile and sat where Callie had been.

"We don't usually see many visitors past Labour Day," he said.

"I'm on business."

"Oh?"

"Looking for someone. Thought he might have been through here last week sometime." Callie came back out with a cup of coffee for John. He accepted it with a smile and fondly touched her hand. He had found paradise.

"Had a lot of people here last week. Mostly regulars, folks from the city for the summer. What's this fella look like?"

"He's from the city too. Would have been coming through probably on Wednesday. Headed towards Balaclava." I took a show card Pearl had given me out of my pocket and handed it to John.

He studied the picture for a second, then said, "Sure I seen him. Thursday or Friday I think it was. But he was headin' away from Balaclava, not towards it."

"Are you sure?"

"Oh yeah. I remember cause his clothes was all torn up when he got here. Looked like he'd been to hell and back. And mutterin' the strangest things. Thought he and the uncle woulda got along just fine. Course, he weren't out front last week."

"How'd he get here?"

"Didn't see no car, or horse. Musta been afoot."

I finished the last of my coffee and thanked Callie and John. They followed me to the front. The uncle began to chuckle softly as soon as I came through the door.

"What's with him anyway?" I asked John softly, once Callie had gone back inside.

"They say he was born with a caul. He's always been a little strange. But we keep him around 'cause sometimes he sees things."

"I thought he was blind."

"He is. I mean he sees things. The future. Y'know stuff that ain't happened yet."

"Oh."

★★★

From Leith, it was a ride due east, up a long hill to the village of Annan. It was late morning by the time Scotty and I got there. So I decided to ride north towards Balaclava, before stopping for lunch. About half a mile out of the village, there was a waterfall. A restful spot, I knew it'd be perfect for lunch.

The waterfall was a quarter mile or so off the road. I stopped Scotty under a big old oak tree. I took his saddle and bridle off, and let him roam around looking for things to eat. He made straight for an old, twisted apple tree that stood not too far away.

"Just don't eat too many of those," I called. He ignored me. I propped the saddle against the base of the oak and leaned back on it. Then I pulled lunch out of my saddlebag. Thick slices of beef on fresh bread. A wedge of peach pie to top it all off. It was pretty squished from the ride. But it tasted good anyway.

"Braaaap." The Lugan had been feeding Scotty corn again. Didn't agree with him at all. It was awesome, the gas he developed. I'd often thought that if I'd taken him to war and fed him corn, he could have single hoofedly defeated the Germans.

Lunch finished, I stood and stretched. Walked across to the waterfall and had a look. It wasn't as big as Inglis Falls, which was south of Owen Sound near Rockford. There the Sydenham River cascaded down the side of the escarpment, dropping nearly a hundred feet on its way to Georgian Bay. Slattery's Creek only fell about 30 feet. But it was still a pretty little spot. I sat back down under the tree. Lunch made me sleepy. I was in no hurry. So I closed my eyes and had a little rest.

An hour or so later, I was back in the saddle. We'd only gone a little way, when I felt Scotty tense, his ears at the alert. I couldn't hear anything. I pulled my field glasses out of their pouch and took a look. Nothing to the north, so that meant it was coming from behind. I pulled the old boy around to take a look. Sure enough, a car was coming. A Packard by the look. We waited for it to pass but it slowed to a stop in front of us. Sean O'Malley poked his grinning head out of the driver side window.

"Wanna race?" He and his partner laughed.

"Ha ha," I was unamused. "With guys like you protecting our roads, who needs hijackers?"

"Seen any?"

"I thought you said they were the Lost Tire Gang. Not the lost hoof."

"Yeah well," he said. "With that horse of yours thinkin' he's a car, I thought they mighta made a play for ya."

"Not yet."

"Where ya' headin?"

"Balaclava."

He paled slightly. "Stay away from Dun Wurkin. That's all I can say." He revved the engine and pulled away before I could ask him what he was talking about. Accelerating hard, he sped off down the road. It was all I could do to hold Scotty.

There was a new Presbyterian church just outside Balaclava. Johnstone Church, the sign on the front of the red brick building announced. I already knew that. The Reverend A.J. Orr was a regular in *The Sun Times*. He was head of the Sydenham Dry Forces and one of the most vocal leaders of prohibition. I resolved to ride straight by. I was afraid he might know I liked the occasional drink, just by looking at me. The last thing I needed was a sermon on my mount.

I nearly made it. But just as I was passing, a head popped out of the shrubbery on the north side of the church.

"Hello," it called with a thick German accent.

"*Guten Tag,*" I called back.

A smile crossed the face attached to the head and a whole body followed it out of the bushes. "*Sprechen Sie Deutsch?*"

"*Ja,*" I said. The man I was facing was not the Reverend Orr, who was a tall, gaunt looking Scot. There was nothing gaunt or tall about this fellow and he definitely wasn't a Scot. He did have a dog collar on. Short and blond, he tended towards the heavy side of the scale. He had an open broad face and smiled a lot.

"*Wie gehts?*" How are you? he asked.

"*Sehr gut.*" Very good, I answered.

"It's nice to meet someone who speaks my language," he continued in German. "Where did you learn it?"

"During the war," I explained. "From the prisoners."

"Oh," he looked apologetic.

"Where is Reverend Orr?"

"I am his summer replacement," the man beamed. "Reverend Klingenberg, from Queens University. Reverend Orr needed a rest after the great battle against the alcohol."

"Oh that," I said dryly. It was ironic the biggest bootlegger in the county was situated less than a mile away from the head of the local dry forces. I didn't say so. Probably the two Franks went to church here. Repent on Sunday. Recant on Monday. It fit.

"Will you have a cup of tea? Or some water?"

"No thanks, padre," I said. "I've gotta meet someone up ahead."

"*Gruss Gott,*" he said. God Bless.

"*Auf Wiedersehen,*" I replied, giving Scotty a kick.

Balaclava was a crossroad. On each of the four corners there was a business. Directly ahead of me on the northeast corner was what appeared to be a small inn. Or at least it had been at one time. Boards covered the windows and there were no signs of life. Across the road was a wagon maker's shop. It was very much in business, as was the blacksmith on the southwest corner. It filled me with nostalgia, hearing the ring of the hammer and anvil. I'd have to be sure to stop in.

Wm. Van Wyck Dry Goods and Sundries stood on the southeast corner of the intersection. I was pleased to see a hitching rail in front and gratefully dismounted. I'd been too long out of the saddle. Once I'd been able to ride for a full day without any ill effects. Not any more. I was going to be sore. I could feel it. I hoped Mr. Van Wyck had a comfortable bed.

The store was a rambling, three storey building. A set of steps led up to a wide porch in front. Large display windows on either side of the door were packed with merchandise. Tinned goods from Smart Brothers in Collingwood. Lydia E. Pinkham's Vegetable Compound. Lux Soap. Borax. A display of McDonald's Cut Brier tobacco. More tobacco for the money, the display told me, at 85 cents a half pound. There was hair tonic. Clothing. Brownie cameras. The other window was filled with hardware items. Axes, hammers, nails, screws, pots, pans and a gigantic new cookstove. I opened the front door. A bell tinkled as I stepped through and a muffled voice called from somewhere, "Be right out."

The inside of the store was as much a wonder as the windows had been. There was merchandise everywhere. Shelves reaching from floor to ceiling ran down either side of the store and they were piled to overflowing. The shelves in the centre of the store were in similar shape. Adding to the visual mayhem, a wide variety of things—mostly food—hung from the rafters. Pork chubs, smoked ham hocks, dried herbs and fish. I wandered towards the back, in the direction I'd guessed the voice came from. A glass display counter held the latest in weaponry. Guns and ammunition of all types. Behind the guns, a shelf was laden with undertaking supplies.

"Good afternoon sir," a polite voice said from behind me. "Is there something I can help you with?"

I turned to look at the owner of the voice. "Are you William Van Wyck?"

"Yes," he looked at me questioningly. "Have we met?"

"No." I pulled the letter of introduction from my pocket and handed it over.

Van Wyck was about five foot ten and less than two hundred pounds. Blond hair, blue eyes. Though he was near my age, his hair had started greying. I wouldn't hold that against him. Better grey than gone was my motto. He had a friendly face and as he finished reading I could see he had a warm smile.

"Well, Mr. Murphy, I don't see any problem."

"Great. And call me Murph."

"Okay Murph. You can call me Van. Everyone does. C'mon, I'll show you a room where you can drop your kit." He turned and led me through a set of curtains, into a spacious sitting room that doubled as an office. He had a pronounced limp and at one point I wondered if he'd make it up the narrow set of stairs at the back. I remembered Sil had told me he was a veteran.

"You get that leg during the war?" I asked, hoping my direct approach wouldn't offend him.

"Uh huh," he said over his shoulder as he led me along the upstairs hallway. It ran down the centre of the building. There were four doors, one for each bedroom and another smaller one I assumed led to the attic. He pushed one of them open to reveal a homey little room, well appointed with a bureau and matching writing desk. A large brass bed stood against one wall, a fireplace dominated the other.

"When the inn closed I bought some of the furniture. Even if there wasn't enough business for them to stay open, I figured there'd be some occasional trade. Whyn't you drop your stuff, then c'mon back downstairs?"

"Sure, fine," I said as he left, closing the door.

I slung my saddlebags and rifle on the bed, then opened the top drawer of the dresser and disarmed myself. I thought I'd talk to Van for awhile and get the lay of the land before I rode out to Dun Wurkin. I peered out the window into the side yard. There was a barn. I'd have to get Scotty unsaddled and moved in.

I went back downstairs and into the sitting room. Windows on both sides of the room let in lots of light. In one corner there was a woodstove and not too far from it was the desk. Bookshelves covered most of the available wall space and in the centre of the room were several comfortable looking overstuffed sofas. Van sat at one, a bottle and two glasses on the low table between the sofas. I sat down across from him.

"Mr. Johnson said in his letter that you're a veteran too?" It took me a split second to realise that Mr. Johnson was Sil.

"Yes," I replied. "I went to sign on with the infantry. When they saw how big I was, they made me a gunner and sent me to Toronto. I guess they needed someone who could manage those big howitzer shells."

"I was infantry. Got hit my first month at the front." He poured some booze and handed me a glass. "Fallen comrades," he said.

We drank and he continued. "I was in the front line trenches. It was a bad night, you know, rain and all that. I couldn't see anything through the trench periscope. So my C.O. sent me over. Just to look around. Me and three other guys. The Huns were sending up flares, they were so afraid of trench raids. So when I saw one go up, I thought it was a dud. Until it hit."

"Jesus," I said. "A Moaning Minnie." Moaning Minnie was the name given to Minenwerfers. They were slow and had a short range. Two hundred pounds of high explosive. The craters they made were usually about ten feet deep. And you only needed to be near one when it went off.

"I was lucky," Van continued. "There was nothing left of the other three. Nothing at all. Not even enough to send home. I got a leg full of shrapnel. And a discharge. I was the lucky one."

I finished my drink. "I guess that wasn't what they call Clabba Killer?"

Van laughed. "This sir, is the finest Scotch whisky that money can buy. Better than that Canadian rye that Mr. Johnson drinks." He poured two more, then asked, "What brings you up here?"

"The two Franks." Van stopped pouring and set the bottle down with a thump. His surprise lasted a second and then he regained himself and handed my glass over.

"Are you buying or selling?"

"Neither."

"They won't want to see you then."

"They'll see me." Van listened quietly as I told him about the investigation so far. He only interrupted once to ask a question.

"This Gas Head Willy, what's he look like?" I told him. "Geez," he said. "I've seen him around. He used to come up and visit John Edmonstone on the 10th Line."

"John Edmonstone?"

"He farms. Also runs booze for the two Franks."

"That fits. Willy was supposed to be comin' here for some Clabba Killer. When's the last time you saw him?"

Van rubbed his chin for a second then said, "Last week, I think."

"How do I get to the two Franks from here?"

"They're just up the road a mile or so. Wait 'til after dinner. That way you'll catch 'em before they really start boozin' out there. Might not be as bad."

"What's the story with them? Why are they so mean?"

"Oh, you know. Their father was their uncle, their mother an aunt. Somewhere in the mix, warm feelings towards others got left out. Not to mention brains. What you wanta watch out for is Little Frank. He's the nasty one. Big Frank just generally goes along. Doesn't have many ideas of his own."

"Big Frank and Little Frank? Those their real names?"

"Yup. Their Daddy wasn't much on originality. But he started that business they got. So he must have had somethin' going for himself."

"Have they got an army out there?"

"Pretty much. At least a dozen men. Pretty heavily armed, I hear."

"How far is it from here?"

"Just a mile or so." Van stood and stretched. "I guess I'll see about supper. If you want to, you can take your horse around back and hobble him in the yard. No sense puttin' him to stable if you're just going out again." I took Van's advice and moved Scotty to the back. Him standing out front was a lot like advertising I was there. Around back, Van was busily stoking wood into a fieldstone fire pit. The yard was an acre with a large vegetable garden running down one side. On the other side was a small barn, good for a couple of horses and some feed. Beside it stood a low stone building that looked like a root cellar. I walked Scotty between the buildings and the garden, then loosened his saddle and turned him out.

"Stay away from the garden." I warned him. He gave me one of those oh-you-think-you're-so-smart looks, then turned and wandered away.

I walked back up to the fire pit and sat in a wide wooden lawn chair opposite the one Van was in. The afternoon had turned golden. A light breeze rippled through the trees that marked the acre surrounding the store. It was warm, not too warm, just pleasant. Perfect weather for sitting around and not thinking too much. I was sorry I'd have to leave after dinner. It was the kind of day that would get better once the sun went down.

"This is some place."

"I like it," Van said. He was scrubbing potatoes in a bucket of water at his feet. "When I first got back from the war, I was in so much pain I couldn't work the family farm. So when this place came up for sale, my folks lent me the money to buy it. Been here ever since."

"Business good?"

"So far. If they ever fix the road I may be in trouble. Everyone'll drive into Owen Sound for their shopping."

"You'll have to open a garage. Sell gasoline."

"What about you?" he asked. "How'd you get into the investigation business?"

"The car did me in. Before the war I was a young man with a trade. Blacksmith. When I got back, half the shops in town were closed, including the one I worked at. So many people are driving cars now, there isn't much need. Some of the guys I used to know, they just switched from the forge to the garage. I'm not much of a tinkerer though."

Van nodded. The potatoes clean, he shoved them into the coals. Then from another pail he pulled out corn that had been soaking and did the same. He went into the root cellar and returned with two slabs of beef and a couple of bottles of beer.

"Made it myself," he said, handing me a beer.

As we drank the brew, we talked about recent goings on in Owen Sound. Van was most interested in the new Legion of returned men. It was a good idea for people who had shared the common experience of the Great War to have a place to meet. A lot of people at the town hall meeting Monday night had felt the same way. He laughed when I told him about the riot that had ensued when the coppers arrested a legless veteran for public drunkenness. Inside an hour there were six hundred men outside the police office demanding his release. Violence was averted when the police let the vet go without filing charges.

"How'd you get this home?" Van asked, admiring my Lee Enfield. Dinner over, I'd gone upstairs to retrieve my arsenal.

"I took two of them apart while we were in England, waiting to be shipped home. When our orders came, we got gauze and plaster of Paris and strapped them to a friend's leg, then made it up to look like he'd broken it. As soon as we were at sea, we took it all off and tucked the guns into our kits. Worked like a charm."

"I'd be mighty interested in buying it. I could add it to my collection."

"I think I'll be needing it. Maybe soon."

"Good point. Maybe you could will it to me?"

"Thanks for your confidence," I said mounting up.

"Seriously," he said, grabbing hold of the reins, "be really careful with these guys. They're bad customers. Especially if they think you're a threat to their business."

"Thanks. Tonight is just reconnaissance. I may stop in to say hello, but nothing more. I'll be back before dark."

"Straight up the road towards Vail Point," he said. "Dun Wurkin is on the left. Won't be hard to spot. There's barbed wire everywhere. It looks like no man's land."

Chapter Six
Dun Wurkin

The fence started right outside Balaclava. It wasn't a new fence, but it was well tended. Five feet high. Barbs as big as a man's fist. The two Franks were serious about keeping people out. Or in.

I had no plan, as Scotty and I strolled through the early evening. There was no proof Willy was in the area. Though he had been. John Walter had seen him. Heading back into town, he'd thought. Despite that, the two Franks had come up in too many conversations to be ignored, especially now that I was outside their place. I figured I'd just drop Willy's name and see what kicked loose.

At any other time, I might have enjoyed the ride north of Balaclava. It was a land of low rolling hills and trees. A light breeze blew up from the bay, which wasn't too far away. The early evening was still and quiet and we didn't see any other riders.

If I hadn't been looking for it, I might have ridden right past the gate. It was set back from the road, in a copse of trees. I was going to go on. But the sound of a gun cocking somewhere in the trees sounded like a challenge, so I stopped right in front of the gate.

I sat absolutely still and didn't say a word. There was no point begging to be let in. And if I was dealing with a lesser, I decided I might as well establish my authority right from the start. We sat there for three full minutes. I could sense the guard's growing exasperation.

"Well?" he finally said, in a rough voice.

"I'm here to see Frank."

"Which Frank? There's two."

"Doesn't matter."

"What's your business?"

"My business is with him. Not some lackey."

"Ride on," the unseen lackey called.

"No."

"I said ride on!" He was shouting now and that was good.

"I'm not going anywhere until I see Frank."

"I told you," he shouted, "THERE ARE TWO FRANKS!" A shot rang out and a slug crashed into the ground at Scotty's feet. To his credit, he didn't budge. He was probably thinking about mounting a gas attack to disable our unseen foe. But there was no need. Within a few seconds of the shot being fired, I could hear horses thundering up the lane.

"What the hell is it?" I heard someone call.

"Someone at the gate," I heard the first guard answer.

"What does he want?"

"Says he wants to see Frank."

"Which one?"

"Won't say. Won't say why, either."

A horse and rider came into view from behind the trees. He was lean and hard looking, the kind of sinewy fellow you never want to get on the wrong side of.

"Whaddya want mister?" he called across the fence to me.

"I want to see Frank." No shots fired. My single Frank reference didn't bother him at all.

"What about?"

"Are you him?"

"Am I who?"

"Frank."

"Nope."

"My business is with him."

"Mister," he started, "I wouldn't be playin' any pissy ant games with me. I'd just as soon kill ya' as look, but you say you got business. Now, you either ride away, or you tell me what that business is. 'Cause there's no way you're gettin' through this gate 'less you do."

"I'm looking for Willy Robertson. Gas Head Willy."

It might have been the light, but I'm sure he looked uncomfortable.

"What's your name, Mister?"

"D.B. Murphy. What's yours?"

He thought about it, then decided it would be okay to tell me. "Jericho Myles. Wait here. I'll be back."

He nodded, then pulled his horse around and galloped up the lane. The early evening silence returned, but there was a certain malevolence about it now. It seemed to come from the general direction in which the first guard was hidden. Jericho Myles came down the road at a fast gallop within a few moments. In a low voice he whispered some instructions and a sour faced man in greasy overalls came out of the woods, rifle held at the ready. He opened the gate and came out.

"Ah, the mystery guard," I said, " and a delightful sight you are, sir."

"Don't get used to it, you ain't gonna be usin' them eyes too much longer less'n I miss my bet. Now git down offa there. I gotta take yer guns 'fore you can go up."

I looked at him dubiously, then at Jericho Myles.

"You'll get 'em back before you go."

I dismounted and unloaded both the rifle and my automatic. No point getting killed with my own guns. I handed them over to the hired man. The way he looked wasn't nearly as bad as the way he smelled. "Got no baths up here?" I called to Jericho. He laughed aloud and from farther back in the bush I could hear more laughter. The first guard gave me a flat look.

"Mister," he whispered. "You better watch out. I'll kill you for that."

"You're welcome to try." I smiled at him and mounted up.

The road was a good one and it showed a lot of use. On either side, the bush was too dense for passage. So even if one managed to scale the perimeter fence, there was no way to sneak around. There was only one road in.

The hoofbeats sounded flat and dead under the canopy of the forest. I hoped my gamble at the gate would pay off. It was never good to make unnecessary enemies, but in this case I'd achieved a couple of goals. I'd won, at least temporarily, the respect of the rest of the gang by calling Stinky down. And the exchange had rattled him enough that he didn't bother to check my saddlebags or boots. So I wasn't riding into Dun Wurkin unarmed.

After about half a mile we started up a short hill. The trees were thinning out and by the time we reached the top there were very few. I saw why immediately. The log walls of a palisade stretched out on either side of a high gate. Dun Wurkin was a fortress.

We rode through the open main gate and into the compound. It was about fifty yards across. Gates at each point of the compass provided access to the surrounding fields and bush. A catwalk ran along the top of the palisade. Perfect for defence. If anyone got past the first fence, they wouldn't just stroll into Dun Wurkin.

The compound was dominated by a fieldstone house. There were also barracks, barns and two low stone buildings which likely housed the stills. I based that guess on the fact that the air coming from that direction smelled boozy.

We rode straight to the house and dismounted in front of the wide front porch. Most of the riders wandered away, leaving their horses. I took that as a good sign. They expected to escort me out again. I stood there for a couple of minutes looking around at the compound, before a voice called from the porch.

"C'mon up here Mister." I started up the stairs. At the top, two men were sitting in the premature dusk of the porch. Jericho Myles stood behind them. Each man had a drink in front of him on a small table and at the far side a third glass stood empty. An open bottle stood in the centre of it all. The larger of the two gestured to it.

"Sit down. Have a drink with us, Mister," he said in a gravelly voice. It was clear to me that the two of them were related. Closely related. They were both big men, around my size—one slightly smaller and one bigger—and both had red hair. The smaller of the two was unshaven and wore dirty coveralls over his clothing. In contrast, the speaker was clean shaven and wore a fine suit of clothes, though he had no jacket on. The meaty fist he offered was scabbed over at the knuckles, evidence of a recent fight which I pretended not to notice.

"I'm Little Frank," he said. "And this is my brother Big Frank."

"D.B. Murphy," I said, shaking hands. There was something wrong. Aside from the fact that Big Frank was little, and Little Frank was big, I'd been to Griffins Theatre often enough to know bad acting. Little Frank could hardly move in his suit, it was so tight. Big Frank couldn't meet my eye as he muttered a greeting. I decided to be really careful. This was, after all, reconnaissance.

Little Frank poured a drink. I picked up the glass and sniffed. It didn't burn the lining of my nose right away, so I took a cautious sip. It wasn't Clabba Killer. It was good.

"It's imported," Little Frank said in response to my questioning look. "My brother here brews up some pretty mean stuff. But we sell it, we don't drink it ourselves."

"Unless there's nothing else around," Big Frank corrected.

"I've experienced the wonders of Clabba Killer first hand," I smiled at them both. "In fact, it's what brings me here in a sort of indirect way."

The two of them exchanged a glance.

"I'm looking for a fellow called Willy Robertson. Gas Head Willy."

"Why come here?" Little Frank asked, the words slithering out of his mouth and into the evening air.

"I have information that he was headed up here. For Clabba Killer."

"Never seen him," Little Frank dismissed the whole topic with a wave of his hand. "Maybe he went to Badjeros."

"Or Blantyre," Big Frank said.

"Berkeley."

"Bognor."

I hated to interrupt when they were having so much fun. "You sure?" I asked. "He's been seen in the area."

A flicker of interest passed between the two. I was getting close to something. "He didn't come here."

I decided to take a risk. "I think he did. And I think you know exactly where he is." The buildup of tension was so fast it seemed to lock us in place for a second, like a tableau. There was a look of amazement on Jericho Myles' face. Nobody questioned the two Franks. As for the brothers, Little Frank looked thoughtful. Big Frank was suddenly boiling, flushed with anger in that way so particular to red heads. It was the anger that broke the spell around the table.

"Now look you…" Big Frank slammed his drink on the table and jumped up. He clenched and unclenched his fists, a towering rage threatening to immolate him where he stood. Little Frank jumped up and grabbed his arm across the table. Jericho Myles looked amused. I stayed put.

Little Frank said a few quiet words in his brother's ear, then turned to me. "Mister Murphy, you've made a mistake. You ain't going to find any Gas Head Willy here. Now I think you'd best leave. Before my brother gets mad."

I got up and left the porch, Jericho Myles right behind me. The other riders had materialized at the end of the big scene, as if on cue. Like at a performance. I looked up at the two Franks on the porch. There was something wrong but I wasn't sure exactly what.

"Don't you come back here, Mister," Little Frank called. The horsemen rode with me as far as the gate at the road.

"You wanta watch yourself," Jericho Myles said while Stinky went to retrieve my guns. "Nobody likes a smart alec."

"You laughed."

"That may be true," he smiled, "but I don't give the orders around here. I just carry 'em out."

"I'll try and remember that next time."

"Next time?" He looked surprised. Stinky arrived with my guns before I could follow up the thought and that was okay. I wanted to keep them guessing. It was one of the few advantages I had.

I was followed all the way back to the store. I didn't see anyone; the lengthening shadows of dusk made it easy for them to hide. It was more the sensation of being followed, plus the logic of it. The Franks were certainly interested. They weren't actors. I wasn't sure what their angle was, but they'd been lying. They knew Willy, and they were interested in him. But why?

I'd already resolved to visit John Edmonstone in the morning. If the Franks hadn't really seen Willy, Edmonstone might have. At least from what Van had told me. After all, if he was bootlegging for the Franks, Willy could get his Clabba Killer there just as easily. And there was a known relationship between the two. It was possible Willy had dropped by and stayed on for a bender. That I'd ride right up there in the morning and find the two of them drunk as lords. Case closed. Back to Owen Sound.

Of course, things rarely worked out that well. But it was fun to fantasize. I went straight round to the back when I got to the store. Van had suggested I put Scotty into the small barn for the night. I went inside and quickly tied his lead to a post, then pulled the barn door shut to a crack. It wasn't long before Jericho Myles sauntered past on his horse. He was headed down the road towards Annan, pretending not to be interested. Once he saw I hadn't continued down the road, it wouldn't take him long to figure out where I was. Balaclava wasn't that big.

I saw Van come to the screen door at the back of the store and peer towards the barn. He looked ready to come out, so I opened the door and waved him back. I'm not sure if he understood why. But knowing I'd been to Dun Wurkin, a guess was close enough. He stayed inside and waited.

About five seconds later Myles came back up the road, this time making no secret of his search. He slowed to a stop at the corner and looked from building to building. He looked at the store, gave a slight nod and moved along. I lost sight of him behind the store, but I heard his horse gallop off in the direction of Dun Wurkin.

Van came out of the house and slipped into the barn. "Mr. Myles seems fairly interested in your overnight accommodation. You must have made an impression." He reached up to a centre beam, pulled down a coal oil lamp and lit it.

"I don't think they'll forget about me right away," I said, relating the rest of the story to Van. I finished it at about the same time we finished bedding down Scotty.

Van shook his head. "I've never seen Little Frank in a suit. And you say he was clean shaven? They sure handed you a line. Or thought they did. Are you going back?"

"I expect so," I said as we walked from the barn to the store. "But first I'm going to go out and see John Edmonstone. He may know what's going on."

"But will he tell you? That's the question," Van said, pulling open the door and stepping inside.

"People always tell you things. Even when they don't want to. Take the two Franks. Their bad acting told me a lot. They either know where Willy is. Or they want to know where he is."

"Does it matter which?"

"Not really. 'Cause one way or the other, I'm going to find him. Tomorrow. I hope."

"Drink?" Van asked as we stepped into his study.

"Sure." I set my rifle and saddlebags on the low table between the sofas. Van poured two drinks, then sat down. He picked up the Enfield.

"Do you mind?" he asked.

"Go ahead." He carefully unloaded the gun, and checked the bore. Putting it up to his shoulder he said, "Y'know this brings back a lot of memories. Our snipers loved the Ross." He sighted down the barrel. "But like you said, the boys in the trenches hated it. More than one of our boys dropped his Ross and picked up an Enfield when he came across a Brit who couldn't use it anymore. It's a better gun for trench fighting."

We stayed up late, drinking and talking about the war. When I finally struggled up the stairs sometime after midnight, I fell into bed fully clothed and slept until sunup.

After breakfast, Van gave me directions to the Edmonstone place. I saddled up and rode out just before seven. I wanted to catch John before he could go anywhere. For a brief second I wished he had a telephone. Then I thought better of it. The longer it took for that pest to arrive, the better. What was really needed was electricity. Ontario's electric commissioner kept promising everyone would have power. But sometimes it was hard to believe they'd bring it so far into the country for so few people.

The Edmonstone place was east of Balaclava. The sun was in my eyes, the bay at my back as I rode. It was another perfect, cloudless morning. Dew hung heavy everywhere, sparkling in the sun. I wondered about the last time Willy had been this way. Which direction had he been going? Back to town? I found myself watching the sides of the road as I travelled. Watching for a pair of feet sticking out of the undergrowth. I gave that up quickly. There were too many old logs, bushes, anthills and clumps of grass that looked like something. Besides, I reasoned, if Willy had met with foul play, his body was likely to be well off the road. Like the other one.

I came to the unmarked lane Van had told me led to the Edmonstone place. There was no house visible from the road. Scotty and I rode up the narrow lane. About a hundred yards along there was a bend in the road and around it was the house. At first glance it looked totally unfinished. But as we got closer, I could see it was in various stages of construction, depending which part of the house you looked at. The roof was only half shingled. All the windows were in, but there was no front door. The front porch was framed but not planked. A twelve-inch board led from the steps to the entrance. Piles of lumber and scrap stood all around the yard. In the back, open fields. Closer to the house, an apple orchard.

I stopped Scotty in front of the house and yelled a greeting. The house stood mute. Silence descended on the clearing. If there was anyone around, they weren't answering. I dismounted, and walked towards the front of the house. I went up the steps and stepped onto the plank. As I crossed it, I realized I had been wrong about the missing front door. It was there alright, but smashed off its hinges and lying in the front hallway of the house. I pulled my pistol and went inside.

The house was a mess. Broken bottles and dishes were everywhere. In the kitchen, there was a large pool of dried blood in the middle of the floor. It was old, no telling how old, but dry as rust. If Willy had been there, I couldn't imagine he'd be alive. On one side of the kitchen, a single bullet casing lay near a trap door. I cocked my gun and, using the steel ring embedded in the centre, pulled the door up. A makeshift set of wooden steps led into the murk of a dirt floor basement. I went down. As my eyes adjusted, I could see stacks of bottle-filled crates. Nothing else. I opened a bottle and the unmistakable smell of Clabba Killer wafted out. Across the room, there was a broad hole in the stone foundation, an unfinished door.

I went back upstairs and checked the other rooms. Empty. Which brought me back to the kitchen. Hanks of rope hung lifeless from the sides of one of the kitchen chairs. Below the chair, drops of blood. Directly ahead—the big puddle. I thought about it, then leaned forward. If I'd been shot sitting in that chair, I'd fall just about where the puddle had formed.

I decided Willy was probably okay. Then thought about a dark-haired man lying in a ditch, his eye shot out.

★★★

It was close to ten when I got back to Van's place. I left Scotty roaming the backyard and went in. From the front of the store I could hear the murmur of voices. I left my guns in the study and went out. Oddball was there.

"Hello, Murph!" he called, pulling a slobbery unlit cigar out of his mouth. It was the same one. I was sure of it.

"Oddball," I replied, then nodded a greeting at Van, who stood behind the counter. "What brings you out here, constable?"

"Found out who that stiff was," he said pleased with himself. "The one from the other day."

"John Edmonstone."

"Wha…? How…? You said you didn't know who he was."

"I didn't. Now I do."

Behind the counter Van was trying to take it all in. "Wait a minute," he said. "You mean to tell me John Edmonstone is dead?"

"That's right," I said.

"Shot through the eye," Oddball added for effect.

"I need a drink," Van said, heading for the back room.

"How'd you know he was dead?" Oddball asked, as we followed Van.

"I was out to his place. Just got back." While I told him about what I'd found, Van poured us drinks. I finished my story by pulling the shell casing I'd found out of my shirt pocket and throwing it to Oddball. "That'll be from the murder weapon."

"Hmmm. A .45." He turned the shell over in his hands. "I'll tell you something you don't know," Odd said, a superior smirk on his face.

"Well?"

He downed the last of his drink and held the glass out for another. Van complied. We both waited while he sampled.

"Well?" I repeated a bit more forcefully. I hated it when someone with a piece of knowledge enjoyed their own suspense too much.

"John Edmonstone was a Temperance Act Enforcement Officer."

"A dry cop?" I turned to Van. "Didn't you tell me he was running booze for the two Franks."

"That's right." He seemed as surprised as I was.

"The basement of his farmhouse was full of booze," I said, turning back to Oddball. He was really enjoying himself.

"It was his cover," he leaned forward conspiratorially. "He didn't really sell any of the booze. Just stashed it in the basement, until his coppers picked it up. The government give 'im the money an' then he paid the Franks."

"Guess they caught on," I said. A dead cop. Someone was in trouble.

"Did you see any money when you were there Murph?" Oddball asked, finishing his second drink.

"Nope."

"Coulda been a robbery then I s'pose. Edmonstone's men have been waiting in town. He already had the money to pay for the booze. They were just waitin' for him to call 'em to pick up the hooch."

"I guess I can look forward to you coming up here and messing up my investigation?" I asked.

"No, no. Not at all. Someone else'll be doin' that."

"Who?"

"The other guy. The inside man."

"Edmonstone had a partner?"

"Yup."

"Who is it?"

"Don't know," he said standing. "I gotta go."

"So you're not going out to Dun Wurkin to do any investigating of your own?" Van asked.

"Naw," he said. "I've got a car patrol to check up on. Could take a few days. Now if Murph here comes up with anything," he gestured with his cigar, "why I'd be happy to do something then."

"What balls," I said to his back as he pulled the door open. Slowly he turned, and fixed a look on me. He reached up and pulled the cigar out of his mouth.

"Ball, Murph," he said. "Ball."

I spent the rest of the morning sitting at the back of the store, enjoying the sunshine. Around noon, Van brought out beef sandwiches. We washed them down again with bottles of his beer, cool from the root cellar.

"I'm going back out there," I said when we had finished.

"I figured," he said picking his teeth.

"They won't be as happy to see me this time."

"To say the least."

"Have you got any dynamite?"

Van gave a sly smile. "Oh yes," he said, "and so much more."

CHAPTER SEVEN
THE PROPOSAL

"Keep ridin'!" The words barked out from a hidden spot within the grove of trees.

"Here to see the Franks."

"Issat so?" the voice sneered. "Well they don't wanna see you."

"I think they do."

"Oh yeah?" the voice countered. "Why?"

"John Edmonstone."

"Wait there." The bush fell silent, and once again I was left sitting in front of the gate. If things went according to plan, I'd know a lot more in a few minutes than the two Franks wanted me to know. The trick would be getting out of Dun Wurkin once I figured their angle. That's where Van came in. He was waiting down the road, out of sight of the gate. By the time I was ready to make my getaway, half the fence in the south field along the road would be wired to blow. Just in case.

I'd decided that Willy probably wasn't at Dun Wurkin. He'd probably never been there. Though it was obvious the Franks knew who he was. Scotty shimmied a little underneath me, as a group of riders approached. Again, a lone rider came to the gate, the rest remaining hidden by the trees.

"Every time you come to this gate you manage to say something interesting," Jericho Myles said.

"It's a curse," I said, "to always be saying interesting things."

"People come to expect it of you," he replied.

"In the end you always end up disappointing them."

"I hope not," he said dismounting. "The Franks don't take disappointment well." He opened the gate and Scotty and I walked through. He did a quick search and found the .45 hidden in my saddlebags. The .32 was still in my boot, but I'd left the other guns behind. I didn't expect to be stopping at the front gate on my way out. And I didn't want to lose them. "I believe you know the way," he said mounting up and gesturing for me to lead on. The gang fell in around us. Stinky rode ahead of me, a nasty grin on his filthy face. I brought Scotty to a stop and the rest of the gang held up. Myles gave me a quizzical look.

"I want him," I pointed at Stinky, "downwind. Or else I ride out of here." There were snickers all round and a murderous glare from Stinky as Myles ordered him to the back of the pack.

It was hot as we rode into the compound, the high walls containing the heat of the mid-afternoon sun. I couldn't help feeling like a condemned man, riding in there with the odds so much against me. I thought of Lori and how much I loved her. And resolved to mention it the next time we were together.

We rode straight up to the house and dismounted. This time though, the horses were removed, Scotty included, to a corral around the side of the still. That was disappointing. I'd sort of counted on him being left out front, so I could make my getaway.

Little Frank stood at the top of the front steps, big arms over his head, holding onto a beam. He looked relaxed and threatening at the same time. I heard a door slam open on the other side of the compound, and saw Big Frank come striding out of the still. A black look crossed his face when he saw me.

"C'mon up and siddown Mr. Murphy," Little Frank called from the top of the stairs. "Have a drink with us." I couldn't help but notice the menace in his gaze, as I climbed the steps. Out of the suit he'd been wearing, one could see how dangerous it would be to mess with him. He was the epitome of a rural boy. Red neck. Big arms and chest. Fists like bricks. And a temper.

"I see you lost the monkey suit," I said as I sat down in the same chair I'd occupied the night before. He splashed some booze into a cup for me and I could smell right away it was Clabba Killer. They weren't wasting any more of the fancy stuff on me. Too bad. Big Frank stepped onto the porch. He took off the leather apron he was wearing and hung it on a nail. He sat and we all drank.

"Now," Little Frank said, slamming his glass down. "What the hell do you want?"

"I want to know what's going on here."

They looked at one another, then back at me.

"Whaddaya mean?" Big Frank played dumb. It suited him.

"You two are the worst actors in the world. Your performance yesterday didn't fool me for a second." They looked at each other again. This was getting really boring.

"I think you've made a mistake, Mr. Murphy," Little Frank said. I heard the distinct sound of a gun being cocked. Under the table. I had to guess it was pointed at me. "We aren't going to tell you anything. You're going to tell us."

I smiled and picked up my cup of rotgut. Took a small sip. Then said, "Why'd you have me followed?" They looked at one another yet again, but this time I detected some confusion. Best to keep that ball rolling, I decided. "John Edmonstone is dead," I said. They relaxed. Obviously familiar ground.

"So tell us something we don't know," Big Frank said with a sneer.

"He was a dry cop." It was a little scary sitting between two redheads with bad tempers when you've just dropped a bomb. Of course I was just the messenger. But somehow I didn't think that was going to matter. Both men exploded into a tirade of obscenities, directed at one another and the world in general. I listened for a second then said with a smile, "You asked me to tell you something you didn't already know."

It was clear by the way they looked at me that I'd worn out my welcome. Time to go. I tossed my nearly full cup of Clabba Killer into Little Frank's face. He screamed. I heard the gun drop to the floor, as he clapped his hands to his eyes and started rubbing furiously.

Big Frank dealt me a stunning blow to the side of the head. I fell forward onto the table, and grabbed the bottle. It shattered into about a million pieces when it met his head.

I stood up, kicking the table away. Still sitting but partially blinded, Little Frank was feeling around on the floor for the lost gun. I kicked him and he went over with his chair. The wind went out of him in a gust. Before I could recover though, my left foot was grabbed and I was twisted around onto my back. A look of rage and hatred on his face, it seemed as though Big Frank was determined to tear my leg off. It hurt. So I pulled my right leg up under me and retrieved the .32.

"Let go!" I ordered. He laughed until I cocked the little automatic. "This'll kill you just as dead as any gun," I said. Behind me Little Frank wheezed, his breath returning. "Now let go of my leg, or I'll kill you."

"Murphy," Big Frank glared as he let go of my leg. "You're as good as dead."

"If we could kill you twice," Little Frank hissed, "we would."

"Thanks for the sentiment boys," I said standing. "There's nothing I like better than making new friends." I kicked Little Frank's gun off the side of the porch. My head throbbed where Big Frank had hit me. I seemed to be taking a lot of abuse lately. And I didn't much like it.

I leaned against the porch rail, keeping the two of them in my sight. I looked around as well as I could. The fight hadn't attracted any attention. I guess it made sense, since everyone had probably known I was due for a working over. Not a word had been said during the entire scuffle. So everyone probably expected the two Franks to be in control. Like they always were.

"Two against one," I said to them. "Where's the fun in that?"

"The fun," Little Frank said, "is going to be seeing you try to get out of here."

"Watch this," I said, giving a loud whistle. I heard a shout from the vicinity of the still. A second later Scotty appeared, ears pricked, flanks trembling. The jump over the corral fence had barely winded him. I kicked a leg over the porch rail and dropped straight onto his back.

Instead of heading out the way we had come in, we rode straight for the south gate. The shouting began before we got even half way across the compound. I looked over my shoulder in time to see the two Franks running for horses. I leaned over Scotty's neck and said, "Get me out of this, and I'll let you race a car."

The next time I looked, there were at least half a dozen pursuers and they were closing. Front and centre were the two Franks. I turned in the saddle and fired a couple of shots. I didn't hit anything but it slowed them. Until we broke from the trees and into the open. Then they started firing back.

We were in the field, the one I'd first seen riding up the road to Dun Wurkin. I made straight for the farthest corner, where Van was waiting. The gang was drawing closer, but its marksmanship wasn't much better than mine. No matter how easy they make it look in the pictures, it was darned difficult to hit something from the back of a moving horse.

As we neared the southwest corner of the field, I started looking for Van. Waving my arms. Shouting. Nothing happened. We were coming closer to the fence and all I could think about was the barbed wire on top. Scotty had jumped the five foot corral fence, no trouble. I wasn't as confident of his ability to clear the perimeter fence with me on his back.

"Van!" I screamed. "Blow it! Blow it NOW!"

Nothing happened. I suddenly realized I'd never considered the possibility of capture. Then I saw him. A rifle at his back, Van was being marched straight up the centre of the road by Jericho Myles who was on his horse. I aimed Scotty in their direction and jammed my heels into his side. It was up to him now. I could hear the sounds of laughter coming from behind. I looked and the pursuit had all but stopped. They thought I was trapped. The fence came up fast. I wanted to close my eyes. Decided I should be more supportive of my steed. So I screamed. At the top of my lungs. And we sailed right over the fence and onto the road beyond. Nearly on top of Van and his captor, who were forced to scramble out of the way.

I looked over my shoulder in time to see the gang riding up the field at top speed, headed for the gate. Van was running back down the road. Jericho Myles was bringing his rifle up to his shoulder. So I shot him.

He toppled off his horse backwards. I didn't stop to see if I'd killed him. Scotty and I slowed long enough to pick Van up. I risked a glance back and saw the posse thundering through the gate and onto the road. Good as Scotty was, there was no way we could outrun them. So I started looking for a spot to make a stand.

"Down the road," Van was out of breath. "Hurry! I've gotta get my bicycle."

Scotty laboured under our weight. I wasn't sure we'd be able to get away. But I was fairly sure Van wouldn't outride the Franks on his bicycle.

"I don't think you'll be able to outride these guys on your bicycle," I shouted over my shoulder.

"No time to explain," he was out of breath. "Stop here!"

We'd only gone thirty yards. Jumping down, he crossed the road into the trees on the opposite side. He emerged a second later pushing his bicycle. At first, I couldn't believe my eyes. There was a machine pistol, mounted between the handlebars. Van fired a short burst over the heads of the approaching gang. Which abruptly stopped. Turned. And beat a path back to the gates of Dun Wurkin. They picked up Jericho Myles on the way past. Just before they went in, Little Frank stopped his horse and regarded us.

"This ain't over," he shouted. Then he turned and followed his men.

Van was smiling.

"Murphy, meet the Revelli submachine gun. Italian design, built right here in Canada." He jumped onto the bicycle and started back towards the store.

I headed back to Owen Sound mid-afternoon, after helping Van get his armoury back to the store. "It's a hobby, like stamp collecting," he'd said about his guns, as we carried a load into the basement. He lit an oil lamp and I let out a low whistle. Van was better equipped than the Canadian army. Guns and weapons of every description lined the walls. In the centre of the room was a large work table.

"You make bullets?" I asked, staring at the equipment.

"The winters are awfully long out here. A guy's gotta have something to do." He locked the outside door with a heavy padlock and we went round to the front of the store. Inside, Van offered me a drink.

"No, I'd better get going. It's a long ride back to Owen Sound. Say," I asked, "what about the two Franks? Aren't you worried they'll come down here and do you?"

"Not really," he smiled. "You've seen the basement. Besides, I'm too useful to them. They buy all their supplies here. I clean and repair their weapons. In fact, I sell them all the guns they need."

"Oh."

"But," he added, "I think I might go away for a couple of days. I've got some friends I've been meaning to visit."

"What happens to the store?"

"I'll just close it down." While Van got himself ready, I went upstairs and collected my things. I didn't want to be caught on the road after dark. In case the Franks had some ideas about having me followed again. Though it certainly wouldn't be Jericho Myles.

I came downstairs and dropped my stuff on the floor. "Which way you ridin'?" Van asked.

"Back down the Lakeshore Road. Still got a few things to check on. You?"

"I think I'll go over to Meaford. Then maybe to Owen Sound."

"You ridin' that bicycle?"

Van laughed aloud, and clapped me on the shoulder. "That'd give the Lost Tire Gang something to think about."

"Well thanks for your help." I shook his hand.

"Don't be a stranger," he said as I rode away.

An hour's ride later I was at the Leith General Store. The uncle was there, sitting out front. I wondered if he ever moved. Dismounting, I tied Scotty off and went inside.

"Hello?" I called. Callie Walter came in the back door and stood uncertainly as her eyes adjusted to the light.

"Why Mr. Murphy," she said. "It's good to see you back. How'd you make out in Balaclava?"

"It's a long story. But fine. I wanted to buy one of these apples here," I gestured to a barrel in the centre of the room, "and I had a few questions to ask your uncle."

Callie came into the room and stopped at the barrel. "These for Scotty?" she asked.

"Yes."

"Penny apiece," she said, searching through the top layer for the biggest, juiciest ones.

I dug a nickel out of my pocket and traded it for the apples. When Callie came back with the change, there was a puzzled look on her face. "What you wanta talk to Uncle about?"

"I just wondered if he remembered anything. About when Gas Head Willy came through here last week."

"You can try. But I don't know if you'll get a straight answer outta him."

"Ma'am," I said, "at this point a crooked answer'll be better than what I've got."

"Go ahead then," she smiled. "And good luck."

"Does he have a name?"

"Uncle. Just call him Uncle."

I went outside and gave Scotty an apple. I think he swallowed it whole. I went to the bench and sat down beside Uncle. His head tilted in my direction, in the manner of one who sees with his ears.

"Uncle," I said, "I was here the other day. Looking for Gas Head Willy. John Walter said Willy was through here last week and I forgot to ask if you remembered him."

"Willy?" he said in a cracked whisper.

"Yes, that's right," I encouraged. He settled back on the bench. Fumbled in his pockets and finally came up with a match. Scraped it across the bench and lit his pipe. Puffed for a minute or two. Then he turned and looked directly at me with his unseeing eyes.

"Guilty the man who removes his head. Malice, pride and vanity, another lies dead."

"What the…? What does that mean?"

Uncle sat back and held another match to his pipe. He puffed furiously to get it going, rolled his eyes and chuckled.

"Told ya," Callie said from the door.

"Do you know what he means?" I asked.

"Nope. That's the problem. You can hardly ever figure out what he means. Except for sometimes. Like last year. Plain as day he said, 'Tom Martin gots a two header'. Couple days later we went up and seen a two-headed calf at the Martin place."

"Two heads? Really?"

"Plain as the nose on my face."

I unhitched Scotty and mounted up. "Well, thanks," I said.

"Hope that helps ya," she called. "Wish he coulda spoke it plainer for ya."

"Maybe he did," I said. "I've just gotta think about it."

I took the ride from Leith to Owen Sound at an easier pace. I wasn't going to be home in time for dinner, so I couldn't see much sense in pushing it. The evening was pleasant, with a light breeze coming off the bay. I thought about what Uncle had said. Guilty the man who removes his head. Malice, pride and vanity, another lies dead. I'm not sure what I'd expected. Maybe for Uncle to say 'look here' or 'you'll find him there'. The rhyme was something else again. It smacked of magic, and that scared me.

It wasn't much of a leap to guess the dead man was John Edmonstone. Guilty is the man who removes his head? No idea. Malice, pride and vanity included about four-fifths of the population.

The sound of a gunshot broke my reverie. I was coming around a big curve in the road, not far from Owen Sound. I urged Scotty to a trot, then a gallop when I heard a second shot. I pulled my pistol out. Just in case.

There were two cars in the roadway as we came around the far side. Two people were beside the car closer to me, a man on the ground and a woman trying to help him. On the other side of them, two men were throwing a spare tire into the back of a late model coupe. Catching sight of me, they jumped into the running car and sped off.

"Are you shot?" I yelled, jumping off Scotty and running to the aid of the couple. The woman looked up, fearful when she saw the gun in my hand. "Don't worry," I reassured her. "I'm here to help."

"They beat Freddy up and robbed us." I could see blood on the face of the young man on the ground.

"You're not shot though?"

"I'm okay," he said through mashed lips.

"I heard shots."

The woman pointed at steam hissing out from under the hood of the car. "They shot the car."

"Start walking back to town," I shouted over my shoulder as I jumped onto Scotty's back. "Remember my promise this afternoon?" I whispered in his ear. "That sounded like a Ford."

He ran like every demon in hell was on his heels. We didn't even get close enough to take a shot. They'd had too big a head start.

We got to town in a big hurry. I went straight to the Grey County Courthouse. It was locked, so I rode over to Oddball's house. He lived in a bungalow on 5th Street East, right along the Sydenham River. I left Scotty standing in the yard and knocked on the front door.

"Murphy," Oddball said without surprise when he opened the front door. "How goes the search?"

"The same," I said. The smell of cooking wafted past him straight into my nose. I was hungry. "How's the murder coming?"

"The same," he said. It was obvious he was anxious to get back to whatever it was I smelled.

"Came across your Lost Tire Gang, just outside town on the Lakeshore Road. There's a couple out there, walkin' in."

"Shit," he muttered under his breath. "There goes dinner." He reached inside the door and grabbed his hat and coat from a peg. "They okay?"

"The boy got beat up some. Car got shot. Otherwise they seemed okay."

"Get a look at the highwaymen?"

"Nope. We tried to catch 'em. They had too much of a head start."

"Damn." He opened the door of his car. "By the way," he said, "you hear about Jamieson Johnston?"

"I've been out of town."

"He's dead."

"Really?"

"Yep. Died Labour Day. When he got home from the speeches at town hall. Lockjaw, the doc says." Johnston had made his money in lumber. That's likely why I'd met him with Silas Robertson on Labour Day. Birds of a feather and all that.

"There anything funny about it?" I asked.

"Don't know. That's city police." He started the car and with a great grinding of gears got it into reverse. "Just out the Lakeshore Road, y'say?"

"That's it."

"Right. See you later Murph. And thanks." Oddball pulled out of his yard and rolled down the street to the corner. I retrieved Scotty and we headed back downtown to the City Hotel.

The wide stable doors were open and we rode inside. The Lugan threw a switch, chasing the early evening murk out the door with electric lights.

"Groom him like always," I said, "and give him double his oat ration. He's earned it." I reached into my saddlebag for the tiny bottle Van had pressed into my hand as I was leaving. "And here," I handed it over. "Try some of this on him."

"What's dis?"

"Horse shampoo."

"Oh." He looked as though he was waiting for the punch line. "That it?"

"Almost," I said, grabbing him by the grubby lapels. "No more corn!"

"He wants to run faster than cars," the Lugan sniggered.

"What?"

"They got gas. So does he." He cackled like a mad fool and I've got to admit that I smiled too. I let him go.

"No more corn," I shouted, as I left the stable.

★★★

Dinner had been over for some time. Marth and Sil were sitting at the kitchen table drinking tea.

"The traveller returns!" Sil cried.

"Are you hungry?" Marth asked.

"Yes and yes," I said pulling out a chair and sitting down.

"How was Balaclava?" Sil asked.

"Now William," Marth scolded. "He just got home. Let him catch his breath." She pulled a plate of food from the oven, where it had been warming. "I saved this," she said. "We thought you might get home tonight."

"Thanks, Marth. I would have been home earlier, but I came across a robbery. Out on the Lakeshore Road." I told them all about the Lost Tire Gang while I shovelled dinner in. I saved Balaclava. After dinner, in a well established pattern, I would tell Sil the story while we drank in his study. He would tell Marth later.

"Did I miss anything while I was away?"

"Did you hear about Jamieson Johnston?" Sil asked.

"Yes. But not much."

"The paper says he collapsed Labour Day, right after he got home," Marth said, adding, "his wife found him. Poor woman."

"He'd had all his teeth pulled last week. On account of pyorrhoea."

"Pie what?" I asked.

"Gum disease. Doc says he got an infection and died of lockjaw."

"They weren't married that long, were they?" I asked.

"No, his wife was just young," Marth answered.

"Too bad," Sil said. "So young. And all that money."

"Oh Sil, you're bad!" Marth threw her dishwashing cloth and hit him square in the face.

Everyone laughed and I excused myself to go wash up. Lori would be wondering where I'd gotten to. She'd probably decided I'd use Balaclava as an excuse to miss the coming wedding. But of course I had every intention of attending. The fires of hell would be tolerable, if Lori was beside me.

She was sitting on the front porch when I came up the cement walk in front of the Storey house.

"Murph!" Lori jumped up and threw herself into my arms. And gave me a melting kiss right there in the open. It was wonderful.

"I've missed you," I said when I could breathe.

"Come inside," she said. The house was quiet. We were alone.

"Where is everyone?" I asked.

"Getting ready for the fall fair."

"Oh, yeah. That's next week, isn't it?" We sat down on the sofa in the parlour.

"You know very well it is. You're taking me, remember? The midway?"

"I'm taking you to the midway? I don't think so."

"What!" Lori sat up in surprise.

"I'm not sure your husband would like it."

"Husband?" Lori asked, unsure of my game. "I haven't got a husband." She sat back and folded her arms across her chest. A tiny pout twitched her bottom lip. I couldn't stand it. I knelt on the floor in front of her.

"Well maybe it's time you had one. Will you marry me, Lori Storey?"

Tiny pouts can become big smiles amazingly fast.

CHAPTER EIGHT
TICKETS PLEASE

"You're full of surprises," Sil said, handing me a drink. It was after ten and we were sitting in his study. I had just come home from the Storeys and told him about my evening. He opened the door and called softly across to the parlour. "Marth?" There was a murmured reply which I couldn't hear, then Sil said, "Come in here and join us."

I heard her footsteps cross the hall. She came in with a questioning look. "What have you two been up to?" Sil smiled and closed the door. He crossed to the small bar and poured a glass of fine sherry from a decanter.

"Murph has something to say," he said handing her the glass. She looked at me expectantly.

"Lori and I are to be married."

"Oh, Murph!" she set her glass down and rushed to hug me. "Congratulations Daniel. This is wonderful news." She kissed me lightly on the cheek, then went back for her drink. "A toast," she cried, "to Murph and Lori."

"Murph and Lori," Sil chimed.

We all drank, then sat down. "When did you ask her? Tonight?" Marth asked.

"Yes. When I went over."

"Well, what happened?"

"I asked her. She said yes. We'll do it next summer."

"Oh, I can't believe it," she said clapping her hands together. Marth loved weddings. "Wait a minute. I'm not sure we have room for another lodger."

"Ha!" I laughed. "The Murphys will live on their own."

"Who'll play with the boys?" Marth asked.

"You'll just have to send them over."

"I hope there'll be little Murphys for them to play with?" Marth teased. I smiled and maybe blushed a little.

I was saved from answering by Sil. "Say, I found something out about the Robertsons."

"What?"

"There was a big scandal. Before the war. Willy embezzled money from his father's accounts. When he was managing them. He'd cut trees on private property and sell the lumber. Instead of handing their percentage over to the owners, Willy was keeping it all."

I remembered what Lori had told me. About her father owning forests. "Jack Storey got caught on that one. Lori's dad."

"A lot of people did. Silas made Willy enlist, to get him out of the way. Then Willy came back ruined. It's killing his old man with guilt."

"I wonder if someone from Willy's past finally caught up with him?"

★★★

By eight the next morning, I was at the office. MacLean was out front, sweeping as usual.

"Good morning, Mr. Murphy," he said cheerily.

"MacLean. How's business?"

"Couldn't be better. And you?" he asked. "How goes the sleuthing?"

"Passably well," I said. "You sweep this walk much more, you'll wear it down to nothing."

He laughed as he put the broom up and began unrolling the canopy. "Long as you have enough business to pay the rent," he said. "That's my only concern."

"I'll be able to. Especially after today." I went past him and in the side door which led up to my office. I had a hunch about Willy and the ticket for the *Michipicoten*, which I planned to put to the test. The steamer was due to leave Cole's dock at around ten o'clock and I was going to be there.

There were a couple of newspapers piled in front of my office door. I picked them up. With a rattle of keys, I opened the door and went inside. The office was musty from being shut up for almost a week. I tossed the newspapers on my desk, and threw the windows open wide. Below me, I could hear MacLean under his canopy setting up displays of fruit and vegetables. A car went by trailing a blue haze of smoke. So much for fresh air. I left the windows open and turned back to my desk.

The most recent issue of *The Sun Times* carried a report on the death of Jamieson Johnston on the front page. DIED SUDDENLY FROM LOCKJAW, the headline shouted. The paper was a couple of days old. He'd been buried while I was still in Balaclava.

Looking to the top of the front page, my heart nearly stopped. THIS HORSE WAS A REAL LEADER the headline read. The story about Scotty and I leading the parade wasn't much better. I decided it was probably good that I'd been out of town the past few days. The story beside that said the Murrell brothers had broken out of jail in London. Sawed through eight one-inch steel bars to make their escape. They'd grown up in Owen Sound. Armed and dangerous, the newspaper warned. I'd have to keep my eyes peeled. Could be another job.

Entertaining as it was, I set the paper aside. The pile of junk on my desk was exactly as I'd left it. I hunted through the newspaper clippings and found the Chinese laundry ticket. It was for Lee Sing's which was on my way to Cole's dock, in a tumbledown building on 1st Avenue East. I pulled the .32 out of my boot and checked the load. I didn't like carrying a piece while I was in town, but after my run in with the Balaclava Boozeheads I'd decided it was better to be safe, rather than sorry. I didn't know the Franks well, but I couldn't help thinking I might see them again. I didn't think they would let me humiliate them on their own turf, without taking a shot at me on mine.

On the way out of the office I grabbed a bag full of dirty shirts. As long as I was going to the laundry, I thought I might as well get them done.

I locked the door behind me and headed downstairs.

The thing I loved about Owen Sound, most days, was being able to walk down the street and know just about everyone. On this day, however, it felt like I was running a gauntlet. I made up my mind to have a word with Scotty.

"Hey Murphy!" Dave Taylor called from across the street. He was lowering the canopy in front of his watch repair shop.

"Hello Dave," I called.

"Seen any good parades lately?" he laughed. "No one else has."

"Ha ha," was about the best response I could muster. I turned in time to avert a head on collision with the Mayor, who was strolling up the sidewalk directly in my path. He wasn't paying attention. Likely caught up in weighty city council matters.

"Good morning, Mayor Patterson," I said.

"What? Oh, Murphy isn't it? How's that horse of yours?" He smiled like a trout. "Y'know, the one with no sense of direction?"

Lee Sing's Chinese Laundry was in what had once been a warehouse. It was built of the limestone which had been excavated when the first harbour wall was built, before the turn of the century. Narrow and tall I'd often suspected the only things that kept it standing were the buildings on either side of it.

To get to the laundry, you went through a battered wooden door as old as the building itself. Above it, the hand painted 'Chinese Laundry' was fading.

The first thing that struck me when I went to Lee Sing's was the smell. The building had been damp and musty to begin with. Now that general mustiness was overlaid with the stink of heavy duty laundry soap. Lee Sing didn't have much use for Lux, I guessed.

The main floor had once been wide open, but a blanket hanging about ten feet from the front door now divided it. Behind, all the washing and living went on. In front, Lee Sing's wife Mai Ling sat at a small desk.

"Good morning, Mai Ling," I said with a smile. As a bachelor I was no stranger to Lee Sing's.

"Hello Murphy," she responded in heavily accented English. "You bring a shirt today?"

"Yes. A couple. And I need at least one for a wedding tomorrow."

"Okey-dokey." Mai Ling handed me a ticket exactly like the one I had in my pocket. I pulled it out and handed it to her.

"Maybe I can collect this while I'm here?" I said. She studied the ticket, then nodded and went behind the curtain. I waited for a few minutes, before Lee Sing came out with a small, paper wrapped package, tied with twine.

"Hey, Murph," he said. "It about time you come."

"What?"

"A man, he left this here. Paid me. Said look after it 'til you come."

"Until I came?"

"Yes. He said you would come to get it."

"When was that?"

"Last week. Friday maybe."

Lee Sing handed me the package. I decided to open it right there. I was heading over to Cole's dock next, and didn't want to be carrying it. I used a pair of scissors on the desk to cut the twine. Carefully I opened the package, to reveal a bundle of rags. I dug through them and finally came to a revolver. It was a .45. I checked the load. One shot missing. I dug through the rest of the rags and examined the paper carefully. There was nothing else.

"Thanks Lee Sing," I said sticking the handgun into my coat pocket. "I've got a ship to catch."

The *Michipicoten* was one of the first ships bought by the Owen Sound Transportation Company. Primarily a cargo ship, it had a small above-deck cabin, with rooms for four passengers. Once a week, the *Michipicoten* made the run from Owen Sound to Meaford, Thornbury, Collingwood and all the way around to the Soo, before it returned home.

It only took me a few minutes to walk over to Cole's dock from Lee Sing's. As I approached, I could see the bustle of last minute loading. Off to the side of the dock, a knot of people stood. Too many to be taking a trip on the small vessel. I stepped out of sight at the corner of a building, just a hundred feet from the gangway. If I was right, the wait wouldn't be long.

Just before ten, I saw the first officer come out of the wheelhouse and down the gangway. One man emerged from the knot that had been waiting and, amidst "goodbyes" and "see you soons," he boarded and his well wishers departed. The first officer pointed to a cabin door and the man disappeared. The first officer checked his watch. Looked up and down the dock. Another ticket had been sold. He knew it and was waiting.

My watch said 10:01 when he checked his again, shrugged and went aboard. I could hear him issuing orders to a couple of his shore crew, who pulled the gangway up. A puff of black smoke popped out of the *Michipicoten's* stack, as it pulled away from the dock. The shrill steam whistle bid Owen Sound farewell, as the boat chugged past ship after ship and headed towards open water.

The dock was deserted. But only at that spot. All around, loading and unloading continued. I stepped out to lean against the now idle gangway. It was only a moment before I saw him. Coming down the waterfront towards me from the north. His eyes never stopped moving, looking from side to side, questioning, perhaps curious. He lurched along as though he was drunk, but I didn't think he would be. His hands twitched and fluttered as he walked, two uncontrollable birds attached to his wrists. When he got close enough, I could hear a constant stream of muttering, his internal monologue having somehow broken free.

He stopped in front of me and grinned in recognition.

"Hello, Willy," I said.

"Murphy. Ya did 'er. D'ya get the gun?"

"C'mon." I grabbed his elbow and dragged him along. "This is too open. Let's find someplace a little quieter so we can talk."

"Big Frank kilt John Edmonstone."

"How do you know?" We were down a short alley between two warehouses. Bales and crates were piled all around, and we stepped into a small space among them. No one could see us. I was sure of it.

"I seen it." His eyes twitched and rolled as he talked, never quite focussing on any one particular object.

"Do they know it?"

"Yes. That's why I been hidin'."

"Why didn't you just come to me? Why the cloak and dagger?"

"Scared. No time. Had to use what I 'membered. They seen me. So I went back up to Mudtown. Put out the word I was going to Balaclava to look fer a killer."

I laughed.

"What?" he asked.

"The general knowledge in Mudtown was that you were going to look for some Clabba Killer."

"Oh. Mebbe that too." He licked his lips.

"Okay," I said. "Let's go back to the beginning." Willy sat down on a crate. It seemed to ease his symptoms. Physically he looked okay. But he twitched and fidgeted like a man possessed. No wonder he'd been nicknamed the Gas Head.

"I visited my friend John last week," he started, "to get me some bootleg. He always had it in his cellar and didn't mind sharin'. From the Franks. Anyways, I was down there gettin' a bottle, y'know there's a trap door, when I heard the front door come in. I mean it got broke in, wasn't no knockin'."

"What did you do?"

"I stayed the hell where I was. There was a lot of yellin' and things breakin'. It was the two Franks. They was fightin' and beatin' John up something awful. Yellin' about some money and stuff. That's when I heard Little Frank say 'you hold 'im'. Then I heard the shot."

"And then what?" Willy's eyes glazed over, and his mouth hung open, as though the soul had suddenly departed the body. "Hello?" I waved a hand in front of his face. No reaction. I waited and watched. His whole body heaved, the kind of twitch you get just before you fall asleep and he was back. He jumped up, eyes rolling wildly. I heard him suck in a big breath, to scream I thought, so I jumped up and clamped a hand over his mouth before he drew attention to us. We struggled like that for a moment and it ended as quickly as it began. I let him go, and he slumped back onto the top of the crate he'd been sitting on. After a few minutes he continued.

"There was a lot of shoutin' about searchin' the house. They left the kitchen and I peeked up through the trap door. He was dead. John. Them Franks ain't scared of any dry cop. The gun was lyin' there on the floor next to him. So I grabbed it. For proof."

"This gun?"

"Yup. Anyhow, I grabbed it. Then I ran for it. You been there?"

"Yes."

"Then you seen the hole. I ran out it and inta the woods. They seen me though. Them two Franks. 'Cause there was a lotta shoutin."

"When did you buy the ticket?"

"When I came back to town. Friday. Dropped the gun at Lee Sing's then too."

"And why didn't you just come to me? Or go to the police?"

"Too scared," he said. "Them Franks, they know too many people. They'll kill me if they find me. And the cops, well who can trust them? You know. You put the chief in jail. I hadta hide."

"It's the Franks who should have hidden," I said. "It doesn't matter who they know. They can't get away with killing a dry cop."

"That's right," he giggled, hugging himself. "They are going to burn. Those two Franks."

"Forget them for now. I think we should get you home. Your family is pretty worried."

"Pearl you mean."

"No, your whole family. I saw your father Labour Day. He seemed pretty worried."

"About himself. And his precious reputation. Where'll he send me next? Where's there a war?"

"There aren't going to be anymore wars. Everyone says it. In any case," I stood, "let's get you out of here and home. That'll be about the safest place for you until we can round up the two Franks."

"Still gots my ticket?" he asked.

"Yes, why?"

"I got no money. Old man won't give me none. I could cash it in and buy a coupla bottles."

There was a big fuss when I got Willy home. Pearl and his mother Anna bawled. His father, who was in mourning for his friend Jamieson Johnston, gruffly shook his hand. It was hard to tell whether Willy was happy to be there. He just took it all in, without offering anything back.

I'd marched him straight up the main street. I wanted to get the attention of the Franks. If they were having us watched, the sight of Willy might draw them out. They were, after all, the only remaining loose ends. I thought it would be kind of nice if I could just deliver them to Oddball myself.

"Murphy." Silas had the tone of a man who was used to being obeyed. "Step inside."

2nd Avenue West was one of the rich streets in town. The Robertson house fit right in. The foyer was open through to the second floor. In the ceiling, a stained glass skylight coloured the foreboding mood of the mahogany panelled walls. A broad staircase led to the second floor. I followed Silas through a door under the stair, into his book-lined study.

He closed the door behind us, effectively cutting off the noises of the house. And I expect, cutting anything we might say off from everyone else.

"So your faithful steed got you to Balaclava and back."

"Yes."

Silas sat painfully at his desk. He had trouble holding the key in his twisted, arthritic hand, but finally got a lower desk drawer opened. "How much?" he asked, lifting a cash box onto the desk top. When he opened it, I could see it was literally stuffed with money. Bills of all denominations. It seemed like a lot of cash to keep in a desk drawer.

"Ten dollars a day, plus expenses. I'll bill you for it."

"Oh," he said, carefully counting out five twenties. "Well, here's the bonus I promised.

I reached for the money, but before I got to it, he'd picked it up. "It's a lot of money," he said.

"Yes, it is."

Robertson leaned forward and whispered, "Is he in trouble?"

I stood there for a moment and wondered whether I was about to see my bonus disappear because of fine print I hadn't been privy to. "I have my doubts about his story. I'm not sure why. But at this point it looks as though he's in the clear."

He relaxed, and shoved the money back into the cash box. "No bonus yet," he smiled like a weasel. "Not until you can say my son's in the absolute clear."

"Fine." I decided I didn't like Silas Robertson much. I didn't like anyone who changed the rules in the middle of the game.

"Mr. Murphy?" he called as I turned to leave the office. "It could be worth considerably more than a mere hundred dollars to clear my son's name."

"So you found your pigeon." Razor Eddie slouched against the bar at The Manjuris.

I took a drink. "Yeah. But I'm still not too sure about what's going on."

"I just hope ya took my advice an' stayed away from the two Franks."

"Um, more or less."

"Which is it?"

"Less." I told him about my two visits to Dun Wurkin. He listened in amazement, especially to the parts involving Van, refilling my glass when it needed it. When I finished we both stood in silence for a second.

"So that guy's got his own arsenal?"

"Yup."

"I just may have to visit him. We could do business." He paused thoughtfully, then continued. "So what'd that old man at Leith mean?"

"The dead person must be Edmonstone. Beyond that I'll be hanged."

"You better watch out. I never known anyone to have the better of the two Franks. They ain't the type to let things go."

"You think they'd come to town to settle up?"

"Don't know. They might. Or they might wait for you to leave town. Y'know, go somewhere outta the way. Where they wouldn't need to worry 'bout the law."

"Hmmm."

"What're you gonna do?"

"I'm going to take your advice."

"You want me to ride shotgun?"

"No thanks. But I'll take a shotgun if you've got one."

It was mid-afternoon by the time I got to the stable at the City Hotel. The Lugan was there as usual and I got him to bring Scotty out. I saddled up and led him out of the building.

We headed out 3rd Avenue East at a walk. I wasn't sure whether anyone was following me. I planned to find out. If the Franks required special circumstances to confront me, I was going to ensure they had them.

I tried to make it easy. Didn't look around much as I rode and tried to seem oblivious to everything.

Nearly through the warehouse district, I decided if nothing happened by the time I got to Mudtown, I'd have a drink at Maisie's then head back into town. I needn't have worried. Predictable as all bullies are, the Franks didn't disappoint me. Just beyond the stove works, four riders came thundering out of an alley and surrounded me. Stinky was in the lead. I smelled him before I saw him. Jericho Myles was close behind him, his arm in a sling.

"Well, well, well. Lookee here boys!" Stinky shouted, wheeling his horse around Scotty, who barely blinked.

"You don't smell any better in town than you did out of it," I said to my aggressor. "I thought maybe they'd delouse you at the city limits. You're a regular health hazard."

"To you, wise guy," he said pulling a revolver from his belt and cocking it. "You better just watch yourself. I'm in charge here now. Long as he's carryin' that bullet you give him."

I looked at Myles, who was clearly unhappy with the state of affairs. "You don't look like you should be on a horse," I said to him.

"And miss a chance at you Murphy? I think you should be worryin' about yourself right now."

Stinky grabbed the reins from me, and we rode back down the alley they'd come from. Our final destination was the waterfront. Between the warehouse district and Mudtown there was a no man's land of scrub trees, boulders and refuse. As we approached it, I could see three more riders. One was slumped over slightly in his saddle. It was Van. As we got closer, it became evident he'd been worked over pretty good. Big and Little sat one on each side.

"Nice of you to ride out," Little Frank spit on the ground in front of me. "Saved us a whole lot of trouble. In tryin' to catch you in town, that is."

"I knew you'd be here."

"Yeah well, just take a look at the storekeeper," Big Frank grabbed Van by the hair and yanked his head up, "and you'll see what's in store for you. Only difference is," he leaned forward in his saddle, "we like him."

Little Frank nodded. Simultaneously, four pistols and one rifle were pointed and cocked. Stinky stuck his pistol in the waistband of his pants and jumped off his mount. He gestured for me to dismount, which I did, and then frisked me. He took both automatics. And the shotgun Eddie had loaned me.

"This boy was packin'," Stinky yelled to the group, as he gestured to the pile of guns on the ground. He swung around and drove a fist into my gut, hard.

"Not here!" Little Frank yelled. "Get him out of sight before we start." Stinky jammed his pistol into my back and pushed me behind the trees, so we were right along the water, where we couldn't be seen from the warehouses. As we pushed through the brush I heard the rest of the crew dismounting. My gut throbbed, but I was getting my wind back. As Stinky pushed me into a clearing, I heard voices.

A group of children was playing. I recognized a couple from my last visit to Mudtown. They lit out when they saw us. "Yeah, you run!" Stinky cackled. I looked around quickly to see if there was anything I could use to defend myself. Stinky looked over his shoulder. No one else was in sight. With a cold smile he swung his gun, catching me hard on the jaw. It hurt. No broken teeth, but a split lip. Lots of blood.

"You better be sure I'm dead after this," I said through the blood, "because if I'm not, you will be."

"My pleasure to he'p you out with that," he smiled. The rest of the gang came into the clearing, dragging Van with them. They shoved him across to stand beside me.

"You okay?" I asked.

"Sure," he said under his breath. "You be careful."

"Stay awake," I whispered, "and be ready when I move." Little Frank handed his guns to one of the men. He took his jacket and shirt off.

"Strip." Stinky waved his gun at me. I took my jacket and shirt off. The other four gunmen ranged themselves around the clearing at the points of the compass. Stinky hid his gun inside his pants. He pushed Van across the clearing to stand beside one of the guards. Off his horse, Big Frank was looking at the pile of weapons Stinky had taken from me.

"Hey!" he exclaimed, finding his gun, the one I'd retrieved from the Chinese Laundry. He looked at me, then back at the gun. Then at me. "I lost this. Where the hell'd you find it?"

"A Chinese Laundry."

"What?"

"A Chinese Laundry. Must've wanted the blood cleaned off."

"What?" He didn't seem to get much. "Alright."

Little Frank flexed his impressive arms. "Let's go." He smiled a chill my way. Stinky stepped forward with a ten foot length of rope. He looped one end around my waist, the other around Little Frank's. He drew it tight until there was three feet between us.

"Slugfest," I heard Stinky mutter under his breath. I didn't need a mailorder degree to figure that out. Slugfest. At Ryerson I'd beaten the school bully, Johnny Baker. He'd tried me again and again over the years. Aside from that, I hadn't been much of a fighter. Slugfest. Little Frank started swinging and hit me with a couple of solid body shots. Rib crunchers. I responded by kicking him hard in the knee. When he fell into me, I swung an upper cut to his jaw. He head-butted me in the guts, like a billy goat. We both fell. My mouth and eyes filled with dirt. He hit me again. I jammed an elbow into his eye, then tried to clear the dirt from mine. Little Frank dragged himself up. He kicked me hard in the gut and I lost my wind. Another kick, then another. When he tried for a fourth, I grabbed his foot and twisted. He went down hard. I got to my feet. Gave him a swift boot to the ribcage. I dove and hit him in the face as hard as I could.

Blood spouted from the nose I'd mashed. He snarled and brought a knee into my crotch. I fell off him and curled into a ball. Through a haze of pain, I saw one of the guards fall down. Someone I knew came into sight. I couldn't think who it was. Little Frank kicked me in the kidneys. He was about to stomp my thigh when I heard a familiar voice shout, "Enough!"

Little Frank stopped. I propped myself up on one elbow. Rufus stood in the middle of the clearing, gun held at the ready. "You wanna get up? Or are you just gonna lie here all day?" he asked. Slowly I got to my feet. The pain was just beginning. I wavered for a second, a black cloud obscuring my vision. A deep breath and the cloud began to recede. A few more deep breaths and I was sure I'd be able to stay on my feet. But I was starting to feel sick.

"Where'd you come from?" I wheezed.

"Doan worry 'bout that now. We gots ta get outta here."

"Not without him we don't," I pointed at Van. Rufus handed me a knife and I cut the rope connecting Little Frank and I.

"You'd best just kill me now," he glowered, "'cause this ain't gonna end until you and me finish this."

"Don't tempt me," I said. "This is over as of right now."

"Not quite!" Big Frank had a knife in his hand. He overhanded it at Rufus, who fired a shot. Big Frank went down with a groan. Little Frank dove straight at Rufus, who was trying to pull the knife out of his shoulder. Next to me, Stinky reached for his gun in a hurry. It was with great pleasure that I swung my arm hard. He screamed when my elbow met his nose. I left him where he fell. Van was toe to toe with the guard who had been nearest him. Rufus had dropped the gun. With the haft of the knife still protruding from his shoulder, he and Little Frank grappled hand to hand.

I searched the ground for his rifle. Before I found it, I heard the alarming sound of a gun being cocked right beside my ear. Jericho Myles pressed the barrel of a pistol to my temple and said, "I guess that's about it. Stop right now, or he gets it!" he shouted at the grappling men.

The fighting stopped. For an instant the clearing froze into a violent tableau. Then Little Frank shoved Rufus to the ground and kicked him. I winced, having so recently been on the receiving end of those boots. "That's enough Little Frank," Jericho Myles said. Little Frank gave him a look aimed at freezing blood.

"What?"

"All I mean is, your brother needs help." Big Frank lay where he'd fallen when Rufus shot him. He hadn't moved from what I could see. Little Frank knelt down next to him.

"Big? Hey, Big?" he called softly. He felt around the prone man's clothing, looking for the bullet wound. He found it in the midsection, and pulled the shirt away. It had passed cleanly through the fleshy part of his hip. Little Frank laughed, then leaned forward and slapped his brother's face. "Hey, wake up."

Big Frank's eyes opened. "Am I dead?" he asked.

"You ain't dead. You're shot, that's all."

"Shot? I'm gonna die," he moaned.

"You're not gonna die," Little Frank stood. "You fainted is all." Our eyes met, and he gave me another one of those smiles. Stinky moaned and stood up. Myles backed off, leaving me standing in the middle of the clearing.

"Tie his hands," Little Frank barked. The man Van had wrestled with stepped in and tied my hands. "Where's the bullwhip?" Little Frank asked.

"Stinky has it."

Little Frank turned to Stinky. "Nose broke, Stinky?" he laughed and his men joined in. "You should thank Murphy. Least one of us here won't be able to smell you no more." The bullwhip was tied off at the side of Stinky's saddle. Little Frank grabbed it and unrolled it with a vicious crack.

"Okay boys," a voice said from the bushes and half a dozen deputies stepped into the clearing, guns at the ready. Oddball followed them in and stepped right up to Little Frank. He pulled the ever present damp cigar out of his mouth and leaned over until they were almost nose to nose.

"It ain't polite to poke fun at the misfortunes of others," he said, gesturing towards Stinky.

"Took you long enough to get here." All activity in the clearing stopped at the sound of Stinky's voice.

Oddball stepped over to him and shook hands.

"Gentlemen," he said, "allow me to present Captain Philip Caldwell of the Temperance Enforcement Branch."

CHAPTER NINE
ONE MORE TIME

I burst out laughing when I saw the look on Little Frank's face. They'd been shocked enough when I'd told them John Edmonstone was a dry cop. It was nothing when compared with this.

"What…? You…? Stinky?"

"Philip Caldwell. And I'll be damned happy to leave Stinky behind."

"But how…? You've been with us nearly a year," Little Frank spluttered.

"Regretfully. I shan't consider it a lost year however, now that you'll be out of business."

Little Frank gave a confident smile. "We'll be back in business before we make bail."

"Bail?" Oddball asked. "I don't think so."

"Less I'm mistaken, bootleggin' ain't no hangin' offence."

"Murder is," I spoke up.

"I haven't killed you," Little Frank sneered. "Leastaways not yet."

I was grateful his hands were shackled together. The clearing was mostly empty. Sean O'Malley and the other deputies had taken everyone away, including the wounded Big Frank and Jericho Myles.

"You and your brother killed John Edmonstone."

"Says who?"

"Says Willy Robertson. He heard the whole thing."

"You found him?" Oddball was surprised.

"Sure. He's been hiding from these two for the past week."

"Where is he now?"

"At home. I'm sure he can tell you whatever you want to know. If you check inside Big Frank's coat, you'll find the gun they used to kill Edmonstone."

"We didn't kill no one," Little Frank said.

"Go on." Oddball urged him.

"I ain't saying nothing till I see my shyster."

"You don't have to say anything," Philip Caldwell offered, "as it seems the evidence is against you. You killed John Edmonstone. And the money you took belonged to the government. Those are hanging offences. Take him away constable."

Oddball led Little Frank back through the trees. Caldwell looked at me. "Sorry about the nose," I said.

"It's an offence to assault a peace officer."

"I didn't assault a peace officer. I hit a disagreeably odorous member of a nasty gang."

"True," he smiled, "and I did get a few licks of my own in. No teeth missing, I trust?"

"Nope."

"Good. Now tell me, why did the Franks kill John?"

"I thought you'd know."

"Uh, uh," he shook his head. "They didn't talk about it. Least not to me."

"Money is a powerful motivator."

"But they were going to get that anyway."

"Maybe they found out he was a dry cop," Van offered.

"That would have made quite a ruckus around Dun Wurkin. I'm sure everyone would have known."

"Say, what's going to happen out there?"

"We'll have a troop of men move in to take it apart. Still, stockade, the works."

"What for?" Van asked. "Someone else'll set up shop within a week."

"And we'll close them down too."

"And on and on it goes," I said.

Caldwell shrugged his shoulders. "It's a job." He turned and left the clearing. I looked at Van, then Rufus. The big man had a hand clamped to his shoulder. Blood seeped between his fingers.

"You okay?" I asked.

"Ain't nuthin next to the beatin' you laid on me."

"You want to come into town, have the doc look at that?"

"Naw. I'll stitch myself up."

"Thanks. For saving me."

"If you was dead, how'd I get a rematch?" He smiled. I put a hand on my bruised ribs. I hoped none were broken.

"I might need a little rest before I take you up on that."

"Lotsa time," he said, turning towards Mudtown.

"Who was that guy?" Van asked.

"Rufus Jones. The Mayor of Mudtown."

★★★

Van and I walked our mounts back to town. I was in so much pain it was easier than riding. Caldwell had galloped ahead, eager to file his report and question the two Franks. Or maybe he wanted a bath. He'd asked me to bring Willy down to the police office in the morning, for a formal statement.

"How do you feel?" Van asked.

"I'm alive. I just hope I clean up okay. I've got a wedding to go to tomorrow."

"You aren't marked up too badly," he said scrutinizing my face.

"Say, how'd they get hold of you anyway? You said you were riding for Meaford."

"I was. I was about halfway there, around Woodford, when they caught me. They thought they were following you."

"Oh. Sorry about that."

"Listen, when I stepped onto that road with my machine gun, I became a part of this. Now I won't have to worry about them anymore. Not for a while, anyway."

"What are your plans now?"

"Don't know. Up until a few minutes ago I expected to be lying in a ditch for the night."

"C'mon back to the house. You can get cleaned up there and spend the night. It's the least I can do."

We stabled the horses, then walked back to the house. It was nearly dinnertime when we arrived and we created quite a stir with our appearances. The boys thought it looked like fun. Sil and Marth wasted no time in hustling Van into the house and getting him set up in the spare room with some wash water and bandages. My ribs were hurting pretty badly, so I wound a couple of yards of tape around them. It helped considerably, but I was feeling stiff. In need of medication.

Changed and cleaned up, I don't think either of us looked too bad. We went straight to Sil's study for a much needed and well deserved drink.

"To the conclusion of your first case." Sil offered a toast, and the three of us drank. The rye hit my stomach and spread warmth throughout my limbs.

"This should be bottled and sold as a restorative," I said.

"It is," Sil laughed, "available by prescription from fine physicians throughout the province."

"You wanna watch who you say that to," Van said. I told Sil about our day.

"Do you ever do anything only partway?" he asked when I'd finished.

"Not unless I halve to," I joked. They both groaned.

Sil raised his glass again.

"An amended toast…to surviving your case." We all laughed and drank, then crossed over into the dining room.

To my surprise, Lori was helping to set the table.

"Hello beautiful lady." I gave her a peck on the cheek.

"And who might this be?" Van asked.

"This is Lori Storey, my girlfr…my fiance."

"Fiance? When did that happen?"

"Last night. After I got home from your place."

"I'm pleased for you both," he said. "Congratulations."

Everyone found a place and sat. Dinner was a roast that Marth had cooked to perfection. Melt in your mouth stuff. We all ate far more than we should have and over dinner I was forced to tell the whole story again.

"So Willy was hiding from the two Franks the whole time?" Lori asked.

"Yup," I mumbled between mouthfuls.

"Why didn't he just come to you in the first place? Why the ruse?"

"He needed me to go to Balaclava to flush out the two Franks. I think he was afraid that if I knew where he was, they'd get it out of me somehow."

"Agnes Macphail will be speaking again next week," Lori changed the topic. "Marth and I are going."

"She's the woman I was telling you about," I said to Van, happy for the change in subject, "running in the election for the United Farmers."

"Do you really think she has a chance?" he asked Lori.

"Yes, I do."

"Why?"

"First of all," she said, "she's not just a women's candidate. She plans to represent farmers and returned men too. All the people who haven't been properly represented by the government. She's smart and plain talking. She'll do circles around those snake oil salesmen in Ottawa now."

"Do you really think the country is ready for women in politics?"

"Women have been running this country from behind the scenes since 1867. I think it's high time we got our due and moved to the front and centre."

"Here, here!" Marth cried, applauding Lori.

"You tell him, Murph," Lori said to me. "You saw her on Labour Day."

"She's quite a speaker," I said to Van, "and if applause is any indication, she's got a lot of support. I don't think the men who are running against her know what to do. Half of them dismiss her as a joke and that's a mistake. The other half just pretend she's not there. I think that's an even bigger mistake."

"Where is she speaking?" Van asked.

"At the fall fair. Just informally."

"I think I'll have to travel back down. To see what it's all about."

"Then you can attend one of the Legion meetings," I added. "They're electing the first ever board of directors next week."

"This is great," Van said, "that they're finally doing something for returned men. It's just too bad it's taken so long."

"What returned men need," Sil jumped in, "is jobs. Not clubs."

"That's right," Van said. "It's too bad the government's forgotten about us already." There was a hint of bitterness in his comment. I'd heard it expressed many times by men returning from the war and I'd felt it myself. All that horror. And when you returned, no one seemed to want you. I looked at Lori and thought about how lucky I was.

Marth got up and started clearing dinner away. Lori helped. Van and Sil continued talking, the conversation shifting from the war to commerce and a comparison of the prices they were paying suppliers for various goods.

After dessert and coffee we all ended up in Sil's study. Later, when I got the look from Lori, we excused ourselves.

"How did you happen to be over to dinner?" I held her hand as we walked slowly in the direction of the Storey house. It was a beautiful warm evening and a light breeze rippled the leaves in the maple trees as we walked.

"Marth sent the boys over for me."

"Oh, I see."

"She wants me to feel like one of the family."

"Do you?"

"Yes. They make it easy."

"They're good people."

"She's afraid of losing you. After we get married."

"What?"

"She and Sil are afraid they'll never see you."

"They will."

"I know that. I told her I'd make sure of it. Of course it won't be so hard once we have children of our own." We were passing a giant maple that stood at the centre of a vacant lot. Lori pulled me off the walk and under the tree. She pressed her back against the trunk and turned her face up to mine.

"Kiss me," she whispered.

"I love you," I said, pressing my mouth against hers. Some time later we arrived at the house on 4th Avenue, arms wrapped around one another. We went up the front walk and kissed at the door.

"What time will you pick me up tomorrow?"

"What?"

"For the wedding, silly."

"Oh. Right. It's at four? I'll be here around three."

"Are we walking?"

"No. I'm borrowing Sil's Democrat."

"A buggy ride. That's nice. Three then. 'Night." She kissed me again and disappeared into the house.

An insistent knocking at my bedroom door woke me. I groaned as I rolled over to look at the time. I was sore all over. Six-thirty. Much earlier than I'd planned on waking.

"What?" I called. Sil poked his head in the door. "Pearl Robertson was here. She says Willy has disappeared again."

Half an hour later I was fully dressed and on my way to meet Pearl at the Robertson house. I turned the bell in the front door. Pearl opened it immediately. "I saw you coming," she said.

"Willy disappeared early in the morning," Pearl continued, "after another one of his screaming nightmares." She'd heard the front door slam and when she'd gone to check had discovered him missing.

"I need to see his room first." She took me up the ornate staircase to the second floor. Antiques and richly carved wooden furniture cluttered the wide hallway.

"Papa believes in investing his money in things," she said, embarrassed.

"Hmmm," was the best I could do. I was tired and sore. I'd already found Willy once. His father was trying to rook me out of the bonus he'd promised. I really didn't want to be there at all. The bed in the room she showed me hadn't been slept in. Everything was perfectly neat and orderly. Just as the maid had left it. I crossed to a bureau and pulled out a few of the drawers.

"Would you know if anything was missing from here?"

She looked in the drawer I was holding open, then went methodically from one to another.

"Well it looks as though there's some things gone," she finally said, "though I can't say as what. Underwear. Socks. Maybe some shirts."

She crossed the room to a huge wardrobe and pulled the doors open to reveal a row of suits, ties and, on a top shelf, hats. Shoes were lined neatly across the floor. "Papa bought all this stuff when the war ended. Thought Willy'd come home a changed man, join the family business."

"He was changed."

"Maybe. Oh, look, there. His duffel is missing." Pearl had moved the suits aside, to reveal a set of shelves and drawers in the back of the wardrobe. I moved in for a look. The shelves held a variety of items, some books, shirts and his uniform. In one of the drawers there was a pile of .45 calibre shells. No gun.

"They're for his service revolver," Pearl offered. "It's usually in that drawer too."

"Is anything else missing? From the rest of the house?"

"I don't think so," she said. "Papa's downstairs. He wants to see you. We'll ask him."

Pearl showed me into the same small study I'd met Robertson in before. He sat at his desk, a cup of coffee in front of him, a cigarette in his hand. "Murphy. Thanks for coming."

"Well?"

"Cup of coffee?"

"Yes. Okay. Thanks."

"You heard the man, Pearl. Get him a coffee." Pearl left. Silas took a long drag from his cigarette. "Smoke?" he asked.

"No. What do you want?"

"I want you to find my son for me."

"I already found him once. And I still haven't been paid for that."

"I'll pay you."

"When?"

"Before you leave."

"No. Now. Right now. Or you can find yourself someone else." He gave me a hard look, then bent to his desk drawer, the one I'd seen him take the cash box from before. Pearl returned with the coffee. When Silas screamed, she did too, and dropped the cup and saucer, right there in the middle of the floor.

The old man sat at his desk, mouth agape, the lid of the cash box hanging open. I didn't need to look. It was empty. "FIND HIM!" Silas was standing, his face contorted with rage. "I want you to find my son and I want you to bring him to me."

"It'll cost you double," I said.

"Just find him."

"Write it down. On paper. So there'll be no mistake." He sat down at the desk, pulled out a cheque book, hastily scribbled in it and tore off the sheet.

"Three hundred dollars," I said reading the cheque. "Thank you. That'll do nicely."

"Just find him."

"I will." It was just after nine when I left the Robertson house. I went straight downtown at a brisk walk and stopped at the stable. I told the Lugan I'd be back in fifteen minutes to pick Scotty up. Then I went over to Oak Hall and gave the cheque to Sil. "Put it in your safe. I don't want to carry it around with me all day."

"Sure," he said. "What's up?"

"I've got a hunch. But I'm going to have to go to Meaford to prove it."

"Don't forget the wedding."

"I know, I know."

CHAPTER TEN
GAS HEAD WILLY

The newly paved Meaford Road became Sykes, the main street, which cut through the centre of Meaford parallel to Bayfield, the waterfront road.

I decided to follow Sykes Street to the town hall and leave Scotty there. A man on foot would draw less attention on the waterfront. Just past Morrison's Theatre was the market square with the town hall and the fire hall on the other side.

I rode past it to the grassy verge in front of the new town hall. The pride of Meaford, it boasted an opera house on the upper floor. The old town hall had burned to the ground in 1907.

Some old timers were sitting on the benches. There weren't any hitching posts. So I tied Scotty to a bench.

"Be good," I whispered in his ear.

I set off down Nelson for the waterfront, a short block away. It was eleven forty-five by my pocketwatch. I'd have to move fast. I had no idea where the *Michipicoten* would be.

I walked past the fire hall, then a couple of houses. At the end of the street, where Nelson and Bayfield met, was the Meaford Planing Mill. The waterfront was directly ahead.

On the east side of the harbour was a wooden grain elevator. Rails led from it to a train station and beyond. A new concrete arch bridge spanned the Bighead River where it let into the harbour. Right in front of me, the Meaford fishing fleet was moored. Boats with names like *Elsie M*, *The Alice G*, and *The Belle*.

The west side of the harbour looked the best bet. Next to the planing mill was the blacksmith, a man called Raven. A couple of fish houses and more boats. At the base of the next street, Collingwood Street, the *Michipicoten* was moored against the concrete harbour wall. The gangway was down and town men were loading Meaford apples onto the craft.

I made for a pile of crates stacked on the dock near the *Michipicoten* and watched the men load for a few minutes. The first officer came to the end of the gangway and checked his watch.

"Excuse me?" I called walking from my hiding spot.

"Yes sir?" He smiled pleasantly.

"I'm looking for a friend. He missed you in Owen Sound and may have boarded here. William Robertson?"

"Cabin Four. Around the other side. We sail shortly. Please don't be long."

"Don't worry."

He stepped aside and let me pass up the gangway.

There was a small porthole set in the centre of the door. I peered inside. The cabin was small, with a bed, night table, bureau and chair. Everything was bolted down.

There was no sign of Gas Head Willy. He'd been dropped like a cheap suit of clothes. The William Robertson I was looking at seemed more a country gentleman, off for an early autumn vacation. He sat on the chair, reading a newspaper. A pipe and tobacco were laid out on the table beside him.

With a shock, Uncle's words came back to me. Guilty the man who removes his head. Malice, pride and vanity, another lies dead. Looking at Willy, I knew Uncle had been right after all. I might have gotten it sooner if he'd said, guilty the man who removes his gas head. Because that was exactly what Willy had done. And malice, pride and vanity now described him perfectly.

I pulled my pistol and opened the door.

"I hate being played for a sucker."

"What the…?" Willy dropped the paper, but relaxed when he saw it was me.

"Hello Gas Head." I pulled the door closed behind me.

"I knew you were smart, Murphy. But you were only supposed to find me once."

"You knew John Edmonstone was a dry cop."

"So? Everyone knew that."

"The Franks didn't know until I told them. That was a few days after you disappeared."

"Maybe I saw it in the papers."

"Maybe. But I doubt it. I think you went up there to rip Edmonstone off for the money he owed the Franks. You found out he was a dry cop. So you shot him. With a gun you stole from Big Frank."

"I...well...um, I..." he stammered.

"Just shut up and listen. You cried poor so I'd give your ticket back. It might have worked. If you hadn't got so greedy and robbed your father too. All I want to know now is, was it worth it?"

"Four thousand dollars, give or take."

I whistled. "Not bad. Must be your biggest scheme ever."

"So far," he amended

"Oh?"

"Don't be naive, Murphy. It's a big world. Lotsa suckers out there just dying to be parted from their hard earned cash."

"Suckers like John Edmonstone?"

"Bad choice of words. Besides, that wasn't his dough."

"How long have you been planning this?"

"You ever spend any time in the trenches?"

"Not much. I was a gunner."

"They used to say up front that if the Hun didn't get you, the trenches would. You know how many guys tripped and drowned while entire platoons marched over them? Have you ever stood in water waist deep in the middle of winter? And how about eating? Ever tried to chow down some bully beef, while the maggot infested corpse of your best friend writhes next to you? Huh? Have you?"

"No."

"Didn't think so. Time took forever to pass. All I could think about was crime and punishment. Because he sent me there. To pay for some money I'd stolen. Said it'd make me a man. But I'll tell you Murphy, there is no crime that fits that punishment. None."

"I can understand you wanting revenge on your father. But what about the two Franks and John Edmonstone?"

"I needed a stake. So I could leave Owen Sound forever. Edmonstone didn't have as much money as I thought he would. Only a thousand dollars or so."

"That's still a lot of money."

"Not enough to start a whole new life."

"So you decided to rip off your father."

"He started keeping whatever cash he hadn't invested at home just before the war. Said banks couldn't be trusted."

"So why'd you hang around? Why not just take his money after you killed Edmonstone and get away?"

"The two Franks were looking for me. I needed you to take care of them."

"You had it all figured out. Every step of the way."

"Yes."

"Except for one thing."

"You."

"Exactly. Let's go."

"What? Where?"

"I'm taking you back."

"Back? No, no. Just wait a minute now." He reached for a black travelling case under the chair.

"Easy does it," I warned him.

"No, look," he opened the bag up. It was stuffed with cash.

"How much?" he asked, hopeful.

"Excuse me?"

"How much? To let me go?"

I thought about the cheque Sil was holding for me. "You said your father doesn't believe in banks."

"That's right."

"This morning he wrote me a cheque. To pay for this job."

Willy started to laugh. "It's worth about as much as the paper it's printed on."

"Alright then, I'll take three hundred dollars."

"No, c'mon. You have to take more than that. Here, take half."

He held the bag out to me. It was tempting.

"Three hundred. Count it out."

He pulled three one hundred dollar bills out of the bag and handed them to me.

"Thanks. Now get up. We're going."

We heard the footsteps outside the cabin door at about the same time.

"Help! HELP! Robbery," Willy shouted before I could shut him up.

The door opened and the first officer took in the scene. Me with a gun. Willy in the chair, a bag of money at his feet.

The sailor jumped me and tried to take the pistol away. Willy bolted out the door.

"I'm a detective. You just let a murderer get away."

"Sure buddy."

We struggled across the tiny room and fell. I twisted and landed on top of him, on the tiny bed. A left to the chin with my free hand convinced the man to give up the struggle.

No more than thirty seconds had passed, but Willy was nowhere in sight when I got on deck. I tucked my gun away and quickly scanned the dock. There was nowhere for him to hide in the open. A dandy with a big bag of money would draw some attention. I had to look somewhere less public.

Across the road, the main floor double doors of the planing mill stood open. The faint whine of a big saw drifted towards me. I decided it was worth a try. I walked down the gangway and across the road.

★★★

My eyes were slow getting used to the light inside the mill. Machinery came into view first. It stood in pools of electric light throughout the building. Sashes, doors, shingles. Lumber in various stages of finish was piled all around the place. It smelled good, all that wood. At another time I might have closed my eyes and taken a deep breath. Instead I pulled the clip out of my automatic and replaced it. With a single Manstopper.

I wound my way around some pallets of shingle and came to the first piece of machinery. A big saw. It was running. Next to it, on the floor, a pair of feet stuck out from under a worktable. The saw operator. Alive. But out cold.

I stayed in the shadows. Beyond the saw, doors stood row on row. It was close. Like in a trench.

I came out at the end of a row, near a planer. Next to it, another set of double doors led into the lumberyard.

I was nearly blinded when I stepped into the daylight. Something hit me over the head. From behind.

Face down in the dirt I must have blacked out for a second. When I rolled over Willy was standing over me, my pistol in his hand.

"Guess I'll be leavin' after all," he said.

All I could think about was the Manstopper. The sure thing. Which was aimed at me.

"I wouldn't be so sure."

"Oh?" A look of pure amusement lit his face.

"Might have something up my sleeve." As I said it, I looked around desperately for something that could help. The bag full of money lay at Willy's feet. Next to it was a hefty piece of lumber, likely the one he had clubbed me with. I thought of Lori the way I'd seen her last. The way I'd felt her last. I had to think of something.

"Killing me won't achieve anything. You'll still get caught."

"You may be right. But I've already killed a peace officer. Don't suppose the gallows are gonna kill me any deader if I've got two murders on my head." On the other side of the building, the *Michipicoten* sounded her steam whistle.

"Well, gotta go. I'll have that three hundred back. You won't need it."

I reached into my pocket. Willy leaned over to retrieve the cash. Over his shoulder, I saw the first officer from the *Michipicoten* walk squinting into the sunlight. Surprise showed on his face as he paused for a second to take in the scenario. Then he sprinted towards Willy, who whirled an instant too late and fired. The big slug flew wild and smashed a hole right through the thick plank wall of the mill. The Manstopper. Willy steadied his aim and pulled the trigger again. The first officer hit him as the hollow click sounded in the yard.

I left Willy Robertson and his money, minus my three hundred, with the Meaford town constable. After checking with the Temperance Enforcement Branch, he'd agreed to hold the fugitive until Oddball sent someone in a car.

It was one-thirty when I walked from the police office to the front of town hall. I'd have to hurry. I rounded a corner and arrived at the grassy verge. Scotty was nowhere in sight. I put two fingers in my mouth and blew. The loud whistle startled the single remaining old timer.

"Say mister, you lookin' fer a hoss?"

"His name's Scotty. Have you seen him?"

"Scotty? What kinda name issat fer a hoss? S'no wonder he ran 'way."

"He ran away?"

"Durndest thing I ever seen. Young Tommy Callendar, he come racin' round the corner in that Durant o' his. That hoss, he took one look an' he lit out like someone set his tail afire."

"Which way?" I sighed.

"That way," he pointed. "T'wards Ow'n Sound."

Towards Owen Sound. At least he was headed in the right direction.

THE END

A fast paced detective thriller set in Owen Sound and Wiarton, circa 1922

THE LOST TIRE GANG

A D. B. Murphy Adventure

PACIFIC HOTEL

PACIFIC HOTEL

Richard J Thomas

Chapter One
The Limb

It was a Packard. Sunk to the axles in the Bognor Marsh. "We chased 'em up 'ere from Bognor an' lost 'em," a geezer wheezed in my face. "It's that Lost Tire Gang."

"How many men?"

"Three."

"They armed?"

"Yep."

I pulled the Webley & Scott .455 from the holster under my suit jacket. The clip dropped into my hand with a slap and I stuck it in my pocket. The geezer whistled when I pulled out the back-up.

"Manstoppers!" he exclaimed.

I rammed the second clip of bullets into the big gun.

"If I'm going in after those men, I'd best be ready."

A man from the group that had gathered gave me a leg-up on my horse, Scotty. I nudged him around the Packard and we started into the swamp.

The Bognor Marsh was an insult to farmers. It stubbornly defied attempts to tame it. Men bought the land over and over again. Arriving in Sydenham Township after a day's train ride, maybe three days by wagon, they would see what they had purchased. Sensing defeat, some just moved on, never to be heard from again.

It was said one could get lost in Bognor Marsh and never find a way out. I'd been all around it as a boy. It wasn't that big. The knowledge didn't make my ride any more pleasurable. The mosquitoes and black flies were thick. They clung everywhere flesh showed. Neither Scotty nor I liked it much.

We rode east towards Walters Falls. It was more than half an hour before we picked up any sign of the car's occupants. A clear path cut straight through a patch of wild raspberries. I swung round to one side, to spare Scotty the aggravation.

There were no tracks at the far side of the patch. The men hadn't come out. I dismounted and left Scotty standing at the edge of the thicket. The raspberry canes clung, tearing my clothes. There was no way to be quiet. It didn't matter. A gunshot sounded close enough to make my ears ring, shattering a limb three inches from my nose. I yanked my pistol out and fired a quick round. The flat head of the Manstopper whistled as it tore through the bushes, smashing everything in its path.

I crouched, trying not to move. It was difficult. The bugs lit on me, drawn by the smell of blood oozing from dozens of scratches. The normal sounds of the marsh, silenced by the gunfire, resumed. There was no breeze to stir the oppressive air. The minutes dragged by. Sweat trickled into my eyes. My thighs started to ache, the big muscles protesting the sustained crouch. Just when I knew I couldn't stand it any longer, a mosquito buzzed maddeningly into my ear canal and I moved.

At the same instant I heard the shot, I felt the burst of pain. Blood gushed into my eyes. A graze, luckily. Blinded, I fired wildly and heard a yell not far away, then a wild thrashing through the bushes. I jumped and ran, swiping an arm across my face to clear my vision.

I made it only ten yards or so before I tripped and fell. The crashing of the retreating men grew distant. I lay for awhile to catch my breath. When I finally got to my knees something under a nearby patch of goutweed caught my attention.

What my eyes saw, my mind didn't want to believe.

It was half an hour before we got back to the road. The boys from Bognor had tied heavy ropes to the undercarriage of the Packard. Their horses snorted and flexed. Steel yielding to flesh. The thought made me touch my forehead. The flow of blood had stopped. I was fairly sure I would live.

There was a car on the other side of the road. Oddball leaned against it, a Havana Stogie hanging from his mouth. The cigars were made in Owen Sound by the Cooke Cigar Company and, in all the years I'd known Marc Scott, I'd never known him to light one. He just sucked them to a pulp. The High Constable of Grey County, he'd earned his nickname as a rookie. An unfortunate accident with a gun tucked into the front of his pants had left him one short of a set. It was his one deficiency. That and the fact he generally needed a bath. Oddball had a ready, open smile. Blue eyes. Red hair. At thirty-seven, he was six years my senior.

He saw me coming and strode my way. The usual jibe died on his lips. His jaw dropped so fast the cigar was lost. It bounced off his foot, leaving a wet spot on the dusty toe of his police boot.

"D.B. Murphy. What happened to you?"

"Hello Oddball."

"These good fellows, the ah…Bognoronians have been filling me in. You find those guys?"

"Bognorites."

"What?"

"Them," I gestured at the villagers. Each now had a rope as well. "They're Bognorites."

"Oh," he said, squinting. "Like in the bible?"

"Those were Israelites."

"Oh. Did you find 'em?"

"They got away. Cut through the Red Sea."

"Huh?"

"The Israelites."

He looked at me like I was a fool. Maybe I was. I dismounted, and started working at the rope I'd used to tie a package across the back of my big Ferguson saddle.

"Well, are you gonna tell me or not?" Oddball sounded exasperated.

"I found them," I said. I was having trouble getting a knot undone.

"And?"

"They had shooting in mind, not conversation."

"No wonder, the way these boys chased them up from Bognor. They prob'ly thought you were tryin' to rob 'em."

"Not the kind of thing I'd expect to worry a gang."

"That's the thing," he laughed. "Might not be the gang."

I stopped fiddling with the rope.

"What?"

"Seems this here Packard…" he gestured towards the car. The Bognorites were clustered around, having given up trying to move it. Several looked sheepish as Oddball continued, "This Packard was comin' through Bognor. Someone seen it had no spare tire, so they naturally thought…"

"That it was The Lost Tire Gang," I finished.

"Right. So we really don't know what them boys is up to. Might be innocent."

I went back to work on the rope. All at once the knot gave. The arm fell out of the package. There was a collective gasp. One man lost his bean supper. His retching had barely ended when the laughter began. Tentative at first, it quickly gained a hysterical edge. Tears streamed down faces as the truth hit home.

"Jeez D.B.," Oddball exclaimed. "You shot some guy's wooden arm off."

Staring under the bush I'd thought of throwing up too. A man's arm. Shot off below the elbow. By me. I choked the bile back down and crawled in for a look. The closer I got, the less real it became. My stomach settled down when I saw the leather straps that had attached the prosthesis to its owner. The owner. Whoever he was, he'd gotten away lucky. The buckle used to secure the straps was shattered, the top portion of the arm split. Another three inches and he'd have needed to replace the arm with a longer one.

The trail they left while escaping was broad. There were three sets of tracks in the soft ground. Every right bootprint of one set showed blood. I was lucky with both shots. It would have been easy to follow the men. With dogs. I had none. Nor had anyone else.

"So we're looking for a one-armed guy." The sound of Oddball's voice brought me back.

"Unless he had three arms to start with," I quipped.

"Don't get mad at me. Yer the one that shot him. A one-armed guy. Like he didn't have enough problems already."

The Bognorites had given up on the Packard and left. Not before promising to return in the morning with a team of heavy horses. They'd get the Packard out. Whole or in pieces.

Oddball was back in his car, with the engine running. "You want to ride in with me? You can tie Scotty to the bumper."

"No." I was still embarrassed. It wasn't every day you shot a guy's peg off.

"Any idea who it belongs to?" Oddball gestured to the package that was on the seat beside him.

"Nope."

"Didn't see them?"

"Nope."

"They see you?"

"I don't know." That hadn't occurred to me. I'd just assumed because I hadn't seen them, they hadn't seen me. I had also assumed the shot that hit me was wild. Like the ones I'd fired.

"Well, watch your back on the way into town."

Oddball switched his headlamps on. With a thrashing of gears the car began moving. "Come on into the office tomorrow," he shouted over the noise of the engine. "I wanta know what you're gonna do next."

I could feel Scotty's sudden attentiveness as Oddball pulled away. He was a strange horse. Loved cars, and he'd race them any chance he got. I mounted up just to be sure I wasn't left behind if he did take off. I needn't have worried. It was too dark to race.

★★★

I'd been in the detective business since the summer of 1921. Purely by chance. I'd left for the Great War a blacksmith, but had come home to find the automobile had limited my job prospects. Like many returned men, I spent a long time waiting for something. There just weren't many jobs in the post-war economy. Farming, if you could stand the hours and the toil. I tried it for awhile. The low wages hardly made it worth the effort. Eventually my brother Kevin had given me a job. An insurance man, he and his partner were being threatened. I couldn't save the partner. But I solved the case.

I'd opened my own office on the heels of that success. Right away, I had a case—to find a missing veteran known around Owen Sound as Gas Head Willy. Another success, and things had been set. I'd been busy over the winter with small jobs, enough to pay the rent on my minescule office above MacLean's Marketeria on 2nd Avenue East.

Now it was 1922. In early spring, Oddball had come to my office. Looking for help with the Lost Tire Gang which had terrorized motorists on county roads throughout the previous summer and fall. The ruse was simple: they dropped a tire in the centre of a remote section of road. When an automobile stopped, armed men would rob the driver and passengers. There hadn't been a murder yet. But winter was over and cars were back on the roads. Oddball was worried. It was only a matter of time.

"Need someone to help out on this thing," Oddball had said, sitting on the only good chair in my office. He'd learned early on to avoid the other one, the one with the split leg.

"What about O'Malley? Your patrol car idea?"

"Don't seem to be workin'. Gang's too smart or somethin'. What we need is a spy.

"You need someone they don't know."

"So you'll do it?"

I looked at my desk. Empty, but for the newspaper I'd been reading. I had nothing else to do at the moment.

"Sure," I said, "but it'll cost you. The standard rate."

"Jeez, Murphy."

"I can always find something else to do."

His answer was a measure of his desperation.

"Okay. Ten a day, plus expenses."

"And a twenty dollar advance. Up front."

Glaring, he'd dug down into his pants pocket.

"One more thing," as he'd handed over twenty dollars in assorted small bills. "When you catch them, I get the glory. County doesn't actually know I'm hirin' you."

"Who does?"

"Just you an' me."

I thought for a second. Then decided glory was overrated.

"Deal," I said.

★★★

The lights of the city looked like stars reflected in a pool of water. They were a welcome sight. With the exception of an occasional passing car, the dark had been complete on the ride back. Not that I minded dark. But light had its place.

Situated on Georgian Bay, the city of Owen Sound was divided in two by the Sydenham River. On the east was the centre of commerce, downtown. The west side was residential. North of 10th Street, both sides of the city were equally devoted to commerce. Railway tracks, factories and warehouses lined the waterfront. Ships were moored port to stern. There were days you could almost walk across the inner harbour without getting wet.

Scotty and I rode down the 6th Street hill and turned north on 2nd Avenue. We went straight to the City Hotel Stable where I handed Scotty over to the care of the Lugan. I didn't know how he'd gotten the name, but the stooped redhead with the hump and ribald sense of humour knew horses.

"Murphy!" he exclaimed as we rode through the open door. "I was wonderin' when you'd get ole Windbag back. Jeez, you're a mess."

"Thanks Lugan. There's some blood on the saddle that'll need cleaning. And don't call him Windbag. You know he's sensitive about that."

"Oh yeah. I keep forgettin'."

I walked from the stables down the block to MacLean's Marketeria. The canopy was rolled up. My portly landlord, James MacLean, was collecting the last of the fruit from his outdoor display.

"Closing so early?" I asked as I dug in my pocket for the office key.

"What on earth?" He didn't bother with a greeting.

"A graze. It only looks bad."

"Enough for a doctor."

"We'll see. What'd I miss?"

"Five more feet."

"Really?"

I turned to look across the street at City Hall. Timing the construction of the new clock tower had become a local sport. Hardly a day passed when there wasn't some comment on it. Not unusual, given the fact that the City Council had devoted nearly a year of debate to it. The brickwork had finally started. Now the game was to guess how much would get done daily, and when it would be finished. They were taking bets at The Manjuris.

"They really outdid themselves. Should see if any of the bricklayers are in on the betting."

A look of surprise and concern crossed MacLean's face.

"Do you think? No, no I'm sure they…well that just wouldn't be fair." He was getting worked up.

"I was only joking."

"Oh, well. Oh, I see." MacLean returned to his task. Less than amused. Some people just can't take a joke.

I pushed open the side door that led to my second-floor office. I gave the wall switch a twist and the narrow stairway burst into brilliant electric light. MacLean had been one of the first in the downtown to switch from gas. The stairs creaked as I went up. The hallway was musty, the stale air of a long Owen Sound winter trapped inside. I'd have to talk to MacLean about getting the storm windows off.

The keys rattled and the office door creaked open. Another twist and a bare bulb lit a room that was equally bare. A desk, two chairs in front and one behind. Battered three-drawer oak file cabinet. Filled with junk mostly. A coat tree I'd added at the start of winter. And two windows that looked out over 2nd Avenue.

I picked my mail up off the floor, quickly learning there was nothing that required immediate attention. So I added the letters to the heap already covering one side of the desk, and kicked the door shut.

I pulled out my pistol. The strong smell of gunpower stung my nose as I unloaded it. A brief flash of the arm flickered through my mind. Manstoppers. At seven hundred feet per second, they were slow but, weighing a thirtieth of a pound, they were one of the most lethal bullets ever made. They'd been outlawed in Europe during the war. Politicians called them inhuman. I'd gotten a supply when I bought the Webley & Scott. I didn't use them all the time. But I couldn't see anything inhuman about saving my own skin.

I opened the top desk drawer and dropped the gun and both clips inside. Doffing my jacket I took off my holster and left it there as well. The .32 automatic I carried in my boot stayed where it was. Few people knew it was there. It had come in handy more than once. I slid the drawer shut and locked it.

It was a warm night. Sil and Marth were sitting on the verandah when I arrived at their big house on 5th Street.

"Hello you two," I called as I started up the front walk.

"The boarder walks," Sil said drily. Marth failed to supress a giggle.

Sil had married Marth right out of high school. He'd once joked to me it was because she was the only woman tall enough for him. Pretty, with blue eyes and a ready smile, she was perfect. Kind and generous to a fault, she was a good mother to their two boys, eight-year-old Finn and six-year-old Aidan.

I'd moved in with the Johnsons after the war. I had returned to Owen Sound with few prospects. They'd offered me a spare room. I'd gratefully accepted their help.

"What the hell happened to you?" Sil exploded when I was close enough to be seen in the dim light cast from inside the house. He and Marth both rushed to the top of the steps.

"Gunfight in Bognor Marsh. And I didn't get the worst of it."

After bringing water and bandages, Marth insisted on cleaning the wound, which was on my forehead right at the hair line. I'd had a lucky escape. While Marth worked, I told them about my evening.

"If it wasn't the Lost Tire Gang, then who was it?" Sil asked after they stopped laughing about the wooden arm.

"And why were they shooting at you?" Marth added.

"I don't know. But it shouldn't be too hard to find out. I just need to find the one-armed man."

CHAPTER TWO
CITY LIFE

"There are a lot of one-armed men around. One-legged ones too. One-eyed. One-eared. The war you know. Lotsa boys missin' pieces."

Doc Evans turned back to his bag and continued pulling out dressings. I'd stopped in at the General and Marine Hospital, hoping to get a lead on the one-armed man. The Doc had agreed to talk, but only if I let him re-dress my head wound.

"Lots lost more. Than pieces, that is." I winced as he pulled the bandages off my head.

"What are ya? A baby?" the Doc teased. "This ain't more'n a scratch."

A new dressing later I left the hospital and headed across town to the County Courthouse. It was a great day. The kind of May morning that feels like a reward for surviving winter. I stopped for a moment on the 10th Street bridge. The harbour was alive with activity and likely had been since dawn. Boxes, bales and barrels travelled up and down the 1st Avenues (East and West), in trucks horse-drawn wagons and handcarts.

Three blocks away was the Grey County Courthouse, an imposing yellow stone building. The date etched on it announced to one and all that justice had been served there since 1856. Behind the building, backing onto 4th Avenue East, was the high stone wall of the jail.

My footsteps echoed down the long granite hall as I approached Oddball's office. It was about halfway along, on the main floor. The frosted glass in the door announced "High Constable, County of Grey" and then "Marc Scott" in small letters at the bottom. I twisted the brass knob and entered.

I could only go as far as the door opened. A chest-high walnut counter prevented any further incursion into the office. At the back, opposite the door, was a holding cell. Empty. The rest of the office was crowded with desks, chairs, coatracks.

"Yer up bright an' early," Oddball said from his desk in the back left corner of the office. He looked comfortable, tilted back in a chair, feet propped up. Sean O'Malley was sitting at the desk next to him.

I lifted the hinged section of the counter, and went in. I'd first met Sean O'Malley when he was a city cop. A large, homely Irishman, he had somewhere around a dozen kids. He'd been caught up in the insurance case that had sent his boss, the chief of police, to the Kingston Pen. I'd kept Sean out of it, but he'd lost his job. Oddball had hired him on for his new car patrol.

"Will you have a cup o' tea?" O'Malley asked.

"No. Thanks. I'll be headin' over to The City next. Want to save myself for coffee."

I pulled up a chair in front of Oddball's desk. "Well?"

"That Packard was stolen."

"That explains it."

"Explains what?" O'Malley asked from behind the huge tin mug of tea that obscured his face.

"Why anyone would drive a nice car like that on county roads in the springtime. Most of them haven't been fixed yet. Just the highways. Where'd it come from?"

"Wiarton. Alexander McNeill. Doesn't know when it disappeared."

"You think it's the gang?"

"Could be," O'Malley said. "Last year they started in the Shelburne area and moved north. They mighta moved right up there t'wards Wiarton over the winter. Less people. Easier to hide."

"So far we got three confirmed robberies," Oddball continued. "All of 'em between Owen Sound and Wiarton."

"Find out who that arm belongs to?"

"Nope. It's a nice one though. Custom job. You can't get 'em outta the Sears and Roebuck, that's fer sure. By the way," he added with that I-know-something-you-don't smirk of his, "Coupla boys in custody up in Wiarton. Runaway Barnardos. Caught 'em drinking in public."

"So?"

"Could be part o' the gang."

"That so?"

"Yep. Caught 'em with a pistol. Matches the description from one of the heists. You oughta go up there and check it out yourself."

"I guess I will."

★★★

I walked from the courthouse to The City Cafe on 10th Street. A small diner, just a dozen or so tables, The City was like a second home to me. The food was cheap and good. I ate breakfast there every day. Sometimes lunch too.

There wasn't much of a crowd when I stepped through the door. The breakfast rush was over. I sat at a table in the corner, by the window, so I could watch 10th Street. Before I was settled Dolores had a cup of coffee in front of me.

"Hey good lookin'." Her morning smile turned to a look of motherly concern. "What happened to you?"

"Just a scratch," I smiled back.

"Sure. His head's nearly gone and he calls it a scratch. The usual?"

"Sure. Thanks 'Lo."

Bill Van Wyck arrived before my food did. Of average height and weight his blond hair was greying prematurely. He walked with a pronounced limp, the result of a war injury. I'd met him the summer before. An acquaintance of Sil's, I'd stayed with him at his store in Balaclava while I was looking for Gas Head Willy. It turned out Van had an excellent and useful knowlege of guns. He'd been inadvertantly dragged into my fight with a couple of local bootleggers. In retaliation, they'd burned his store to the ground. So now he worked for me. Until he decided what to do next.

"Hello Van," I stood and shook his hand.

"It looks like you found something, D.B. Or it found you."

"Sit down. Have some breakfast."

"Or lunch," he replied.

"Whichever. Been able to find anything out?" Van had wanted to be a spy during the war. His injury had dashed that hope. I'd gotten approval from Oddball to bring Van in undercover. For nearly two weeks he'd been in the Wiarton area, snooping.

"Tell me what happened to you first."

My breakfast arrived, so between mouthfuls I filled him in.

"So the car was stolen from Wiarton?" he asked when I'd finished my story.

"Yup."

"That fits then. I've spent a lot of time in the Pacific Hotel up there. Rumour is the gang is holed up somewhere nearby."

"There's something I need you to do. But you'll have to go back today."

"What is it?" He sopped up the rest of an egg with his toast.

"You have to get arrested."

Van stopped chewing mid-mouthful. After staring at me for a second he continued chewing. When he finished he didn't ask why. Just said, "How?"

"That's up to you. But head back there now. I want you in a cell this afternoon. Make friends with the two boys in the lock-up. Oddball thinks they're gang members. I'll come get you the day after tomorrow."

I stepped out of The City and back into May. The streets had been cleaned by one of Owen Sound's hired men. At the intersection of 10th Street and 3rd Avenue, near the Seldon Hotel, potholes were being patched. A fresh breeze sliced up from the harbour. To the north, a ship's whistle sounded. The day always seemed better after coffee. And breakfast.

Between 10th and 7th Streets, 2nd Avenue was three blocks of progress. Shops. Lawyers. Doctors. Insurance agents. Chiropractors. All the professions. There were ticket offices—rail and shipping. Land surveyors. Restaurants. And The Manjuris. I crossed the street, cut between two angle-parked cars and went through the pool hall entrance. I thumped on the door at the top of a narrow and dimly lit set of stairs. A panel slid open. The eyes that peered out into the gloom took a moment to adjust. The panel closed. Muffled by the door, I heard Red shout my name. The door opened and I went in. Red smirked a greeting.

Play at all the tables stopped. Razor Eddie was leaning over the table in the centre of the room making what looked to be a big shot. He stood before I got to him.

"Murphy," he said. He turned my way with a smile on his face.

"Hey Ra…" The greeting died in my mouth. The left arm of his suit jacket hung empty at his side.

"What?" he demanded.

"Your arm."

He looked at the empty sleeve and screamed, "My arm! My arm!" He tore at his coat. Then, in a calm voice, he said, "Oh. There it is."

The room erupted in laughter. I'd been had. The Razor waved at me with an arm that I could now see was fully intact. I charged at him. He scrambled around the table to put it between us.

"Hey, I got ya good, Murphy!" he laughed from the safety of the far side.

I laughed with him.

"News travels fast," I said, as he came around to my side of the table.

"'Specially when yer dealin' with Israelites."

Eddie had grown up with Sil and me. We'd gone off to war together. He was in the infantry. I was a gunner. Eddie had left an ear behind. An angry scar slashed down the left side of his face nearly to his chin. While I looked for work after the war, Razor Eddie was busy setting up his bootlegging empire. Prohibition was on and business was good. He got his stuff by boat from Montreal. There were still people who wanted quality booze. Not swamp whisky.

Most days, Eddie was at The Manjuris. At night he did business. At the waterfront. And at a dozen homes throughout the city. Shorter than me by a head, he was lean and muscular. He dressed well, in suits tailored to hide the pistol he carried. He was also going around with my soon-to-be-wife's sister. Razor and Dori made a good couple.

Eddie signalled Red as we stepped over to the bar. A couple of drinks appeared.

"You're gonna like this." Eddie picked one up. I took the other.

"The right to bear arms!" he laughed, tossing the drink back.

I took mine at a gulp. It was smooth. Not like the usual stuff Eddie got.

"Good stuff," I said. "It's not rye."

"Nope. Irish whisky. The best money can buy. Got it fer a party. Up near Wiarton."

"Oh?"

"Yeah," he leaned closer. "At the Corran."

"The what?"

"The Corran. Big stone mansion. They got twenty rooms. Servants. Outbuildings. And roses. Acres of 'em."

"Who owns it?"

"Some politician," he shrugged, accepting another drink from Red. I took one too.

"When's the party?"

"Friday."

"Are you going?"

"Sure. He's payin' me a fortune."

"The politician?"

"It's fer him. But his manager, Alf Lewis, come to see me 'bout it in the name of Angus Peacock."

"Who's he?"

"Don't know. He lives up there. On a remittance."

I'd heard of remittance men, though I'd never met one. Often bad sorts, second and third sons, they were paid a small allowance to stay away from home. Many came to Canada where living expenses weren't as high, to make the most of their money. Some would work to make something of themselves. Some, I'd heard, made additional money in not so friendly ways.

"What's his game?"

"Don't know. Don't care."

"He paid cash."

"Uh huh." Eddie smiled.

I suddenly remembered the purpose of my visit.

"Can you come to Wiarton early? Say the day after tomorrow?"

"You wanna come to the smoker tomorrow night?" Eddie answered my question with one of his own.

"Okay. I'm seeing Lori tonight. So I don't think she'll mind me going to the smoker."

"Good. Bring the Sergeant Major. What're we doin' in Wiarton?"

"A jailbreak."

Eddie threw his head back and laughed. Red poured more drinks.

Owen Sound had been talking about Kate McDermid for weeks. So had Lori and I'd bought tickets to see the show. Miss McDermid, according to the *Daily Sun Times*, was a singer of the highest regard. She was much in demand in Europe and her recent performance at Toronto's Massey Hall had received the longest ovation in that building's history. McDermid's concert at Owen Sound's Classic Theatre was a sellout. A good thing too. The theatre needed to help its image in the community, having so recently been the centre of a scandal.

Alburtus the Mesmerist had planned to put a woman into hypnotic sleep in the front window of a 2nd Avenue shop. When the public uproar began, the store quickly backed out. Undeterred, Alburtus moved his show to the Classic Theatre lobby. The police commission tried to stop the stunt, but Alburtus went ahead, though he performed the hypnosis by telephone. The woman went to sleep. And the uproar leading up to the event proved to be the most exciting part of it.

The Storey family owned a big house on 4th Avenue West. Dori, Lori and Glori all still lived with their parents. Jack Storey was a shift supervisor at the Kennedy Foundry. A veteran of the Boer War, Eddie and I called him the

Sergeant Major. A big man with iron grey hair, he wore a cookie duster on his upper lip. He answered the door when I knocked.

"Gunner Murphy," he saluted.

I snapped off a smart salute and clicked my heels. "Sergeant Major. Sir!"

Jack laughed and held the door open. As I stepped inside, my nose filled with the wonderful smell of dinner. In a room to the right of the entry hall, I could hear someone practising their scales. Lori taught piano.

Jack led me into the parlour. A room I was more than passingly familiar with—the one where Lori and I spent much of our time. Door open of course. I'd proposed to her there less than a year ago.

"Sit down, sit down, my boy," Jack blustered.

"Thank you, sir."

"Been in a fight, have you?"

I involuntarily touched the bandage on my forehead. "Hazard of the job."

"What're you doing this week?"

"Same job. For the county."

"Dastardly business. Haven't caught those fellas yet?"

"No sir. I'm working on it."

The front door banged open. Jack was on his feet and into the hallway in a flash.

"Where have you been, young lady?" he shouted in full Sergeant Major voice.

"Out," was the curt response from Glori, the youngest of the Storey girls.

A strong-willed teen, she was a concern for the family. According to Lori, the battles between her younger sister and parents had been growing in frequency and intensity. They seemed to be about the usual problems. Glori was rebelling, and like most teens felt that rules, especially those laid down by parents, were made to be broken.

"Just you hold on a minute, Miss!" The Sergeant Major grabbed her arm as she tried to brush past him.

"Ow! Let go."

"Is that gin? On your breath. I smell gin!"

I jumped to my feet, sure the scene was about to come to blows. Glori squirmed out of his grasp and rubbed her arm.

"You don't have to break my bones you know."

"Answer me. Have you been drinking?"

"Maybe. Maybe not. Anyway it's none of your business if I have."

"As long as you live under my roof, you live under my rules. What don't you understand about that, Miss Fancy Pants?"

The Sergeant Major advanced on his daughter. It looked to me as though he was going to turn her over his knee right then and there. Before he could do anything, Mrs. Storey and Lori were both in the hallway shushing. Both combatants departed for other areas of the house.

"I'll be in as soon as I finish," Lori smiled, pretending not to notice the bandage on my forehead.

We had met by accident. Lori's sister Dori had witnessed the murder of my brother's partner. I'd come to the house one day hoping to find her. What I found instead was the woman of my dreams. Pretty, with brown hair and blue eyes, Lori smiled a lot. Her great figure was complemented by wit and intelligence. She had a good sense of humour and a voice like summer sunshine. I'd been smitten instantly.

"Is there something I can get you, Danny?"

Mrs. Storey had come into the room. They didn't keep any booze in the house, so I knew a drink was out of the question.

"No thank you ma'am."

"Dinner won't be but a few minutes," she said with a smile. "As soon as Lori's finished."

"That'll be fine."

"Don't mind Jack," she lowered her voice. "Glori can be a handful."

"Is it always that bad?"

"I'm afraid it's getting worse."

"I'm sorry. But don't fret too much. She's a good girl. She'll come around."

"Are you a fortune teller as well as a detective?"

"No. But I think I know how she feels. I went through a rough patch at the same age."

"I'd best get back to the kitchen. Today's paper is there."

She left. I picked up the paper. The front page was dominated by the usual stories of stills, drunks and illegal booze. I wasn't sure prohibition had done much to stop people from drinking. It just made more drinkers into lawbreakers.

The search for the Lambton was continuing. The government steamer had disappeared mid-April, in heavy Lake Superior ice. Captain Alex Brown was from Owen Sound, as were many of the crew.

The population had increased by 347 during 1921-22. There were now 12,360 people living in the city of Owen Sound. A high proportion of them were without work, especially returned men. So the City Council had decided to offer cash incentives to any business that decided to locate in Owen Sound. Ads would be going in the national newspapers in Canada and abroad.

Further inside the paper was a small story about the Kate McDermid concert. She and her accompanist Mr. Angel had arrived on the late train the night before. Miss McDermid was said to be looking forward to “the performance of her life” in Owen Sound. After the show she’d be proceeding up the peninsula for a short vacation and private concert.

An advertisement for the Old Time Smoker was on the back page. It was a fundraiser: the Legion was trying to make enough money to buy a building. The card included three fights, the last one a barrel fight between Battling Young and Kid Nicol. The YMCA boys would be tumbling, and local musicians would entertain. I’d have to remember to convey Eddie’s invitation to the Sergeant Major. It might put him in a better humour

“Anything interesting?” Lori asked from the doorway

I jumped to my feet as she entered the room. Then we were in each other’s arms. The world and its concerns grew distant. For a moment, the two of us were all that existed.

We sat down and I folded the paper. It drove me crazy when people left them in a mess. I tried not to do it myself.

“What on earth happened to you?” Lori asked, touching the bandage on my forehead.

“Chasing a couple of boys. In the Bognor Marsh.”

“You’re beginning to sound like a bad risk, Mister.”

“No risk, no reward.”

“I’m definitely looking forward to the reward,” she leaned closer, for another kiss. Footsteps in the hallway arrested her motion. The Sergeant Major came to the door.

“Dinner,” he said, turning on his heel before he got into the room.

“Don’t mind him,” Lori said. “It’s this business with Glori. It upsets him.”

★★★

After dinner we took a walk. It was a nice night, though still cool. Our hands were warm together. “I go for another fitting this week,” Lori said.

“Better stay away from the Candy Kitchen.”

“Smarty pants,” she gave me a playful poke. “Do you have your tuxedo yet?”

“Sil has it at the store. I just have to pick it up.”

“I can’t wait to marry you.”

“Me either.”

“You can’t?”

"No. Every morning I look at myself in the mirror and I can hardly wait to marry me."

"Maybe you should go for the fitting this week," she teased.

"White isn't my colour."

We wandered down 2nd Avenue West towards the mill dam. It was a street of big houses, the biggest and most expensive in the city. My brother lived in one. I didn't see him much. The Robertsons also lived on that stretch. As we passed, I wondered how Gas Head Willy Robertson was finding life in prison. Probably not too bad. Though he'd stolen from his father, I'd heard the old man was putting a considerable amount of cash into the system to ensure his son's comfort.

"What are you thinking about?" Lori asked. It was getting dark, and when she turned her face towards me, all I wanted to do was kiss her. It would have to wait.

"Where do you want to live?" I answered her with a question of my own.

"Anywhere."

"No really."

"I mean it," she said. We were walking down a narrow pathway to the mill dam. We'd cross the river, then walk downtown from there. Lori stopped and put her hands on either side of my face. She pulled me towards her, until our lips were nearly touching. "It doesn't matter," she whispered, "because wherever you are, that's my home."

I took her in my arms. Hidden in the roar of water cascading over the dam, sheltered by the early twilight of the trees, we kissed for a long time.

CHAPTER THREE
THE PLAN

2nd Avenue East was something to see after dark. It was lit right up, being the only place in town with electric street lamps. Their canopies long since rolled up, many of the shops remained open. Lori wanted to stop at every window. Between 8th and 9th Streets, I could see light spilling onto the street from the lobby of the Classic. Off to one side of the doors, Sil and Marth were waiting.

"We were beginning to think maybe you weren't coming," Sil quipped as we arrived.

"And miss the show of a lifetime?" I asked.

We went inside and abandoned our coats and hats to the coatcheck girl in the lobby. I could hear the low buzz of conversation as we rounded the corner, and entered the plush theatre. It was nearly full. We got into our seats, and hadn't been there more than a minute when the lights went down. An expectant hush dropped over the crowd.

The stage lights came up and a man of medium height crossed the stage. Mr. Angel had white blond hair and piercing blue eyes. He moved with a lithe grace as he sat down at the piano. Flipping open his music book, he began to play—*Consolation No. 6* by Franz Liszt, according to the program. I'd never heard anyone play the way he did. His long fingers caressed the piano keys, coaxing and controlling them. The song built and rose until it towered over the audience, filling the theatre completely. Then it was over and, as the last note died away, thunderous applause filled the void. Mr. Angel stood and took a small bow.

"I wish I could play like that," Lori whispered in my ear.

Then the diva took the stage. She joined the audience in saluting Mr. Angel's considerable talents. The audience joined Mr. Angel in welcoming her to the stage and Owen Sound.

Miss Kate McDermid was stunning. Her platinum blonde hair was cut in a short bob. Her gown, which she filled admirably, was complemented by a low neckline. Cut well above the ankle, it was shorter than anything previously seen in Owen Sound. She had sparkling blue eyes, a straight nose and full red lips. I tried not to stare. If she sang as good as she looked, we were in for quite a show.

Mr. Angel turned another page and began to play *Pur dicesti, o bocca bella*, according to the program. It was immediately clear that Miss McDermid's was the best voice ever heard in Owen Sound. Song after song, the audience expressed its appreciation. When she finished, there was an ovation of the type that had never been seen in the Classic. Watching her, I thought Miss McDermid might have been slightly overwhelmed. The audience called for encore after encore and might have kept her there until the following day. Finally however, it was too late to continue. After a last standing ovation, the performance ended.

Everyone was in awe as we waited to collect our things in the lobby.

"That was quite a show," Sil said.

"It was," Marth agreed. "Do you think it's the latest fashion to wear a dress that short?" she asked Lori.

"It must be. I'll have to get mother to help me with some hemming."

"Really?" I asked. "I must caution you, Miss. I may not be able to resist you."

"You already can't," she smiled sweetly.

"Good point. I guess I'll just want you even more."

"Are you saying you don't want me as much as you possibly can already?"

"I'd be careful D.B.," Sil said, a smile on his face. "Dangerous territory."

"Thanks for the help," I said. Lucky for me we had reached the front of the line to retrieve our things from the coatcheck. By the time we were on the sidewalk in front of the Classic the conversation had been forgotten.

"Did you want to come out for a cup of tea?" Marth asked.

"Sorry, we can't," I said.

"Too much in love to have a drink with an old married couple?" Sil teased.

"It's not that," Lori said. "I have to go to a reception for Miss McDermid that the Women's Music Club and the Music Teachers' Association are putting on. And of course, I must have an escort."

"A reception with Miss McDermid? It's D.B. who needs the escort," Sil laughed.

"Or a chaperone," Marth added with a giggle.

"I'll deal with you two later," I called after them as Lori and I headed up the street in the other direction.

The midnight reception was at the home of Mrs. Eudora Filbert who lived five or six blocks away, on the Sydenham River by Harrison Park.

"Who does the arm belong to?" Lori asked as we walked.

"Thank you for not laughing." I'd watched her carefully as I told the story. "I don't know. No one's shown up to claim it."

"What do you mean?"

"Oddball has it. In his office." We walked on for a couple of minutes in silence.

"Sometimes I worry about you," Lori finally said.

"Don't."

"Why not? Give me a reason."

"I can handle myself."

"What about all the people who keep shooting and throwing knives and punches at you?"

"None have succeeded."

"Yet."

"Darling," I stopped in the middle of the sidewalk and took both her hands in mine. "There's an element of risk in anything worth doing. All I can do is try and minimize that risk by outsmarting the people I deal with."

"Like in the Bognor Marsh?"

"Okay. That was stupid. I shouldn't have gone in alone."

"And what about Wiarton?"

"I'll have Van to watch my back. And Eddie's coming up for awhile too. Are you having second thoughts about marrying me?"

"No. I love you."

"And?"

"No and. I just worry a little." We continued walking.

"As long as it's just a little worry," I said.

"It is."

I wanted to tell her I was always careful, and there was no way I would let anything happen. When I was with her I felt charmed. And as long as we spent our lives together, nothing could happen to me. It just wouldn't be right. What I said instead was, "Okay," and we walked the rest of the way in blissful silence.

Cars lined the street in front of the elegant Filbert residence. We strolled up the front walk and into the house. It was alive with chatter. Glasses tinkled. Somewhere, a piano played.

"Lori Storey!" a matronly woman exclaimed, rushing into the entry hall.

"Mrs. Filbert," Lori responded, shaking her hand. "May I present my fiance, Mr. D.B. Murphy."

Mrs. Filbert gave me a quick up-down, then smiled and extended her hand. I took it and said, "A pleasure."

A serving girl appeared and took our things.

"Upstairs with the rest, Esther," Mrs. Filbert called, guiding us into the parlour. It was filled to bursting with music lovers. Mrs. Filbert began introducing us to many people we already knew. Owen Sound was like that. We worked our way slowly across the room, until we arrived at the corner in which Miss McDermid had taken up residence. Mr. Angel was close to her side. He apparently took his duties as accompanist seriously.

Mrs. Filbert introduced us, then bustled off to greet the newest arrivals.

"Miss McDermid, it's so nice to meet you," Lori enthused. The songstress offered an elegant groomed hand to each of us.

"Quite a show," I said.

"Thank you, Mr. Murphy." She was even more beautiful up close. "May I present my accompanist, Mr. Samuel Angel?"

Angel shifted drink and cigarette and offered a hand. "Sam," he said. "It's a pleasure."

"Murph," I said. "Mutual."

"Your performance tonight was wonderful," Lori said to the singer. "Will you come to Owen Sound again?"

"Actually," Miss McDermid said, "we'll be in the area for some time now. The day after tomorrow we're going to Wiarton for a short vacation stay at Alexander McNeill's mansion. I hear the flowers are divine."

"Are you performing?" Lori asked.

"Yes. At a private function later this week."

"Well, good luck," Lori said. Then we had to move on, because the line waiting to meet the star had grown long behind us.

We left after an hour or so. On the walk back to the Storey house Lori said, "I'm sorry."

"For what?"

"Before. I do want to marry you. No doubts. It's just that sometimes things bother me."

"Okay."

"I know there are no other jobs."

"None that I could make money at. None I'd like as well either. Except blacksmithing. We know that's not going to happen."

"No."

"I was thinking we should start looking for a house."

"Really?" She stopped in the middle of the sidewalk and turned to face me. She was excited.

"Sure. Why not? We're getting married. We'll need to live someplace."

"Can we afford it?"

"Prices dropped during the war. They haven't gone back up. I've got some money saved."

"There's a sweet little house over by the library."

"The brick one?"

"Uh huh."

"Why don't we go and look at it tomorrow?"

"Could we? Could we really?"

"I'd like to. Yes."

By the time we were at her front door, Lori was buoyant.

"What time will you come for me?"

"What time are you free?"

"After lunch. I don't have any students until school gets out."

"Okay. I'll see you then."

★★★

The next morning I started out at the County Courthouse."You want me to what?" Oddball asked.

"I want you to tell the Wiarton Police Chief I'll be up tomorrow to break Van out of jail."

"Why would I do that?" he thundered. "And what the hell's Van doing in jail?"

"While you're at it, tell him I'll be taking those two boys out with me."

"What?" Oddball jumped up so fast that, for the second time in a week, his cigar hit the floor.

"Tell him that I'll be taking those two boys. It's my only way into the Lost Tire Gang."

"Oh." Oddball sat down, opened a desk drawer and pulled out a fresh Havana Stogie.

"So you have a plan."

"Yes, I have a plan. All you need to do is listen."

"Right." He leaned back in his chair and put his feet up on the desk. His eyes closed as he chewed the cigar furiously.

"Are you going to sleep?"

"Of course not. Just tell me this plan of yours."

"We'll earn their trust by breaking those boys out. Hopefully they'll be so grateful, they'll take us to their hideout. We can join the gang."

"And then?"

"Go out on a job. Once I've got the goods on 'em I'll haul 'em in."

"I like it," Oddball said, nodding.

I knew he would. It fit his plan perfectly. I'd do the work. He'd take the glory. I didn't care as long as I got paid.

"Can you square it with the law in Wiarton?"

"I'll use the telephone right away."

"No."

"What? I can. They've got the telephone up there now."

"With how many exchanges in between? Nope. Too many people listening in."

"Never thought of that." He scratched his head. Sitting up straight, he snapped his fingers. "I'll send a wire."

"Good idea." I stood to go.

"When you gonna be back?"

"Don't know. Hopefully before the end of the week."

"Going today?"

"Nope. I'm going to the smoker tonight. I've got tickets on the morning train."

"Tickets?"

"Scotty's coming too."

"Oh."

The Royal Canadian Legion had begun in 1921 when Owen Sound and Toronto formed the first branches simultaneously. The two communities fought constantly about which came first. Chicken and egg, as far as I was concerned. The important thing was, there was now an organisation for returned men. With so few of them working and so much time on their hands, they needed something to keep them out of trouble. I knew. During the past two years, I had felt desperate a lot of the time, even though I had Sil and Marth. Some weren't as lucky.

During its first year, the Legion met all over town in any space that was available. Now it was trying to purchase a home of its own. Events like the smoker were organized to raise money.

The air at City Hall was already thick with smoke when Eddie, the Sergeant Major and I arrived. All three of us were veterans and supporters of the Legion. Al Cowling and Bertie Waltham, army buddies of the Sergeant Major, were on the door. They gave us each a Legion pin. I tacked mine to the collar of my coat. The Sergeant Major stayed to chat with his buddies. Eddie and I each took a cigar and moved inside.

A boxing ring had been set up in the centre of the hall. Rows of chairs surrounded it. Most were full. Eddie and I stopped just inside the door. I got my pocket knife out and trimmed the end from my cigar. I handed the blade to Eddie. He did the same. I watched as he struck a match on the bottom of his fancy shoes. Two-tone chocolate and beige wingtips. Purchased on a trip to New York, there was nothing like them in Owen Sound. I struck a match on the bottom of my boot and used it to warm the end of the cigar. I fired up a second match and used it to light up.

There was a band off to one side of the hall. The Plaza Orchestra. It was playing *Baby Face*. The sign on an easel standing beside the band urged readers to SUPPORT YOUR LEGION. A drool bucket on the floor in front of it was filling quickly. With cash. Of all denominations. Eddie and I went over and forked some in. He pulled a silver flask from his hip pocket. We each took a slug of the good whisky inside.

"Whaddya think?" Eddie smiled around his cigar.

"I can see why they call 'em smokers. The rate this place is filling we won't be able to see the fight."

"You'll see it," he pointed to the large electric lights that had been rigged above the ring.

We found three seats.

"I'll go tell the Sergeant Major," I said.

"Sure." Eddie had the flask in his hand.

I wove my way through a crowd of familiar faces. At the door a crush of people blocked the way to the Sergeant Major. I tried to push my way through and found myself face to face with Silas Robertson.

"Mr. Murphy," his greeting was curt.

"Mr. Robertson," I responded. He looked older. Greyer.

"Don't expect me to thank you for your help last year."

His son was Gas Head Willy. I'd been hired by Robertson to find him. I had. And Willy had landed in jail for murder and fraud. I hadn't seen the old man since.

"I got paid. I don't expect anything else."

"He'll die in there." The old man's voice rose. Bystanders began to notice. I was getting angry. I didn't like it when people blamed their messes on others. Especially me.

"He killed a cop. Stole money."

"He's my son," the old man screamed. Spittle flew from his lips as he raised his walking stick to me.

"Here now," the Sergeant Major boomed from behind Robertson. He grabbed the stick and gave the old man a shove. Jack Storey had been caught in one of Willy's money-losing schemes before the war. A lot of money had been involved. "Your son didn't get nothin' more than what he deserved," he hissed.

The Sergeant Major gave the stick back and pushed Robertson away, towards the door. Someone in the crowd propelled him along. People started talking again, as we turned and headed towards our seats.

As far as I could tell, Eddie hadn't moved. The cigar was still in his right, the flask in his left.

"Drink?" he asked the Sergeant Major as we sat down.

"I believe I will," he surprised us both.

He took the shot like a pro and handed the flask back.

"What's wrong boys? Didn't think an old fella like me'd take a drink once in a while?"

I couldn't think of anything to say, so I laughed and slapped him on the back. He was still smiling when he finished choking.

The orchestra stopped playing. Jim Simpson got up and gave a speech about the Legion. The hubbub in the room eventually quieted. "…the object is not self seeking. The Legion exists only to unite the men who have served at war, for King and country. To do this we hope soon to secure permanent quarters for the Owen Sound Branch of the Royal Canadian Legion."

Cheers went up around the hall. Near us, Billy Taylor yelled, "Then we'll have us a place ta drink!" which received an even louder cheer.

The first bout of the evening was light. Jack Adams and Joe Stewart bashed each other during three two-minute rounds which ended in a tie.

Rupert Legate sang two humorous songs during the intermission. The cigars were doing fine and we all had a few more drinks.

"Those two guys really socked the hell out of each other," I said.

"They did not," Eddie replied. "It ain't a fight unless there's blood. The more the better."

"Good point. But they did sock the hell out of each other."

"Yeah. They did."

The Sergeant Major was staring into space. Eddie noticed and lowered his voice.

"They're really worried about Glori, eh?"

The bell sounded. Our conversation was lost in the roar. Two apple barrels had been rolled into the ring. Two big barrels. Two colours. They stood a foot and a half apart. A man climbed into each. The ring cleared.

"Gentlemen," the announcer bawled. "Presenting a barrel fight. No old time smoker is complete without one." The crowd roared. "In the blue barrel, Battling Young, and in the red barrel, Kid Nicol."

The bell sounded. The crowd exploded onto its feet. The bruisers in the barrels started swinging. Leather slapped flesh. Battling Young landed a heavy body blow. Kid Nicol fell back and his barrel tipped, spilling him onto the canvas. The mob howled with laughter as two men tipped Kid's barrel upright. Young tried to land another quick body shot but missed. Kid gave him a shove. Over he went. And so it continued, but only for one round. The smokers and the jokers were both laughing hard at the end of it.

The last bout was swift and brutal. Real boxing. George Faleris against Curly Scott.

"He related to Oddball?" Eddie asked.

"Don't know."

"Find out."

"How?"

"Don't ask me. You're the detective. If I was you though, I'd be in the locker room after."

I walked right into it. "Why?" I asked.

"You can check his bag." He ducked the fist I sent his way.

Ten seconds later Faleris downed Scott with a right to the jaw. Scott beat the ten-count. The bell went. Three minutes gone.

For the next four rounds Scott was on the offensive. The smoke was so thick it seemed like a dream. All mist and motion.

The final bell went. Bathed in sweat the two men stood in their corners. The judges passed an envelope to the referee. The bout was declared to have been, "an excellent example of the fistic arts, and a draw."

★★★

Eddie and I left City Hall together. The Sergeant Major went with friends. He'd seemed in better spirits at the end. Spirits being the operative word.

"When you goin' up?"

"Tomorrow morning. By train."

"Train?"

"I want Scotty fresh. I don't know how far we'll have to ride once we get there."

"Where we meetin'?"

"The Pacific."

"Good. The stuff's comin' in by water. I'll lay up in Clavering 'til the party. Got a place up there."

"What's the idea?"

"Nice time for a vacation."

"And of course you'll tell me where to find you."

"Just in case."

"Of course."

CHAPTER FOUR
KIDNAP

The morning train left at ten. I arrived just before nine to get Scotty loaded into a boxcar. He'd seemed more excited than usual. Likely the prospect of a train ride. I was excited myself, even though the ride would be short. The trip to Wiarton only took an hour. Maybe a little more depending on the stops.

The Grand Trunk Railway Station was on 1st Avenue West. Across the street, I could hear Kennedy's Foundry—the roar of the big furnaces, the shouts of men working and the clang of steel on steel. On the other side, four sets of tracks separated the station from the harbour. Boxcars and flatcars lined the siding closest to the docks. A constant stream of loading, unloading, carting, hauling and packing was going on. The day was warm on the wooden platform. I stopped on a bench for awhile. The world kept on moving.

At nine-thirty a car pulled up. It was a big black McLaughlin Buick. The driver hopped out and opened the door. Sam Angel emerged. I watched him help Miss McDermid out. The driver unloaded their bags as she sat down on the other bench on the platform. Mr. Angel went inside. The driver pulled away after taking the bags into the station.

We sat awhile longer. Neither of us made a move to say hello. Which wasn't a surprise. I was trying my best to look the part of a desperate man. It was the only way the jailbreak would work. In my riding boots, coarse pants and worn leather jacket, I didn't look much like the man Miss McDermid had met at the party two nights before. The only way she might have known me was the bandage on my head. But I had my hat pulled low, to conceal it. My disguise was perfect.

A car I recognized pulled up. Oddball. The county had purchased him a new four-ninety Chevrolet sedan. It was his pride and joy. It had everything, including Gutta Percha tires from the Owen Sound Vulcanising Works.

The driver's door opened and the High Constable stepped out. He hitched his pants up and squinted around the platform. Spotting me, he started over. Then he saw Miss McDermid and the walk became a swagger. Before Oddball got to her, Mr. Angel came out of the station with tickets in hand. They arrived at the bench occupied by Miss McDermid at the same time. I saw Oddball introduce himself. Hands shook all around. There was chitchat. I saw Oddball nod in my direction. And the whole party looked at me. A moment later Oddball detached himself and strolled over.

"What was that all about?" I asked.

"What?"

"I'm sitting here hoping no one will notice me and you point me out."

"Oh that," he smiled. "I told 'em you were suspected of bein' a felon. An' I was here to check ya out."

"A felon?"

"Sure. A member of the notorious Lost Tire Gang."

"Great. What's up?"

"It's all squared in Wiarton. They'll pretend like it's a real break-out."

"How many people know?"

"Just the chief I think."

"What happens if we don't tell anyone else?"

"The inspector will come from the provincial police. Maybe call a dragnet."

"Perfect. It's just what I need."

"Yeah well, I'm not so sure he is."

"What do you mean?"

"Inspector Blood is not a happy man. Ever since they egged him in Hanover, he's been pretty nasty. Not that he was a daisy before that."

"They egged him?"

"Sure. He gave a coupla boys tickets cause they didn't have license tags on their cars. Buncha kids gave him an eggin' before he got on the train back to Walkerton." Oddball leaned closer to me. "I hear he pulled his gun."

"On a bunch of kids?"

"Uh huh."

"That seems unnecessary."

"Yup." Oddball looked over his shoulder towards Miss McDermid and Mr. Angel. "Nice lookin' travellin' companion. He her husband?"

"Her pianist."

"What?"

"Her piano player."

"Oh. Right. I knew that. Well, I suppose I better shove off. How'd ya like the car?"

"Looks real nice."

"She is. I'll take ya fer a ride sometime. If yer horse'll let me, that is."

A whistle blew and the train engine chuffed along the inner harbour to the station. The others stood. I stayed put. They still had to load coal and connect the cars. Departure wouldn't be for a while yet.

"Oh, say," Oddball added. "About that arm. It ain't no normal wooden arm."

"We knew that."

"Sure, sure. But what I mean is, it's worth a lotta money. It didn't just fall off some Johnny-come-marching-home. Nope, it's off a rich feller. Hasta be."

"That should make things easier."

"Eh? How so?"

"Well obviously if we're looking for a one-armed rich fella it eliminates a lot of suspects."

"Oh. Sure. I knew that."

"Right. Are you comin' up to Wiarton?"

"Not really my jurisdiction. But I may do. I just may do. Why?"

"Well, I thought if you did, you could help Inspector Blood. You being such an expert on the Lost Tire Gang and all."

"If I helped him, wouldn't we catch ya quicker?"

"Not necessarily."

"Oh, I see. You don't want a dragnet. You want a goose chase."

"Exactly."

"See what I can do."

"Great."

"How'll I get hold of you? If there's somethin' I need to tell ya?"

"Leave a message with the barman at the Pacific Hotel. That's where I'll leave word for you."

"Right."

He strode off, leaving me alone on the platform. A manhunt would give my whole plan an air of legitimacy. As long as Oddball could prevent Inspector Blood from actually finding us. I had no doubt that he could. I didn't want anyone to know Oddball had an undercover man. Newcomers would be turned away from the gang. They might even be killed. Van and I needed to gain their trust for my plan to work.

The conductor stepped out of the passenger car with a footstool. He set it in front of the high iron step and helped Miss McDermid into the car. Mr. Angel and a couple of other passengers followed.

"All aboard!" I stood when the conductor gave his final call to passengers. Shouldering my saddle, rifle and kit, I crossed the platform and climbed up.

The passenger coach was well appointed. Brocade seats. Carpet. A pot belly stove in front for heat during winter. Miss McDermid and Mr. Angel sat forward in the car. They eyed me as I went by. Still no recognition. I went back halfway. Opposite side. I humped the saddle and gun onto the rack over my seat. My coat stayed on. No point letting anyone know I was armed.

I slumped into the seat by the window. A hissing of air brakes and clanging of the bell warned everyone the train was about to start rolling. The engine lurched and couplings rattled the length of the train. Then it caught and we began to move. On to Wiarton. A dozen places between, too.

I could feel the straining of the engine. It was four cars away. We rolled past the G.T.R. sheds. Next to them, Imperial Oil. I could smell the Northern Varnish Company before I could see it. Rich, thick and chemical. It left a sharp afterburn in the nose. Then we were past. On the west side, away from the water, there were rows of houses. Factory district houses. Small, wooden. Not like the big brick ones downtown. The North American Bent Chair Company blotted the view as the train moved by. A brief glimpse through an open door. I saw hundreds of chairs piled high. From Owen Sound to the world.

We crossed the Pottawatomi River on a rattling iron bridge. The water that oozed below was inky. A hundred yards east it was swallowed by the blue of Owen Sound Bay. Henry Kelso's beach was an oasis in the sprawl. The train chuffed up the first of many grades. Sunshine sparkled on the clear water to the east. It was bright enough to hurt. Across the bay, I could see the smoke coming from the stack at Keenan's Woodenware. It ran two shifts now.

North Owen Sound came next. It had been called Brooke. Then in 1921, Owen Sound became a city and swallowed the tiny community. The train was still travelling slowly. By order of the G.T.R. president. In the spring, when he'd made an unscheduled visit to Owen Sound, his train had ploughed into a herd of cattle at five in the morning. He tried to blame the farmer. The city fathers didn't hold with him. Trains now moved through the city at ten miles an hour.

At the city limit the locomotive picked up speed. After the first big hill, we raced across the flats, toward the second and more dramatic climb. Up the escarpment to Benallen. I felt myself pressed back into the seat as we started up. Slowing, the train laboured its way to a near standstill at the crest. Over the top, it settled into a gentle rhythm.

Inside the car a number of conversations were going on. Miss McDermid had shifted around to the seat facing Mr. Angel. She was reading a book, *Three Soldiers* by John Dos Passos. Myself, I'd have preferred Zane Grey.

But I hadn't brought anything to read. I looked out the window. We cut straight across Keppel Township, through Shallow Lake. At Park Head the train stopped, while someone jumped off and threw a switch. Then we headed north towards Wiarton.

★★★

I must have dozed. One can only look at so many cows, so many fields. The train was stopping. In a hurry. Steel screeched. I looked out. Three men on horses were right beside me. They accelerated past my window. The first leapt from his horse onto the stairway between the cars. He was out of my sight. The train was nearly stopped. The second man had an easier jump.

They burst through the door, guns drawn. Both wore riding clothes. Hats were drawn low, concealing their eyes. Scarves covered the lower part of their faces. Both were average height. One was thin. And young. The other was heavy. Older. Wide shoulders. Bowed legs. His forehead sloped to a single eyebrow. He scanned the car with flint-coloured eyes.

A woman screamed and an uproar started. One of the men fired a shot into the ceiling. The car fell silent.

"Nobody moves, nobody gets hurt," one of the men growled.

The boy grabbed Miss McDermid by the arm and dragged her up. Pain flashed across her face. Anger followed.

"How dare you!" she hissed. "Get your hands off me." She wrenched her arm out of his grasp. Mr. Angel jumped up. The wide man's gun stopped him from doing anything else.

"Not so fast, pretty boy." He held the gun level with Angel's eyes.

The car door slammed open. The third man limped in. His identity concealed the same as the others, he was favouring his right foot. He appeared older than both of them. I barely noticed. I was busy looking at the empty sleeve of his jacket. I followed it to his shoulder, then on up to his face. Like the others, his eyes ranged around the car, looking everywhere at once. It was only a matter of moments before he saw me. I had no proof he would know me. No proof that he was my one-armed man. It wasn't a good situation. I was beginning to feel uneasy. I reached carefully into my jacket and pulled my pistol out. I felt reassured right away.

"Get her up," said the one-armed man, turning to address his confederates. He spoke with an Irish accent. "Be careful of her throat," he added a warning. "She won't be worth a penny to us damaged." He looked at Angel. With a swift motion he used his stump to push the pianist back into his seat.

"No point wasting a whole arm where just half will do," he said, glancing back towards the other two. They laughed. He turned and started to walk out. The wide man followed. Two backs turned.

Angel seized the opportunity. Jumping up he gave Miss McDermid a quick shove into the wide man's back. He was grappling with the boy when I leapt to my feet.

"Hold it!" I shouted swinging my pistol in plain view. The kid freed his gun hand. The shot he fired went through the pianist, deflected off the ceiling and landed on the seat beside me. The shot I fired killed the kid. I didn't have to check. I knew. The one-armed man stepped back into the car, gun drawn. I aimed carefully.

"Hold it right there," I shouted. A mistake. He looked directly at me. Surprise gave way to hatred. The emotions didn't really matter. The recognition did. He flung his arm up and fired. I hit the floor. The shot went wild. By the time I looked up, the two of them were gone. I ran the length of the car, vaulting over the dead gunman. When I got to the stairway they had already mounted and were riding away from the train. I fired a couple of rounds. Then I climbed back into the coach to see what I could do.

Miss McDermid cradled the body of the fallen Angel in her arms. The dead kidnapper hadn't moved. No one else seemed to be around.

I went forward into the next car where I found the conductor. Blood oozed from an ugly lump on the side of his head.

"Where are we?" I asked.

His eyelids cracked to slits. "Huh? What?" His voice was weak. I wished I had some salts. "One-armed guy hit…" The conductor sagged back into unconsciousness. Carefully I laid him back on the floor. Rushing forward, I left the car. My boots clanged on the metal stairs. I nearly landed on the engineer who had hurried back at the sound of the shots.

"Jeez, what happened, eh?" He panted and blew much like his engine.

"Why'd you stop?" I shouted.

"They got the tracks blocked. Coupla trees. Is it bad back there?"

"Two men dead. One of them a gang member I plugged. Your conductor's in a bad way too."

"You shot one of 'em? One of the gang?"

"Yes."

"C'mon up front. And help me git that stuff offa the track."

I followed him to the front of the train.

"Where are we?" I asked his back.

"Near Clavering."

One of the places everyone thought the Lost Tire Gang was hiding. I wondered if there could be a connection.

We came round the front of the engine. Two large cedars had been dropped across the tracks. The engine was less than ten feet from them. The engineer grabbed an end. He started grunting, trying to heave the timber off to the side. I put a shoulder to it and dug my heels in. We got rid of it in a shake. Same with the other.

"I've gotta get out of here," I said as we walked back to the engine.

"Whaddaya mean?"

"I mean off the train. I can't show up in Wiarton on the train now. There'll be too many questions."

"Whaddaya want ta do?"

"I've got to get my horse out of the back. I'll ride up from here."

"Can't. It's 'gainst regulations. 'Sides, we gotta get these people up ta town."

"Those two guys are dead. They'll be just as dead when you hit Wiarton. As for the conductor, he'll live."

He pulled off his cap, and scratched his head. Dandruff fell like snow. "I jes' don't know. S'gainst the rules."

A couple of men walked up from the back of the train.

"What's goin' on Leo?" one of them asked the engineer.

He filled them in and ended by saying, "And this here fella wants his horse off now. I tol' him it's 'gainst the rules."

"Look fellas," I started. "My name's Murphy. I'm an investigator."

"Like a Pinkerton's man?" one of the boys piped in.

"Yes. I'm on a case. I'm headed to Wiarton to break some boys out of jail. They might be part of this gang. They don't know I know. I'm going to spy on them. So no one can know who I am. If I come in on the train it'll be about five minutes before the whole town of Wiarton knows I shot that boy in there. You are just going to have to break the rules, Leo."

"I don't know," the engineer scratched his head.

"Hey, what's that pin? On your collar there?" the man who had been silent asked.

"This?" I grabbed my collar and showed them all. "It's a Legion pin. I'm a member in Owen Sound."

"You a returned man?" the fellow asked.

"Uh huh."

"Well c'mon back. I'll open up that car for you. Any man who fought for his King and country deserves all the help he can get from the G.T.R.."

"There'll be hell to pay when we get to Wiarton…" Leo the engineer started.

"Just you never mind," my helper said. "In France my specialty was getting into places I wasn't supposed to be."

"Great. Thanks," I said to him. The two of us turned and ran to the back of the train. Here and there passengers were hanging out of open windows, trying to see what was going on. Some were outside looking around. I sprinted back into the coach I'd started the trip in. The dead man was still lying face down in the aisle. Someone had thrown a lap blanket over his head. There was blood on the floor. Miss McDermid sat alone. She was crying. The body of the late Mr. Angel was across the aisle in another pair of seats. I grabbed my saddle and rifle and left.

Three cars back the helpful trainman had opened the big door on a livestock carrier. Inside it looked as if the only thing missing was Noah. Luckily, Scotty was up front. He was surprised to see me. Probably hadn't finished his oats. I got him saddled up. The G.T.R. worker helped with a ramp. It was steep and narrow. Scotty made it down without any trouble.

"What's your name?" I asked.

"Charlie Virgo," he replied.

"You live in Owen Sound?"

"Yep."

"Come see me some time. I'll buy you a drink."

Up the line, the passengers were being reboarded. The airbrakes hissed and the bell started to clang. Charlie Virgo put the ramp away and closed the boxcar door. I gave him a wave, then Scotty and I slipped into the trees and started for Wiarton.

CHAPTER FIVE
SAWDUST TOWN

We arrived just after the noon bell. Scotty was happy to be out of the train. Both times a car passed us by, I could feel him tense. Ready for a race. He was a strange horse.

The town limit was at the top of a hill. Most of Sawdust Town was below, on the shore of Colpoy's Bay. The nickname came from Wiarton's seven sawmills. The waterfront beach was buried in mill refuse. Wiarton Road turned into Berford Street as we went down the hill. It was the main street. All five hotels were either on it, or close by. So were five churches, the city hall, the fire hall, the police station, the post office and most of the town's retail businesses.

If you lived in Wiarton, and somewhere around five thousand did, you either lived "on the hill" or "on the flat." There were telephones and electric streetlights. Wires were strung on poles from the generator at Sauble Falls. There weren't a lot of cars in town. All the roads to Wiarton were still dirt. It was an issue of much contention at Bruce County Council. For those who owned automobiles.

Scotty and I rode down the Berford Street hill onto the flat. There was a silent policeman in the centre of the George Street intersection. An iron post, it directed horses, wagons and automobiles to the right hand side of the road. Owen Sound had them everywhere. As I cut around it, I looked down the next block on George. There was quite a commotion at the G.T.R. Station. The train was in. I could see a crowd had gathered. I wanted to go over and look. But I decided against it. One of the passengers might recognize me.

We continued along Berford until it intersected with William. The Pacific Hotel was on the northwest corner. On the William Street side there were hitching rails. I tied Scotty off and went in.

The beverage room of the Pacific was spartan. A couple dozen tables. Sawdust on the wooden floor. A bar stretched across the wall opposite the door I'd come in. A gigantic mirror covered the space above it. To my left, a mangy bear's head was mounted over the fireplace. There was a stuffed groundhog on the mantle. Nearby, set up on a table, was a locked glass case with a Massassauga rattler inside. It got fed a rat every Friday night. In Wiarton, that passed for entertainment.

Lunchtime and the place was packed. A player piano in the corner slammed out *I'm Just Wild About Harry.* I could barely hear it above the din of the crowd. A lunch counter was set up across one wall. Meats, cheeses, pickled eggs and herrings were available free to the drinkers. But the real attraction was the springtime specialty of the house. A lean roast raccoon with a spiced crabapple in its mouth.

The going was slow, but I finally made it to the bar. Men stood three deep around it. For prohibition, there was a lot of drink in sight. I thought maybe I should yell out "dry cops!" and throw a scare into the crowd. Then I decided I'd rather live awhile longer.

Behind the bar, a large man was pouring shots from a brown jug. A small paper sign announced the going rate was a nickle a glass.

"Howard!" I shouted above the din. The bartender turned his head. I waved. He hadn't seen me all winter and it was easy to tell he had no idea who I was. Then he smiled. I couldn't hear him but I saw him mouth, "Murph." He grabbed a shot from the counter and passed it down the row of men in the front of the bar. He was specific about who the drink was for. His size got it to its destination. I fired it down in one swallow. Rotgut. Not the worst I'd had. Pure turpentine compared with the stuff I'd recently imbibed at The Manjuris.

The bartender was Howard Monck. We'd met during the war when I was on leave in London. Eddie and I had arranged to meet. He arrived with Howard in tow. We'd stayed in a hotel on Trafalgar Square and had had a rousing good time. Wine. Women. Song. I had a bath every day. After the trenches I'd do anything to stay clean. After the war Howard and Eddie did some importing together. Once in a while Howard would come to Owen Sound. We'd meet at The Manjuris. I'd decided to use him as my contact while I was hiding with the gang. It'd be easy to go unnoticed in the Pacific. Besides, Howard could be trusted.

Ten minutes after I'd arrived the place was empty. I sat down at a table to wait. Howard came over. He brought a bottle and two glasses.

"This is the good stuff," he said, pouring.

"I was thinking how much I needed another drink. To take away the taste of that first one."

Howard laughed but didn't apologize.

I took a sip. Better, no doubt.

"It always like that in here?"

"Mill workers get a twenty-minute dinner. In shifts, starting at noon. Lots of 'em beat it over here. They drink all they can, then go back to the mill."

"What about prohibition?"

With a sly grin he said, "A special arrangement. It costs me. But I make it back."

"And then some, I'm sure." I sipped some more whisky. "Seen Eddie lately?"

"No. Is he comin' up?"

"Meetin' me here. Any time now."

"He should have called. I coulda put somethin' special together."

"For you and Eddie maybe. I'm workin'."

"Here? On what?"

"A jailbreak."

"What?"

"Got a friend in jail. I'm going to break him out."

He laughed again. "You're as crazy as Joe Hunt's dog!"

"What?"

"Joe Hunt's dog didn't like bein' away from home. Real particular 'bout his dish too. He swam across the bay to get a drink o' water out of it. Crazy, that dog."

"I'm not crazy." I laid out the whole story for him. Eddie arrived as I was finishing the tale. Howard got him a glass and poured.

"So you want me to pass messages back and forth?" Howard asked.

"That's right. Eddie's going to be in Clavering until Friday. If I need help I'll get word to you. You get word to him."

"How?"

"Why don't I set one of my boys up here?" Eddie asked. "You need me, any time of day or night, just send him."

"Okay. What about the cops?" Howard asked.

"The only one you talk to is Oddball Scott."

"The Grey County Constable?"

"That's right. You know him?"

"Nope."

"Don't worry. You'll recognize him," Eddie said. "He's an amputee."

When we stopped laughing, I let Howard in on the joke.

"Don't tell anyone else about this. And watch out for a cop called Blood. Provincial Police Inspector out of Walkerton. A real tough one from what I hear. He might put the squeeze on you if he thinks you're in it."

"How long you gonna hide out?"

"Week or so."

"Okay."

"One more question," I said as we stood to go. "Any one-armed men in Wiarton?"

Before he could answer the door banged open. Another torrent of working men poured in. Second dinner shift at the mill.

"Gotta go." Howard dashed back to the bar. I stopped at the door and looked back. All I could see was the top of his head bobbing above the sea of men crashed against the bar.

I bought three sturdy horses at the Livery. "Oddball is gonna like you when he pays for them," Eddie said.

"You want one while I'm at it?"

"Naw," he said. "My car's outside the Pacific."

"You just gonna drive out of town after pulling a jailbreak?"

"No."

"Good."

"I'm gonna walk back and have another drink with Howard. Then I'm gonna drive out of town."

"You're as crazy as Joe Hunt's dog," I said.

"What?"

"Never mind. Are you crazy?"

"No. You got it all fixed with the cops. I don't gotta run away."

"The cops have to make it look real. Otherwise no one will believe it."

"They'll have four desperadoes on horseback to chase. But I'll tell you what. I got more clothes in the car. I'll change. No one'll know it was me."

"You'll have to cover that face."

"Of course."

We rode south a block to George Street, stashing the horses across the street in an alley called Louisa Street. There weren't many people around. We crossed George to the town hall on the southwest corner. It was a new building. The first one had burned down in 1912. The Public Utilities office was in the front end of the building, the town offices were upstairs. In the back of the building, the police office and jail. The top half of the wooden door was glass. POLICE, it said, in large golden letters. Eddie ducked down and stood on the other side. He quickly tied a scarf around his face. It concealed everything including his scar. I did the same, then pulled my Webley & Scott out. Eddie reached inside the long coat he was wearing and pulled out a Thompson submachine gun. He grabbed a pannier of ammunition from a deep pocket and snapped it into place. My eyes bulged. I felt them.

"Where on earth did you get that?" I whispered across the door.

"From a friend."

I shrugged. There would be no reason to use the gun. Its looks would menace the stupidest of cops into compliance.

"Ready?" I asked.

Eddie nodded. I grabbed the knob, gave it a turn and shoved the door into the office. Eddie and I followed it.

"Hold it where ya are!" I shouted as we strode in.

CHAPTER SIX
JAILBREAK

"Where is everyone?" Eddie asked, looking at me. I looked back at him, and the two of us began to laugh like a couple of fools. The office was empty.

I pushed the door shut behind us.

"They must be at the train. I didn't think everyone would go."

"Probably the first stiffs these boys've ever seen," Eddie quipped. He was moving slowly through the office, eyes scanning everything.

"I doubt it," I said.

The office was small. Three desks. A couple of file cabinets. A gun rack, full. A stove in the corner. There was a bag of pastries on one desk. In the back wall there was a heavy wooden door with a small peep door at eye level which Eddie popped open. He nodded through the bars.

"Van's ready," he said. He went to the nearest desk and began to open and close drawers.

"What are you doing?" I asked.

"Looking for the keys."

"What for?"

"So we can break these guys out. What else?"

"I was kind of hoping to do it while the cops were here. For better effect."

"If you take them now, they'll think you set up the whole train thing. To get the cops out and make the break."

It hadn't occurred to me.

"I guess that's why I brought you along."

I pulled out the centre drawer of the desk that was closest to me. There was a gun in it. Couple boxes of ammo. Citation book. Pens. Lots of other junk. No keys. I closed it and opened the top right.

"Jeez, this guy's got guns in every drawer."

"The one in the bottom left is missing," a voice said from the doorway.

I looked up. A uniform was blocking the opening. A large pistol was levelled at the space between Eddie and me.

I'd shifted my pistol to my left hand to search the desk. It was out of his sight. Not that it mattered. He had us dead to rights. And I'm not much of a shot with my left hand. I looked at Eddie. The Thompson was hidden by the big jacket.

"You the chief?" I asked, knowing full well he wasn't.

"Chief's at the G.T.R. station."

"He tell you about a telegram? From Marc Scott?"

"What telegram?"

We had a problem. Eddie knew it too. Being careful of my left foot I fired a shot into the floor. The blast was deafening. The uniform jumped with fright. Then thought to bring his big gun around to fire a shot at me. He didn't get the chance.

"Ever seen Swiss cheese?" Eddie called out. The uniform's eyes widened. I stopped cringing. Eddie had the machine gun levelled. The cop's gun clattered to the floor. I rushed around the desk and shut the door behind him. I pulled the blind and locked it. I grabbed his shoulder and pushed my gun into the small of his back.

"The key!" I said into his ear.

He was scared dumb.

"Where's the key?" I said it louder.

"Wha…what?" he finally stammered.

"The key. For the cells."

"On the side of the gun cabinet." His eyes never left the machine gun. He trembled as we walked over. Without the support of my hand on his shoulder he might have fallen. I felt bad for him. He was just a kid. And the chief hadn't told him. I was afraid someone else he hadn't told might come in. We opened the door and went back.

"About time," Van said from inside.

There were two cells side by side. Each about eight feet square. The only things in them were bunks. And people. I shoved the cop into a chair. Van was in the cell on the left. I let him out first.

"Good work!" He clapped me on the shoulder and limped out.

"Save it. We gotta get out of here. Now." I turned to leave.

"Ain't ya gonna get us out too?" a voice asked from the other cell.

The speaker was a boy. All freckles and red hair. A huge set of ears set at right angles to his head. Skinny, he was fourteen or fifteen. Rough clothes. He was white knuckling the bars. A hopeful smile revealed a mouthful of crooked teeth.

"You're just a kid."

A second boy came to the bars. He had dark hair and eyes. Stocky build. He was good looking, in a brooding sort of way. Sixteen, I'd guess.

"Pete?" The second boy looked at Van.

"The redhead is Jug. The other one's Davey. You're right. They are just kids. That's why ya should let 'em out," Van said from beside me. "Besides we can prob'ly use their hideout for a coupla days. 'Til the heat's off. Right boys?"

"Yeah. Sure," Jug said. He spoke with an Irish accent. Behind him, Davey grunted.

"Okay." I gave Van the key. "Hurry." I herded the uniform into Van's cell. The door clanged shut behind him. He walked to the back and stood facing the wall. I wanted to say something but couldn't.

"C'mon. Let's go," Van said as the three of them rushed out of the room. I followed in time to see Eddie pop the front door open and wave them through.

"Across the street into the alley," I heard him whisper.

He followed me out and pulled the door shut. We hid our weapons, and pulled our masks off.

"See you later," I said. "Enjoy Clavering. I'll check in with Howard if I need anything."

"Good luck," he said and walked away.

I ran up the alley. The other three had already mounted. I grabbed Scotty's lead and jumped into the saddle.

"Which way?" I asked Jug.

"Oxenden."

"Right. Frank Street. Go south on Berford. Turn left."

"In broad daylight? Verle, are you crazy?" Van asked, looking straight at me with a smirk on his face.

"As Joe Hunt's dog," I said in my best Verle voice. I jammed my heels into Scotty's sides. He leapt out of the alley.

The streets were still relatively free of traffic. The whole town had to be at the train station. The undertaker's wagon rolled by as we came down the hill to Berford Street.

"What's 'appening?" Davey asked.

"Couple stiffs on the train," I said. Another jab of the heels. Scotty picked it up to a gallop. The four of us thundered straight up Berford and cut across a lawn at the corner of Frank. I looked over my shoulder once. We weren't being followed.

★★★

Frank Street turned into a county road at the town limit, running northeast along the bay. The water was on our left as we rode. To the right the cliffs of the escarpment rose a hundred feet in the air. The road was in bad shape. Dirt. Rutted. Potholed. We were forced to a walk in places. The two boys led. In the rear I watched where we'd been.

"They must have found that uniform by now," I said.

"Those guys never stray from their bag of pastries for long," Van said.

"Shoulda let Johnnie blast it with that Tommy gun. Cops woulda been too busy mourning to chase us." I got a good laugh.

"Pretty convenient the train pulling in with a couple of corpses," Van said over his shoulder.

"Wasn't it?" I replied.

"Cleared the cop shop at just the right time. You have anything to do with it?"

I nodded. "Something."

"I can't wait to hear it."

"Yeah, me too," Jug called back over his shoulder.

I put a cautionary finger to my lips. Van nodded.

The banks of Gleason Brook had been badly undermined.

"Beaver," Davey informed us. "Folks have been talkin' about it for months. They say it's huge. But no one's ever seen it. Keeps blockin' the crick."

Before I could laugh I saw the dust cloud chasing us.

"Pete!" I called. Van turned and I gestured behind us.

"Company, boys!" he shouted to the other two.

I pulled Scotty up. I looked as hard as I could. A car. And two horses. They were putting on a good show. Or else the Wiarton Police Chief hadn't actually received the telegram. I was beginning to wonder. I gave Scotty the boot and caught up with the others.

"I suggest a little speed." We broke into a trot, then a gallop. Our pursuers gained on us.

"Where are we going?" I shouted.

"Not much farther. Into the woods." Davey shouted.

I nodded. That would take care of the car, leaving just the horses to contend with.

There was a gunshot and a piece of hot lead sizzled past.

"We better hit those woods now," I shouted.

We raced off the road and across a field. I thought we were going to make it until Davey flew off his horse. They both hit the ground hard. A grunt and a snort and the horse was up. Its front right leg swung like a pendulum. A jagged edge of the cannon bone dripped blood. We circled around for Davey. He was on his feet but looked shaky.

"Hit some kinda animal hole," he shouted, angry.

"Get him up with you, Jug, and ride!" I shouted. Davey staggered his way towards us. I dismounted and threw Scotty's lead to Van. I looked across the field. The car had stopped but the two men on horses were still coming. I looked at the horse then back at Van. He shook his head. There was no helping it. A break like that was the end of a horse. I pulled out my pistol and fired.

The cops stopped riding. Uncertain. I lifted the gun and fired a couple of shots over their heads. I grabbed the lead from Van and jumped on Scotty's back. When I looked over my shoulder they were right behind us. Guns drawn.

CHAPTER SEVEN
BRUCE'S CAVES

The other two were waiting in the bush. Jug lashed his horse when they saw us coming. We rode up a slight slope and into the forest. At the edge, the light was a luminous green. The deeper we rode, the darker it got. The trees grew close together. Maples, tamaracks, spruce and cedar. We were at the bottom edge of the escarpment. Rocks gnarled with cedar roots loomed above us. Moss crept everywhere, deepening the green. There didn't seem to be a trail. But Davey led his horse surely, first in one direction, then another. All the while we were hidden by rocks and trees. In the distance I could hear thrashing and cursing. The law wouldn't find us. Except that we were the law. Van and I were the only ones who knew it.

We rounded an outcrop. The noise of our pursuers disappeared. Everyone relaxed.

"That horse," Jug whispered, shaking his head.

"Break like that there's nothing else to do," I said.

We rode deeper into the forest and closer to the cliff bottom. A small cave stank of something rotten. A second was shallow, scooped out of the cliff bottom. We passed more caves. Finally we had to dismount and lead the horses across the uneven ground. Around an outcrop, there was a huge cave. Fifty feet deep, its ceiling was a cathedral.

"In here?" I asked and the cave answered.

"A little ahead," Jug said twice.

We went around another outcrop and directly ahead was a smaller opening. We led the horses to the back of a narrower, deeper cave.

"We'll wait here 'til dark," Davey said.

"How will we know?" I asked.

"Bats," he said, pointing up. I couldn't see them. When everyone was quiet I could hear them. Rustling. The sound of paper-dry leaves rubbing against one another. I had chicken skin in a flash. I hated bats. I must have looked sick. Fortunately no one could see me. They'd laugh for sure.

I dropped Scotty's lead. There were no cars to chase. We walked to the back of the cave and up an incline to a sandy flat. Six feet wide and ten deep, it was perfect. We hunkered down.

"This where you boys hide out?" Van asked.

"Don't be daft," Jug said.

"We're goin' there after dark. Them coppers might still be blunderin' about in the woods. Can't risk 'em findin' the camp." Six or seven feet away, Davey was the deepest in the cave.

"They won't find us," Jug said. "Boss says no one comes out here."

"You fellas know about these caves?" I asked the dark.

"No," one of them murmured.

"They're called Bruce's Caves."

"Who's Bruce?" Jug asked.

"Robert Bruce. He was a hermit. Owned these caves."

"You fellers from around here then?" Davey asked.

"Yes," I said. "Back around in that big cave is where he lived. In a hut outside."

"Yeah?" I could hear the wonder in Jug's voice.

"He'd go away in summer to work on the railroad. In winter he came back to live in the hut. Smoked forest leaves he'd collect up himself in fall. His clothes were made from flannel blankets sewn together. Stripes at the cuff."

"Get off it," Jug said.

"Really. Wore a pillow case for a hat too. People'd come up here and have their pictures taken with him. They paid for it."

"What happened?" Davey asked.

"Died. Before the war. Buried over at Oxenden."

"These caves are named after him?" Jug asked.

"Yes."

"Tell them about that other grave," Van spoke up.

"What other grave?" Jug was loving it. So was I.

"The murdered stranger?"

"Yeah," Van said. I held my tongue for a second.

"Are you gonna tell us or not?" Davey asked.

"Sure. About forty years ago, a drifter shows up in Oxenden. Rough shape. Ragged clothes. Carpet bag hanging off a stick. He looked to be tow-headed under the moth-eaten hat he was wearing. He was thin and six foot six."

I paused in the story and stood. Feeling my way down to and around the horses, I reached into my saddlebag. The bottle I'd brought had survived the trip.

"Hey, what are you doin' there, Verle?" Davey called.

"I'm talking too much," I said, shaking the bottle Eddie had sent with me. Murmurs of approval greeted the sloshing sound. I pulled the cork and stuck it into my pocket. In case we needed it again. I doubted we would. I took a long pull, then passed it to Jug.

"So a week or two later, there's this fire. At the John Dance farm. Tenant farmer named John Bailey and his hired man died. The hired man was tall. Thin. Ragged clothes."

"Someone burnt 'em?" Jug asked excitedly.

"Cut them up first," I said.

"Murder!" Davey cried.

"Rumour is, it was a triangle. Farmer Bailey, pretty little Miss Ellen McLeary and another man. The murdered stranger was an innocent bystander."

"A couple of provincial detectives were called in," I continued. "Dressed as pedlars. One of them pretended to be sweet on Ellen McLeary. Next thing he's bedding her."

"She confesses while they're doin' it." Van was enjoying himself. "All the while his partner's under the bed taking notes!"

We roared with laughter. The bottle made another round. If the police were anywhere within a mile, they would have heard us.

"I knew the coppers liked their pastries," Van joked. "I guess they like tarts too!" Another roar of laughter and more bottle passing.

"I've been thinking about a career with the cops," Jug smirked.

"You'd be needin' a bigger nightstick," Davey parried.

We laughed so hard I thought I might split. The bottle made another round. I was starting to feel pretty good.

"Tell them about Jamieson Johnston," Van said.

"Another murder?" Jug asked.

"In Owen Sound. Last year just after the Labour Day celebration. A rich old guy, Jamieson Johnston. Didn't feel well all afternoon and after the speeches and such went home and died. He'd just had all his teeth out. He was gettin' a fake set. The sawbones that looked at him called it lockjaw. Except a week later his pretty young widow gets married to Johnston's hired man."

"Not in the least suspicious," Van put his two cents worth in.

"So they dig him up. And check again."

"And?" If he'd had one, Jug would be on the edge of his seat. I heard the bottle tip up at Davey's end of the cave.

"Poisoned. With strychnine."

"The wife?" Davey asked.

"No. They think it's the hired man. Took his boss over to the Patterson House for a drink. They say he put the poison in when the old man wasn't lookin'."

"Why'd they do it?" Jug asked.

"Love."

"Of money," Van added.

"Yeah. Prob'ly."

"What happened?" Jug took another slug of booze.

"In court right now. Be to the jury before the end of the week."

"Whew!" Davey exhaled. "Just like home."

"Where's that?" I asked.

"London. England."

"I was there once. It wasn't so bad."

"You were? When?" Davey asked.

"During the war."

"You fought? In the war?" Jug was excited by the prospect.

"Both of us did. It's where Pete there got his limp."

"What was it like?"

"Hell," Van said, "I was only there a month. That was long enough. Mud. Water. Rats. Corpses. Corpses everywhere."

"Ya kill lotsa the Hun?" Davey asked.

"A few maybe. You never knew. They nearly got me."

"How?"

"Bomb. That was how most of the boys got it. In the trenches you were pretty safe. The first thing you learned was not to stick your head up. Didn't help though. One night I was looking through a trench periscope at the Hun. A bomb came down right on top of me. Blew my clothes off. Tore my leg up. The end of the war for me."

"How 'bout you Verle?"

"I was a gunner, in back of the lines. My howitzer killed the Hun. But I never saw them."

"I woulda joined up," Jug said, "But I was too young."

"How long you been in Canada?" I asked.

"Since 1915."

"Where are you from?"

"County Kildare. Then we moved to London."

"We?"

"Me family."

"They here with you?

"No."

"Oh."

"Me da was killed in an accident. That's why we moved to London. Then mam got sick. That's when I heard of the Ever Open Door."

"The what?"

"The Ever Open Door," Davey said. "He's talkin' about the Barnardo home."

Canada was built on the backs of children. Many of them were Barnardos. For forty years they'd been coming. Boys first. Then girls. Orphans and street children. Taken into the homes started by Dr. John Barnardo in 1867, when he found eleven street urchins freezing on a London rooftop. His first mission was to provide shelter. Then he provided a new life, by sending the children to Canada. Immigrant labour indentured to Canadian farmers. A new life at a price. Some, like Jug and Davey, disagreed with their new homes.

"How long you boys been on the run?" I asked. The cave fell quiet. Grew uncomfortable.

"He's okay boys," Van said into the dark.

"Just asking," I said.

"How'd you know?" Davey demanded. In his anger he jumped up. His head wasn't as hard as the rock it hit. He'd forgotten we were in a cave. He swore, madder than before.

"I read newspapers."

"Eh? What's that got to do with it?"

"Hey, hey, easy now boys," Van said. "Verle here has been my friend a long time. If I say he's okay, he's okay. You wanna fight, I'm gonna take his side."

If I was going to win their trust this was it. "I knew a boy who was a Barnardo," I explained. "I read his *Ups and Downs*. You've read it, right?"

The pain had caught Davey. In the dark, I could just make him out. He was holding his head between his hands.

"You okay Davey?" I asked.

"Fine. What is *Ups and Downs*?" he murmured.

"A newspaper. For Barnardo boys and girls."

"Sounds stupid," Jug said. He probably couldn't read.

"It's got stories. About other kids. It helps families find each other."

"How?" Davey asked.

"You can write in letters. If you're missing someone. They print them. Maybe your someone finds you. Maybe not."

"I got a sister," Davey spoke in a low voice. "Our da died too. There was four of us and mam had to give up us two youngest. The older ones could work for themselves. We was a burden. My sister, Rose, she's here too. But with another family. I don't know where."

"When did you see her last?" Van asked.

"At Hazelbrae. The home in Peterborough. When the trains came they said we couldn't go together. Nobody wanted two."

"Whyn't you write a letter?" I asked.

"Can't," he said.

"I'll do it for ya. Then in a day or two I'll go into Wiarton Post Office," I offered.

"Would ya?"

"Sure."

"Wait a minute," Jug interrupted. "Where's she gonna find him? Out here in this bush?"

"Naw, she can just write to him at the Post Office. Wiarton or Big Bay."

"If she ever sees it."

Davey groaned. I passed the bottle to him.

"It's getting dark," Van said. "Shouldn't we get going?"

"Yeah, let's," Jug agreed, standing.

★★★

It was dusk by the time we were mounted and moving. Not long after we started Davey finished the bottle and tossed it end over end into the bush.

"Say," he called back from the front, "who was the other guy?"

"Other guy?" I played dumb.

"What other guy, he says!" Davey threw his head back and laughed, nearly unseating himself. I'm not sure if it was the booze, the bump on the head or the fall off his horse. Probably all of the above.

"Just a friend."

"Yeah, where'd he get the Tommy gun? That's what I wanna know."

"From another friend."

"You got lots of friends, have ya Verle?"

"What's it to ya?"

"I'd just like to get me one of them guns. That's what. I could really do somethin' if I had one. Whaddaya think?"

"I guess you could."

"No, I mean can you get me one? Maybe two?"

"Three," Jug chimed in.

Van looked back at me and winked. We had something they wanted. That was good. I'd been worried about what might happen when we got to the camp. Just because we'd sprung these two boys didn't mean the rest would want to take us on.

"Maybe," I said.

I was beginning to get a little concerned about the riding. At the base of a cliff, dark came on fast. It was getting difficult to see where we were going. I needn't have worried.

A half mile or so from the cave Davey stopped and dismounted. In front of us was another shallow cave. A circle of piled rocks and logs blocked the entrance. A corral. The rock face to one side was obscured by a pile of hay. It looked as though it had been dropped down from above. On the far side of the enclosure I could make out a wide sloping path that cut up the side of the cliff.

We dismounted quickly and moved our horses inside. There were three others already there. Lots of room. I stripped Scotty and gave him some oats. I patted him on the neck. He was a good horse.

The others finished their tack and motioned us to follow. I felt tense. This was it. Whether we were in or out depended on the next few minutes. I looked at Van. He reached into the side pocket of his jacket and showed me the butt of his pistol. I nodded and loosened mine in its holster. It was too big to conceal in a pocket. But I wanted to be ready.

We shouldered our saddles and followed Davey and Jug. It was full dark. The boys blocked up the corral while we watched. They finished and led us over to the ramp which was carpeted with moss. My feet sunk in as we walked. About halfway up there was a natural sort of landing. We stopped and Jug whistled. Twice low, once high and loud. The response was enthusiastic. They hadn't been expected back.

"C'mon," Jug said. In the dark I could hear his smile.

Van and I followed, as the two of them led us up the slope.

It was the best natural camp I'd ever seen. By the time we reached the top of the cliff, it was pitch dark. The heavy canopy overhead let few stars in. Directly ahead of us was a bonfire. The light was visible to us but the half circle of rocks at the far side would shelter it from prying eyes. We walked up.

My eyes adjusted to the firelight. There were three people. Two were girls. One jumped up and ran, shouting "Davey" until he caught her in his arms. She was younger than him. Jug smirked as they kissed. He shook the hand of a man, hidden in the shadow of the rock. I couldn't see his face.

The second girl looked eighteen. Pretty. Dark hair. Wide round eyes. I couldn't tell their colour. Full lips. She gazed into the fire, having taken little notice of our arrival. She'd been crying.

Davey and his girl came up for air. Arm in arm they walked over to us.

"This here's Shelagh," he said.

"Hello." Her voice was honey.

"This is Verle and I'm Pete." Van held a hand out. She offered hers. He bent and kissed it. She blushed and we all laughed.

"Well isn't this cosy," a voice rasped from the other side of the fire.

I looked as Jug and the hidden man stepped into the light. He was heavy, with dark hair. A low sloping forehead ended where the single eyebrow slashed across his face. The nose had been hidden the last time I saw him. It was ugly, like a turnip. Wide shoulders. Bowed legs.

My heart slammed. The surge hit my brain with the force of a hammer.

Standing less than ten feet away from me was one of the men who had tried to abduct Miss McDermid.

CHAPTER EIGHT
THE LOST TIRE GANG

The saddle slung over my shoulder hid my hand from them. I reached inside my jacket and grabbed the butt of my gun. Beside me, Van saw. He slipped a hand into his pocket.

"Well?" the big man grunted.

"These fellas sprung us from jail," Davey said.

"Jug tol' me."

Unlike the others, this man spoke with a Yankee twang.

"We told 'em they could come to stay."

"Didja also tell 'em I'm the one who says what's what around here?"

Jug and Davey looked uncomfortable.

"Sure," I said. Turnip nose looked at me. I searched his face, but saw no sign of recognition.

"Did they then?" he asked.

"Yes. We knew it was a chance."

"You bet it was a chance!" he shouted across the fire. "You don't know how much of a chance."

His turnip flushed purple. He reminded me of the peacocks at Harrison Park. Always a big show.

"Listen," I tightened my grip. "If you don't like us that's okey dokey with me. We'll leave in the morning. But busting these two outta the pokey has gotta be worth one night."

He glowered across the fire at me. A little man with a little power. He'd convinced himself he was big. I couldn't wait to set him straight. Minutes passed. We stared at one another. Finally he spoke.

"Nope," he said turning his back.

"They can get Tommy guns," Jug spoke up.

"What?" The big man whirled and looked me in the eye.

"Maybe," I said.

"Maybe? You can or you can't."

"We do favours for people. Sometimes."

"Well?"

"For friends."

"Whyn't you say so? Pal." He circled the fire, hand outstretched. "C'mon, sit down," he said after we shook. "Jug get these fellas a snort."

We followed him around the fire. I'd trust him about as far as I could carry him. I dropped my saddle against the rock then leaned against it. In front of us, we could see the treetops below the cliff. A narrow band of stars filled the space up to the trees above us. It looked something like the movie screen at Griffins. Both of my hands were in sight. So were Van's. We were okay for the time being. He hadn't recognized me. I hoped my luck would hold.

Jug came round the fire with a couple of soda bottles. He passed one to Van and me. Then sat next to the big man and opened the other. Davey and Shelagh sat between us. I used my teeth to pry the cork out of the bottle. Whatever was inside, it wasn't soda. The whiff I caught burned its way clear into my head. I held my breath the best I could and took a drink. It was raw and kicked like a mule. I tried not to wince as I passed the bottle to Van.

Jug shuddered openly as he drank. The big man didn't flinch. He drank a second time and wiped his mouth with a grimy sleeve.

"What's with her?" I gestured at the quiet girl across from me.

"How'd you boys manage to break into the jail?" he countered.

"Pete was in there. Had to get him out," I said.

"What about the cops?"

"They were busy."

"Oh?"

"At the train station."

A shivery moan escaped the quiet girl. It made the hair on the back of my neck rise.

"Shut her up," the big man growled at Shelagh. She crossed round to the other girl and tried to comfort her.

"How'd ya happen to have four horses? When you was just comin' to rescue Pete there?"

I wasn't ready for the question. There was no convenient lie on my tongue waiting to be thrown.

"I told him about the boys." Thinking fast, Van jumped in.

"How?"

"Carrier pigeon. Now why's she crying?"

He considered the answer for a moment. I doubt he believed any of it. Then he said, "Derry's gone."

"Gone! Where?" Jug stood. Shocked, Davey looked from the big man to the girls. Both were crying. He turned back to the big man.

"What've ye done?" he cried.

There was something off about their reactions. I'm not sure what it was. I returned my hand to the comfort of the gun. Davey was on his feet. He advanced towards the big man, who remained sitting.

"Settle down," he said.

"Don't you tell me to settle down," Davey growled.

"When we got up this morning he was gone. Ask them." He gestured at the girls.

"Well?" Davey demanded.

"Took his kit and left. Before dawn," Shelagh said.

"Where?"

"Didna say. Just left." The other girl wept.

"Not Derry. He wouldn't do that." Davey sat back down.

"He's just gone off," the big man said in a placating tone. He clutched the half empty bottle in a meaty fist.

"You're right, Goldy," Jug said. "He's just gone off. He's gonna be back. He wouldna leave without word. Not Derry."

"Prob'ly be back in the mornin'." Goldy smiled, the crisis averted.

"Yeah." Jug scoffed a drink from the bottle. "In the mornin'."

★★★

We drank in silence. Colleen's tears had stopped. The cool night air was punctuated by the crackling of the fire. The liquor was having an effect. Tension was carried off with the smoke. Jug jumped up and threw a stack of fresh cedar boughs onto the flames. They caught with a fury. The light could be seen thirty feet further at least. Not to mention the noise. Fresh cedar kicks up a real fuss when it burns.

Goldy looked disapprovingly at him, but said nothing. I was surprised. He was the kind of man who would have an opinion on every topic. The right opinion.

"You boys'll have a turn standin' watch t'nite," he said to Van and me. Every time he looked my way I relaxed a bit more. If he hadn't recognized me right off I didn't think he would. Everything on the train had happened too quickly.

"When?" Van asked.

"Artie is down there now. One o' youse can go down an' relieve him. Jug'll show ya."

"Great," Van replied. Artie? The one-armed man? I hoped so.

"So can you get Tommy guns? You know where?" Goldy came back to the subject closest to his heart.

"Maybe," I said.

"Jeez, don't start again. Can ya? Or not?"

"Suppose I can? Then what?"

"Oh, I dunno. I could find some use for 'em."

"Around here? What for, hunting woodchuck?"

Jug sniggered into his hand. Davey laughed aloud. So did Colleen.

"We got ourselves a sweet little deal cooked up," he said. "Don't we boys?"

They looked at him, wary. Nodded in agreement.

"What?" I asked.

"None o' yer damn business!" he said, smiling.

"Can't help you then," I said.

"Why not?"

"Say I got you the guns. Then you and the boys here, you decide to kill me and Pete. Wouldn't be too smart would it? You killing me with the guns I sold you."

"Hadn't thought o' that."

"Right."

Everyone relaxed and went back to their drinking. It wasn't the last we'd hear of that topic. Goldy seemed inclined to let it slide for the time being. Davey left the fire and came back with a guitar. He tuned it, then struck a chord. Jug produced a penny whistle from his pocket and joined in. Then he lowered it and sang:

Fare thee well my lovely Dinah

A thousand times adieu,

For we're going away from the holy ground

And the girls we all loved true.

We'll sail the South Seas over

And we'll return for sure,

To see again the girls we love

And the Holy Ground once more.

To the girls I do adore

And I still live in hope

To see the Holy Ground once more.

His voice was untrained but pleasing. He sang two more verses. They recounted the tale of a fierce storm that nearly battered the ship apart. Surviving to reach port. Drinking to the Holy Ground. Money spent going back to sea. The song ended. So did the spell. We were back around a campfire in Keppel Township.

"What was that?" I asked as we applauded the pair.

"Irish folk tune," Jug said.

I looked at the boys with admiration. I loved music and respected those who had mastered it.

"You boys should be on stage at Griffins," I said.

"Where's that?" Davey asked, tuning his guitar again.

"Owen Sound."

"Not that far away," he mused.

"No."

He plucked aimlessly for a second. Slowly he came round to a tune and began to sing.

I have seen the lark soar high at morn, to sing up in the blue,

I have heard the blackbird pipe its notes, the thrush and the linnet too.

But none of them can sing so sweet, my singing bird as you.

Ah—my singing bird as you.

Everyone listened with rapt attention as Davey sang. His voice was trained. As raw and unpolished as Jug's, Davey's voice was smooth and perfect.

If I could lure my singing bird from its own cosy nest,

If I could lure my singing bird I would warm it on my breast.

And on my heart my singing bird would sing itself to rest,

Ah—would sing itself to rest.

I thought about Lori. I loved her. No doubt. I wanted to marry her. A log on the fire shifted. The fragrant smell of pine hung on the night air. I wished Lori and I were sharing the fire. Goldy didn't look the cuddling type. The song ended and everyone was silent. Colleen was crying quietly. I felt sorry for her. The missing Derry was the man I had shot on the train. I was sure of it.

"Time to change the watch," Goldy said. "Pete can relieve Artie. Then it's to bed. We've work ta do tomorrow."

Van and I exchanged a glance. If Artie was the one-armed man, things could get lively.

"Have ye got a gun?" Goldy asked.

"Yes," Van said. I knew he had several.

"Go back the way we come in," Jug said. "At the edge go right fer ten feet. There's an outcrop."

Van walked into the dark without looking back. I found I was holding my breath. Van wouldn't confront Artie alone, of that I was sure. If he was our quarry.

Davey and Jug struck up another tune. In the middle of it, I could hear the crunch of footsteps coming through the woods. I slipped a hand inside my jacket and gripped the butt of my gun. A man strolled into camp. I relaxed. Artie had two arms. He was tall and fair. A ready smile after I was introduced. I'd have to keep looking.

A couple more songs and Goldy made us pack it in. I didn't mind. It had been a busy day. The moonshine the boys fed me was good. I didn't anticipate any problem with sleep. I stretched out on the ground and used my saddle for a pillow. Covered myself with a blanket. Stared into the fading fire. I was out before it was. I fell asleep with a hand on my gun.

Van shook me awake sometime before dawn. I yawned and asked, "Where to?"

"Straight ahead. You can't miss it." He yawned too.

I stood and shouldered my blanket. I was stiff from sleeping on the ground. The path was clear in the pre-dawn light. I was surprised how close the edge was. In the dark it seemed farther. To the right of the cut the cliff inclined. Just a few feet away a ledge jutted out from the rock face.

It was three feet long and the same wide. A blanket padded with straw sat across the centre. Directly below was the junction where Jug had whistled our arrival the night before. Legs up, the lookout would be invisible from below.

For three hours I watched the forest come to life. When the sun climbed above the trees below it got warmer. A red squirrel scolded me, I'm not sure why. The .455 would have splatted it. I was going for the .32 in my boot, thinking it would make a nice bit of breakfast, when it ran off. An occasional bug came along. I was hungry. It was still early. A crow landed with a rusty croak on the topmost branch of a nearby pine. More of a frond, the weight of the crow caused it to swing crazily from side to side. The crow gripped hard with its scritchy toes and hung on. I was staring it down when Shelagh arrived. She was carrying a double-barrelled shotgun.

"Morning," she said in a pretty way.

"Hello," I said. "I've been staring down this crow. I hope you don't mind taking over."

She looked at me for a long moment. Then decided.

"Sure. Goldy wants to see ya."

"What about?"

"Don't know."

I moved off the outcrop so she could take up her watch.

"It won't take long to stare him down."

"What?" she said sharply.

"He's got a tough exterior. Inside he's mush."

"Who is?"

"The crow." I pointed at the feathered pest.

"Oh. Him." She brushed by and sat down on the outcrop.

"Will he let us stay?"

"Why would ya want to?"

"Need to be somewhere."

"I guess."

"Well?"

"Goldy don't have much say," she said. "It's up to the boss who stays and who goes. Not Goldy. He's the number two man."

"The boss?" New hope of finding the one-armed man.

"Said more'n I should already."

"Who is the boss?"

"Better get yerself over there," she said, uncomfortable.

"Okay, sure." I turned to walk away, then looked back at her. "You a Barnardo too?"

She looked surprised. Taken aback.

"They told ya?"

"Sure. We spent the afternoon drinking while we hid from the law. Got to know each other real well."

"Oh."

I waited a moment. "Well?"

"When my father died there were six of us kids. The three young ones stayed with mam, and the rest of us lived with our Auntie May. When she got sick, mam had to send us oldest three away. We went to Miss Maria Rye, and she sent us to the Western Home, at Niagara-on-the-Lake. That's where me and Colleen met."

"How'd you get in with this bunch?" I asked. Before she could answer I heard Goldy's harsh voice call "breakfast" from the camp.

"You'd best be goin'," Shelagh said. "You don't want to make him mad."

"Right," I said, getting up.

By daylight it was easier to admire the genius of the camp. Hidden by the ring of rocks it was difficult if not impossible to see it from three directions. Anyone coming from the west had to get past the lookout. The dense trees surrounding the camp provided further cover.

There was coffee on the fire. A battered tin cup filled to the brim made me feel human again. There was nothing to compare with the first coffee of the day. Especially if it had been cooked over a campfire all night. One cup and you were set for several days.

Van sat on an upturned log in front of the fire. Goldy was nearby. Jug and Davey were both rolled up in their blankets. Colleen wasn't there. Nor was Artie. I wondered if they were together. Van gestured to the stump next to me. I sat down and sipped my second coffee.

"You wanna be careful with that stuff," Van warned.

"Huh? Why?"

"I been out to the bushes twice already."

"Keeps you regular."

"Too regular."

"Don't complain."

"If you two girls is finished whinin'," Goldy spoke. I'd almost forgotten he was there. I looked over. He was slicing chunks of bacon from a piece of pork. I'd have to remember to add rustling to the charges against them.

"What about those guns?"

"Eh? What?" I played dumb. I'd have to watch myself. I was getting good at dumb.

"I'll pay."

"How much?"

"Whatever it costs. I just need 'em. Two. No. Three."

"You'll pay whatever it costs?" This was getting more interesting by the moment. So far I had them for car theft, attempted kidnapping, murder and making booze. Another charge more or less wouldn't make much difference. But it would make Oddball look exceptionally good.

"Whatever it costs."

"Where you gonna get the cash?"

"Ain't your business. You get the guns, I'll get the dough. That's all you need to know."

"Okay."

"Okay?" Goldy said meaning one thing.

"Okay?" Van said, meaning another.

"Yeah. Sure. I'll get them for you. A hundred bucks apiece."

"A hundred!" Goldy jumped up, scattering raw bacon everywhere.

"You said you'd pay anything. That's the price. Sears and Roebuck sells them new for a hundred and seventy five. I'm giving you a bargain."

His outburst had woken the others. Goldy leaned towards me and asked, "Why? Why give me a bargain?"

You just can't make some people happy. "A guy I know has some. Hot. He wants to get rid of them. Cheap. They'll probably come in pieces. But Pete there, he knows his guns. He can put them together for you."

"Alright," he grumbled. "Three at a hundred apiece. I'll get the dough today."

"Hold on," I kept my voice low. "It's gonna take at least until tomorrow. I've gotta go into Wiarton. Arrangements have to be made."

"He stays with us," Goldy said, pointing at Van with the sharp knife he was holding. A simple gesture, but ominous. Van nodded in response to my look. He could handle himself.

"Alright. I'll head out after we eat."

Davey was on his feet first. He slept fully clothed. He stretched and scratched. Headed into the woods. Jug groaned where he lay.

"He always come around this slow?" I asked Van.

"Don't know. Jug!" he called, "You always this slow gettin' up?"

"It's sleepin' out in the air," he said.

"It sounds like he'd rather be in jail," I said to Van.

"Sounds like you'd rather be in the pokey," Van called to him.

"Naw. Not me. I'll take this any day. Thanks again fellas," he said with some feeling.

"Why do they call you Jug?" I asked.

"Lookit his head. Them ears is like jug handles." Goldy pointed and laughed.

"Why are you called Goldy?" I pressed on.

"His name's Goldfinch," Jug called. The big man scowled at him. Davey returned from the woods.

"We goin' out today then, Goldy?" he asked.

"Yeah," the big man said. His nose looked even more like a turnip in the daylight.

"Are ya not worried about the coppers?"

"While they're up here lookin' fer youse, we're gonna be somewheres else makin' our trade." He gave a loud guffaw at the end of it.

"They comin'?" Davey asked, pointing at Van and me with his coffee cup.

"Pete there is. Verle's got business." Goldy looked my way and winked. We were cohorts.

Breakfast was bacon, eggs and cakes cooked over the fire. After we finished I grabbed my saddle and walked down to the corral. A pebble bounced off the brim of my hat. Shelagh smirked and waved at me from the perch.

At the bottom I climbed between two cut saplings and into the corral. Colleen was there. Sleeping in the hay. By the light of day she was beautiful. Hair I had thought mousy by the fire was actually strawberry blonde. Her brows were the same color. A strong nose. A chin that balanced her face perfectly. I guessed her eyes would be green. I didn't wake her.

I slipped past into the cave. Scotty seemed none the worse for his night outdoors. Colleen was awake when we came out. Her eyes were green. Hair and clothes were a mess. It made her more appealing.

"Hello," she said with a shy smile.

"Hi."

"Leaving?"

"Just for a while." I dropped Scotty's lead and sat down next to her.

"So you're comin' back?"

"Uh huh."

"That's nice. You're big. Strong looking," she said with open admiration. I was a little embarrassed.

"I used to be a blacksmith. Before."

"Before you became an outlaw and jailbreaker?"

"Before the war."

"Oh."

"You okay?"

"Uh huh," she said. Her eyes gave the lie away.

"Sure?"

"Yes." She tried a smile. Suddenly I felt sorry for her. Sorry for them all.

"Okay." I stood up and brushed bits of hay off my pants. "I'll see you later then."

"Let me help you." She got up and moved the two saplings that blocked the way out.

"Sure you're comin' back?" she lilted.

"By tonight. They've got breakfast up there you know. Best go get some. Won't last long with Davey and Jug awake."

"Yes," she smiled fondly. "Those two are a pair of mongrels."

"See you," I said, mounting up.

"Sure. Ride careful now. Mind the coppers."

"I will."

★★★

I rode south towards Mountain Lake. The morning was beautiful. Farms lined the road on either side. I saw few people. Lots of beef cattle. The settlers of Keppel Township had learned that cropping was not a means of survival. Stoney Keppel they nicknamed it, while trying to clear land to farm. And truly, in every field, along every road, there were rocks. Huge rocks. A fresh crop of them every spring. Rocks that a hundred years of blasting, chipping and sweating would never move. Not ready to give up, the settlers of Keppel adapted. They cleared what fields they could. Then imported beef and dairy cows, hogs, sheep and goats. Marginal for crops, the land was perfect for livestock. So Stoney Keppel thrived.

It took me an hour or more to get to Mountain Lake. Turning west I rode out to Wiarton Road, coming out near the spot I'd started riding from the day before. After the murders on the train. I wondered how Miss McDermid was. Mr. Angel had sacrificed himself to save her. It was a weight she'd carry for the rest of her life.

I wondered where the one-armed man was hiding. I guessed he might turn out to be the boss who ran the gang. But what were his motives? Why try and kidnap Miss McDermid? I'd have to figure it out quickly. Goldy hadn't recognized me. He'd not had time to stare at me in the daylight either. The longer I stayed the more likely my cover would be blown.

Near the main road I eased Scotty into a fragrant stand of pine. I didn't want to get caught crossing in the open. I left him about thirty feet from the road and carefully made my way forward. Concealed behind a tree, I had a good look both ways. Nothing coming. I ran back and grabbed Scotty. I led him across on foot and into the bushes on the other side. Leaving him inside the trees again I went for a another look. It was all clear.

We rode through the bush and back onto the sideroad after about half a mile. If we continued straight along it, the road would angle up towards Boat Lake. Eventually we'd arrive in Oliphant. On a regular day that might be alright. I'd been to the tiny fishing village before and liked it. But there was work to be done. So after another mile we turned north. The sideroad we were on ran parallel to the main road and would take us straight to Wiarton. It would allow us to approach from the west. We wouldn't have to ride through the downtown, and could slip into the Pacific Hotel virtually unnoticed. I hoped.

It wouldn't matter if we did get caught. We were on the right side of the law. Assuming the law had finally heard from Oddball. I was worried about the one-armed man. I still didn't know who or where he was. He could be waiting in the tap room at the Pacific. Waiting for me. He knew who I was; he'd recognized me on the train. I didn't want to get caught in an ambush. When I got to the Pacific I'd go straight to Howard. To set me up with Eddie's man. I didn't fancy the idea of buying Tommy guns for the gang. I wasn't even sure Eddie could get them. I had no idea how long I would be with them. So I decided to do what I could to make the ruse appear genuine.

We hit the town line before noon. My timing was perfect. The Pacific would be packed. The dinner rush. In the confusion I hoped not to be noticed. I hid Scotty and walked in on foot. The police would be looking carefully at all horsemen.

As I walked, I couldn't help but notice the houses on the hill looked the same as the houses on the flat. I wondered how the residents of Wiarton had come to make a distinction between the two. It was clear the hill was considered superior to the flat. Similar to the East versus West argument in Owen Sound. Divided by the Sydenham River there was a long standing rivalry about which side of Owen Sound was best. It was all the same.

The Pacific was packed to the rafters. The roar of the men at their dinner was deafening. I pushed my way through to the bar. Howard was pouring lightning like lightning. Thirsty men bellied up and grabbed their glasses as quickly as they were set down. I waited by the bar. I don't know how, but Howard saw me. Leaned over in mid-pour and said something to one of the other barmen. Busy as he was, the man left. Howard kept pouring. The barman came back. He grabbed a couple of shots. Led me to a table near the front corner of the room. I couldn't believe it was empty. I sat.

The crowd milled around me. Laughing. Drinking. Gossiping. Talking tough. Liquor sloshed out of glasses as the constant movement of the crowd jostled elbows. They were hard working, hard drinking men of all nationalities.

They cut lumber for a living. When the lumber was gone, they would be too. West with the rails.

The wall of men near my table opened like a door and Sil walked through. My jaw dropped.

"What are you doing here?" I asked in surprise.

"Nice to see you too," he smiled as we shook. "To change," he added, grabbing one of the shots off the table.

I saw stars. It was lightning. White hot. The most potent moonshine I'd ever had. When I could see again I looked at Sil. His eyes were watering.

"Whoaaaa," I wheezed. I'd have to talk to Howard about that stuff. "So what are you doing here?"

"Oak Hall has been sold."

"What?" Oak Hall was Sil's life.

"Oak Hall has been sold. We're doing inventory. I'm off for a couple of days. Eddie asked me to help out. So did Lori."

"Hold on. You saw Eddie? He was in Clavering."

"He came back when…oh…you don't know. Glori has disappeared."

CHAPTER NINE
TEMPTATION

"What?"

"She got into a Packard. The same one you chased into the swamp."

"I've gotta get back!"

Sil stopped me before I could leave the table. "Hold on. Sit down." He half forced me back into the chair. The barman brought a bottle. I hardly felt the next two shots.

"What happened?"

"Glori and the Sergeant Major had another fight. The name-calling kind. She took off. Someone saw her get into that Packard. Headed for Wiarton."

"The cops had that car."

"Someone came to get it. For the owner."

"He's from Wiarton."

"Uh huh. Alexander McNeill."

"The politician?"

"The politician."

"The cops on it?"

"Inspector Blood. And Oddball. Since it was on the highway, it was technically in both counties.

"Well?"

"Nothing. The car was picked up by McNeill's son. Malcolm. No one can find him. Off on some bird hunt. Blood says he talked to another guy up there, Peacock, I think it was, who says Glori wants to stay. Showed Blood a note that said so."

"Where's Eddie?"

"Clavering."

"I guess I better go to McNeill's place."

"The family wants you to."

"Can you and Eddie help?"

"Yes. He's supplying a party there. Friday night."

"Of course! At the Corran. McNeill's place. You said the politician, but I didn't make the connection."

"We're gonna grab her."

"Okay." I poured us each another drink. I thought of Lori. I should be with her.

"She wants you to stay and do this," Sil read my mind. It was something about growing up together. Always knowing someone's mind. "Will you be through with the gang by then?

"Yes. I need Eddie to get me some machine guns."

"How many?" he asked, when he got over his surprise.

The smell of broasting chicken drifted past my nose. Hunger poked at my gut. I took another drink.

"Three. Tomorrow."

"Jeez, Murph. That's short notice."

"I need at least one that works. Otherwise, just fill a bag with old gun parts. I'll bluff."

"Where you want to pick 'em up?"

"I'll come to Clavering. Noon."

"Looks like a conspiracy." A voice broke into our conversation. Oddball sat down beside me. Without waiting for an invitation he grabbed the bottle and took a long hit. It was good he never actually lit those stinky cigars he liked. He would have blown us all to kingdom come.

"How's it going?" he asked, replacing the bottle. "Hello Sil."

"I'm sure you know some of it."

"I do," he said authoritatively. "Angel got his wings. Derry Wallace ate a slug the size of my thumb. From your gun, is my guess."

"They were trying to kidnap Miss McDermid."

"I know."

"It was the one-armed man."

"I know that too." A packet wrapped in butcher's paper and tied with twine thumped onto the table in front of me. The wooden arm.

"I want you to give that to him for me. When you find him. After you're done with the gang."

"I think he may be their boss."

"So much the better. I want him in my jail."

"More than you want the gang?"

"If he's the boss, he is the gang."

"Exactly," I said.

I told him what had been happening. At the end he let out a low whistle.

"So you mean ta tell me this Goldy's the same guy as was on the train? The number two man?"

"Yes. That is what I mean to tell you." Some days I wondered how Oddball kept his job. Compensation for his injury perhaps.

"How soon will you be done with the gang? And Goldy?"

"Two days. Thursday afternoon. Then on Friday I've got to go to the Corran. To get Glori."

"I heard about that. Blood says she's a guest up there."

"Yeah, well, her parents want her home. By the way, what are you doing here? Wiarton is in Bruce County."

"Keppel Township is in Grey. That's where the hideout is."

"At Bruce's Caves."

"See. That's what I thought." A pulp that had once been a cigar rolled between his lips. "Here's what I want ya to do," he said. "Get enough on the gang so we can haul 'em in. The one-armed man must be the boss. Maybe you'll catch him right away. If you don't I'll squeeze Goldy while you go up to the Corran. He'll sing. After you've got Glori you can go after the real prize."

"The one-armed man."

"Bingo," Oddball said.

"Okay, it's a plan." The place was beginning to clear out. "I'd better go."

"Keep in touch," Oddball said.

"By the way. What'd you tell the cops here about the jailbreak?"

"Oh, yeah," he chuckled. "The chief forgot. Said it seemed more realistic anyways."

"A little too realistic. I had to shoot a horse at Oxenden."

"Don't worry. County pays. See you." He walked off with barely a wobble. Sil and I had another drink.

"Have you seen the paper?" Sil asked when Oddball was out of sight.

"No," I said. "I've been in the bush."

Sil unfolded a copy of *The Canadian Echo*, Wiarton's contribution to the world of journalism. On the front page the headline "Hero Identified" topped a photo of me.

"What!"

"It came out yesterday."

"This could be a problem."

"Especially if the boss saw it."

"Why do we have to have reporters?" I asked.

"There's always muck to be raked," Sil responded.

I folded the paper up and handed it back to him. "At least none of the gang will see this. I'm not even sure they can read. What I need to do now is wrap this case up before the boss meets with Goldy again." I suddenly remembered what Sil had told me when I arrived. "What do you mean, Oak Hall sold?"

"New owners. We're doing inventory. I decided to come up here for a few days."

"You're not out of a job, are you?"

"I don't know."

"Are you worried?"

"Sure. What'll happen to Marth? And the boys?"

"You can resurrect that daredevil act of yours to make money."

"What?"

"Balancing on bridge railings."

"Very funny."

"Sorry," I said, "but I don't think you've got anything to worry about. You're a good man and if the new owners of Oak Hall can't see that, they don't deserve you."

He laughed. "Right. I'll keep that in mind."

"Good. See you tomorrow. By the way, can you mail this for me?" I asked, handing him the letter I'd written for Davey. It was addressed to *Ups and Downs*.

"Sure," he said, taking it with him.

★★★

The ride back was uneventful. I arrived at the camp late in the afternoon. I'd stopped beside Gleason Brook to hide the arm in a tree. Arriving with it would be a bit too obvious. I'd pick it up later, when I went after its owner.

There was no one around as I unsaddled Scotty. I decided to take a look in the cave. Following the smell of wood smoke, I wandered back. Triangular in shape, it wasn't deep. Along one wall a fire smouldered. Over it a large pot of mash bubbled. The earthy smell of fermentation filled the air. A copper tube led from the top of the pot into a deep chasm in the wall. The temperature couldn't have been more than 50 degrees. A large brown jug collected the moonshine from the other end of the tube. I turned from the still. Along the back wall were cases of food. Cans of fruit and vegetables from Smart Brothers in Collingwood. Tinned beef, fish and chicken. They were supplied for the long haul. I hated to disappoint them.

The horses grew restive. Someone was coming. I crossed back to Scotty and picked my kit up. Bottles clinked in my saddlebag.

"Whatcha got there, Verle?" Jug called from the front of the cave.

"You startled me," I said.

"Saw ya come in. From the perch. Seemed to be takin' a long time. So I come down."

"I went back and looked at the still. Nice set up. Stuff it kicks out is pretty wicked."

"The deadly green shit."

I laughed. "It's green?"

"Guess ya couldn't see that by the firelight."

"What are you using for mash?"

"This 'n' that."

"Oh, I got some whisky. In Wiarton." My saddlebag made that delightful clinking sound again.

"Great," he said as we left the cave and started up the path.

"Did ya get them guns?" he asked.

"What's it to you?"

"I never fired one before."

"I did. In the army. Who's the boss?"

"How d'ya mean?" he asked innocently.

"It's not Goldy. He's not smart enough."

"Bad news," he said, ignoring me.

"What?"

"Goldy wants to fight ya. He tol' me."

"Does he."

"Yeah. Anyone bigger'n him, he's gotta whip 'em."

"To show just because he's short, it doesn't mean he isn't tough. Right?"

"How'd you know?"

Standing less than an inch over six feet, I'd run into Goldy's type before. What they lacked in height, they tried to make up for in power. "I just know. So who is it? The boss."

A look of hope crossed his face. "You gonna take over? When you get the guns?"

"Maybe. Who is it?"

"Don't know. Really."

"Who does?"

"Goldy. And Derry too. At least he did."

"Did?"

"He's not here any more, is he."

"Where'd he go?"

He gave me a funny look. "Don't know. Don't care."

A shower of pebbles from above stopped us. We were right under the outcrop. I looked but couldn't see anyone.

"I thought you were on watch," I whispered.

"I am."

"Who was up there?"

"I don't know," he said, pale. "I just hope whoever it was didna hear us."

But for the clinking of the bottles, we walked the rest of the way to the top in silence.

★★★

Everyone was around the fire. Jug had gone back to his perch. A chorus of shouts welcomed me. Van jumped up and shook my hand. Across the fire, Colleen smiled at me. Goldy looked grim, as always. Artie ignored me.

The air around the camp was thick with the good smell of stew cooking. It was coming from a pot that hung over the fire. I wondered if a man could drown in his own saliva. Dropping my kit, I pulled a bottle out. Crossing around the fire, I sat down next to Goldy. I yanked the cork out with my teeth and spit. After a long slug I passed the bottle to Goldy. He grabbed it away with a grunt and made me look like a rank amateur.

"T'anks," he muttered. After another drink, "Well?"

"Maybe tomorrow. I have to go see. Got the cash?"

"I got yer moola. You ain't gettin' it 'til tomorrow. And then Pete and Artie is goin' with ya to make sure ya come back."

"Whatever." I took another drink. Without his noticing, I looked Goldy over. Thick arms and chest. Legs like tree trunks. Hands like stone. I didn't want to fight him. I supposed it was inevitable. It always was with guys who had something to prove. I left the bottle with him and took two more out to pass around. Then I sat down next to Van.

"We've gotta talk," he said.

"Go ahead."

"Goldy wants to fight you," he continued in a low voice.

"I know. What did you do today?"

"What do you think?"

"Rob a car?"

"Two."

"Two?"

"Uh huh. Near Big Bay."

"What was the take?"

"Forty-two dollars. I think." I whistled inaudibly. Van caught my meaning.

"It's a lot. Most honest jobs are worth less than five a day," he said.

"They disable the cars?"

"Yeah and I can see why they want the machine guns. They just stood there and plugged shot after shot into the cars. Took a long time but they finally shut both down. Machine gun would do it a lot faster."

"Three hundred dollars is still a lot of money to spend if they're only taking forty or fifty bucks a day."

"Goldy said something while we were out. Sort of like he was gloating. Said they wouldn't be living on chicken feed much longer."

"You think they're planning something else?"

"Trying to kidnap Miss McDermid from the train was a definite step up."

"True."

"It's just a feeling, and I haven't got anything to confirm it but I think they're gonna hold up a train, or a bank maybe…"

"What are you two boys whisperin' about?" Colleen asked from directly behind me. Her hand rested on my shoulder.

"Just talking," Van said.

"Goldy broke his left knee once," she said in a conversational tone. Her breath felt warm in my ear. Too warm. At the hint of his name in the air, Goldy's head shot up. He'd heard it. By the look on his face he had no idea who'd spoken it.

"Thanks," I said. She left her hand on my shoulder. Van passed the bottle to me and I passed it to Colleen. While she drank, Davey and Shelagh moved closer to us. Davey had a deck of cards and from inside his jacket he produced a homemade cribbage board.

"You boys play?"

"Yes." I said.

"Spent a lot of time playin' while I was in the hospital," Van said. "While I was recoverin', eh."

"What happened to ya?" Colleen asked, passing the bottle back into the circle.

"Bomb fell on him," I said.

"Really?" Colleen asked.

"Yup," Van responded. "Only lasted a month at the front. A bomb dropped on me and some of the boys. I was lucky."

"How long were ya in the hospital then, Pete?" Shelagh asked.

"Five months. Maybe more. I kinda lost track."

Davey shuffled and dealt the cards. I got skunked in the first two games and gave up. Van was too good for me.

The others kept playing. I got up to stretch my legs. Leaving the fire, I walked east, away from the edge of the cliff. Cedar gave way to hardwood. The boulders I'd come to associate with Keppel Township were everywhere. Sunlight slanting through the leaves cast a brilliant green light. A couple of hundred yards from the camp I came to a three-foot stone fence. A falling branch cracked like gunshot. The cattle on the other side of the fence stared. When nothing else happened, they went back to grazing. I watched as they wandered aimlessly. I heard another branch crack. I'd hoped Goldy would follow me out. Thugs like him weren't always as tough without an audience.

I turned expecting the worst and instead got the best. Colleen was coming towards me through the trees. Perspiring from the walk, she glowed with effort. Her smile and her eyes were bright when she got to my side. For a moment I wished it had been Goldy. He would have been easier to deal with.

"What're ya doin' out here?" She leaned against the stone fence and ran a hand through her hair. It shimmered in the sun.

"Needed a walk. To clear my head."

"Ya don't mind me joinin' ya?"

"Of course not."

"They can be pretty nosy," she said.

"What?"

"Them cows." They had in fact come a lot closer.

"Must get pretty boring. Just standing in that field all day, chewing."

"Sort of like hiding in the bush all day. With nothing to do." She smiled an invitation.

I'd always liked redheads. I tried not to think about it. Thought instead about being engaged. "It doesn't allow for much of a social life."

She snorted. "You and Pete are the most excitement we've had in two months."

"Where were you before? During the winter?"

"An abandoned homestead. Down country. We wintered there. Came here when the snow went."

It was difficult not to notice her figure.

"Why?" I asked.

"Why what?"

I tried to focus. "Why here?"

"To be closer to the boss. We hardly seen him at all down country. Now we can't get rid of him."

"I thought no one knew him. Just Goldy. And Derry."

The pain on her face made me wish I hadn't said it.

"That's true," she said. "Just Goldy. He's always goin' off to meet the boss. I'm not sure where. Can't be far. He's never gone long."

Important information. But I couldn't be alone with her any longer.

"I'm starving," I said. "Let's go back and get somethin' to eat."

Goldy met us outside the camp. His habitual scowl was deepened by drink. He looked at Colleen and then me. Knowing what I'd been thinking, I could imagine what he was thinking.

"Git back ta camp," he barked at Colleen.

"We're goin'," Colleen said.

"Not him. You." He pointed a stubby finger in the direction of the others.

"Go on," I said in response to her questioning look. Goldy didn't like her consulting me before following his order. More fuel to whatever fire was simmering inside him.

When she was gone, he advanced. He got so close I could feel the heat coming off his body. He had to look up to talk to me. "You and me. Now." Spit flew from his lips. I barely managed to not wipe my face.

"You don't want to fight me, Goldy."

"Yes I do." His teeth were clenched.

"You'll lose."

He moved closer and spit some more.

"Did not!" Before Goldy could speak, a scream from near the fire cut between us.

Goldy moved quickly. I arrived at the fire right behind him. Jug had returned from his watch. He and Davey were fighting.

"Liar." Jug threw himself on Davey. It was an awkward move and Davey countered with a punch to the gut. Jug dropped like a rock. Davey was on top in an instant. He peppered the fallen boy with combinations. Van tired of watching and waded in. He dragged Davey up by the arms.

"Verle, c'mon and help me here," he called over his shoulder.

"Sure." I brushed past Goldy and into the camp. Bent down to see how Jug was. He winked and smiled. Then groaned.

"Oh, my guts. Jeez, Davey, ya kilt me." Thoroughly confused I helped him up.

"S'matter Pete? You don't like a game o' fists?" Goldy asked, stepping back into the circle of the fire.

"I thought they might kill each other," Van said.

"Ha!" Goldy slapped his knee and laughed. "These boys is always fightin'." He sat down and drank. Everyone relaxed. Van winked at me.

"Drink, Verle?" he asked.

"Sure," I said. We went back to my kit and sat down. Van drank and passed me the bottle.

"Their idea," he whispered.

"The fight?"

"Uh huh."

"Why?"

"Colleen told us what was happenin'. They figgered Goldy was gonna make his move."

"He was."

I looked at Jug and Davey. They were drinking together and laughing. Jug caught me with another wink. I winked back. I owed them.

★★★

Supper toned things down. Food always did that. It's why socials had a lunch at midnight. Quell the combat with cuisine. By dark, things were cleaned up. Goldy had cooled off a bit. He was still drinking. Looked like he could pass out at any time. Davey pulled out the guitar. The music was as enchanting as it had been the night before. Rather than folk songs, he played some popular tunes. We sang along with *Baby Face, Ain't We Got Fun, When My Baby Smiles at Me,* and *A Pretty Girl Is Like A Melody*. Colleen got a sweater and a rifle and went for her watch. Measured in empties, the night went on a long time. Goldy checked out early. A full moon rose. Night was day until it passed over the clearing.

I fell asleep. Hands nowhere near my gun. In the early morning I woke and Colleen was beside me. I thought she'd come to get me for watch. Until she spooned in behind me and wrapped her arms around my waist.

"I'm cold," she whispered.

CHAPTER TEN
GANG AT WORK

The sun was barely up when Van woke me. His hand was across my mouth. Colleen was gone. The fire had smouldered down to an angry looking pile of coals.

"Someone out there," he whispered in my ear. He took his hand off my mouth. Got up and melted back into the shadows. Goldy snorted and rolled over. I wondered where Colleen had gone as I followed Van into the woods. He was waiting by the overhang.

"Who is it?"

"Sil."

"Is he crazy?"

"As Joe Hunt's dog, I'd say."

"Where is he?"

"Straight out. Thirty yards."

"What's he want?"

"Haven't seen him."

"What?"

"He gave me the whistle."

"From when he and I were kids?"

"The same."

"Okay. I'll go out. If anyone comes, start shooting."

"Like he's running and you're chasing."

"Try not to hit us."

"Right."

★★★

Dawn hadn't touched the bushes below the cliff. The going was tricky. Rocks covered in moss. Wet with dew. Here and there a crevice. Not to mention the thickets of cedar. In the end, Sil and I blundered into one another. He was going around a thicket one way, I the other. We met in the middle.

"If you hear shots, run."

"I'm not gonna ask."

"I am. Do you know the risk? Why are you here?"

"There's a delay on the guns. You can't get them until dark."

"Why?"

"Eddie can't get them sooner."

"Okay. You better get out of here."

"There's one more thing."

"What?"

"Lori is on her way up."

"What!"

"She'll be in Clavering on Thursday. Then she's going to the Corran on Friday."

"The Corran!"

"The Sergeant Major is coming too."

"What! Why?"

We heard the shot at the same time the slug ripped through the trees above us. Sil was off. He shouted at me over his shoulder.

"The stone school in Clavering. At dark."

"Right." I said to the spot where he'd been standing. I pulled my pistol. Moving as quickly as I could in another direction, I fired two rounds.

"Over here!" I shouted at Van.

He fired a couple of shots in the direction I'd headed. I ran fifty yards then turned back to the camp. Partway, I ran into Goldy. Literally. We both hit the ground. He was up and snarling in a second. I was up. But I didn't snarl.

"Whoever he was, he got away."

"Did ya see 'im?"

"Nope."

"Did ya hit 'im?"

"Don't think so."

"Let's see yer pistol."

"Why?"

"I wanna see it." He was getting aggressive. His breath stank. I pulled the pistol so he'd shut his mouth.

"Hand it over," he demanded.

I pulled the clip out. I didn't want to be shot with my own gun. I'd seen what it could do.

"Hmm, interesting." He pretended to know what he was doing. After a moment he handed the weapon back. I took it from him and reloaded. When I looked up I caught him smiling.

"Let's get back to camp." He turned and headed off. I stared after him and wondered about that smile.

★★★

"When ya gettin' them guns?" Goldy asked after breakfast.

"Tonight."

"I thought you said noon."

"Must have heard me wrong. Tonight's what I said."

"Fine. You can go out with the boys. Do a spot o' work."

"Sounds like fun."

"Be even more fun after you an' Jug see ta them horses."

★★★

We were careful not to talk near the overhang. Anyone could be listening. Jug spoke once we got inside the cave.

"Colleen fancies ya."

"Yeah. So?"

"So what about it?" He said it casually, as though it didn't matter. But every muscle in his body, every move he made told the truth.

"I've got a girl."

He relaxed and picked up a shovel.

"Thanks for last night."

"We seen Goldy at work before. Knew just when to start. To keep you from gettin' hurt, that is."

"Did you get hurt?"

"No more'n at the farm."

"Where?"

"My situation. With Barnardos."

"Why'd you leave?"

"The farmer, he didn't have no patience with me."

"He was rough with you?"

"Yeah." Jug shovelled up a pile of dung. "I thought they'd fix it when Barnardos come ta visit."

"What happened?"

"No one came."

"Someone from the home was supposed to visit you? And they didn't?"

"I don't hold it against 'em. They got me outta the gutter."

"So you left."

"Yeah." He stopped shovelling and pulled his shirt up. Before it was over his shoulders I could see the scars. "I didn't see that I needed no more o' this."

"He whipped you?"

"Had nearly two years left on me contract. Knew I wouldn't live to see the end."

I finished the feeding and watering. Outside I leaned against the corral while Jug finished mucking out.

"How'd you hook up with the gang?"

"Met Davey in Shelburne last fall. We went on the bum together. Coupla months ago we run into Goldy at the Munshaw House. You know it?"

"That's the hotel in Flesherton."

"Right. Well the boss was there too. He stayed upstairs. We only seen Goldy. He offered us work and board. Easy money. So we came."

"How about the girls? Where'd they come in?"

"Derry found them on a trip to Shelburne before Christmas. They was in a bad way, so he brung 'em back. They spent the winter down in some house near Ceylon. That's what I heard, anyhow."

"So was Shelagh Goldy's girl before you and Davey came along? Or Artie's?"

"Naw. Goldy and Artie don't seem too interested."

"How about the boss?"

"Never met him. I heard he's a gentleman. These ain't the kind of girls for the likes of him."

"You've never met the boss? How can you rob folks for someone you don't know?"

"I got lots of money. Before I had nuthin'."

"You're breaking the law."

"Fat lot of good the law done me on that farm."

"There's jobs."

"Is that what ya think it's all about?"

"What else?"

"After I ran, the farmer told people I done things."

"Did you?"

"No. But they're gonna send me back to the street!" he said in a voice that was raw with pain. It was the driving force in his life. Not to go back.

"London was bad," I said.

"You'll never know how bad," he said. But he was wrong. His face told it all.

"All done? Good. Saddle up," Goldy called out from behind us. He was on his way down the ramp.

Jug started saddling one of the gang's horses.

"We going somewhere?" I asked.

"Work."

"Saddle's up top," I said.

"Git goin'. And hurry up. Times a wastin'."

The village of Hepworth was a crossroad. To the north, Clavering and Wiarton. To the south, Park Head. Lake Huron was west. Shallow Lake and Owen Sound were east. There wasn't much to the place. Tavern. Bank. Dry goods. A small hotel.

"Here. This is good," Goldy said.

We were north of the village. A heavily wooded stretch of the Wiarton Road. Trees came right up to the gravel. In some places they crowded it to one lane. The spot Goldy had chosen was near Shepherd Lake. We took the horses twenty yards back from the road. Davey had the tire strapped to his saddle. A rope ran through the spokes and around the horn. He undid it. The heavy wheel thudded to the ground.

"Okay. Let's go." Goldy led the way back to the road. Davey picked the wheel up and we followed, cutting through to the road's edge. Goldy and Jug crossed to the other side and hid behind the trees. Davey dropped the tire in the middle of the road and came back to where Van and I were hidden.

"Now what?" I asked.

"We wait."

"How long?"

"Until a car comes," Van answered.

We hunkered down. Davey pulled out a bottle and passed it around.

"The drivers give you trouble?" I asked.

"Sometimes. Depends how many of us there are."

"Safety in numbers, eh?"

"Right."

"Jug told me how you guys met Goldy. What's your story?"

"Who cares?"

"Jug gave me his angle. I just wanna know yours."

"Jug talks too much. It's gonna get him in trouble."

"He was in a black humour. That's all."

"The coppers'll send him home."

"You too?"

"Naw. They want ta send me to another farm. I'd rather do somethin' else."

"I know what you mean. After the war I couldn't find work. So I went to a farm. Didn't last. You planning to stick with these guys long?"

"Naw. I'm savin' my take."

"How much do you get?"

"Ten percent."

"Each?"

"Yeah."

"So you got four bucks yesterday?"

"And twenty cents. Tonight it'll be less. There's more of us."

"What's that got to do with it?"

"Boss gets half the take. Goldy gets twenty per cent. We get the rest."

"You guys need a union. What's the boss do for his cut?"

"He's the boss," Davey answered, as though it explained everything.

Van sat up. I heard it too. A car. It had already started gearing down. By the time it stopped we were at the road's edge. The driver left the engine running while he stepped out to look at the tire. A moment later, Goldy was on the road behind him. Gun drawn. His face was hidden by the same mask he'd worn on the train. I suddenly had the urge to arrest him then and there. Teach him a lesson. I couldn't. I had bigger fish to fry.

The rest of us surrounded the car. The female passenger screamed. The driver whirled around and found himself staring down the barrel of a .45 calibre. Goldy was on the other end.

"Empty yer pockets."

The man reached into his pockets. He turned out a small amount of money. A few bits of paper. Nothing else. Her bag held even less. A compact. Handkerchief. A lipstick. A couple of coins.

"Wasn't even worth stoppin' ya," Goldy shouted at the man. He strode to the car and started firing at the engine. Six shots and it was still running. I pulled my gun out and took aim. Compared to the .45, my gun sounded like a cannon. One shot and the car died. A cheer went up from the boys. Much to Goldy's disgust.

We left the hapless couple and their wounded car. Rode southeast through Hepworth. Towards Shallow Lake and Owen Sound.

"We'll catch the next car before it gets to that one," Davey explained.

"What if someone comes up the Bruce County Road? Or from Sauble Beach."

"More come this way. The odds are in our favour."

We rode half an hour before Goldy picked a spot. It was identical to the last one. But we didn't have to wait as long. A fast coupe pulled to a stop moments after we set the tire out. I couldn't see the cursing driver from my hiding spot. But I knew the voice well enough. No one could swear as well as Razor Eddie.

"What the…" Eddie reached for his gun.

"Go ahead mister. Try." Goldy stuck a gun in Eddie's face. Eddie froze. "Empty yer pockets."

Eddie had to know I was with them. Even so, I was afraid he might try something brave. So I stepped over to the car. Sil was in the passenger seat.

"Empty yer pockets!" I shouted an inch from his face. I thought he might laugh.

"No need to yell, Goliath," Sil said, emptying his pockets. I looked back at Eddie and Goldy. Eddie was staring Goldy down. While he was emptying his pockets.

"Look in back," Goldy shouted at me. Davey and Jug moved in on Sil. I went round and gave the knob on the trunk a twist. The lid popped, revealing three boxes. Machine guns.

"Anythin' there?" Goldy shouted.

"Nothing." I slammed the lid down. I hoped he wouldn't check.

"Alright you. Back in the car." Goldy pushed his pistol in the small of Eddie's back. Jug and Davey had retreated with the loot and the tire.

Eddie dropped to the ground and mule kicked Goldy. I guess he didn't want his car shot. He hit the knee Colleen had told me about. Goldy went down hard. Gears ground, the engine revved. Sil jerked the car forward. Eddie hurled himself into the vehicle as it roared past Goldy.

"Shoot!" Goldy screamed.

I brought my pistol to bear, confident I would miss. Before I could shoot I heard a commotion in the bushes. Jug and Davey were yelling. Then Scotty came crashing through the brush. The revving of the engine had been too much for him. As the speeding car passed he took off after it. The blue stinking vapour of the car hung in the air. In the distance Eddie and Sil's laughter carried over the sound of the car. Then they were out of sight. Scotty hot on their trail.

"That's some horse," Goldy said.

"I'll see you back at camp."

"Wait a minute." He grabbed my sleeve as I walked past. "Where d'ya think yer goin'?"

"I won't be much use to you without a horse."

He looked at me carefully, then he let go of my sleeve.

★★★

It was mid afternoon when Scotty and I arrived back at camp. I'd found him in a field south of Wiarton. It was as good as life got for a gelding. A car to chase, a field to pillage. We'd ridden back along the shore road and hadn't seen a soul. The boys were back. Van told me they'd taken another car at Poverty Corner. Lorne Saunders' place.

Lorne's farm was at the intersection of Clavering Road and County Road 17. He'd done just about everything in life a man could do. Worked on the Fort Churchill and Flin Flon railways. Homesteaded in Saskatchewan. A cop and a firespotter. Despite the name, Poverty Corner had twenty-three outbuildings. A pond at the back had a live alligator in it. The reason most people knew him was because of his pet armadillo. Lorne had brought it back from one of his many trips. It was young and took Lorne to be its parent. Followed him everywhere.

"When he heard the shootin' Lorne came runnin' with a muzzle loader," Van said.

"Did ya ask him if he wanted to sell it?" I asked.

"Sell it?" Davey was eavesdropping.

"Pete here collects guns."

"Oh."

"We didn't hang around long enough for me to ask. Maybe I'll go back some other time. Like when we're not pulling a heist in his front yard," Van laughed.

"What happened?"

"It misfired. We rode away."

"Surprised he didn't sick the 'gator on ya."

"The what?" Davey asked.

"He keeps an alligator in his pond."

"What's that?"

"It's a fish ya daft bugger." Jug arrived, bottle in hand.

"It eats fish," Van said.

"And men," I said. Jug stopped laughing.

"It's eight feet long. Got a mouth this wide, full of teeth." Van held his arms apart.

"Get off!" Jug said. "I seen it followin' him. It was long, sure, coupla feet. But its head was tiny. Just had that beaky thing."

"What about its skin?" Davey asked.

"That was his armadillo," I said. "Comes from Florida. Same as the gator."

"I thought they was nocturnal," Goldy interjected from across the fire. Everybody stared at him in complete silence. There was something unnatural about Goldy knowing that. Conversation continued as if he hadn't spoken.

"So this 'gator thing is bigger?"

"Uglier too. Pass me that bottle." We'd drunk all the whisky the night before. The rotgut burned its way down.

"Now what?" I asked the boys. They looked at me blankly. I let the sound of conspiracy slip into my voice. "What are your plans, I mean? Y'know, for the future."

"Are you gonna take him out?" Jug whispered, looking sidelong at Goldy. They were in a hurry to be rid of him.

"Doesn't matter," I said. "The question is, what are you boys gonna do?"

"I liked farmin' well enough," Jug said. "Just the situation I didn't like."

"What about robbery, thieving and the like?"

"It's temporary," Davey replied.

"Stop. Now."

"And what?" Jug asked.

"There's always a place for a strong back and willing hands. We've had it with Goldy. Come with us." Van nodded his head in agreement.

Jug and Davey exchanged an unhappy look.

"Boss said he'll kill us if we try to leave. Or if we do anything against him."

"You let me worry about him. How many arms does the boss have?" I asked.

"Huh? What?" Jug said.

"Arms?" Davey asked.

"Never mind."

"Supper!" Shelagh called from beside the fire.

"The girls'd have to come too." Davey said.

"Of course," I said. "Think about it. We'll talk later, after I get back with the guns."

★★★

We rode hard to Clavering. I wanted to get back as quickly as possible. Davey and Jug were convinced. If I could draw them out of camp with the girls, I could take care of Goldy alone. I'd arrest him. At gunpoint if necessary.

We rode down the 12th Line all the way to the Clavering Road and followed it west across the Wiarton Road. The Clavering stone school was a couple of miles along. We got to it just past sundown. I left Artie and Van in the woods. Artie to warn me if anyone uninvited showed up. Van to watch Artie.

Eddie was waiting.

"Sssst." I heard from the deeper shadows of a tree. It was full dark under the canopy so I had to wait for my eyes to adjust. The first thing I picked out was the gleaming barrel of a gun. It wasn't a Thompson.

"What is that?" I asked.

"Just what you ordered."

"It's not a Thompson."

"Naw. It's a Fiat. Made by the Canadian General Electric Company."

"Just one?"

"All I could get on short notice. I've got a bag of parts for you."

"Thanks. How do I load these things?"

Eddie picked up the Fiat. It was two feet long. Double barrelled. From his pocket he pulled a square metal box.

"Detachable magazine." He showed me.

"How many rounds?" I took the gun from him. It weighed about twenty pounds. I unloaded then reloaded it. I tied it and the bag of parts to my saddle horn.

"I think I've got the boys convinced to leave. They think the boss killed, or had Goldy kill, Derry. I'm gonna send them down here tonight. Can you keep an eye on the place?"

"Sure."

"Take them somewhere safe. Then watch for me. I'll be down later. Once I take care of Goldy."

"Okay," he said.

"What about Friday?"

"All set."

"Are Lori and the Sergeant Major here?"

"Tomorrow."

"Okay. See you later."

"Be careful."

"I will."

★★★

Artie begged, so I let him carry the machine gun. It didn't worry me. He hadn't enough ambition to turn the weapon on us. It was dark and the going was slow at first. Then the moon rose and we were able to quicken our pace. Even so, it took time. More than I liked.

We rode single file. Artie was in the lead and I was right behind him. We were at the halfway mark when something began crashing through the bush to our left. The sound grew closer. In the dark it was impossible to see what was coming, but it made a big sound. Instinctively we closed the gap between our horses and waited. Whatever it was, it was headed our way.

It wasn't until I heard his machine gun cock that I realized how frightened Artie was.

"No!" I yelled, too late. My words were lost in the roar of the gun. Artie kept his finger on the trigger even as he fell off his bolting horse. There wasn't much left of the whitetail deer he landed on.

"Nice hunting, Ace," I said looking down on him.

"Thanks."

I dismounted and yanked the gun out of his hands. The barrel was hot enough to make me change my grip.

"That was a stupid thing to do. Have a nice walk."

"Walk?"

"Your horse is gone. We won't make time if we have to carry you and the guns. So I'm taking the guns. You can walk back.

Van chuckled at the hapless Artie as we rode away.

★★★

It was after ten when we got to the base of the cliff. "Leave the horses saddled," I said.

"Do you want me to stay down here?"

"I think…" A shrill scream from the top of the cliff cut me off mid-sentence. Van and I were already running when we heard the shot.

Chapter Eleven
The Boss

Davey was on the ground by the fire with Colleen leaning over him. She pressed her bloody hands against his wound, trying to staunch the flow of blood. Shelagh was screaming. So was Davey. I bent over for a look. He'd taken it in the side. A clean wound. The entry and exit were close together.

"Stop yelling. It's only a flesh wound."

"I'm not yellin' about that. It's the boss! Goldy took Jug ta see the boss."

"Van, get something to wrap it with." I pointed at the wound. "Shelagh, boil some water." She jumped up and set about the task.

"They're gonna kill 'im. I know they are." Davey said. "No one's ever met the boss and lived." I had a flashback to the news that Derry was gone. Now I knew why everyone had been so upset. Meeting the boss wasn't a good thing.

"Where are they?"

"The stone fence."

"Where we met. Yesterday." Colleen said.

I looked at Van. "As soon as he's patched up, take them to Clavering."

"Where are you going?"

"To save Jug."

I ran almost all the way, slowing down at the last so my feet wouldn't betray me. In the clearings, the moon lit my path. It'd be easy to ambush someone from the shadow of the trees. I wished I'd brought the machine gun. A couple of bursts could really break up a party. Van and I had dropped it in our haste to get to the top. I still had the Webley & Scott. Its weight felt good in my hand. Close to the wall I dropped to my knees and crawled.

"He's a detective." A harsh voice broke the silent night. My head tingled. The boss. "What did you tell him?"

"Nuthin'. I swear."

"Give 'im another shot," the voice ordered.

Goldy made a fistic statement. Jug cried out in pain. I spotted them. In the weak glow of a lantern. On the other side of the wall. In the cow field. Behind a piece of beautiful stoney Keppel. Jug was slumped against the rock. Barely on his feet. Goldy stood in front of him. His raised fists were bloody. Beside the rock, the boss was a shadow.

"What did you tell him?" The voice had an educated sound.

"Nuthin'," Jug half sobbed.

"Liar. Goldy overheard you. Confessing to him like he was your priest."

Goldy swung. The air hissed out of Jug like he was a bad tire. As he drew his arm back to punch again, I hoisted myself up and over the wall. The blow and I landed at the same time. The blow with Jug. Me with the ground. I lay still. Listening to see if I'd been caught.

"One more chance," the boss said in a menacing voice.

"I'm tellin' the truth!" Jug screamed.

The boss appeared to consider this. The silence drew out. Goldy concentrated fiercely on Jug. His fists remained up. The snick of a bolt being drawn back broke the silence. Jug moaned.

I got to my feet and fired at the boss. The rock above his head shattered. I sensed rather than saw him jump back in surprise. I dropped and rolled. He returned fire. Hot lead cut through the spot I'd most recently occupied. I fired again and moved closer to the lantern. Ten feet away, I was as close as I could be without being seen. Not close enough to rescue Jug. A second shot rang out and the gun was torn from my hand. I yelled in surprise. Goldy charged.

The boss grabbed Jug and pulled him away from the light. Goldy flung himself towards me with arms spread wide. I ducked, hoping he'd go right over. Instead he bounced off my back, winding me. He hit the ground with less force than if he had gone over. So he was up faster as well. He sent a double shot to my mid-section. His fists didn't just look like stone. They felt like it too. I slapped away his next blow and crossed with a right that rocked his head. I backed away to gain advantage, still waiting for my wind to return. Goldy shook the blow off more quickly than I liked and came again. This time I was ready and hit him with a one-two combination to the mid-section. Then I mashed his turnip with an elbow. He leapt back from me, hands clenched across it.

"Ya broke my nose," he yelled in a distinctly nasal voice.

"It'll only get worse."

"I'm gonna kill you."

"No. You're going to lose. Give up now and I'll only arrest you."

"There was somethin' off about you right from the start."

"You should have done something about it. Now it's too late."

"No it ain't." He dropped his hands. The nose was flat and oozing. He charged like a bull. Head down, shoulders bunched. Fists clenched, arms driving his squat body forward. I waited until he wouldn't have time to react and fell flat. He tripped over me and landed right beside my gun. I got up in a hurry and jumped on him. A left-right combination to the head rattled him. Suddenly it went dark. The lantern was leading the boss and Jug through the bush. They'd been watching from the shadows. The boss knew what I'd told Goldy was true. I was going to beat him.

He twisted his powerful frame and flung me off. I landed hard near my gun. My left shoulder slammed on a piece of rock. My fingers went dead. I heard Goldy scrabbling around in the dirt. On his hands and knees, he was trying to find me. A hand caught hold of my left boot. I instinctively lashed out with my right. It was a good move.

"My eye! Aaaah, my eye," Goldy cried into the night. I gave him another kick for good measure.

"Goodbye, loser." I said feeling around on the ground for my gun. "Follow me and I won't stop to talk. I'll shoot you. Plain as that," I said towards the fallen thug. Then I found my gun and set off through the woods in the direction of the lantern.

The boss wasn't much of a woodsman. Even with the lantern he was making an awful racket. I heard them long before I caught up to the light. The boss was limping for the edge of the cliff. The camp was somewhere off to our left. I hoped Van had gotten the others moving. I followed at a dead run. There was no point in being quiet. I doubted they'd hear me anyway. Though the boss undoubtedly knew I'd be coming. The feeling was back in my left arm. But my shoulder was sore.

I caught up to them at the cliff's edge.

"C'mon, faster." The boss was angrily trying to get Jug moving. His back was to me. I could see Jug alright. He was scared.

"I can't. My ribs. He hurt 'em bad," Jug cried. His breath was whistling in and out.

"You deserved it. I took you in. Treason is what I get back."

"I never…" Jug protested.

"Shut up! You've already done too much talkin'." The boss pulled a gun out of his overcoat. I stepped up behind him and jammed my gun in his back.

"That's enough," I said.

"Not nearly," he replied.

Jug caught sight of me standing behind the boss. Relief swept across his messy face.

"Drop it," I said.

"Why?" he asked. "Maybe I'll kill him. Then you can kill me. Maybe at this range you'll get it right." He waggled his stump for emphasis.

"I'm not going to kill you. That'd be letting you off too easy. No, it's the pokey for you, my friend. Kingston is nice this time of year."

"I won't be going to prison."

"No?"

"Of course not. You can't beat me, D.B. Murphy."

"So you know my name. Big deal."

"From a name, one can learn so much."

I chopped his good arm hard with my gun hand. He cried out in pain and dropped the pistol.

"That's more li…" A yell from behind surprised me. Goldy pinned my arms. It hurt. The boss snarled and grabbed Jug by the scruff of the neck. In a hurry he propelled the boy towards the cliff. I snapped my head back as hard as I could. The sound inside was deafening. Goldy held on. The boss and Jug were at the edge. No time to spare. I squeezed the trigger and removed much of Goldy's right foot. He let go with a roar of pain. I ran.

"Don't!" I shouted, gun raised. At this distance there wasn't much question of me hitting the boss. But there was a problem.

"You won't shoot," he said in flat voice.

"I will."

"At this range, with that gun, you'd kill us both."

He was right. But I wasn't beaten.

"So what do we do now?"

"I suggest you back up," he said. Slowly I bent down.

"And?"

"I will leave."

"Just like that?"

"You can try to follow."

I switched the Webley & Scott into my left hand. I bent and snagged the .32 I carried in my boot.

"I now have a different gun. It won't kill the boy. Surrender."

"Never."

Goldy slammed into me for the third and final time. As I fell, the boss shoved Jug, who went over without a sound. I rolled onto my back and fired with both guns. Goldy died before he hit the ground. I scrambled up and ran to the edge.

"Jug!" I screamed into the night. "Jug!"

The blackness below was untouched by the moon. I couldn't see a thing.

"Jug?" The question came back at me unanswered an instant later. I listened for breathing from below. Moans of pain. Anything. Nothing. Jug was gone. I was seized by fury. There was no time to feel sorry for the boy. His killer was within my reach. And he had been right. He wouldn't be going to Kingston. He wouldn't be leaving the bush.

Unlike the boss, I'd spent a lot of time in the bush. He was city bred, no question. Irish like everyone I'd met so far. But genteel. Superior. Obviously infallible. In his own mind, above the law. I was about to teach him a thing or two, in the only language he understood.

I ran east along the edge and found the lantern in less than five minutes. I crept forward slowly, confident he wouldn't be anywhere near it. He was hoping I'd be stupid enough to walk right up to it. He'd plug me from behind a tree or rock.

I crawled forward until I was about twenty feet away. I set the small gun on the ground and felt around until my hand closed over a baseball-sized rock. I hurled it like a grenade. Smashed the lantern to bits. I hadn't planned it. A lucky throw was all.

A gunshot from close by split the air. The acrid smell of gunpowder burned my nose. The bullet whined off a rock and spent itself in a tree trunk. The muzzle flash had been less than ten feet away. On my right.

I fired. He'd moved and shot back at me from a different spot. I jumped out of the way. The bullet caught the trailing edge of my jacket. My index finger fit through the hole. He was using a big gun.

I moved away from the spot I'd been in. I found a good-sized tree and stood behind it. Not knowing where the boss was, I resolved to stay put until I heard or saw something.

The night settled down. A faint whiff of coal oil came from the smashed lamp. A bat dashed haphazardly past. Somewhere a chorus of tree frogs started singing.

For a long time nothing happened. I tried not to breathe. Apparently the boss was doing the same thing. I'd lost all track of time when I finally spotted the silhouette of his hat, hidden behind a fallen tree.

I decided to circle through the bush and try to come up behind him. It would take longer, but had better potential as a plan.

It took ten minutes. I was quiet on my hands and knees. When I got around and in position, I could see clearly that the log was in fact wearing the hat. The boss was not hiding behind it. Which meant I was in the open again. And he was somewhere nearby waiting. I started to back up. His voice stopped me cold.

"Well, well." He was right behind me. I looked under my right arm. His position was perfect.

I kicked down hard on the toe of his right foot. The scream and the jump were simultaneous. I was right. One of my bullets had caught him in the swamp. He hopped onto his left leg, cursing. I rolled hard and took it out from under him. He fired wild. I kicked and scored another point on the sore foot. He cursed and fired again. This time the shot was closer. It was bad luck when I stumbled getting up. My pistol fell to the ground. I thought I had time to grab it, right up until his gun connected with the back of my head.

I couldn't see a thing when I came to. I was on my back, being pulled by my feet. Dirt and twigs grabbed and tore at my clothes. My arms dragged above my head. There was a bag over my head. That's why I couldn't see. It didn't matter. I was still so far out I couldn't move anyway. I tried issuing a few orders. The head and the hands weren't yet connected. I was pushed into a sitting position.

"Goodbye," the boss said. Then there was nothing but air under me. I landed on a tree. An evergreen of some sort. Branches broke, smashed and cracked as I fell. My clothing was shredded. I twisted and turned, thrown like a straw doll from limb to limb. Each slowed me, but hurt more.

I finally hit one that didn't break. The abrupt stop knocked the wind out of me. I grabbed the branch and hung on. With one hand I tore the bag off my head and stuffed it inside my coat. I felt dizzy. Glad I couldn't see the bottom. Worried I might fall, I shimmied towards the trunk and wedged myself. I rested for a while. Or maybe I blacked out.

I don't know how much time passed. When I finally started moving again, an inventory revealed cuts and abrasions. Sticky with blood or sap. Maybe both. An egg was ready to hatch on the back of my head.

It took me a while to climb down. At the bottom, I decided I should have slept at the top. I hadn't felt bad just lying among the branches. Falling twice more on the way down I felt really good. I started inching my way along in the impenetrable darkness. I couldn't imagine the boss had dragged me far. I thought I'd find Scotty a couple hundred yards away. Jug would be closer.

I looked up once. The trees at the top shone in the moonlight, mocking. Above them stars. Millions. I pushed on, feeling my way from rock to rock, the progress slow. I fell often. I may have walked within feet of Jug, but I didn't see him. Too dark. I hurt too much.

"Scotty," I called in a low voice.

He answered from not too far ahead.

“Keep talking so I can find you.” It took me a second to realize how stupid that sounded. Then I laughed. The cliff curved to my left. I followed and walked smack into one of the fence rails.

“Scotty?”

He shuffled over and gave my face a wet snort. Smelled the pine sap. He was still fully saddled. We’d dropped everything in a heap when Davey was shot. I stumbled into the cave and fumbled across cans, boxes and barrels. Eventually my right closed around the neck of a bottle. I dragged it out. Hoped it wasn’t kerosene. I had my limits. I got the rail down. Shoved the bottle into my saddlebag. Got onto Scotty with some difficulty.

We left the place. I’d have to send the boys back at first light to find Jug. Some new life he’d gotten when he crossed the Atlantic. I doubted there had been anything in his Barnardo days that prepared him for robbery and murder.

I let Scotty find the way. Every step jolted me with pain. The smell coming from the bottle was unmistakably from the deadly green shit. I had some. No surprise when the edge came off my pain immediately.

My existence had boiled down to one goal. Find the one-armed man. The boss. He would pay for the things he’d done. As soon as we had Glori, I’d go after him. He was somewhere nearby. It’s all I needed to know. I’d contact Oddball and get a troop of men out if I had to. We’d find him.

I went back to Oxenden and turned south. I drank some more. I seemed to be drifting in and out of reality. I saw faces. Heard voices. I’m not sure if it was the pain or the deadly green whisky. I saw sunset. Bats flowing out of the caves like smoke. Munitions. Fireflies in the dark. A piano. Lori’s hands. The one-armed man. Jug falling.

I jolted awake. We weren’t moving. I didn’t know where we were. Scotty was eating grass. There was bush in front of us. I looked at the sky. There was light in the east. Dawn was near. Turning in the saddle I waited for my eyes to adjust. It took longer than usual. I had another drink and felt better.

Eventually I thought to look over my shoulder. It was the schoolyard. We were near the back of the property. The school was at the front of the property. I dismounted. Realized as I hit the ground that both of my legs were asleep. I landed in a heap. Pain woke me up in a hurry. There was no one else around. They’d probably left when I didn’t show up.

I got myself under one of the maples and propped my saddlebag against it. I was sleeping before my head got to it.

It took me a long time to wake up. I know because when I opened my eyes I was surrounded by a gang of kids. Schoolchildren arranged around me in a semi-circle. Staring. Before I had time to be surprised, the teacher arrived. She pushed her way through the children. We looked at one another. Midway past five feet. Her look was dour. A real teacher look. Little black framed glasses perched on the end of her nose. Her mouth narrowed.

"Well?" she asked with authority.

"Sorry ma'am." I stood up slowly. Her look said she appreciated the cost of the gesture.

"All right children. Go and play." She clapped her hands to break it up. Protective, a couple of bigger boys hung around. "That's all right Bert, Harry," she said to them. They turned and went off in the direction of a group which had gathered around Scotty. They were giggling and pointing at his bald spot.

"Do you know where you are?"

"The stone school in Clavering ma'am."

"What are you doing here?"

"Meeting someone. Ma'am."

"Mrs. Hargrave."

"D.B. Murphy, ma'am. Mrs. Hargrave. I'm working for the High Constable. Marc Scott. I was spying on a gang not far from here. There was trouble."

"You don't need to tell me that young man. You're in pain, I can see that. When I came to see what the children were looking at, all I could smell was liquor. I thought you were a common drunk. I can see you're not."

"Thank you."

"What can I do for you?"

"Nothing. I'll be going."

"What about your rendezvous?"

"If anyone comes looking, I'll be in Wiarton. At the Pacific."

"Fine. If anyone comes I'll let them know."

"One more thing," I said.

"Well?"

"If the man looking for me only has one arm, be extra sure he gets the message."

She gave me a strange look. "Fine." She walked back towards the school. A moment later the bell began to ring. Boys and girls of all ages flocked to the doors.

I picked up my saddlebag and the bottle. I didn't suppose Mrs. Hargrave would think too kindly of me if I left it behind for her students. At that moment, it was the last thing I wanted to see. The night's relief had become the morning's pain.

In the full daylight what I could see of me looked bad. My pants were torn and bloody. The leather jacket I wore had protected my upper body. I wasn't sure what damage my face had suffered. My ribs ached. Bruised but not broken. I'd have to think about charging Oddball for mileage.

I felt like a pine, walking over to Scotty. My limbs were stiff and sore. The bending parts didn't want to. Which complicated the process of mounting.

I made it up after a couple of tries and rode off without looking at the school. I didn't want to know if anyone had seen how goofy I looked.

I arrived at the Pacific long before the dinner rush. Howard took one look at me and ran to get Sil. Soon they were both in the bar. Sil had his suitcase in one hand.

"What happened to you?"

"I killed Goldy."

"What?" He dropped the case and led me to a chair.

"It was self defence. The one-armed man killed Jug. I tried to catch him. That's when I had to kill Goldy. The one-armed man ambushed me and threw me off the cliff. I landed in a tree and here I am. I want something to eat. I want to go to bed."

"I was just leaving. Going to Eddie's. Why don't you come too?"

"You couldn't get me on a horse."

"Okay then. What about a bath?"

"Later. Just get me some food and a bed."

I slept all day. Before supper, Sil woke me. Half an hour in a tub of hot water and I didn't feel too bad.

"You need a doctor?" Sil asked after I was dressed. The room was the one in which he'd spent the week.

"I'll see Doc Evans when we get home. Got any tape?"

A search of the Pacific turned up a roll. I taped some of the larger problems.

"Lori is coming up tonight," Sil said.

"To Clavering?"

"No. Here. She's in Clavering. While you were asleep I rode out and told everyone what happened. It was all I could do to keep Lori from coming right away. I told her you needed sleep."

"I did. Oh." Out of habit I'd started to put on my shoulder holster. I suddenly remembered I'd dropped my gun. And something else.

"Did they find Jug?"

"I left before they got back from Oxenden."

"They?"

"Eddie and his man Red went out there with Davey as their guide. Left Shelagh and Colleen with the Sergeant Major and Lori."

"How'd they take it? About Jug, I mean."

"Hard. What'd you expect?"

"Just that." In my mind's eye Jug went over the cliff again. Again. Again. I was always too late.

"Nobody blames you."

"I do."

"You tried to save him, Murph."

"Tried."

"C'mon." He put his hand on my shoulder. "You can't do this to yourself."

"He died because he talked. To me."

"He would have died anyway from what you've told me of the one-armed man." Sil was right. But I'd been right there. I'd seen him die and couldn't do a thing about it.

"What now?" I asked.

"Can you ride?"

"Might have to go slow."

"Let's save Lori the trip. Go down to Clavering for the night."

"Okay."

Eddie's place was in Bruce County, not far from the stone school. A hundred-acre lot. The house near the road. It was a big fieldstone job. Probably built in the '70s. Older than me by a long shot. I could see a chicken coop, several outbuildings and a large new barn.

We rode straight up the lane. Lori came out onto the big front porch and waved. My spirits lifted. I waved back and kicked Scotty to a trot. I wanted to jump off and into her arms. I decided against it. The brief trot had reminded me of a few injuries. I dismounted with due care. The Sergeant Major, Eddie and Van had come onto the porch. Shelagh, Colleen and Davey followed.

"Oh, Murph," Lori said and wrapped her arms around my neck. She kissed me on the mouth. Clung to me for a moment. Then stepped back, looked me over and said, "You're a mess."

"Should see the other guy," I said.

"Hey Buddy," Van slapped me on the shoulder. I tried not to wince.

"You're late," Eddie said, smiling. Everyone else crowded around. I gave up trying to answer all the questions at once. Lori grabbed me by the hand and led me into the house. It was quieter inside the cool dark hall. Lori's mouth was hot against mine.

"Everyone else went around the back," she said when we came up for air.

"Except Sil. He went back home. Been away too long already."

"I'm sure Marth has her hands full with those two boys."

We kissed again.

"I'm glad you're here," I said.

"Me too."

"Should we go outside?"

"I like it in here just fine."

There was a fire roaring in an open pit when we went out back.

"Finally," Eddie shouted.

Wooden lawn chairs circled the fire. To one side of the dirt yard the harsh clang of metal on metal announced horseshoes. Van and Davey were playing. The girls were watching. Colleen looked at us over her shoulder then quickly turned back. Eddie and the Sergeant Major were sitting beside the fire. Eddie poured Lori and I each a glass of what they were drinking.

"What is it?" I asked.

"Smell it," Eddie said with a sly grin.

I took a hesitant whiff expecting the lining of my nose to burn.

"That's not Clabba Killer," I said. Smooth, it carried the hint of a peat fire. I took a sip. It was the first time whisky had ever caressed my throat on its way down.

"Oh my," was all I could think to say. Eddie and the Sergeant Major, having watched carefully for my reaction, laughed.

"Gad man," the Sergeant Major said. "The finest Scotch in the Empire. All you can say is 'Oh my'." The giggle at the end of the sentence gave him away. The Sergeant Major had been sampling. So had Eddie. He was in his shirtsleeves. Or maybe that was because of the country air.

"Did you find Jug?" I lowered my voice so I wouldn't be heard at the horseshoe pit.

"Nope," Eddie said. He stood up and struggled in one of the pockets of his jacket. He pulled something out and threw it my way. My pistol. It landed at my feet.

"Found that," the Sergeant Major said. "No sign of the boy. None at all."

"Musta fallen down a hole," Eddie said. "Lots of 'em around there."

"I'll have to get word to Oddball. He can send some men out to search tomorrow."

"While we're at the Corran," Lori said.

I slipped my pistol into a pocket. Took another drink.

"I'm not so sure about you going up there," I finally said.

"Why not?" Lori demanded.

"It might be dangerous."

"That Inspector…what's his name?"

"Blood."

"Glori told him she wanted to be there. What's dangerous about that?" Lori asked.

"Do you really think she does?"

"I don't know. She could. The way she's been behaving lately. She and daddy did have a fight. But that's beside the point. Do you think I can't handle myself?"

I was in trouble. I knew right away. The Sergeant Major and Eddie weren't going to save me. The Sergeant Major harrumphed and stood up, weaving his way over to the horseshoes. I hoped he wouldn't try and play. Eddie beat it out of there into the house.

"Are you going to drink that?" I pointed to Lori's untouched whisky. She shook her head so I picked it up and took a swallow. It was a taste I could get used to.

"You just never know how these situations are going to play out. It could end up dangerous."

"If so, it'll be dangerous for you too. I'm not saying you can't go."

"But…"

"But nothing, D.B. Murphy. We're going to be married. You have to learn I have a mind of my own."

"Alright." She was right. Besides, there was no way I could win.

"That's more like it. Now why does that girl keep looking at you?"

"What?" I spilled whisky all over myself.

"That girl. Colleen I think her name is. She keeps looking at you."

"It's…"

"Well? Everything settled?" Eddie dropped into his chair.

"I'm coming," Lori said.

"Great," Eddie smiled. He'd known the answer all along.

"What'd I miss?" Van asked. The game of horseshoes finished, he'd found a chair across from us.

"We were talking about tomorrow."

"Is there a plan?"

"Not yet," Eddie said. "They was just layin' the ground rules."

"So you're coming," Van said to Lori.

"I told you so," she smirked.

"Am I that transparent?" I asked the world in general.

"See through," Van said. Eddie cranked up a thumb of approval.

"Not transparent," Lori's smile melted me a bit. "Honorable."

"Sensible," Van added.

I looked at Eddie.

"I ain't gonna say a thing," he said, pouring a drink.

"I will. What's the layout for tomorrow?"

"Party starts at seven. We gotta leave here around two. Give us time to set up."

"How many people?"

"Fifty."

"Just to hear Kate McDermid sing?" Lori asked.

"Partly. A lot of bluebloods gonna be there."

"Snoot galore," Eddie quipped.

"What's the main attraction?" I asked.

"Sir Robert."

"Borden?"

"The same."

"Jeez, an ex-Prime Minister. How you going to get us in?" I asked Eddie.

"Followin' the unfortunate demise of her piano man, Miss McDermid called to Owen Sound looking fer a player. One is on her way as we speak."

Lori gave me an aren't-I-clever look. She was.

"The piano player, a young lady, is of course accompanied by her father. For safety reasons," Lori said with a smile.

"Won't Glori run when she hears you're coming?"

"She won't hear."

"Miss McDermid wil…"

"She doesn't know who's coming," Lori cut me off. "She called Mrs. Filbert and asked her to send someone."

"Oh. What about the rest of us?" I asked Eddie.

"I told them I'd be bringing two men. To serve drinks."

"What about you?" I asked.

"I'm gonna circulate."

"What if Glori isn't at the party? What if she's not a voluntary guest?"

"I'll circulate. If she ain't in the house I'll check the other buildings."

"What about them?" I looked over at Davey, Shelagh and Colleen.

"That's for you to say."

"I guess."

"Oh, Murph! You can't turn them in," Lori grabbed my hand and squeezed.

"It's what Oddball hired me to do. Bring in the Lost Tire Gang." The thing of it was, they were right. I didn't want to turn in a bunch of kids.

"They came here to start a new life," Lori added.

"Some life," Eddie said.

"They're just kids," Lori said.

"She's right," Van jumped in. "You spent time with them. They don't deserve jail."

"Besides, what happened wasn't their fault. They were corrupted." Lori's view on the next course of action I should take was fairly apparent.

"By the boss." Van clinched the argument. "Find him. He's the guy for Oddball."

"Jeez!" I slapped a hand to my head.

"What?" Lori asked, concerned.

"I left his arm out there."

"What?" Van asked.

I told them about Oddball giving me the arm. "I hid it near Gleason Brook."

"Okay, so you know where his arm is. Where's he?" Van asked.

"I don't know. He met Goldy once a week or so. To collect his take. He's close by."

"So catch him. Let the kids go," Lori said.

"What do you suggest I do with them in the meantime?"

"My man Red can bunk them down until you get back. Then we'll figure out what to do with them," Eddie said.

"What'll I tell Oddball?"

"Make somethin' up," he laughed.

"Right."

Van cooked beef and potatoes on the fire. We ate in our chairs. After, there was coffee. Better than the stuff the gang made. The three of them were off to one side. Grief. Fear. Uncertainty. They needed to be close to one another. Away from the rest of us.

"Have you figured out what you'll do when you find her?" I asked Eddie. He topped up his coffee.

"Sergeant Major sees me go, he puts me on the clock. After twenty minutes, he's outside waiting."

"He'll take Glori out?"

"Right. Lori comes back with us."

"Okay. Red can take care of these kids. I'll decide what to do with them when I come back to town."

"How long you gonna be gone?" Eddie asked.

"Don't know. A week maybe."

"Until we find that one-armed menace," Van sneered like the villian in a penny novel.

I stood and stretched. My back end was sore from the chair, but otherwise I didn't feel too bad. All things considered. I filled my coffee cup and went over to where the kids sat.

"Hello Ver…uh, Murphy," Davey said.

"How you three making out? Need anything?"

"What's gonna happen to us?" Shelagh asked.

"You're not sending us back are you?" Colleen asked.

"Are you a cop?" Davey asked.

"I'm a private investigator. How's your wound?" I asked Davey.

"It still hurts. But it'll heal up okay."

"Are we goin' to jail?" Shelagh asked.

"Slow down," I said. "The gang is done. I killed Goldy after he…well, just after. I'm looking for the boss next."

"What are ya gonna do to him?"

"He's killed a few men. Probably more than we know. Justice has to be served."

"He's tough."

"So am I."

"And smart."

"I'm smarter."

"So what're ya gonna do with us then?" Shelagh asked.

"Did you see the big fella, the one we call Red?"

"Yah. He was here when Van brung us in," Davey said.

"He works for Razor Eddie. He's a good man. You're gonna go with Red down to his place near Owen Sound. He's gonna put you up for a few days out in the country. A place called Inglis Falls. Stay with him until I come for you."

"What are ya gonna do with us?"

"I'm gonna keep you out of it. If I can." They sighed in three-part harmony.

"Thanks," Davey said. "What about Barnardos? The home'll send us back to England."

"Do you still believe in it? The Barnardo dream?

"A bad day here is still better'n any good day in the gutter," Davey said with conviction. The other two agreed.

"Alright then. I'm gonna find some people to take you in. People I know. Places you'll be safe."

"A second chance?" Shelagh asked tentatively.

"Best part is, I'll visit. To check up. Be sure you're all staying on the right side of the law. Now why don't you move in closer to the fire here? Davey, where's that guitar?"

Davey and Shelagh jumped up and ran into the house. Colleen and I were alone. I looked quickly over my shoulder. Lori had gone inside with the others.

Colleen stared into the fire. I cleared my throat.

"Are you okay?" I asked.

"Don't ask me that," she said.

"Why not?"

"'Cause then I'll have to tell ya."

"I want you to tell me."

She held me for a second with her perfect green eyes. Then broke the contact, blushing. She said something under her breath.

"What?" I asked.

"I'm embarrassed," she said in a louder voice.

"I thought you were angry."

"I've been turned down by men before."

"You see why."

"That's just it. Lori is so nice. If I'd known, I never would have cuddled up with you by the fire..."

She was stopped in mid-sentence by a sharp intake of breath from behind us. I turned to see Lori running back up to the house. She brushed past Davey and Shelagh. They were coming through the door with the guitar.

"What's wrong with Lori?" Davey asked when they got to the fire.

"Nothing," I said running up to the house. I was met at the door by Eddie and Van.

"Hey, where you goin' big fella?" Eddie asked.

"I need to see Lori."

"She's gone to bed."

"I've got to talk to her."

"She said ya would. Said forget it. She'd talk to you in the mornin'. Seemed real upset."

"I better go up anyway."

"Better not. Sergeant Major's up there."

"Jeez." I slammed a fist into my open palm. It was safe to guess she hadn't heard the part where I'd turned Colleen down. What a mess.

"C'mon down to the fire, buddy. Have a drink."

The evening was subdued by murder, misunderstanding and thoughts of the next day. We sat by the fire for a couple of hours, alternately talking and listening to music. I finally had enough and decided to turn in.

"Decided what you're gonna tell Oddball?" Van asked as we walked up to the house.

"I'm sure I'll think of something."

CHAPTER THIRTEEN
THREE HUNDRED STAIRS

Oddball caught up to me the next morning as Scotty and I were riding back to the caves. I needed to take a look around to satisfy myself that Jug wasn't there. I'd tried to talk to Lori before I left. She was out for a walk. I didn't see her at all. Everyone else was getting ready for the trip to the Corran.

Near Oxenden, Scotty's ears pricked up. I stopped at the side of the road. It was a few minutes before I heard it and by then the car was in sight. I knew it was Oddball. I'm not sure how, I just did. His big car clattered to a stop in front of us. He shut it down and stepped out.

"Heard you got beat up a bit."

"Hello Oddball."

"Murph." He stepped closer. "I heard right."

"You heard right."

"How many more people you gonna kill?"

"Just one. Why?"

"It ain't that it bothers me. Keeps the jails from gettin' clogged. County don't have to feed them neither."

"You're full of understanding."

"Where's the gang?"

"Get right to the point don't you?"

"What else do you want me to talk about?"

"Could ask how I am."

"Well, I seen the other guy. You're in much better shape."

"He was my only way to the boss."

"You sayin' this is gonna take a while longer?"

"It might."

Oddball pulled a Havana Stogie out of his pocket and bit off the end. He fired it over my right shoulder. "Van stayin' too?"

"Yes."

"Gonna shoot my budget all to hell."

"Gee. Too bad."

"What about the rest of 'em?"

"Huh?"

"The gang. The rest of the gang."

"One of them's dead."

"Haven't found him."

"I saw him go over. The drop was at least a hundred feet."

"So that's one. Where're the rest of 'em?"

"They eluded capture while Goldy beat on me."

"Get off it."

"Ask Van."

"Where was he when all this happened?"

"I think he fainted or something."

"Fainted?"

"I think so."

"I can't believe that. Where is he? I want to talk to him."

"Back at Eddie's place. But they'll be leaving soon to head up to the Corran."

"Gonna get Glori?"

"Always avoid alliteration."

"Huh?"

"Never mind. Yeah, they're leaving around two."

"I'll go over right now. Where are you goin'?"

"To get that arm you gave me. Had to stash it."

"You stashed it?"

"Couldn't quite ride into the camp with that sticking out of my saddlebag."

"Oh. Right." He finally got it.

"You any relation to Curly Scott?"

"The fighter? Sure. Why?"

"Saw him fight at the smoker. Just wondered."

"He's my cousin. The name's a giveaway."

"He's got that big head too."

Oddball took his hat off. "It ain't that big," he said running a hand through his hair.

"Like a football. Well I better go."

"Me too," he said, still puzzled. He continued to rub his head, then looked inside his Biltmore. After shrugging his shoulders, Oddball replaced the hat. Gave another shake, then said, "Right. See you."

Gleason Brook had disappeared. Scotty and I headed off the road and down the bank. We rode straight up the creek bed fifty yards or so, to the place where I'd hidden the arm. The tree I'd hidden it in was gone. A beaver dam was standing in its place.

I dismounted and looked around. It took me a few minutes to find it. The arm, or what was left of it, was nearby. The beaver had done a good job, likely enticed by the sweet-tasting varnish. Wood. Metal hardware. Digits. I reached into a pocket and pulled out a canvas bag. The one the boss had put over my head before he dropped me off the cliff. Carefully, I gathered as many pieces of the arm as I could.

Filled with shavings, rocks, dirt and metal pieces, the bag weighed about five pounds. I stuck it back in my saddlebag. I couldn't wait to return it.

"Leave your rough clothes on," Eddie said. "We'll change after we unload the boat."

Everyone had been ready when I arrived back at the farm. Evening wear and guns had been packed away in the trunk of Eddie's London Six. It was a luxury ride, built in London, Ontario. Powered by a firetruck engine, the London Six could give the passenger train on the Windsor-Toronto run a ten minute head start and still beat it. It was the perfect car for a bootlegger. Eddie was proud of it, and rightfully so. But I still wasn't going to ride in it.

"It would offend Scotty," I said when he asked.

"C'mon. You're one of my men. Ya gotta ride with me."

"We'll ride along with you."

"Yeah right. You gonna keep up with this?" He raced the engine. It sounded smooth and powerful.

"Been up the road north of Wiarton yet?"

"Nope."

"We'll keep up."

I was right. We had no problem keeping up. It was after three when we arrived at the big iron gates of the Corran. They were set alongside the centre road of the Bruce Peninsula. I'd thought about Lori on the way up. Hoping I'd be able to talk to her before the party, to clear up the mess about Colleen. It would depend on the unloading. Eddie had been mysterious about that. All he'd say was the booze was coming in by water.

Past the gates we followed the carriage-way through a swamp, across a field and into a mature hardwood forest with elm, hemlock and maple. I saw an occasional cow among the trees, caught a whiff of manure here and there. I smelled the tang of cedar before I saw any. Clearings were carpeted with fern. At the edge of the forest, a manicured lawn led up to the house. It was magnificent. The biggest residence I'd ever seen. Huge, and made of cut stone.

I paused before following Eddie's car behind the house, through a set of gates that led to the left. Across the lawn, on the other side of the house there was an orchard. And flower gardens. Footpaths wound their way through both.

The barn was a large stone affair. Next to it a henhouse was alive and clucking. Behind the barn I could hear the low hum of a Delco plant. I wasn't surprised. I'd expect a house like that to have power. It had the phone too. I'd seen the wires when we rode in.

I pulled Scotty up behind the car. Eddie was out and talking to a man in the yard. I dismounted and left Scotty standing behind the car.

"This here's Alf Lewis," Eddie said gesturing to the man.

"Alf." I gave a short nod with my head. He wouldn't want to know too much about us. It made things easier.

"You wantin' to unsaddle yer horse then?"

"You're as Irish as they come," I said casually as Scotty and I followed him into the barn.

"All the staff is. His Lordship brought us over special."

"Leave it on," I said when it looked like he was thinking of taking Scotty's saddle off.

Alf raised his eyebrows. "Goin' somewhere in a hurry, are ya?"

"Be prepared. That's my motto."

After he'd had a drink, I strapped Scotty's feedbag on.

I went out into the yard. Eddie had backed his car behind the henhouse, nose out. Not too far from it was the Sergeant Major's carriage.

"The party starts at eight," Alf was saying when my ears arrived at the conversation he was having with Eddie. I was thinking that meant I'd have lots of time to find Lori when Alf asked, "Can you get it unloaded and up here that fast?"

Eddie stared me in the eye and said, "Sure. That's why we brought muscles here along."

"Okay. The boat's here. I'll show you the stairs."

Eddie, Van and I followed him out of the barnyard and back onto the carriage-way. We walked to the edge of the forest. Through the trees on a broad path, we were always in sight of the lawn. At one point I had a clear view of the house. There was a wide set of steps onto the porch. It covered half the front. The other side was all glass. A conservatory.

"She's quite the house," Alf's voice invaded my reverie.

"I'd like to meet the man who built it."

"You may. He takes quite an interest."

The house went out of our sight. We passed close to a clearing on the other side. A small stone cottage was surrounded by gardens.

"Escott's cottage," Alf said helpfully to all three of us.

"Who's Escott?" Van asked.

"Remittance man who used to live there. Had a market garden. Used to make his own wine."

The bulk of the garden was devoted to vegetables. At one end, grape vines grew up wooden racks.

"Used to?" Eddie asked.

"Dead these five years."

"Someone live there now?" I asked.

"The stairs are just here." Alf walked off without answering.

We were at the cliff's edge. A wooden verandah jutted out. A set of stairs seemed to lead from it to nowhere. Van and I crowded in behind Alf and Eddie. Looking down, I couldn't see the bottom.

"Lot of steps," Van said.

"Exactly three hundred," Alf smiled. "Himself sends me down every morning fer water."

"No well up here?" Eddie asked.

"Sure, sure. But he likes his mornin' tea made wit' lake water."

"And the liquor is down there? On a boat?" I pointed down the stairs while looking at Eddie.

"Right." He grinned a filthy look.

"I don't remember hearing about this."

"Don't remember you askin'."

"How many cases?" I asked.

"Of what?" The maddening grin was still on Eddie's face.

"In total."

"Twenty or thirty."

"Well, I'll leave you boys to it." Alf knew when to get lost. He fairly ran up the path away from us.

"Thirty cases?" I almost shouted.

"Yer in luck," Eddie smiled. "They got a winch. Someone stays up here and pulls 'em in. Someone carries 'em from the boat and ties them on at the bottom." He looked at me as he said the last.

"I don't think I could make it with my leg. Or else I'd go," Van said.

"I was hoping to see Lori and straighten something out," I said.

"Guess it all depends on how fast ya can unload that boat." Eddie was still smiling.

I headed down without another word.

CHAPTER FOURTEEN
THE POLITICIAN

At the bottom of the stairs, I knew Alf was right. Three hundred. Exactly. I wondered how many mornings he'd counted his way down. Or up.

From the last stair it was fifty paces to the dock. The wood walk itself was another thirty paces or so. On the north side there was a boathouse. A disappearing propeller boat was moored next to it. I slowed for a look. I'd only seen one before. Built like a big canoe. Rich looking brass fittings. The motor was amidships. Forward was a large brass handle which raised and lowered the propeller in and out of a special keel compartment. A safety skeg under the boat protected the propeller from rocks, raising it automatically. Paddled in shallows, propelled in open water. It was the perfect boat.

I wandered to the far end of the dock. A couple of fellows were there, unloading cases from a boat. The motor was idling and they were hurrying.

"Problem?" I asked.

"Dry cops," a buzzard of a man spat.

"Where?"

"Everywhere."

"Not here."

"Don't care." He and his companion continued unloading apace. The other fellow was youngish, blond. He snickered behind the old man's back and shrugged his shoulders at me. I shrugged back and picked up a case. Each contained twelve bottles and weighed about twenty-five pounds. I was just thinking I should have taken two when an old man passed me going down the dock. I didn't pay him much attention. Until he came back a moment later carrying two cases.

"Hey!" I pushed myself to a quick walk. Still couldn't keep up.

By the time I caught gramps he was at the bottom of the cliff and had the cases stashed in a net bag at the end of the rope. Breathing hard, I set my case down with a thump. I startled him, as though he'd forgotten toddling past me on the dock.

"Forgive me, sir," he said, holding his hand out to me. "Alexander McNeill." His eyes were alive. Hair, beard and brows were snowy white. He was tall and fit. Sixty I'd guess.

"I'm eighty." My surprise widened his smile. "You look like a blacksmith. Run like one, too."

His grip was pure energy.

"D.B. Murphy," I said. "You're good at reading people. Good skill for a politician. Tupper didn't like you much."

It was his turn to be surprised. I laughed and offered my hand. We shook again. He leaned back and gave the rope a tug. The whisky began its ascent. McNeill looked at my one case. Up at his two. And laughed again.

"I was showing off. You carry the rest. I'll send them up."

★★★

Twenty-seven cases later, the job was done. All that was left were the stairs. I let McNeill set the pace.

"It's true," he said after we'd started up. "Tupper thought I was a pain. Needed me in my seat. Wanted me to shut up and toe the line. I showed him what Bruce County was about," he laughed. It was a happy sound. The pure pleasure of a good reminiscence.

"Lumber, wasn't it?" I remembered from school.

McNeill stopped and stared at me. Continuing up the stairs, I'm sure he was smiling. "You appear to be a young man with potential. Do you mind explaining why you're lugging booze for a criminal?"

"Not if you tell me what you're doing buying booze from a criminal. Which he is not by the way."

McNeill stopped to catch his breath. "Point well taken," he said after a moment.

"He's doing me a favour."

"How's that?"

"What?" I asked.

"You said he's doing you a favour."

"I have a job. It's more than most returned men can say."

"Ah. A veteran."

"Yes."

McNeill started up the stairs again. I hadn't been able to count. I thought we might be near the halfway point.

"A difficult business, war," he said over his shoulder.

"For politicians?" I asked conversationally.

"Sometimes." His tone was light.

"They don't die."

"No. Do you think the war was wrong?"

"No."

"Tyranny must be stopped. It was. We'll never see another Great War."

"I hope not."

"What's your job?"

His question caught me by surprise. I nearly told him. I wanted to. I liked his friendly manner. I hoped I'd be able to meet him again, and explain the lies.

"Blacksmith."

"Hah! I knew it." I could see he was pleased with himself.

"Before the war. Now I work for my brother. Insurance."

"Why aren't you working today?"

"Because I'm here."

"Ah," he said absently. We reached the top of the stairs and he set off across the lawn. A dozen or more dogs sprinted around the corner of the house and headed towards him. Before they arrived he turned.

"There's a nickel tour," he called to me.

"Of the grounds?"

"And the house. Interested?"

"Yes."

"C'mon then." The dogs arrived. Then McNeill was lost in a frenzy of licking and wagging. He indulged it for a moment, then spoke.

"Now boys," he said. The dogs promptly sat in two neatly ordered rows. "Coming?" he asked.

"Yes." Not a nostril flared as I passed the ranks.

"Come along," he said as we walked away. I turned to look. Two lines of dogs walked directly behind us.

"Interesting," I said.

"A trick. Simple after parliament." We stopped in the centre of the lawn and turned to the east. Two great clearings had been made in the trees. To the south, Colpoy's Bay looked splendid. In the north hole, White Cloud and Griffith Islands looked close enough to touch.

"Beautiful."

"Thank you." He led the way up to the house. "Those are the rose gardens. Beyond them, the orchard."

"How many roses?"

"About five hundred. Come inside. I'll show you my favourite." He led me up the wide granite steps onto the covered porch. "Stay," he said over his shoulder. Two rows of canines sat.

A heavy oak door led into the foyer. While my eyes adjusted to the light, I took a deep breath. The smell of delicious food filled my nose. My stomach rumbled. Somewhere, someone was playing a piano. My heart skipped a beat. I still might get a chance to speak to Lori.

"Come in here."

I followed McNeill through a door on the left into the biggest library I'd ever seen. Floor to ceiling, the mahogany shelves held thousands of volumes. Comfortable leather chairs were spaced around the fireplace. Two ten-foot windows lit the room. In front of one there was a huge desk. We passed it and went into the conservatory. Humid and bright. It was a wonderful place. Full of green, full of life. Potted roses in bloom covered shelves on three walls.

"Your first conservatory?" he asked.

"Yes."

"It's not usually so full. These roses are for tonight's party. The bushes outside won't bloom for another month, and I do so like the fragrance," he added. "We'll come back here for refreshment."

Folded wooden deck chairs leaned against one wall. McNeill led me to a set of shelves. One potted rose, prominently displayed, stood out from the others.

"This is my pride."

"Another rose."

"Not just any rose. This one comes from Scotland."

I looked more carefully at the plant. It looked like any other rose.

"It looks like any other rose," I said.

"Until she blooms. It's a black rose. And not just any black rose. This is a cutting taken from the black rose bush Mary Queen of Scots slept under not long before she was executed."

"Which one was she?"

He gave me a funny look and scowled. It sounded like he muttered "colonists" under his breath. We walked back into the library.

"You have more books than the Carnegie Library in Owen Sound."

"Maybe."

We crossed back through the foyer and into the parlour. A couple of servant girls were cleaning in preparation for the party. Everything was opulent. Stained glass. Brocade drapes. Wall hangings. The best furniture. The view of the rose gardens didn't hurt either.

At one end of the room was a grand piano. And Lori. Engrossed in converation with Miss McDermid. They didn't know we were there until McNeill cleared his throat.

"Is everything to your satisfaction ladies?"

Lori pretended not to see me. Miss McDermid saw me. Her look was one of curiosity rather than recognition.

"Fine thank you, Alex. Miss Storey and I met in Owen Sound. You were brilliant to get her." It was clear Miss McDermid liked McNeill.

Lori still hadn't looked my way when I followed him into the foyer. He led me down the hall, past the stairs to the upper floor.

"Nothing to see up there. Bedrooms. And the bathroom of course." He emphasized the last.

"Indoor? Nice."

He acknowledged the compliment with a nod and led me into the dining room. A huge table took up most of the space.

"Rosewood," he answered the question before I could ask.

Across the hall was a small room under the stairs. Eddie and Van were inside. The cases were piled against the wall.

"Gentlemen," McNeill greeted them.

Eddie introduced Van. "And I see you've met D.B."

"He has," I jumped in, afraid they'd think I'd taken McNeill into my confidence. "He thinks I've got too much talent to sling cases for a bootlegger."

"He doesn't know ya like we do," Eddie laughed. Somewhere in the house a telephone rang. I thought I'd seen one in the library.

"I meant to ask you. That cottage, Erwin's was it?"

"Escott's."

"Who lives there now?" Before he could answer, the door at the end of the hallway opened. A woman came out.

"Oh, there you are, sir," she said. "A telephone call for you. Long distance."

"Thank you Mrs. Lewis. If you gentlemen will excuse me."

CHAPTER FIFTEEN
THE PARTY

The room we were stationed in was the cloakroom. Six feet wide by ten long. A small doorway at the back led to a storage area under the front stairs. Cedar lined, it was filled with coats. Hiding us kept up the respectable appearance of the party. While everyone would consume the bootleg, it was considered poor form to display it in any public area of the house. And the kitchen, Eddie explained, was much too busy.

"It's rough fare," the serving boy who brought our supper said. "Cook's busy. There'll be better after the guests have gone."

Fresh bread. Cold chicken. Pickles. Potato salad. Fresh coffee. It didn't seem bad to me at all.

"Why'd you ask about that cottage?"

"Someone brought Glori here. I want to know who."

"Why not McNeill?" Eddie spoke into a chicken leg. "The old geezer seems healthy enough to me."

"It wasn't him. Someone else."

"We'll find him. Whoever he is."

"What's the drill for the party?"

"Teapots."

"The usual, in other words."

"Kitchen staff brings the pots. We fill 'em. They fill the teacups."

"Why are we dressed?" Van asked.

"So you can circulate. D.B. is gonna bounce people out in case they get outta control. You gotta mingle and keep an eye on things."

"You'll go look for Glori once the concert starts?"

"Uh huh."

"Where'll the Sergeant Major be?"

"Look, we been through all this. Don't worry."

"I'm not worried. A little nervous is all."

"You packin'?"

"Of course."

"The big gun?"

"The .32."

"A girlie gun," he ribbed me.

"At party range it'll be good enough. Besides I can carry it in my jacket pocket." I showed them.

"You ain't gonna need it anyway," Eddie said. "This is gonna be a piece of cake."

★★★

The party was swank. Guests arrived from seven until eight-thirty. The house seemed full. Miss McDermid pulled Lori through the room. I watched from a corner as my fiancee was introduced to one and all.

She was beautiful in a white satin gown. Just the right amount of make-up and jewellery. Miss McDermid on the other hand was clad in some European number with a low neckline and high hemline. Her knees were scoring points with some of the older gents. They were headed my way. I hoped if I stayed put I'd get a moment between guests to talk to Lori.

"Sheba! I think I'm in love," a deep voice sounded at my elbow. The talker was a head shorter and slight. His dark hair was brilliantined in place. The beard he wore was trim. Dark eyebrows nearly joined above a straight nose and two blue eyes.

"William Simpson. Land agent." He offered his hand.

"D.B. Murphy. Party goer." He laughed at my glib response.

"What does a land agent do?" I asked.

"I carry out federal government land policies on the Bruce Peninsula."

"I didn't know there were any." I knew a bit about the long and difficult history of timber on the Bruce. Once the government hadn't let anyone cut anything. Then it let everyone cut everything. Soon there would be nothing.

"Good evening gentlemen." Miss McDermid and Lori stood in front of us. I smiled and shook Miss McDermid's outstretched hand. Pure alabaster. She gave me another look.

"D.B. Murphy. Mr. McNeill introduced us earlier today. While you were rehearsing."

"Oh yes, I know. It's just that…nothing. This is Miss Storey."

The ring was still there when I took her hand. I sensed a softening in her demeanor towards me. It was probably the tuxedo.

"Miss Storey," I said.

"Mr. Murphy."

"Your attention ladies and gentlemen, attention please!" McNeill stood in the centre of the room, teacup in hand. "This afternoon I received a phone call from Toronto. Robert Borden will not be joining us. He's been called back to the capital on pressing business."

No one seemed disappointed so he continued, "I'd like to present the real reason for our gathering. Miss Kate McDermid."

There was enthusiastic applause. Miss McDermid accepted the adulation easily. She stepped to the centre of the room and kissed McNeill on both cheeks.

"Have to go," Lori said.

I grabbed her hand and pulled her close. "I have to talk to you." She smelled so good I almost didn't make it back from her ear.

"Later," she said, pulling away from me. Skirting the crowd in a hurry, she made it to the piano before Miss McDermid. Once the diva was in place, Lori struck up the first notes of *The Last Rose of Summer*. Behind her there was a blaze of electric light, and the rose gardens were illuminated. There was an audible gasp in the crowd. Miss McDermid didn't miss a note. Nor did Lori.

I left the parlour and went back to the cloakroom. Van was there alone.

"Is he gone?"

"On schedule."

"I'll wait here until we hear something."

After half an hour I started to worry. Miss McDermid would be taking a break soon. The crowd would begin moving around. I didn't want Eddie caught before he found Glori.

"I'm going back into the party. To see how things are."

"How long do they go on?" Van asked.

"She was going to sing forty-five minutes. Then an hour break while the Lombardo dance band plays. Another forty-five minutes of singing. Then more dancing."

"It's been close to forty-five already," Van said. "I'm surprised he's not back."

"There was a lot of ground to cover. People to avoid."

"I thought all the guests were inside."

"This place has fifteen servants. I think a lot of them are on break while she sings. Who knows where they go." I left the room and headed back down the hall to the parlour.

Miss McDermid was singing *The Night Wind.* The crowd was clearly captivated by the purity of her soprano voice. She finished the song to much applause. Crossing behind the piano she pulled Lori up to share the accolade. I'm not sure Lori was expecting it. She looked a little embarrassed. The applause went on and on, until McNeill finally stepped in and raised a hand.

"Miss McDermid will be back to entertain you shortly. Please, refresh yourselves. Walk in the gardens. Enjoy."

The crowd broke up. McNeill walked over to Miss McDermid and offered his thanks. She hugged him and excused herself, leaving Lori to accept his invitation of a stroll through the garden. My chance of explaining things walked towards the door with them. I saw Lori turn and look my way.

"You saved me!" Miss McDermid threw herself into my arms. In my surprise I caught her. When I looked back Lori was gone.

"It was you on the train, wasn't it?" On vacation, she hadn't bothered to read the local paper. Her proximity was alarming, so I removed her arms from around my shoulders.

"What train? What are you talking about?"

"Oh come on, big fella." She wagged a finger in front of my face. "I've been trying to think where I know you from all day. You saved me on that train. I owe you a lot." She gave my right bicep a squeeze. "Ooooh, I like that."

I pulled her deeper into the corner I'd been inhabiting.

"Look, you don't owe me anything. I did what anyone would have done."

"There were other people on that coach. You're the only one who did anything."

"It's what I do. I'd appreciate it if you didn't tell anyone here about this."

"What are you talking about?" she asked, exasperated. I wasn't adoring her the way I should.

"I'm a detective. On a job. Don't blow my cover."

"That's not what I had in mind. Are you really a detective?"

"Uh huh."

"Why are you here? Looking for bad guys?"

"Sort of. Look, I…"

Van signalled me from the door then disappeared.

"When you pulled it out on the train I couldn't believe the size."

"What?" I hadn't been paying attention.

"Your gun. Do you have it with you?"

"Look, your pianist is my fiancee. You don't owe me anything. I have to go."

I left before she could say another word. Coming around the corner into the hall, I ran headlong into another man. We both careened off balance.

"Oh. Excuse me," I said. There was a sharp intake of breath as though he was going to speak. Instead he stepped through the door. I looked back in time to see his silhouette framed in the entryway. My heart stopped. He only had one arm.

Chapter Sixteen
Heel and Toe

I hurried down the hall to the cloakroom. "Don't panic. Everything's okay," Van said when he saw the wild look in my eyes.

"He's here," I said.

"Borden?"

"The one-armed man."

Van's jaw dropped, his eyes bulged and his nostrils flared. All at the same time. It would have been comical under any other circumstance.

"Here! He's here? Are you sure?"

"I just saw him. In the hall. Where's the Razor?" I was sorry now about the .32. I needed a pistol with authority for what I wanted to do.

"Took the Sergeant Major and Glori out to the car. Then he's comin' back."

"He found her then? Where?"

"She was in that little cottage you were asking about."

"She okay?"

"Unconscious."

"What?"

"Laudanum, Eddie thinks."

The thought of Glori and the strong narcotic made my stomach turn. "Who gave it to her?"

"We aren't going to know until she wakes up."

"I'll bet it was him."

"Who?" Eddie said coming through the doorway.

"The one-armed man."

"Eh?"

"He's here. D.B. saw him in the hallway," Van said.

"We're going to take him. Right now," I nearly shouted.

"Hold on," Eddie said, pushing the door shut. "How do you know it's him?"

"What?"

"You're angry. You're not thinking straight. How do you know it's him?"

"Aside from the obvious?"

"You told me you never saw his face. So there's a one-armed guy here. How do you know he's the right one?"

"Um…" I saw his point. He was right. I was angry. About Glori. About the one-armed man and all he'd done since I chased him in the Bognor Marsh. The Bognor Marsh. "He's got a wounded foot."

"What?"

"One of them left a bloody track when they got away. Then when the one-armed man got on the train he was limping."

"So all you gotta do is ask to see his foot."

"I can't do that. But I have an idea."

★★★

Many of the guests had gone outside. Lit rose gardens on a warm May night. Inside the orchestra played *When My Baby Smiles At Me*. A dozen couples were swinging. Lori and McNeill were outside by the rose garden. Miss McDermid was still in the parlour, surrounded by a group of young men. I interjected myself and dispersed the boys.

"Is it always like that?" I asked her.

"Those guys were nice. Not like the usual stage door johnnies."

"Boys of breeding if I know our host."

"How do you know him?"

"I don't. Just met him this afternoon. Remember when you said you owed me? I'm going to collect after all."

"That didn't take long. I thought it would be at least an hour before you changed your mind." She reached up to put her arms around my neck.

"You don't owe me that much. Just a dance."

"If that's all I can get," she pouted.

"Not with me. Someone else."

"What?" She looked at me like I was Joe Hunt's dog.

"Remember you were asking what I was doing here? This is it."

"Will it be dangerous?"

"It might be." I explained the plan, then got into position. Eddie waited by the door. Van was near the orchestra, which was arranged around the piano. I had my back to the rose garden. As I watched, Miss McDermid crossed the room to the one-armed man. He was engaged in close conversation with two other men. The three of them looked up and took her hand in turn as Miss McDermid introduced herself. She spoke for a moment. The one-armed man joined her on the dance floor, where the band had slowed the tempo. They spoke to one another as they danced. Around and around. Miss McDermid was enjoying her part in the night's little adventure. Dancing with the man who had tried and failed to kidnap her. His back was turned to me when I heard him yell. Miss McDermid's heel was planted directly on top of his toe. She backed away when she saw me coming. Eddie and Van held their positions. We'd agreed they'd act as backup.

He knew the jig was up. I was just about there, when he gave his good arm a shake. A gun dropped out of the sleeve and into his hand.

"Gun!" I shouted as loud as I could. It got everyone out of the way in a hurry. The one-armed man spun and fired. The shot went wide and nicked the support holding the top of the piano. It crashed down amid the screams of partygoers trying to escape the gunfire. I grabbed his gun hand and pushed it towards the floor. With my free hand I punched him in the face. He started to fall. I twisted my wrist and yanked the gun out of his hand. He hit the floor and I jumped on top of him. I would have dearly loved to beat the hell out of him. What I tried to do instead was subdue him. Then we could get him out before anyone else was hurt.

Unfortunately, he didn't think that was such a good idea. I don't know why, but I didn't consider he might hit me with his stump. So when he did, he totally winded me. I fell forward and tried to pin him while I waited for breath to return. The next thing I knew he had my .32 in his hand. He cuffed me on the side of the head. I fell off in a hurry. Then he was up and had the stump of his arm around Miss McDermid's neck. The little gun was at her temple.

"Stay back or she dies." I got up, just a couple of feet from the two of them. I motioned towards the rose garden.

"Go ahead. But you should know, you're not going to get away."

"You think you're man enough this time, do you?" he scoffed, pulling Miss McDermid around so their backs were to the garden. He dragged her along backwards. Her eyes were frightened. I smiled.

"A guy like you can only get away for so long."

"A guy like me? What do you know about it, blacksmith?" He said it like the word was supposed to hurt. I took it as a compliment.

"If that's the best you can do, this isn't going to be much of a challenge after all," I said to him.

They were almost at the door.

"It's not my best by any means, Mr. Murphy."

"That hardly seems fair."

"Fair?"

"You know my name but I don't know yours."

"You introduced yourself to me in Bognor Marsh. I've still got the toe. Where's my arm?"

I decided it was best to avoid that topic for the moment. No point making him any madder. I'd wait until I had the upper hand. So to speak.

"Aren't you going to introduce yourself?"

"No. I'll let my new girlfriend do it."

"How's that?"

"You and I are almost related."

It took me a second. Then I knew.

"Glori."

His smile was full of meaning. Miss McDermid sighed and went limp. When he realized she'd fainted he shoved her into the room. He was out the door before I caught the falling singer.

There were shots outside and screams. I lowered Miss McDermid to the floor.

"Look after her," I shouted over my shoulder as I ran out the door. McNeill was on the ground. There was blood on the front of his shirt. I ran down the steps. He wasn't wounded, just shaken up.

"I'm okay," he said hoarsely, "but he took that young lady. The piano player."

CHAPTER SEVENTEEN
THE CHASE

"Took her? Where?" I shouted in alarm.

The old man pointed towards the water. "That way. The stairs."

I ran from the house straight down and across the lawn. I had no gun. It didn't matter. If he had Lori, I wouldn't be able to risk shooting in the dark. I reached the woods and slowed down. Stopping for a second I listened. All I could hear was the excited babble of voices coming from the house. I moved on, carefully. I didn't want to break a leg.

At the stop of the three hundred stairs I shouted, "Lori!"

"Danny-Boy!" Her cry was followed by a shot. The bullet thudded into the railing near me. I took the stairs three at a time. They were past the halfway point. I had to hurry. I stumbled once and fell. Didn't feel a thing. Was up and running. I had only one thought. Well, two. Saving Lori. And settling a score. With any luck I could do both and still get back in time for Miss McDermid's second set.

My legs and arms ached by the time I got to the bottom of the stairs. I paused and tried to slow my breathing so it wouldn't give me away. The water would hide the sound, but in my own ears I was as loud as a locomotive. After less than a minute, I started down towards the dock.

Pausing at the edge of the bushes I cased the waterfront. Once I left the cover of the trees I'd be a clear target. Nothing moved. I dropped to my belly and started towards the boathouse. I crawled down beside the dock and started into the water. The normally pleasant lapping sound against the piles was annoying. I was near the boathouse when I heard the clink of an oarlock.

I pulled myself onto the dock. The disappearing propeller boat was gone. I ran down the dock to the spot where I'd unloaded the booze and peered into the darkness. I heard the spin of a starter. A pause while the cord was rewound. The second time it caught and an engine sputtered to life. I listened carefully and decided they were heading north.

I ran as fast as I could through the trees and up the stairs. The best my legs could do was two at a time on the way up. When I hit the top I thought they might explode. I wasn't sure I'd ever walk normally again as I negotiated my way across the lawn. Pure lead. But they got me to the barn, and Scotty. Working fast I cinched his saddle and dragged him out the door. Sensing my urgency he didn't put up a fuss. Or maybe it was the tuxedo.

I leapt, or more like lurched, into the saddle.

"Ho! D.B." It was Eddie. "Where to?"

"North. He's got her in a boat going north."

Eddie ran for his car. I gave Scotty a double kick in the sides and he sprinted up the lane.

Scotty and I made good time riding along the edge of the road. A mile north of the Corran, a county road turned east towards the escarpment. It led to the fishing village of Colpoy's Bay. Less used than the centre road, it was in better shape.

I urged Scotty from a trot to a gallop. He covered the half mile to the top of the hill in less than two minutes. The road cut down the side of the steep hill. We took it at speed, finding that it improved in quality near the bottom. It had been recently repaired. A car owner in the village, no doubt.

No sooner had I thought it when I heard the sound of a starter grinding at the end of the street. A yell followed. The engine caught. Less than fifty feet away a set of headlamps came on. Gears ground. A spinning of gravel and it was off. Scotty and I charged down the road past a man yelling, "My car! My car!" I scanned the water side of the road, trusting Scotty to keep his eye on the car. Near the dock at the end of the street, we passed the boat.

Looking back to the road, the car had disappeared.

"Where is it?" I yelled into the night.

The road curved sharply to the left. The tail lights came into view. Silhouetted against the light of the headlamps, I saw one person. A man. The road was still good. The automobile accelerated away. I dropped the reins onto Scotty's neck and leaned forward.

"This is your chance."

I barely got hold of the saddlehorn. Scotty took off so quickly I was sure he must have jumped right out of his shoes. It was a sight to see. If only it had been daylight. His strong legs pumped in rhythm. He truly was a magnificent runner.

The one-armed man fired a shot. I wasn't worried. There was no way he could hit us at that distance with the little .32. Not while he was driving.

But we were going to catch him. And I had no gun. I did have the Lee Enfield in a side mount on my saddle. I still couldn't risk shooting, not when Lori might be in the car. Also, we were riding so fast, I couldn't risk letting go with both hands to get the gun out. I thought of jumping into the moving car. I'd had enough pain for one week. Reaching back with my right hand I searched my saddlebag. We were coming alongside the car. My roving hand found something heavy. I whipped it out and couldn't suppress a laugh at the irony. I leaned low in my saddle. I took aim and swung. The bag carrying his arm connected squarely with the top of the one-armed man's head.

He lost control of the car and went off the road. Striking a tree, the vehicle stopped. Scotty stopped. Prancing over to the car, he gave a sneer, then a laugh. Horse triumphant.

The one-armed man was slumped over the wheel. Out cold. Blood gushed from a wound where his forehead had hit the wheel. I checked the floors front and back. Lori was nowhere in sight. The cooling engine of the car ticked. Underneath it, fluid was leaking.

"Lori?" I called into the night air. I was rewarded by a kicking from the back of the vehicle. I tore open the trunk and pulled my fiancee from inside.

She looked none the worse for wear. A little out of breath.

"Nothing happened with Colleen."

"I know."

"You do?"

"I was mad at first. Then Colleen came to me and explained it all. I just haven't had a chance to talk to you. I'm sorry."

"It's okay." I said. And it was.

CHAPTER EIGHTEEN
PAY DAY

"Where you been D.B.? You missed all the action." I was standing in front of MacLean's Marketeria. Landlord MacLean had just finished sweeping up. It was after eight on Monday morning. Not long before the start of business. He was pointing at the City Hall clock tower. It had grown to full height, a hundred feet, while I was away. Towering over the downtown, the good citizens of Owen Sound would always know the time. I'm not sure I liked that development. We were all slaves to the clock as it was.

"Sure did," I said, opening the street door and heading up the stairs. It smelled fresher. He'd finally gotten the storms off. Windows had been opened.

A Saturday *Sun Times* lay in front of my door. I picked it up. Unlocked the door. Pushed it and a rather large pile of mail into the room. Bright morning light filled the room. I threw the paper on the desk. I'd read it at home.

On the front page a banner headline read "LOST TIRE GANG FOUND" and in smaller print underneath it read "Oddball Evens Score."

As contracted, I'd solved the crime. He'd taken the credit. Called the reporter from *The Sun Times* down to the jail. Shown them Angus Peacock, the notorious one-armed man, leader of the Lost Tire Gang. Had his picture taken with the culprit. Regaled the members of the press with details of his investigation. They embellished to the point that Oddball achieved deity status.

I spent the morning sorting through mail and back issues of the newspaper. The City Council had begun meeting with developers interested in their offer of investment capital. The announcement of a deal that would bring jobs to Owen Sound was imminent, according to the Mayor. A surprise I found was the conclusion of the Jamieson Johnston murder trial. The dead man's wife and new husband had been acquitted by the jury. Their only crime, it seemed, had been getting married too soon after the old man died. The happy couple barely escaped an angry mob when the cops slipped them out the back door of the courthouse.

At eleven my door opened. It was Oddball, right on time.

"How's the best investigator in town? Enjoying his celebrity status?" I asked.

"Yes, I am," he said with a smile. Reaching into a coat pocket, he brought out an envelope. "Your pay."

I looked inside and let out a low whistle. "Looks like more than we agreed on. Lots more."

"I got a raise."

"You got a raise? For what?"

"For bringing a desperate criminal to justice."

"For sitting at home in an easy chair."

"Anyway I decided you should get a raise too. Even though you couldn't seem to catch the rest of the gang." He looked at me sideways.

"If I told you once, I told you ten times. They got away while Bill Goldfinch was giving me the knuckles."

"Sure, sure."

"Have you been putting the screws to Peacock?"

"Uh huh." He pulled a Havana Stogie from his shirt pocket and lit it. He took a long pull, and exhaled a streamer of blue smoke towards the ceiling. "Good cigar needs whisky. Got any?"

I pulled a bottle and two glasses out of the bottom drawer of my desk. I kept them there in case of emergencies.

"I can't believe you lit that," I said.

"Things are going extremely well. I'm in the mood to celebrate."

"Is he singing?" I poured us each a drink.

"Like a bird."

"I'm surprised."

"He knows he'll swing for the murders."

"Well? What's his story?"

"Angus Peacock is McNeill's cousin. He came here from Ireland just over a year ago to live on the estate. He'd gotten into some trouble in the old country. The family wanted rid of him. For McNeill, it was an obligation. He's made it very clear that he didn't care much for his cousin, and virtually ignored him."

"Which meant Peacock could do pretty much whatever he wanted."

"Sure. So he hired the late Bill Goldfinch. Goldy, as he was known to you. He wanted to make a big score. But that kind of thing takes money to set up. That was the one thing he didn't have much of. So they started with the petty stuff."

"What about his remittance?"

"A pittance. The cottage was free, and the family only sent enough to keep him in groceries. Not enough for a man of his ambition."

"So he had bigger plans?"

"Yes. The kidnapping of Miss McDermid was one. He was going to ransom her to McNeill."

I let out a low whistle.

"That's not all," Oddball continued. "We found plans for Molson's Bank in Owen Sound when we searched the cottage. They were going to knock it over with the machine guns they got from you."

"He had to know I wouldn't really sell them three guns."

"That's just the thing. He didn't know it was you who had joined the gang. Not until that story in *The Canadian Echo*."

"I knew that was going to be trouble."

"More than you know. That's how he snagged Glori too."

"Huh?"

"He and McNeill's son."

"Malcolm."

"Right. They picked up Glori outside Owen Sound. She wanted a ride. Anywhere. Everything was fine until she saw a copy of the newspaper lying on the car seat and tried to impress them with her brother-in-law, the hero."

"Peacock knew exactly what to do."

"That's right. She was his trump card. He knew you'd come to get her. What he didn't know was that you would be at the party. You took him by surprise, and ruined his plans for revenge."

"What if I hadn't ruined his plans?"

"He might have killed Glori."

"Yikes. I guess it was my lucky day."

"Or hers."

"I've promised Eddie I'd meet him for a drink. Will you join us?"

"Don't mind if I do."

★★★

The day was warm and fresh smelling. Cars rattled up and down the street. We walked to The Manjuris. Eddie was there.

"Hey, D.B.!" he called. "Get it all patched up with the missus?"

"Wedding's on."

He spotted Oddball coming through the door behind me. "You here on official business?"

"Not on your life," Oddball said. "I come for a drink. He's payin'."

"In that case, step right over here." Eddie led the way to the bar. Red had glasses and a bottle set up. He nodded a greeting and backed away.

"Wedding's on? Good news, eh?" Eddie said. "Let's drink to that."

"Or to our new house," I said.

"You bought that old clunker? The one by the library? It's at least 30 years old. Whyn't ya buy a new place?" Eddie asked.

I laughed. "I'll have to find someone a lot richer than the county to work for, if I want to buy anything else."

"Hey, we paid you okay!" Oddball mocked offence.

"When's the big date?" Eddie asked.

"We can move in any time after next month."

"No. The big date."

"Oh, the BIG date. August."

"Well, here's to it."

"What's everyone drinking to?" Sil asked before we got started.

"Sil!" Eddie was surprised.

"Sil drinking in the daytime? Must be bad news."

"Huh?" Oddball grunted.

"Oak Hall was bought out. Sil met his new boss this morning," I explained. "And?"

"Keepin' me on. With a raise." He smiled. Eddie thrust a glass of whisky in his hand and we all drank.

"That's good," Oddball said, handing over his glass for another. Next thing he'd have the bag of pastries out.

"Van go home?" Sil asked.

"Not yet. He's waitin' for his dough."

"You be sure and get that to him now," Oddball said sternly.

"Right."

The door behind us burst open and one of Eddie's men ran in.

"Big fight outside!" he said breathlessly.

"Who?" Eddie asked.

"Constable Tom Carson."

"Against how many this time?" I asked, gulping my whisky.

"Just two. One's got a shotgun. Over on the 10th Street bridge."

"Let's go." Eddie grabbed his hat and led us down the stairs.

A crowd had gathered by the time we came around the corner. The combatants were on the south sidewalk. One man, bloodied, was on the ground. Tom Carson was face to face with the shotgun carrier. I could have told the shotgun man he would lose. Could have told him that Constable Tom Carson was without question the toughest man in Owen Sound. I'm sure he wouldn't have believed me. So I watched Tom disarm him, then lay him out next to his buddy. The crowd cheered and started to break up. We'd missed the best of it. While Oddball went to help with the mop up, Eddie, Sil and I started back to The Manjuris. As we turned the corner I glanced across the street. I wasn't paying attention and walked straight into a young man.

"Oh. Sorry, I..." I started as I turned to help him up.

"Verle!" the smiling face said.

"Jug!" I dragged the boy up off the ground and gave him a fierce hug. "I thought you were dead. What happened?"

"I woke up in a tree. It was daylight and everyone was gone. So I hitched a ride. Been here a coupla days now."

I took him to dinner at The City. Dolores thought he was cute and told him so. "What about the others?" he asked. "Are they in jail then? Where are they? What's happened?"

"You all broke the law. What do you think is going to happen?"

"Dunno," he said, frowning.

"You could get jail. Or hard labour. What do they do in Ireland?"

"Jail."

"Did you expect less here?"

"I expected more."

"C'mon," I said standing.

We left The City and walked through the downtown. It was lunchtime and there were a lot of people around. We wove back and forth through the crowds until we got to the City Hotel stables. The doors were wide open and a crew was loading supplies onto a wagon. One of the girls screamed.

"Jug. Oh my. Jug!" Colleen burst into tears and scrambled down from the wagon.

"What? Hey…Oh, Jug!" Davey shouted with joy and ran to greet his friend.

Shelagh came round the back of the wagon and joined the fray. Soon they were all crying and laughing and hugging at the same time. Van walked around the wagon and surveyed the scene.

"Room for one more?" I asked.

"Many hands make light work."

At the side of the stable another girl watched, aloof. I walked over to her.

"Hello Glori," I said, giving her a hug.

She hugged me back and, through tears, said, "Thanks, D.B."

"Will you be okay with this crew?" I asked.

She nodded and wiped her eyes. "I think a little time away would be good right now. Mommy and Daddy agree."

"They know Van. You'll be safe with him."

"I know."

"Do you need anything?" I asked. "Have you met everyone?"

"They're thick as thieves already," Van said from behind me. "They'll get along just fine."

"That's good," I said offering a hand. We shook, then embraced. I turned once more to watch as the kids continued loading the wagon.

"Good luck," I said to them. "Build him a nice store."

THE END

THE THIMBLERIG

An action packed detective story set in Owen Sound, 1923.

A D.B. Murphy Adventure

Richard J Thomas

Chapter One

The body was frozen to the cement retaining wall above the mill dam. Encased in ice. The head and shoulders were firmly stuck to the wall. A cop in hip boots dangled at the end of a rope, feet braced against the top of the spillway. Inches below him, the Sydenham River roared over a twenty foot drop.

If Hip Boots went over the edge, it would be days before the black churning water at the base of the dam disgorged him. Stinky George had stayed down more than a week. Perhaps the frozen corpse had known about George, had made one final effort to save himself by clinging to the wall.

At the other end of the rope two cops, fat in their winter gear, struggled to steady their dangling fellow officer who was using a wooden mallet to try and break the body free. Every time he swung, his position became momentarily precarious. The blows sounded like pistol shots in the early morning of the river valley.

Half an hour of effort had failed to move the body, but the noise had drawn a crowd. People lined the road along the top of the west bank. On the east bank, not far from where I stood, a lone dog sat watching the proceedings.

I'd been tipped to the action just before five when the overnight switchboard operator had called. Her tips earned her a small commission from the D.B. Murphy Detective Agency.

"Cops are at the mill dam," she said when I finally dragged myself away from Lori and our warm bed.

"Yeah?" The hallway was cold. I did a little dance as we spoke.

"Someone in the ice."

"A stiff?"

"Very." She disconnected.

Ten minutes later I was shivering with the rest of the crowd at the mill dam.

"They'll never do it," said Constable Tom Carson who was standing beside me. The toughest cop on the force, I'd once seen him disarm two men single-handed.

I was distracted by a fantasy involving hot coffee and breakfast at the City Café. "You never can tell," I said.

"They got no leverage."

His words were still in the air between us when a loud cheer went up. The rope-dangling mallet-wielding copper had cleared enough of the body to tie a rope around before scrambling back to the top of the mill dam.

A sharp February wind sliced up the river from Georgian Bay. Backs were turned against it and shoulders were hunched. A second, stronger gust followed. Trouser legs flapped with a vengeance. Faces were hidden behind scarves and mittens. The wind stopped as suddenly as it started.

On top of the dam the cops started to haul their catch in. First they gave a tentative tug on the rope to be sure it was well attached. Then they put their backs into it. On the third grunt and heave the body came free. At the same time the cop anchoring the rope slipped and lost his footing. He kicked the feet out from under the man in front of him when he fell. The frozen body at the end of the rope dipped below the surface of the water. The cops skidded across the ice after it. The only one of them left standing hit the railing with a bone-racking thud. He wedged into it and saved the investigation. The leather-lined hogskin gloves he wore prevented rope burn as he clamped down to stop the body from sliding further.

The other two officers got to their feet and rushed to his aid. The crowd applauded as the body broke the surface and inched its way back up the mill dam. The mutt barked. It looked like a border collie. It hadn't moved all morning.

A hundred yards upriver around the bend, an ice crew was at work. I could hear the rasping of the big hand saws, even at that distance. Once you learned it, it was a sound you never forgot. The ice would be loaded onto a sledge and drawn downtown to the ice house. Packed in sawdust, the harvest would be used to keep iceboxes cool through the warm summer months. I knew by the temperature the river cutting was almost finished. Within a week the crew would be out on the bay. Some customers preferred bay ice, believing it to be cleaner than the stuff that came from the river. Working in the open, the cutting crew would be as cold as their harvest.

Not as cold as the body the officers hauled up.

"Is it him?" Police Chief Foster asked. Around town he was known as Snake Foster. I'm not sure why.

Constable Carson walked over to the corpse. "Can't tell," he called over his shoulder. "Ice is too thick."

"Get to work," the chief grunted, and Hip Boots stepped forward. In addition to a wooden mallet, he had a chisel in his hands. With the skill of da Vinci, he started on the head.

The crowd buzzed as the sculptor chiseled away. It wasn't likely that art would be revealed. An artist, yes. Of the con variety.

"Well?" the chief asked Carson.

"Well?" Carson queried Hip Boots, who moved aside so the senior officer could step in for a look. "It's him. It's Everett Hall."

The wind was down so his voice carried loud and clear in the river valley. The chief gave a satisfied nod, relief showing on every feature. A cheer went up from the crowd.

CHAPTER TWO

"Take him down to the foundry at Kennedy's. Set him beside the big furnace. When he thaws take him over to Doc Soames at the General and Marine Hospital and see what killed him," the Chief instructed Carson.

The crowd dispersed and I went with it. The dog barked once as I left but when I turned I didn't see it anywhere. I wasn't sure why I'd gone down to the mill dam. Interest, I suppose. The possibility of a job. I'd been following Everett Hall's story since his arrival in town on Armistice Day, November eleventh of the previous year, 1922.

Technically a dry event due to prohibition, the celebration was anything but sober. Everett Hall made his grand entrance late in the afternoon when he rolled up in a McLaughlin Buick. Resplendent in a linen suit and tan bowler, he walked straight up to the mayor and doffed his hat, revealing a fashionable head of silver hair. Piercing blue eyes and a straight nose complemented his boyish face. He addressed the gathering, announcing he had come to Owen Sound to begin a new manufacturing business. "Electric iceboxes, for use in the home," he had said. "A revolutionary idea that will make Owen Sound a world class city."

At City Hall a few days later he had unveiled the plans for his electric icebox. The city fathers had committed twenty-five thousand to the project on the spot. After all, there would be five hundred new jobs. Good for the hundreds of Grey County veterans who had survived the trenches of France only to become economic casualties. The war had been over for years, but many men still hadn't found work.

Within a week, Hall had rented a factory near Mudtown at the northern edge of the city's factory district. Thousands of citizens had lined up for jobs, lured by the promise of wages equal to those earned by workers in Toronto. Machinery for Owen Sound's newest industrial resident had begun arriving by train.

In the middle of his second month in town, Hall had called another public meeting. A decision had been made to offer shares in the new Northern Home Refrigeration Company to the same business leaders who had wholeheartedly prompted the city council to support it. Another twenty-six thousand dollars was collected.

It all went bad the last week of January. No one had been hired and the factory had not opened. Nosey Parker, *The Daily Sun-Times* reporter blew the scheme wide open and revealed the confidence game for what it was. A thimblerig. Hall had disappeared. Now he had turned up dead.

★★★

A car horn brought me back to the reality of 2nd Avenue West in mid-February. "Climb in," the familiar voice of High Constable Oddball Scott shouted over the sound of his Chevy. The county had bought it for him the summer before. He insisted on driving it no matter what the season or weather conditions. The passenger door squeaked open and I jumped in. "You're up early," he said as I slammed it shut behind me.

Outside a dog barked. It was the mutt from the mill dam. I'd been so absorbed with my thoughts I hadn't seen it following me. Good thing it wasn't armed.

"Your dog?" he asked. It was sitting on the sidewalk about twenty feet from the car. Staring.

"Nope. Saw him down at the mill dam. He was alone."

I turned back to Oddball as the car lurched forward. The quiet of the morning was momentarily shattered by the gnashing of gears.

"Damn Chevy," he cursed under his breath as he tried to bring the beast under control.

"Why do you drive this thing in the winter? Stick with a horse."

"We can't all have a horse like your Scotty. 'Sides, they plough half a dozen streets now."

"The county doesn't plough."

"How'd ya mean?"

"You're High Constable of the county, not the city. You don't work in Owen Sound."

"Oh that. Well, I got a horse for the county, don't I?"

Oddball Scott had gained his nickname as a rookie. He'd had a mishap with a pistol he had tucked into the front of his pants when he'd cornered the notorious bank robber Red Ryan. Attempting a quick draw, the gun had gone off a little early, and his "boys" had taken the worst of it. One of them didn't make it, and someone had pegged the involuntary amputee "Oddball".

The lawman slowed down at the intersection of 8th and 2nd and went to the right of the silent policeman. A concrete device meant to direct traffic to the proper side of the road, it had met the fender of more than one car. My office was in that block, across from the city hall.

"Stiff up at the mill dam," I said.

"Oh?" He raised an eyebrow.

"Everett Hall."

His breath whistled out.

"Everett Hall? Someone gave him the business?"

"The works. He was in the water frozen to the retaining wall."

Oddball smiled. He had a friendly face that made it easy to ignore the fact that he wasn't the swiftest dog in the pack. Red hair, blue eyes and average build, he was half a dozen years my senior. Habitually a Havana stogie hung from a corner of his mouth. He never lit them. Just sucked them to death. They were local, not Cuban, made by the Cooke Cigar Company on 8th Street.

"You hired?" he asked.

"The yards hired me to find out who's stealing coal."

"I mean the Hall job."

"No," I shook my head. "Murder was up to the cops in town last time I checked."

"Sure it is. But where's the fifty thousand?"

"The what?"

"The money he stole. Was it on him?"

"Won't know until he's thawed."

"I betcha it wasn't."

"The guy who finds it is gonna be popular."

"The guy who finds it is gonna be rich."

"I hadn't thought of it that way. Guess maybe I have something to do after all."

CHAPTER THREE

I'd been a blacksmith before the war. The family business. Then I'd joined up and gone to Europe for four years. A gunner, the better part of my job had been loading hundred and two hundred pound artillery shells. It was hard work, but better than the trenches.

After the war there was no call for blacksmiths. The automobile and the assembly line had done away with my career. I'd opened my own private investigation office above MacLean's Marketeria on the main street of Owen Sound in 1921.

My landlord was shoveling the sidewalk in front of the Marketeria when Oddball dropped me off. The area in front of my door wasn't cleared.

"What gives?" I asked pointing at the pile of snow. James MacLean put his shovel down and wiped his perspiring forehead on a coat sleeve.

"You don't come to work this early. Not once in the time you've rented. Never once before nine o'clock. Usually not until ten. Sometimes not at all."

"I like to keep you guessing."

"You see the paper yesterday?"

"Uh-huh."

"A golden cat's head!"

"I saw. A Canadian got killed there, too."

"Solid gold! A cat's head." MacLean's eyes glowed, the merchant inside him counting dollars.

For weeks *The Daily Sun-Times* had been filled with stories of the work at Luxor, in Egypt. MacLean and I talked daily about the ongoing excavations. A lot of people did. It kept our minds off the more serious events taking place in Europe. Germany had stopped making reparation payments of coal and timber to France. Miners in the Ruhr Valley, the coal centre of Europe, were striking to protest the worthless deutschmark. A hundred thousand French troops were occupying the Ruhr and there was a real threat of war breaking out again. The thought was horrific. The world couldn't afford the loss of another generation.

"They warned tourists not to go out at night," MacLean continued. "But you're right. It is a shame. Did I mention the cat's head was solid gold?"

I scooped up a handful of snow and threw it at his head. He ducked then made like he'd throw a shovelful at me. I headed for my door.

"They say they'll have Tut Ankh Amen out by the middle of the week."

"Great. More rich conversation," I said, door keys in my hand.

"Oh, by the way…" MacLean said.

I turned, expecting the question.

"Why are you out so early this morning?" His voice dropped to a conspiratorial whisper.

"Everett Hall is dead."

MacLean stopped his work again and smiled.

"He had it coming. Who killed him?"

"Could have been anyone. Lots had reason."

MacLean nodded his agreement. "How'd he die?"

"Don't know yet. He was frozen to the side wall of the mill dam."

"Let's go inside. I've got a fire on."

It was warm inside the store. We went straight back to the stove. Foreseeing the coal shortage, MacLean had loaded up early in the winter.

"There's coffee on the stove," he said. "I need one."

He crossed to the dry goods and pulled a bottle of hooch out from behind some boxes of Bovril. Carrying it back to the stove, he glugged a shot into each of our cups.

"It doesn't surprise me," he said.

"How much did he take you for?"

MacLean's face went dark. "A thousand."

"Holy moly!"

"It's everything I've got. Aside from the store. He took it all."

"That's the way thimbleriggers work. First they make you greedy. Then they take you for everything you're worth."

"I didn't know it was rigged until that article Nosey Parker had in the newspaper." He took a slug straight from the bottle before passing it to me.

"I guess I just hoped that somehow…"

"You'd get it back?" I finished the sentence for him.

"Yeah." He grabbed the bottle back and took another drink. I felt sorry for him, and the rest of the investors.

"It's gotta be somewhere," I said. "Maybe the investors would consider paying a commission to the fella who finds it?"

MacLean thought for a second then started to nod. "If you get it back I'd pay you. Ten per cent."

"I already have a job."

"Looking for missing coal? It'll keep. The shortage isn't going to end anytime soon."

I could barely see my breath in the hallway when I went up to my office. MacLean's stove had heated things up nicely. I heard the scrape of his shovel outside the lower door as I reached the landing.

I picked up a few days worth of mail and newspapers and fumbled keys out of my pocket. They slipped out of my hand and hit the floor with a crash. A flicker of movement behind the frosted glass of my office door caught my eye.

Someone was inside.

CHAPTER FOUR

The Webley & Scott .455 wasn't under my arm. It was cleverly concealed in my desk. I still had the .32 automatic in my boot. In a flash I had it in my hand.

I unlocked the door and turned the knob. Then I kicked it hard. The door whistled open, slammed into the person hiding behind it and bounced back. A muffled groan came from behind the door. A broken nose was my guess.

"Come out." I held the gun and waited.

A masked man appeared. One hand was clutching the spot where I imagined his nose had been. The other held a leather billy. A big one. Six ounces of braided leather could seriously mess up a man. This billy had to weigh a full pound. The hand holding it wasn't tiny either.

"Hands up." I gestured at Broken Nose.

Suddenly another masked man sprang up from behind the desk. Leaping forward, he shoved a chair at me. I jumped out of the way and saved my life. The closet door burst open. A third man dashed out with his arm swinging. His billy, intended for my head, hit my gun arm instead. It struck with a force that sent shards of pain to my shoulder. My automatic clattered to the floor. The third attacker raised his arm for another swing. I kicked his knee so hard it cracked.

"Bloody hell!" he screamed and fell to the floor.

Then the other two were on me. I swung at Broken Nose, forcing him to alter his attack. The second man rammed his head into my stomach sending my wind out in a gust. I managed to twist as we went down. He landed on the bottom. Number Three was on his feet. He caught me in the gut with a clean shot. I saw it coming, but it still hurt. I swung with my left and hit his head. I was winding up for another when the kick landed. Right in the place a man hates to be kicked.

The pain was overwhelming. For a moment I couldn't move.

"Let's teach this nancy-boy a thing or two," grunted Broken Nose. With a furious lash his billy hit my upper thigh. My gut clenched. I barely avoided vomiting.

Number Two kicked me again. I caught his ankle. He hit the ground hard. I struggled to get to my feet. I was slick with sweat.

A fist caught me in the face. Broken Nose grabbed me from behind. He clamped an arm around my windpipe.

"Aw hell," Number Three yelled. "Stick him."

With a click Number Two opened his push button knife. The long steel blade locked in place. The word 'Invincible' was written in raised lettering on the gleaming steel. As the limping man approached, Broken Nose tightened his grip on my neck.

"Keep yer nose outta other people's business," Broken Nose said. Every word was accompanied by a nasal toot from his busted beezer.

"Like you…" I said in an airless whisper.

"Yeah. Stay away from…"

His words were cut off by the sound of MacLean's shovel smashing in the frosted glass of my office door.

"What in hell's name is going on?" he roared.

CHAPTER FIVE

All three assailants charged the door at the same instant. MacLean swung his shovel and caught Broken Nose a glancing blow on the shoulder. He yelped and kept moving. Number Three followed, swinging his deadly billy. He caught MacLean in the side of the head. The stout landlord fell like a Bruce Peninsula pine.

I stumbled to my .32 but they were down the back stairs in a clatter by the time it was in my hand. I fired a shot into the wall above the door anyway. For effect.

Easing MacLean up, I got him into a chair. He came around slowly. Blood oozed from the welt behind his ear.

"I'm going down to get some ice. And that bottle of yours."

On my way back I heard a crash in my office. Thinking our assailants had returned I ran the rest of the way up with my gun drawn. The door was still open. I could see MacLean on the floor but he was alone.

"Which chair did you sit me on?" he asked foggily as I helped him up.

"The wrong one." It was in pieces all over the floor. The leg had needed fixing for more than two years.

I handed him the bag of ice.

"Who were they?" He winced when the ice touched his neck.

"A case."

"The Hall case?"

"They were about to tell me when you crashed the party."

"Oh. Sorry."

"Not at all. If it wasn't for you, those probably would have been the last words I ever heard."

We had a drink and he left with the bottle. I was sitting at my desk aching. I was going to be sore. Pawing through the junk scattered across the top of my desk I located a stack of clippings right where I'd left them. The few times Lori had been to the office she'd wanted to clean. I'd resisted, assuring her I knew exactly where everything was. I was fairly sure I did. At the bottom of the pile, sorted in reverse chronological order, was an advertisement placed by the city council in dozens of North American newspapers. "CASH OFFERED FOR MANUFACTURERS TO RELOCATE TO OWEN SOUND" the headline screamed. An open invitation to every grifter, flim flammer and thimblerigger on the continent. It had been the start of everything.

I read until noon was announced by the clock in the tower across the street in front of City Hall. I got up and took a clean shirt from the closet. A small mirror revealed a mouse under my left eye. A hazard of the job. The newspaper clippings had given me a couple of ideas. One was to visit Nosey Parker. The other was to walk across to City Hall and ask some questions.

I went back to the desk and opened the bottom drawer. It was empty. Unbelievingly, I pulled the drawer right out. My .455 was gone. Along with an entire box of manstopper bullets.

I put my coat back on and headed down the stairs into February. There was no point in moping around. 2nd Avenue East was a river of snow, all currents and eddies. A couple of cars were angle parked in front of shops, despite the weather. Horses pulled skidders full of local hemlock up and down the main street. Some were tied to lampposts. Council had removed all the hitching posts to give Owen Sound a more modern look.

I saw few people as I crossed to City Hall. Owen Sound always appeared deserted during the winter. No one wanted to be out of doors more than absolutely necessary.

I'd decided the best way to find the money was to find the killer. The best way to find the killer was to find out who had lost the most to Everett Hall. It was the kind of information they might have at City Hall. At lunchtime the managers and politicians would be at a trough somewhere, giving me time to exploit city staff with little interference.

I stomped the snow off my boots inside the front door and took off my hat. At the information desk, I gave the bell a good ring. Before the war I'd known people at City Hall. The staff had changed while I was away, and very few faces were familiar to me now.

"May I help you, sir?" A woman had come into the lobby from the office behind. Her brass nameplate said Catherine Ballantyne. She was a brunette of medium height with a pleasant smile.

"I'm looking for some information," I said, handing her my card.

"I'll do my best Mr. Murphy."

"Call me D.B."

"Alright then D.B., how can I help you?"

"I'm investigating the death of Everett Hall."

She didn't seem a bit surprised.

"Yes?"

"Did he have associates? Maybe you have a list of investors?"

"I don't know about associates. He took money from everyone in Owen Sound. Including the city itself."

"I was hoping for something a little more specific."

"Such as?" she asked.

"Names. Amounts. Anything."

She looked thoughtful for a moment, then said, "I could check the information he filed with the Clerk. For his business license."

"It's probably worth as much as he was."

She crossed to a bank of file drawers and, after careful consideration, pulled one open. A quick search and she moved to another drawer, then another. By the time she'd closed the third one she was frowning.

"It's gone. Let me check with our Mr. Williams. He may have it."

She headed for the Clerk's office. I heard murmuring and then Miss Ballantyne returned with a diminutive civil servant. He was less than five feet in height. Black hair was oiled to his scalp. His eyes were framed and magnified by thick glasses. An obsequious little fellow, he was clearly second, or maybe even third in charge. Except during noon hour. Then he was the King of City Hall.

"Yes sir?" he inquired. "How may I be of service?" I'm not sure what it is short men always seem to have to prove. Whatever it is, this guy had it and he was doing his best to look down on me despite his obvious height disadvantage.

He'd already decided not to tell me anything. I could tell by his stance. I could also see that he knew I knew. So did Catherine Ballantyne, but I was committed to the charade.

"I'm investigating Everett Hall's murder. I was hoping to take a look at any information you might have on him."

Mr. Williams barely managed a smile. Waves of bureaucratic condescension preceded his response. "Those documents are confidential, sir. Available only to Council and City Hall staff."

"When there's public money involved the paperwork is usually public information."

"Usually, yes. But there's nothing usual about this, is there sir?" His face closed down and I knew there was no point in further questions.

"Thank you," I said.

"No. Thank you," was the response. "We always encourage people to take advantage of our open door policy here at City Hall." Mr. Williams pulled the door to the inner office closed behind him.

"He isn't always like that," Miss Ballantyne said. "It's just that noon is the only time of day he feels important."

She was holding my card out.

"Please keep it," I said. "If you think of anything, anything at all, don't hesitate to call. Or drop by my office."

"What is it you're looking for, exactly?"

"The money."

"Really? There's nothing I could possibly know that would help you," she smiled. "You'd probably learn more from Everett Hall's girlfriend."

"His girlfriend?"

"Valerie Sutherland. She lives out Brooke."

CHAPTER SIX

I went to the City Café for lunch. It was on 10th Street East between Second and Third. When I was a bachelor it was my second home. Married, I only ate an occasional lunch there. When I was on a case and could expense it.

"Will ya look who it is, Cosmo," a loud voice called as I came through the door. "The married detective."

The café fell silent. Every eye in the place was on me. Behind the counter, Cosmo the Greek grunted as he leaned over the grill.

"She's jealous," I said to the room. Amidst the laughter people started to shovel food again. "Hello Dolores." I followed her to an empty table. While I hung up my coat, she laid the place setting and dropped a menu. Dolores and I had known each other since grade school.

"Special's a hot turkey sandwich."

"Okay," I said.

"Coffee?"

"Sure. Please."

She left and Constable Tom Carson followed a draft through the front door. He took his coat off and came straight over.

"Cold out there," he said rubbing his hands together.

"Tell me something I don't know," I said with a smile. "Coffee's hot."

"I'll have what he's having," Tom called across the restaurant to Dolores.

"Sure you can afford it on a policeman's salary?" she called back.

"He's paying," Carson laughed and gave me a wink.

"I am?"

"Sure." Carson laughed again.

"Isn't that called bribery or corruption of a public official or something?"

"Consider it charity." I thought it over for a moment. So far in the course of my day I hadn't done one charitable thing.

"Okay."

"So what happened to you?" He gestured at one of the bruises on my face. I told him about the attack.

"What'd ya think about this morning?" I had to strain to hear him ask the question.

"It's amazing, the things you find in the Sydenham River nowadays."

"If we don't watch it we'll have to get our drinking water somewhere else."

"What'd he die of?" I asked.

"He's not even thawed yet. It'll be tonight before they can open him up."

We talked over lunch. The subject of Everett Hall didn't come around again. Instead, I asked him about police station politics, City Hall politics and told him about the golden cat's head they'd found in the tomb of Tut Ankh Amen. When we finished eating, he promised to call by the house as soon as he knew the cause of death.

★★★

After lunch I walked back down to the mill dam. The wind was at my back so it didn't seem as cold. At around 6th Street the dog picked me up and followed at a discreet distance.

Before I got to the mill dam I could hear the sound of the big saws. The ice crew was cutting fast while the bitter cold lasted. I climbed down the bank and walked on the ice around the bend in the river, skirting the large hole made by the harvesters. A thin scab of ice had already formed to separate air and water.

There were six men on the crew, overseen by a foreman who was nowhere in sight as I approached. Three of the men were cutting blocks of ice with huge hand saws. The other three, wearing heavy leather aprons, lifted the blocks out of the water onto a sledge.

I thought I was going to make it to the crew when thc stout foreman stepped out from behind a pile of ice and blocked the way. Grey haired and florid faced, he was angry, as always. I'd not seen him for years but he looked exactly as I remembered.

"I thought I told you never to come near me!" he barked.

A man who didn't know him as well might have flinched at the hot anger. I'd known him a long time. I met his gaze and said the only thing I could think of.

"Hello, Uncle Hank."

CHAPTER SEVEN

"What in hell are you doing here?"

There was bad blood between Hank and me going back to my decision to leave blacksmithing for the war. I tried to remain calm as he spat the words in my direction.

"Well?" he hollered loud enough that the cutters stopped working to see what was happening. Uncle Hank barely noticed.

"I'm investigating the death of Everett Hall," I announced in a loud voice. "I need to ask some questions."

The low mutter that rippled through the crew provided a first bit of information. They all knew who the thimblerigger was. Probably most of them had already talked to the police.

"Bugger off." Uncle Hank turned away from me. "You men get back to work," he yelled. "I ain't paying ya to stand around gawkin'."

"My name is D.B. Murphy," I called before they started sawing again. "Some of you know me. I have an office downtown above MacLean's Marketeria. Come and see me if you know something about this murder."

"Any man who does will lose his job," Uncle Hank shouted back.

"Someone killed Everett Hall."

"Had it comin'," my uncle muttered.

"The law doesn't care about that."

"What do you have to do with the law? You're no copper," he said without turning around. "Not a real one anyway."

There's something about family that can make a person weak. The usual defenses fail.

I grabbed Hank by the left arm, to swing him around so we were face to face. He swung at me and I ended up chewing his knuckles. I reacted to the situation without thinking. I cocked a fist. But the look of triumph on his face as he braced himself for the blow stopped me throwing it.

"That was a free shot," I said. "Don't try it again, Hank."

I started across the ice, away from the gang. But he wasn't ready to let it go. I heard his footsteps hurrying behind me.

"BIG MAN!" he screamed as loud as any man could. "Big detective. You're afraid to mix it up with yer poor old uncle are ya?"

I knew Hank well enough to know there was no point in talking. I kept on across the ice. I'd just have to hope that if any of the crew members had information, they'd come to my office. Otherwise it would mean a lot of leg work tracking them all down at their homes.

"Big man! Hey, big man." He was still following but was well back of me. "Who you goin' to beat up on now? Your dad maybe? Gonna beat him up? Oh, I forgot. You can't. He's dead. Isn't he Danny-Boy? Dead."

That stopped me. I turned and shot a look that backed him up a step or two. Then I continued on without another word.

CHAPTER EIGHT

I felt like Everett Hall by the time I got home. Frozen. Stiff. My gut ached. Inside I was still fuming over the encounter with Uncle Hank. In short, I was a mess.

I could hear the muted thump of the piano playing *Second-hand Rose* as I came up the front walk. Students. Lori had kept her students. Sometimes in the snoop business there was money, big money. Mostly though it was nickel-and-dime stuff, barely enough to pay the bills. The money she made teaching went a long way towards putting food on the table regularly.

The door between the living room and the foyer was closed. I struggled out of my things and went to the kitchen. I got the good bottle out, poured three fingers of whisky and drank it straight down. I poured another, then grabbed *The Daily Sun-Times* and went upstairs. It had been an early morning and a long day. A wee lie down would feel good.

Lori's warm hand woke me. She was sitting on the edge of the bed rubbing my cheek. Light spilled into the room from the hallway.

I smiled. "Hello, Mrs. Murphy."

"Hard day at the office, honey?" She pulled the cover down and gaped at the bruises. To her credit she didn't say anything but, "Hungry?"

"For you." I pulled her closer and gave her a vigorous kiss.

I felt like another and as it turned out, so did she.

"I didn't know he hated you so much." We were sitting down to a late supper in our pajamas. It seemed silly to get dressed for just the two of us. A tall candle burned on the table between us. Beef stew and fresh bread. Cold beer for me, milk for Lori. The kind of mid-February meal that's so right it makes you happy just to be alive.

"I don't know how it got started," I said between mouthfuls. "What made it worse was the war. Dad didn't want me to go. I went. He died while I was in France."

"Your dad had a heart attack."

"A broken heart, according to Uncle Hank."

"Hank thinks you're responsible for your dad's death? How could you be?"

"I couldn't. But there it is."

"Doesn't seem fair. Or logical."

"What do women know about logic?" I teased.

"So MacLean and the other investors will pay you a commission to find their money?" she asked, ignoring my comment.

"MacLean will," I said. "He's going to try and get the others to agree."

"And you have to find the killer to find the money?"

"I think so."

"We could pay off the house."

"If I find the money."

"You'll find it. But that means you'll find the killer too. Someone is already beating you up and stealing your gun. I think I should be afraid of what might happen. I'm too young to be a widow."

"I'm too young to be a corpse. From now on I'll be more careful."

"You'd better," she pouted.

I moved my foot until it touched hers. Her smile nearly melted me.

★★★

Tom Carson was at the kitchen door before eight the next morning. "Doc Soames says Everett Hall was murdered."

I sat him down at the kitchen table and grabbed the coffee pot from the top of the stove. Stopping at the cupboard for a second cup, I said, "Not much of a surprise in that. How?"

"Sapped. With a billy. He had a real nice egg behind his right ear."

"One way to stop a guy from swimming." I poured coffee for Tom and sat down to my own.

"If the poison didn't get him first," Tom said after a long sip.

"Poison?"

“Last thing he ate was pie. Poisoned pie.”

I set my cup down in a hurry. “Are you kidding?”

“It was apple.” He took another sip of coffee.

“Somebody really wanted him dead.”

“That’s probably why they stabbed him.”

“What!” I slammed my cup down so hard that coffee sloshed across the table.

“With a filleting knife. Shot him too. Probably a .32. Doc was digging for the bullet when I left.”

“This is incredible.”

“Ya wanna hear the kicker?”

“What?”

“He drowned.”

CHAPTER NINE

The Daily Sun-Times was a few doors down from my office on the same side of 2nd Avenue East. I walked through the front doors just after nine.

"Nosey Parker," I said to the horse-faced receptionist. She gave a sour smirk at the mention of her co-worker's nickname.

"It about a story?"

"Yes."

"Okay. Because he's too busy to see anyone who isn't bringing a story."

"It's about a story. He'll find it interesting."

She nodded at a bench along the wall. I sat down and waited. I sensed rather than heard the thudding presses. The back pages were printed first. Parker was probably still trying to fill the front page with fast-breaking stories. That was the reputation he had. A young newsbreaker on his way to bigger and better things.

The lobby door opened and the receptionist came out. She was followed by an undersized man who was balding prematurely. What he lacked on his head he made up for in his ears and nose. A pencil-thin moustache sat on top of his lip. Below it, a smoldering Roi-Tan was clamped to the corner of his mouth. The suit he wore hung from a set of oversized shoulders. On some men the look was fashionable. On Nosey Parker it was cheap and embarrassing. Nosey Parker was reputed to know everyone in town. He was also reputed to know everyone's secrets.

"If it isn't D.B. Murphy," he said, offering a limp handshake and a sly grin. "I heard you got roughed up. You don't look too bad."

"Most of the damage is below decks," I grimaced.

"Condolences to all the might-have-been future Murphys," he said, laughing.

For a rare moment I was at a loss for words. Nosey filled the gap in conversation without a problem.

"Here to talk about Everett Hall?"

"Yes."

"C'mon in."

We went around a corner and through a set of double doors. I could hear the roar of the presses more clearly. The stench of wet ink hung over us. We strolled down the hallway and into a small office.

"This is just a stepping stone," he apologized for his surroundings. "I ain't gonna be here long."

There were papers and clippings everywhere. It reminded me of my own office. A battered Underwood sat on a small typing table. Parker sat down behind the desk and gestured to the chair in front of it.

"I hear Doc Soames had a look at Hall this morning. He was sapped before he went into the mighty Sydenham."

"Is that so?"

"No, no. This is the part where you confirm what I've heard."

"No."

"No? Too bad," the journalist said, relighting his Roi-Tan. "You got nothing for me baby, I got nothing for you."

"That how you press types get your big scoops?"

"Jeez, you really are a detective."

"Spare me the sarcasm. I've heard there may have been more than one assailant."

Parker sat bolt upright. "Say again?" He picked up a notepad and pencil.

"This isn't coming from me."

"An unnamed source."

"Exactly."

"Okay then. The doctor did look at Hall. Drowning was the official cause of death. But there were a number of other, ah…mitigating factors."

"Hall got the old Rasputin treatment?" Parker asked, recalling the Russian monk who had been poisoned, stabbed, shot, beaten and finally drowned just a few years earlier.

"I can't say."

"Any suspects?"

"A whole town full. Your turn."

"The American Deputy Vice Consul is coming to Owen Sound on the noon train from Toronto."

"And?" I asked, waiting for the punchline.

"Hall was an American."

★★★

I left the newspaper office and walked along 9th Street across the bridge to 1st Avenue West. It was the second day of deep cold. The lack of wind made it seem warm. I headed over to Tenth past the YWCA and the Kennedy and Lemon houses. Crossing the street I continued past the stink of Kennedy's Foundry to the Murphy Ice Works. Uncle Marty would be alone.

The building was straight post-and-beam construction covered with wooden siding. I went around the side and walked through the man-sized door set into the loading doors. The Ice Works was sixty by a hundred feet. It smelled like a wood shop. Sawdust trucked from Keenan's Woodenware was piled nearly to the roof in the back third. It protected ice laid to rest until the summer.

"Hello?" The sawdust deadened my yell. I tried again, louder. "Martin Murphy!"

A head popped up from behind one of the shorter blocks. "Hello?" Uncle Marty squinted in my direction.

"Hey Unc."

"Danny-Boy?" he called scrambling up and across the pile of ice. Marty was nimble as a chipmunk, surprising in a man of sixty. He was the oldest of the Murphy brothers. My dad was next, and would have been fifty-seven. Hank was the baby at fifty-five. Dad had been the only one to marry. Confirmed bachelors, Hank and Marty lived together.

"Is that you Danny-Boy?"

"It's me."

He was all smiles as he strode across the floor. He shook my right hand, and clapped his left on my shoulder.

"How's married life?"

"Good. Thanks for the gun. And the dishes." Dishes for Lori and a gun for me. Marty had known what to get each of us for wedding gifts. The gun was designed by Browning, an M1911 Colt .45 automatic. The best handgun ever made, the Colt had proven itself in the hands of American soldiers during the war. Seven shots. One in the chamber, six in the clip. Just six and a half inches long. It was under my arm, in the place normally occupied by my recently stolen Webley & Scott .455. The ninety-five piece set of dishes was Nippon China. White, decorated with pink and green floral sprays and gold traced edges. Lori assured me it was a highly fashionable way to dine.

"I got the card you sent. But you're welcome on both counts," Uncle Marty said, steering me towards the tiny office in one corner of the Ice Works.

"Nothing has changed," I said when we got inside.

"Nothing ever changes here."

I sat down in one of the chairs in front of the tiny coal fire. Brown coal. It smoked a lot and didn't give off much heat.

"Sorry about that," Uncle Marty said. "It's that damn Ruhr Valley business. Can't get good hard coal anymore."

Uncle Marty poured a couple of drinks.

"It's been too long," he said clinking the edge of his cup against mine.

It was quality stuff.

"That's not cheap," I said.

"Real whisky. We get it from Eddie."

He poured himself another drink. Surprising. He'd never been much of a drinker. Marty had always seemed ageless to me and still did. His hair was iron grey. Brown eyes. Just under six feet tall. He and I had always gotten on well.

"Heard ya bumped into Hank yesterday."

"More like a head-on collision."

"Oh? He told me you barely got away with your life."

"He said what?"

"Why'd you go? You know how Hank feels."

"Heard about Everett Hall?"

"Everyone has."

"I'm on the trail of the money."

"How you gonna find it?"

"By tracking down the killer."

A look of alarm crossed Marty's face. "You can't. It'll…" He stopped for a second, then continued, "it'll be too dangerous."

"That's why you gave me this." I patted the butt of the Colt. "For protection."

"What can I do?"

"Get Hank to come back here for the afternoon. So I can talk to the boys on the crew."

CHAPTER TEN

The Manjuris was about halfway between the Ice Works and my office so it was natural for me to stop in. The local poolroom and cigar store, it also served as the informal headquarters for Razor Eddie, one of the busiest bootleggers in the port. I walked up the dingy stairs and rapped on the door at the top. The Judas door at eye level opened and closed. A rattle of the door knob and I was in, Red smiling a welcome as I went past.

"Eddie's inside," he said, thudding the door closed behind me.

The weak February sunlight barely penetrated the room. Electric light encircled each of the half dozen pool tables. Eddie was playing at one of them. I watched as his arm pistoned back then sharply forward. There was a sound like a gunshot and balls were dropping everywhere. The Razor stood, well satisfied with the shot.

"D.B."

He smiled and handed the cue stick to one of his boys who had been watching the master at work. Eddie was good. He had confidence, a smile and a gang that was loyal.

He was handsome despite the scar that had given him the nickname. If anything, the slash from ear to jaw made him better looking to women. Perhaps it was the sense of danger his face conveyed. Compact and muscular, Eddie moved well. He wore a pistol under one arm.

We shook hands and walked to the bar. Red had drinks and cigars laid out.

"Cubans," Eddie said, lighting up. "Prepare for the best smoke you'll ever have."

He passed the cutter. I sliced the butt off the cigar, then used a match to warm the business end. Another match for ignition and I was inhaling some great smoke. The whisky was as good. It tasted smoky too.

"Heard you got roughed up," Eddie said, looking me over.

"So?"

"Just heard. That's all."

"You hear who did it, too?"

"Actually, yes," Eddie said, with a smile and a tip of the glass. "So what about Everett Hall?"

"That's what I came here to ask you."

"Don't know who did it. Don't know where the money is," was the reply.

"Okay. What do you know?"

"He was stayin' at the Queen's Hotel. He stepped out a lot."

"Who beat me up?"

"Costellos."

"The Costello brothers?"

"That's what I heard."

The Costellos were triplets. Don and Dave were big, with black hair and foreheads that sloped down to a single eyebrow. Doug was the runt of the litter. Slight, with the same hair and eyebrow, he was the brains in the family. That's not saying much. I'd gone to high school with them. Doug and I played field sports together and got on okay. In addition to being ugly, Dave was mean as a snake and we had clashed often. Don ran with a different crowd. I'd always assumed that because he looked like his brother he behaved in much the same way.

"Why would they attack me?" I asked.

"Yeah, a long time since high school, isn't it? What other black crimes you looking into right now?" Eddie asked.

"Pardon?"

"What's the old king's name?"

"Cole? Coal. Of course. Thanks buddy." I shook his hand.

I was on my way to the door when he yelled, "Watch your back. A lot of people are looking for that money. Soon they'll know to look for you."

The Queen's was an east side hotel, just around the corner at 3rd and 8th. I walked up the steps and inside to the front desk.

"What room was Everett Hall in?" I asked.

"Sorry, sir," a fat man in a uniform responded. "We aren't allowed by law to divulge the locations of our guests."

"Even when confronted with one of these?" I passed him a fin. It disappeared. He slid me a key.

"Top of the stairs. Room Seven. Cops have already been here. They didn't find nothing."

The air was cleaner upstairs, away from the public rooms. The law hadn't trashed Room Seven too badly. Drawers were mostly shut. The bed was unmade, the mattress was askew. The draperies and furniture were threadbare. Cheap carpets almost covered the rough wooden floor. A couple of very nice suits hung in the closet. On the floor behind them there was a leather bag. Empty.

I was putting it back when I heard the door open. I went the rest of the way into the closet and eased the door shut behind me. I pulled my Colt and stood in the dark, waiting to see what would happen.

Breathing never sounds as loud as it does when you're trying to do it quietly. The intruder was poking around the room in much the same way I had. Drawers opened and closed as the bureau was searched. I was getting ready to jump out of the closet and confront whoever it was when I heard the outer door open and close. Holstering my gun, I crept from the closet and listened at the hallway door. I opened it quietly, just in time to see a well-dressed young man slip down the front stairs. I followed.

We went three blocks straight down 2nd and then across to the C.P.R. station where he disappeared around a corner. As I went around the same corner, I noticed the train had arrived. There was a crowd on the platform. I caught a quick glimpse of the Police Chief and Nosey Parker standing with a couple of people. I couldn't see my man. I panicked and broke into a run. That's when he saw me and dodged. He turned and fired a shot over the collected heads. I pulled my pistol.

"Everybody down!" I yelled as people screamed and ran for cover. The gunman turned and ran. As I started through the crowd I saw a distinguished looking gentleman who had been standing with the Chief move to cut the gunman off. My size helped me. I was through the scattered onlookers and on his heels in a second.

The fugitive saw what we were trying to do and ran even harder. He disappeared into the darkness of the roundhouse. The older man and I slowed. I reached into my boot and pulled out the .32 automatic. He took it and we split up.

It took a moment for my eyes to adjust to the dark. A train engine was waiting to be turned on the giant turntable. The stranger I was chasing had to be either inside it or on the other side.

There was an ear-piercing shriek of metal on metal and the floor shuddered. The giant mechanism began to rumble and the engine started to turn. I hopped onto the moving platform and started across. The noise was deafening. Coming around the cow-catcher, I saw the end of a hand-to-hand struggle between good and bad. The latter swung a billy which connected with the former's shoulder, dropping him like a sack.

I went straight for the gunman who went straight for his gun. I wasn't close enough to stop him. I shot as he aimed at me. He yelled as his gun flew out of his hand. A lucky shot.

"Lie on the ground. Hands over your head." He did as I instructed. By then, Police Chief Foster and one of his men had caught up to us. They took the attacker away.

I crossed to my rescuer and helped him up.

"Thank you," I said.

"No trouble. Nice shooting."

He was husky, with the kind of build men in their forties seemed to get. They led with the belly. Still he was dignified, wearing expensive clothes and a number of gold rings. He used stove black on his hair but the mustache was a natural grey. He had a friendly enough face, but it was distorted by pain. He wore spectacles, which were on the ground a couple of feet away. I picked them up and handed them to him.

"Hospital?" I asked.

"Who are you?"

"D.B. Murphy."

"Well, D.B. Murphy," he said, handing my .32 back, "It's a pleasure to meet you. My name is Carr. Kenneth Carr. American Deputy Vice Consul."

CHAPTER ELEVEN

A crowd had gathered by the time we stepped out of the roundhouse. A woman embraced Carr.

"Daddy, are you alright?"

His daughter. She was beautiful.

"I'm alright thanks to Mr. Murphy here," he said flashing a grateful smile.

"Mr. Murphy. I'm Nadine Carr."

I took the elegant hand she offered.

"A pleasure," I said.

"He brought the villain to heel," Carr said to his daughter.

She gave a little squeak of alarm and placed the same beautiful hand over her mouth. I thought she would cry.

"I'm sorry Mr. Murphy," Carr said. "My daughter really can't stand gunplay. Excuse us."

The two of them walked down the platform.

"Glad to see you're okay," a nearby voice said.

I looked around but didn't see anyone.

"In here," the voice said from the nearby ticket wicket.

"Uncle Jerry," I said smiling. It was my mother's younger brother.

"Still right at the centre any time there's trouble," he said.

"Sure. You know me, Jerry. Some things never change."

"How's yer ma enjoyin' her trip?" he asked.

After Lori and I married, my mother had gone away. A trip to Ireland she'd been saving for all her life. It was six months from one end to the other.

"Got a letter last week. Says she's having a grand time and wouldn't be back in Owen Sound for all the world. No insult intended."

As Jerry laughed, I saw Tom Carson come around the corner heading straight for me.

"See you later, Jerry," I said.

"Right. Bye Danny."

"Any idea who I shot?" I asked Carson when he got close enough.

"The mook? An out of town boy by the look of them clothes. We'll take care of him."

"A room for one in the ol' pokey."

"Where'd you pick him up?" Tom asked.

"At the Queen's. Everett Hall had a room there and I was checking it out."

"Find the money?"

"Did you?"

"No. Have you talked to Rose Eng lately?"

"Not in years." Rose and I had been high school sweethearts. "Why?"

"She was goin' out with Hall."

"Rose? Come on!"

"Sorry. I thought you knew."

"Excuse me?" A woman's voice said from behind me. I turned to see a pleasant looking woman with dark hair pulled back in a rather severe bun. She was smiling, another question on her lips. She reminded me of a Carnegie librarian.

"Yes, ma'am?"

"I couldn't help but overhear. Are you D.B. Murphy?"

"I am."

"Oh. That saves time," she said, fumbling inside her bag. She eventually pulled out a copy of *Ups and Downs*, the newsletter put out by the Barnardo homes.

"Yes?" I asked, not sure why she was showing it to me.

"I'm Judy Armstrong," she said. "There's a letter in here that says to contact you. It's from my brother Davey. I've come to see him."

I took Miss Armstrong to the City Hotel. "Davey isn't in Owen Sound. I wrote the letter for him last summer when he was living in Wiarton. Now he's up in Balaclava. Northeast of here ten miles."

"He lives up there? Is he still one of Dr. Barnardo's boys?"

"No. He lives with a friend of mine."

Barnardo boys and girls were generally orphaned or from poor families. With nothing but hardship in their home country of England, many were taken in by the Barnardo Society, a well-intentioned organization which trained the young people as farm labourers and servants. Then their passage to Canada was paid by farm families here. The passage would be worked off over a number of years before the Barnardo children were truly free to seek a future in the new land. Some had an okay time of it. Others were little more than indentured slaves.

In my pursuit of the Lost Tire Gang the previous spring I'd come across a group of runaway Barnardo children. They'd fallen under the influence of a couple of bad characters who had forced them into a life of crime in exchange for freedom. I'd broken the ring up and sent the Barnardos out to Balaclava to help my friend Bill Van Wyck rebuild his store, which had been burned down in retaliation for the help he had given me with a case. From all I'd heard, the arrangement had worked out very well for everyone.

I had already suspected I might need Van's help on the Hall case. Now I had a reason to go and ask him.

"How can I arrange passage? Is there a stage?" Miss Armstrong asked.

"In the summer a boat goes to Vail's Point, but there's no official way to get out there in the winter. Do you ride?"

"No."

"Okay. I'll take you out to Balaclava by cutter tomorrow."

"Thank you, Mr. Murphy."

Once Miss Armstrong was safely away to her room, I went down to the City Hotel stable. The big double doors were closed against the weather. A cutter passed down the street, harness creaking and jingling, hoofs pounding in rhythm. I pushed open the small side door and stepped into the stable. It took a moment for my eyes to adjust to the light. Or lack of it. The place smelled of warm horses.

"Hey D.B.!" I heard the voice of the Lugan come from deep within the bowels of the place.

"Lugan." I wasn't sure why he was called that. It could be his name for all I knew. I walked along the side of a warm and horsey stall into the centre of the barn where Scotty was waiting. On my way to the newspaper office I'd set up an eleven o'clock date with my horse.

"I got ol' skinhead here ready to go." The Lugan was red headed and stooped, with a hump high up on his back. He wore a wicked smile, knowing full well I hated it when he called my faithful horse names.

"But for one thing," he went on.

"Uh huh?"

"Might wanna put a toque on him."

I'd had Scotty for years. One of his endearing qualities was the bald patch between his ears. You didn't see that much on horses. Another was his desire to race cars. Hoofs versus tires. I'm not sure why he did it. A friend of mine suggested he feared I might trade him in for a car. Said the horse had something to prove. To me and to himself. I thought it sounded too deep for a horse. Pigs were the philosophers of the barnyard.

"He knows you're making fun of him," I said.

Scotty nickered in agreement.

The Lugan snorted and passed the reins over to me.

"Don't run him too hard. It's cold out."

"Goin' out Brooke," I said. "We'll be back in an hour or so."

Brooke had been absorbed into the City of Owen Sound during the incorporation of 1921. The small west side community had formerly been a part of Sarawak Township. Ten minutes ride from downtown, it consisted of a handful of houses sitting on a bluff above the bay. The Park Head Branch of the C.N.R. divided Brooke down the middle.

Halfway there I noticed the dog from the mill dam was following me at a safe distance. I was beginning to wonder if Everett Hall had owned a dog.

CHAPTER TWELVE

I found the house without any trouble. A small brick affair set back from the road, almost on the edge of the bluff. The name on the box at the road was R. Sutherland. A picket fence contained the front yard. I hitched Scotty to it and went through the gate and up the walk. I knocked on the front door. Nothing happened. I knocked again and it opened.

The woman who stood before me was good looking, in a domestic sort of way. But then, I'd caught her baking. Hands covered in flour. She quickly wiped them on her apron. Dark hair and eyes. She was wary of something. Probably the sight of a large man at her front door in the middle of the day.

"Yes?"

"Miss Sutherland? Valerie Sutherland?"

"Mrs.," she said. "But he's dead."

"Excuse me?"

"Mr. Sutherland. He's dead. You a reporter?"

"No ma'am. D.B. Murphy is my name. I'm a private investigator and I've got some questions about Everett Hall."

"Oh. I suppose I may as well invite you in. 'Cause I expect you're not going to leave unless I talk to you."

"You're right," I said. "Thank you."

I followed her into the house. It was a basic four-room layout. She led me around the stairs into the kitchen. I love pie. That kitchen smelled like heaven.

Mrs. Sutherland went back to her baking. She was rolling dough for another pie. Two were cooling on a rack. There were more in the oven. She noticed my look.

"I do this to earn extra money. Since my husband died. Sell 'em to the restaurants."

"What do you need extra money for? Didn't Hall leave you any?"

“Hah!” she said. “If Everett Hall had money, I never seen any of it.”

“Oh?”

“Mister, he took me for everything my Robert left me.”

I didn’t know what to say to that. So I didn’t say anything at all. She worked the pie dough until it was thin as an onion skin.

“Your mind isn’t on your work,” I pointed out.

“Oh, damn.” She slammed the rolling pin down on the table.

“Who killed him?” I asked.

That’s when she turned on the waterworks and fell in a heap at the kitchen table, sobbing. I waited a few minutes. When it started to look like she wasn’t going to stop blubbering any time soon I left a card.

When I got to the road the dog was sitting a few feet from Scotty. I had the feeling the two of them had been talking about me. Or whatever it is animals do.

“Hello dog.”

His tail barely twitched as he moved off to a safe distance.

He followed us all the way through the downtown to the mill dam.

The sun disappeared behind the escarpment at around three o’clock most winter days. It was twilight in the river valley when I arrived. It wasn’t until I was within a few feet of the ice crew that I noticed steam rising from every man. Perspiration soon to be snow.

I walked over to where the three pilers were working. Muscles bulging, they fished blocks from the water with pikes. Water sloshed off their thick leather aprons. Heaved ice chukked into place on the sledge.

“Titanic Dick!” I called out.

All of the men stopped working and in a chorus said, “Huh?”

Amid the laughter that followed, the man I had recognized from my time on the ice crew waved a gloved hand.

“Hey Danny-Boy,” he said.

Dick had shown up in Owen Sound after the unsinkable ship had gone down. Claimed he’d been working in the boiler room of the Titanic when it hit the berg. He’d tell the story to anyone who would listen. It hadn’t taken long for him to earn the nickname and the snickering that usually accompanied it.

“Is Hank around?” I asked.

"Nope," Dick said.

"Anyone here know anything about Everett Hall?"

"He's dead," a man called from across the ice.

"Anyone see anything that has to do with Everett Hall?" Dick called loud enough for all of them to hear.

There was another pause in the work as they considered the question. It was easy to see the foreman was away. He wouldn't have let them stop, no matter how important the question.

"What about blood?" I asked. "Hall had a few holes in him."

"No blood anywhere," Titanic said. "But you'd really have to ask Hank. He gets here first in the morning."

CHAPTER THIRTEEN

All I wanted was to cosy up to the stove in the kitchen when I got home. Lori was there getting dinner ready.

"No students?" I asked, sitting at the kitchen table.

"Cancelled. I didn't feel too well earlier."

"Do you think it's influenza?" Over twenty million had died worldwide during the influenza outbreak of 1918. More than a few people still twitched at the very mention of the word.

"I don't think so. It doesn't feel that serious. Oh, there was a telephone message for you. A man named Ken Carr. There's a reception of some sort at City Hall this evening. He wants you to go." I changed and put on a tie. For a second I thought about leaving the Colt at home. Then I thought about the Costello Boys. They'd be back. Of that I had no doubt.

"I won't be too late," I said kissing Lori on the back of the neck. "You smell nice."

"Sure you have to go?"

"I do. Sorry. It's work."

"Well, you know where to find me when you're all done."

"That I do," I agreed, giving her a real smooch. "That I do."

Nosey Parker was on his way out of City Hall as I arrived. "Some do, eh?" he asked.

"I haven't been in yet. How do you suppose City Hall knew the Deputy Vice Consul was in town?"

"I don't know," he smirked. "Maybe they read it in the paper. See ya later, D.B. I've got a story to write."

The first person I bumped into was Miss Ballantyne of the City Clerk's department. "Why Mr. Murphy," she said. "Twice in the same day. How nice."

"Thanks for this morning. It was a good tip."

"Did it pay off?"

"Not in dollars. But golden nonetheless."

"Mr. Carr has been regaling us with stories of your derring-do this afternoon."

"It was nothing. Just another hood with a pistol. Anyone with two dollars can buy a gun."

"Well, congratulations anyway." She smiled and took my things to the cloakroom. I went into the Council Chamber.

"And here he is now," I heard the mayor say. The crowd in the room turned to look at me. Then the darndest thing happened. They began to applaud. I felt like a baboon's butt. All red and exposed.

Ken Carr came forward and shook my hand. He led me past the coffee and tea table into the mayor's office. Excellent whisky swirled in crystal glasses and we were soon toasting one another.

"Thank you again for this afternoon," he said.

"I should be thanking you."

"Cigar?" He offered me an expensive looking mahogany box filled with expensive looking cigars.

"Thank you," I said performing the ritual.

"I hear you're looking into the murder of Everett Hall."

"I'm looking for the spoils."

"Excellent," Carr said. "My government has an interest. Hall is well known to us in seven states under as many names."

"Good to know Owen Sounders aren't the only gullible people in the world."

"Not by a long shot," Carr laughed and poured more drinks. "I'd like frequent reports."

"Wait a minute. I'm already employed."

"It seems to me the only way to find the money is to find the murderer. You can make twice as much for the same job."

"Twice as much?"

"My government will match your fee dollar for dollar. How much are you getting?"

"Ten per cent of Hall's take. If I find it. Nothing if I don't."

"Fifty-one hundred dollars. I don't foresee any difficulty there." So far I was only getting one hundred dollars, which was ten percent of MacLean's "investment". I didn't bother to correct him. If he wanted to pay me fifty-one hundred, I was willing to let him.

Nadine Carr entered the room. The only word I could use to describe her is startling. Her black hair was cut in a bob. Her dress was beaded and low cut. Dark eyeliner was offset by rouged cheeks. A perfect nose led to lips that were even more perfect.

"Another sherry please, Daddy," she said. "Who's this?"

"You remember Mr. Murphy, darling," he said. "From the depot today. The hero."

"Oh. Mr. Murphy. Well hello."

I kissed the perfectly manicured hand that was offered to me. When I finished with it, the hand went straight to a pack of imported Turkish cigarettes. At ten for fifteen cents they were pure luxury.

"I'm pleased to meet you, Miss," I said.

"Miss? Well aren't we formal. It's Nadine, honey."

"Well then. Nadine honey it is."

"Quite the little town you've got here. Nothing like Albany."

"That where you're from? Albany?"

"Um hmm. What do the yokels around here do for fun? Are there clubs?"

"Try the Manjuris," I said.

"Is it wet?" she asked.

"Unofficially."

"What's that?" Carr asked as he returned with her drink.

"Nothing, Daddy." Nadine gave me the goodbye look.

"If you'll excuse me for a moment?" I said.

I headed straight to the men's room. I was washing my hands when I heard shots. Three of them. Small calibre. Close by the door. I rushed into the Council Chamber. People were scrambling in every direction screaming.

"What is it?" I called out to a man running past.

"Someone tried to kill Ken Carr." It took me a few moments to cut through the crowd to Carr's side.

"Are you okay?"

"Yes. Where were you?" he asked.

"Taking care of business," I said. "What happened?"

"We came out of the mayor's office right after you. We were talking with the mayor and the next thing I know someone's shooting at me. From over there." He pointed in the general direction of the men's room.

"I heard the shots."

"Is Owen Sound always so dangerous?"

"Two attacks in one day. You might think so."

"I need to keep you close by to protect me, Mr. Murphy."

"Excuse me, Mr. Murphy? Here is your overcoat." Miss Ballantyne was standing behind me, my overcoat across her arm.

"I didn't call for it."

"Oh, I'm sorry…" She looked confused. "Someone told me you wanted it. I'll just take it back."

"No, that's okay. I may as well go."

Many people had left already, but there was still a crowd around Carr. I took my coat and hung it over my arm. As I turned to go something fell from the pocket, clattering to the ground at my feet.

A .22 calibre pistol.

CHAPTER FOURTEEN

I spent a long night in jail. We started in one of the sweat rooms. Two cops, one fat, the other not, a big electric light and me. The sack of meat was Charles Fish. Charlie the Carp people called him when he was out of earshot. He had weight, a problem with his sweat glands and the voice of a neuter. The bone rack next to him was Detective Constable Des Rennet. Out of uniform. Dressed in a cheesy suit.

"Let's hear it one more time," Rennet said in a voice like curdled milk.

"I'm not telling you again."

"Yes you are," Carp squeaked from behind the light. "You're going to tell it as many times as it takes."

"What for? You know I didn't do it."

"Do we now? And how do we know that?"

"I heard of a guy got shot in the head twice point blank range with a .22 calibre Mossberg Brownie like that one."

"Yeah, so?" Carp asked.

"He beat up the two guys who shot him and then walked to the hospital and got the bullets taken out. The .22 handgun is a lady's gun. If I'd wanted to kill Ken Carr I'd have used a gun that could hurt him. Not a .22."

"Maybe ya just done it to scare him," Rennet spat.

"A .22 isn't a threat. It's an irritation. Besides, I told you. I was in the men's room."

"Get this bum out of here," Carp said to Rennet. "Let him cool his heels overnight.

I didn't sleep much so I had some time to think. Valerie Sutherland and Rose Eng had both dated Hall. Neither knew about the other. Hall's body had been found at the mill dam. Near the ice crew and the mill. He had been sapped, poisoned, stabbed and shot. Yet he'd drowned. One very persistent assassin. Or a handful of them. The fifty-one thousand dollars Hall netted in his thimblerig was missing. Taken by the murderer? Or did Hall have a partner? Or partners? Ken Carr might be able to tell me whether Hall had worked with others in the past or not. It was an elaborate scheme he'd been running and he might have needed help. I'd been beaten up. Framed. Soon, somebody was going to get hurt and I didn't want that somebody to be me.

I had to see Rose Eng.

Just after seven the next morning the turnkey let me out. "Goodbye, Murphy," he said. "We all knew it wasn't you anyway. You'd never use a lady's gun. Would ya?"

"Not in this life."

Tom Carson was waiting outside the lock up. He handed back my personal effects, including my unloaded Colt .45 and a clip. I shrugged into my shoulder holster and put the gun away.

"I don't know what those night guys were thinkin'. Obviously it couldn't have been you. You saved the guy yesterday."

"Who can explain what goes through a cop's mind?" I asked in a loud voice as we walked through the police offices. "Promote the smartest uniform cop to detective and he turns into a dolt. Don't ever let them promote you, Tom."

I followed Tom through the hostile, silent squad room and out into the hallway. He was laughing as I pulled the door closed behind me.

"With a friend like you I don't think I'll ever have to worry about a promotion."

I gave a short chuckle. "I get cranky when I miss my sleep. Just ask Lori. She here?"

"Naw. The Razor went over last night and told her you'd be home in the morning."

"Who told the Razor?"

"This is Owen Sound boyo. You forget? Everyone knows everything about everyone else."

"Why didn't they let me out last night?"

"Carp and Rennet accidentally misplaced your paperwork," he said, dropping his voice. "We had to wait for one of them to come in this morning. You find the moola yet?"

"Not yet."

"Let me know. I want the killer. That's all. Just the killer. And listen," he leaned closer. "Keep your nose clean. Carp and Rennet have got it in for you. Don't give them a reason to haul you in again."

I walked straight from the jail to the Eng home on 5th Street East. It was still dark and there weren't many people out and about yet. Lights burned in many of the homes I passed. I knew the lights would be on at the Eng household. I'd eaten breakfast there often enough as a teen.

A milk wagon passed. One of its wheels hit a hole and I was showered with slush. I stopped walking long enough to scrape off what I could. I'd have to mention the state of the winter roads to the helpful Miss Ballantyne the next time I saw her.

Rose Eng had been my first love. We were kids, both of us students at the Owen Sound Collegiate. It had been intense and, as with most teenage romances, it had broken up spectacularly. I hadn't seen her much in the intervening years. I'd often found it interesting that in such a small town two people could avoid one another so successfully. I wasn't looking forward to seeing her now.

Rose's father was Joseph Eng. He was one of the few members of Owen Sound's Chinese community who wasn't in the laundry business. Mr. Eng owned a haberdashery on 2nd Avenue East not too far from my office.

The Eng house hadn't changed. Red brick with green trim and shutters. The lane and the walk were both neatly shoveled. A Model 'T' stood in the driveway.

I turned the bell in the centre panel of the door and waited. My breath frosted the glass panes. I heard a step in the hall, and the electric light above my head was switched on.

My heart beat faster. I hadn't seen Rose in a long time. I'd heard plenty though. She wore makeup and drank. She smoked cigarettes through a carved ebony holder. Most scandalous of all, she wore a brassiere. In short, Rose Eng was Owen Sound's first flapper.

The door opened. Rose's brother peered out at me.

"D.B.," he said with surprise.

"Hello Peter," I said. "Is Rose home?"

"Come in." He opened the door wide. I stepped past him into the warm foyer. Leaving my boots and coat, I followed him back to the kitchen where Mr. Eng was sitting at the table reading a paper. The soft-boiled egg in front of him was untouched. It looked good.

"Ah! D.B. How many years since we've seen you!" he said jumping to his feet. "Please, sit down. Coffee?"

"Thanks." I wondered for a moment whether I looked as bad as I felt, then realized I didn't really care. Peter brought me coffee and toast. It was the best meal I could remember having.

"To what do we owe the pleasure of this visit?" Mr. Eng asked in the over formal manner of one whose first language is not English.

"I came about Rose."

He sighed. "What trouble is she in now?"

"Trouble? I don't know about that. I just need to talk to her. Is she around?"

The old man looked sad. "She has not been with us for some time now D.B. We haven't seen her in days."

"How many days? Since Hall turned up dead?"

"Does this have something to do with Mr. Hall?"

"Yes. Is there anything you can tell me? Anything at all."

"I don't think there is," Mr. Eng began, then he seemed to change his mind. "Last time we saw her she mentioned a reporter had been trying to see her…help me out Peter…"

"It was that guy from *The Sun-Times*. Nosey Parker."

CHAPTER FIFTEEN

"So you think Rose did it?" Lori perched on the edge of the clawfoot tub while I soaked.

"I don't know who did it. And I'm no closer to the money."

She started to rub my shoulders. I'd been in the warm tub for some time and was beginning to feel quite relaxed.

"I've been thinking about doing some work on the spare room. Okay?"

"Work?"

"Just some cleaning up. Maybe a touch of paint."

"Want help?"

"Not right away. I'll let you know when."

"I'm going to bed."

"Tired?"

"I didn't sleep a wink in jail."

"The rowdies keep you up?"

"No." A sudden realization made me sit up, sloshing water over the top of the tub. "There was no one else in there!"

"So?"

"Where was the guy I saved Ken Carr from? He should have been in the other cell."

★★★

It was a good sleep. Too bad it was interrupted. Just after eleven Lori shook me awake. "The Deputy Vice Consul is downstairs. And a Miss Armstrong telephoned. Are you going to Balaclava today?"

"Yes."

"Will you be home for supper?"

"No. But Van will be coming back with me later." I got dressed and went down. Ken Carr was waiting in the foyer.

"Hello, Mr. Carr."

"Ken, please," he said as we shook hands.

"Come in." I led him through to the kitchen. "Coffee?"

"Thanks. How is your investigation going?" he asked as I turned on the stove to heat up some java.

"I haven't found the money yet, if that's what you want to know."

"The money is a concern. We are also concerned that Everett Hall's killers be found."

"Killers?"

"There are many sources of information open to a diplomat," he smiled. "I take full advantage of them. As for my use of the plural as opposed to the singular, is it not fair to assume that with multiple methods come multiple suspects?"

"I suppose. But I still haven't any evidence to support that theory." I told him what I knew, not what I surmised.

"What will you do next?"

"I have to do a favour for a woman who came in on the same train as you."

"Really?"

"Her brother is out at Balaclava. I'm taking her to visit him after lunch."

"Who do you think has the money Hall stole?"

"Either one of the killers or Hall's partners."

"Partners?"

"Why not? It takes a lot of expertise to pull a job like this off."

Carr shook his head. "I don't think so. Working alone was his trademark. Everett Hall was the master of all charlatans, flim flammers and thimbleriggers. He always worked solo."

CHAPTER SIXTEEN

I hired a nag and cutter from the Lugan and trotted round to the front of the City Hotel with Scotty hitched to the back of the cutter. I'd leave it at Balaclava for Miss Armstrong to use during her visit. Van and I could return to Owen Sound on horseback.

She was out front with her baggage when I got there. The dog was sitting beside her.

"Is that your dog?" I asked as I helped Miss Armstrong and her things into the cutter.

"I've never seen it before in my life."

"Oh."

I gave the reins a sharp jerk and we started off down 2nd Avenue East. I pulled a black goatskin driving robe across our knees.

"Is this really necessary, Mr. Murphy?"

"Have you ever been in a cutter?"

"Of course not. In Toronto we have streetcars."

"Sure. I know. Just trust me. You'll be glad for it soon enough."

The day was clear but there was a north wind coming off the bay. As we passed through the factory district and Mudtown the wind started to bite. Miss Armstrong pulled the robe tighter around her legs.

I liked taking the Leith Road to travel north. The trees along the shore from Squaw Point to Leith provided good cover from the winter winds. The other choice to Balaclava, the Annan Road, was a killer in the winter. The wind whipped up to the top of the escarpment, running unchecked across the cleared fields to the road where it hit like a frozen brick.

"How long will it take to get there?" Miss Armstrong asked.

"Two hours. If we're lucky."

"Is the horse behind for pushing?"

I laughed. "Are you kidding me?"

"Yes," she said. "Just because I'm from Toronto doesn't mean I haven't got a sense of humour."

"Sorry."

We rode in silence for a few minutes.

"What sort of work do you do, exactly?" she finally asked.

"Private detective."

"Really? So the other day at the train station..."

"Paid hero."

"I saw that man help you. The one from the train."

"Kenneth Carr. The American Deputy Vice Consul. Yes. He and his daughter came in on the Toronto train as well."

"Deputy Vice Consul?" she asked.

Before I could answer, a shot rang out behind us and a bullet whined past. Our nag screamed and bolted. I looked behind. Three horsemen wearing balaclavas had ridden out of some bushes. Appropriate. And very familiar. Two of them were husky. The third was slight. They looked like the Costellos. Gunfire elevated our dispute beyond a simple warning.

I handed Miss Armstrong the reins and struggled to get my coat undone. The Lee Enfield I'd brought back from the war was in its customary leather saddle holster. On Scotty's back. I finally freed the Colt from the holster under my left arm. There was a six round clip in it.

"She's following the road," I shouted at Miss Armstrong, while pointing at the nag. "Let her run." We were at the bottom of the escarpment outside Leith. It was straight uphill to Annan.

I aimed over their heads with the .45 and squeezed off a couple of rounds. Beside me, Miss Armstrong screamed.

The gun had good balance but it kicked like a horse. I'd need to aim with two hands if I decided to shoot one of them for real.

A bullet smashed through the wooden back of the seat between us. To say I was surprised would be an understatement. It is notoriously difficult to hit anything from the back of a galloping horse. More so if you're a Costello.

Another shot hit the wagon. I was going to have to change my opinion of the Costellos. To make matters worse, they were gaining on us. The cutter had slowed to a walk, the nag was winded.

"They're going to catch us," I said matter-of-factly.

"You sure that horse can't push?"

We were almost at a standstill so I changed strategies. I emptied the clip, dropped it and rammed another one home. I jumped out of the cutter and emptied the second clip as I made my way to Scotty's side. In a second I had the Lee Enfield out. I took aim, let out my breath, and dropped one of the masked riders with a single shot.

CHAPTER SEVENTEEN

We pulled up to the Balaclava General Store late in the afternoon. It looked exactly as it had before the two Franks burned it down. Through the steam that obscured the front windows I could see a variety of products the North Sydenham Township homeowner might need. Along with Magic Baking Powder, Borax and bullets there were traps of all types, heavy outerwear and home embalming materials. Behind it all I saw a face peering out and it was the right one.

The door burst open and Davey flew down the stairs. He'd grown from a husky lad to a well-dressed, solid man in the half year since I'd seen him.

"Judy. Judy!" he cried as he flung himself at her.

"Davey! Oh, my Davey-boy." I turned away, embarrassed, not wanting to intrude on their reunion. Shelagh was coming down the steps to meet her boyfriend's relative. She tossed a shy wave in my direction before Davey caught up her hand and excitedly introduced his sister.

"Well, look who it is!" Van said from the doorway. "Now Sydenham truly is the lawless township!"

Colleen and Jug followed him down the stairs. All three were wearing white shop aprons. Jug carried a broom, which he left at the bottom of the stairs before coming to shake my hand.

"Got a job for me?" Van asked as we shook hands.

"Have I."

"C'mon inside where it's warm. Davey," Van addressed the lad, "get your sister's bags and bring them inside."

"Then they picked him up and rode off." Jug, Colleen and Van were sitting around the wood stove in the shop listening to my story. Davey, Shelagh and Judy Armstrong were in the back parlour talking and crying.

"Does this have anything to do with your case?" Van asked.

"Up until a couple of days ago I was just working on coal theft. Now I'm trying to find the money Everett Hall took. I'm on commission with the folks he took it from. I don't know if this ambush has anything to do with either case. But I think I need some help. Interested?"

"It's a slow time of year."

"When can you leave?"

"I'll get my things."

We hit the road just before dark. It had started to snow. Big, gentle flakes that stuck to everything. The wind was beginning to come up. We'd have to push the horses if we were going to make it to town unfrozen.

"Whose dog?" Van asked.

I looked back. The collie was right behind us. The question was beginning to annoy me.

"Don't know."

"He's a good lookin' mutt."

"Sure he is."

"You and Lori gonna have kids?"

"Someday I suppose."

"Then you need a dog."

"Wrong. I don't need a dog. You need a dog?"

"With the Lost Tire Gang rattling around my place?" Van asked. "Are you kidding?"

"Ah. How's that going?"

"They'll be Canadian citizens before long."

"Good."

"Who killed Everett Hall?" Van asked.

I was so engrossed in our conversation I'd led us due south along the Annan Road and now regretted it. I could barely see Van in the swirling snow. The wind had really come up and was now whistling around us. I had to shout so he could hear me.

"I'm not sure yet."

"But you think the killer has the money."

"Maybe."

"Is there anything you know for sure?"

"Violence seems to follow me everywhere I go."

"That's an occupational hazard, isn't it?"

By the time we got up to the Meaford Road conversation was impossible. Snow whipped across the fields and hit us broadside. We picked up the pace and twenty minutes later we were riding down St. Mary's hill into the Sydenham River valley. Among the buildings downtown the wind dissipated. But six inches of fresh white snow had accumulated since I'd left that afternoon.

We rode into the City Hotel stables after nine. The Lugan took our horses. Van would come home with me. We were just stepping through the gap in the stable door when a boy approached.

"Hey, is that D.B. Murphy?" a young voice called out.

"It is."

"Eddie sent me. He said to tell ya that Rose Eng is at the club."

Van and I shoved our bags back through the door into the stable. The boy lit out for The Manjuris. We followed. At a distance. He was pretty fast.

We were halfway up the narrow staircase when Red yelled from the top. His face was barely visible inside the Judas door.

"Pick it up flatfoot. One two. One two. Left right. Left right."

"Enough out of you. Infantry thug." He laughed and let us into the club.

"I don't know why folks call coppers flatties," he shot after us. "Seems to me fatties is closer to the truth."

Eddie was leaning against the bar watching the action at the half dozen tables.

"She's gone. Left just after I sent Andrew to get you. Hello, Van," Eddie continued, offering him his hand.

"How long ago?" I asked.

He ran a finger thoughtfully along the purple scar that twisted across his jaw. "About twenty minutes ago I guess."

The lad who'd come to fetch Van and I walked by, heading straight to the pool tables. One of the players stood back and immediately surrendered his cue stick.

"He the new boy?"

"In training."

Eddie had a platoon of lieutenants. Every one hand picked. Andrew, the boy who'd come to fetch us, was about to join an elite unit.

"Drink?"

"Only if it's older than fifteen minutes," I replied.

"I think I've got some that's twenty. Red?"

"Sure boss," the big man said, ducking below the bar. He came up with three tumblers and a crystal decanter on a silver tray. I started to laugh.

"You always expect so much more than the usual client when you come here," Eddie snickered. "I like to deliver."

Red poured. We drank.

"What's new?" Eddie asked. I told him about the gunfight near Leith.

"You killed one of the Costellos?" he asked.

"I guess. Although it doesn't seem like coal-theft should call for gunplay."

"Good point."

"How long was Rose here?" I asked.

"Don't know."

"Anyone talk to her?"

"I wasn't here the whole time. Andrew?" he called across the room. "Anyone talk to Rose Eng tonight?" At the mention of his name Andrew handed his cue to another boy and abandoned the game he was involved in. "Sorry boss. What?"

"Rose Eng. Anyone talk to her before I got here?"

"Sure. Nosey Parker was bending her ear a while."

"How'd she take it?" I asked.

"Good until the end. Then she got mad and stomped out." Red poured a couple more shots.

"What kind of shape was she in when she left?"

"She was pretty tight."

"Any idea where she went?" Van had finished both his drinks while we talked.

"Out Brooke, I think she said."

CHAPTER EIGHTEEN

The Lugan complained. Got all flushed, the way redheads do when they get angry.

"I just put them horses to bed." He was ready for bed himself. His pajamas were decorated with ship's wheels and anchors.

"Catchy get-up," I said to him.

"Oh yeah? Wait til you see what yer friends here is wearin'."

Van and I followed him into the stable. It was quite a sight. Every horse in the barn was wearing a set of old City Hotel curtains.

"Like 'em? I thought they'd be more comfortable than itchy old blankets. Look a lot nicer too, don't you think?"

He was almost right. The horses looked nobler in a strange sort of way. But they also looked ridiculous and I couldn't get past that.

"Only in Owen Sound," Van said shaking his head.

The storm had closed right in by the time we left for Brooke. The snow drove across the road horizontally. Drifts were forming and the wind cut exposed flesh. I pulled my hat down low over my eyes and let Scotty do the seeing for us. Though I didn't see him I assumed the dog was following. It had been for most of the day.

Van rode close enough for me to fill him in on my last interview with Mrs. Sutherland. Scotty stopped in front of her house. A cutter and horse were already tied to the picket fence. An Eng family cutter and horse if I didn't miss my bet.

We dismounted and started up the front walk. Van continued around the back. There were several lights burning in the house. The front door was partly open and snow had started to drift across the exposed floor. I looked towards the road for a moment. Just in time to see Scotty and the dog touch muzzles. I was beginning to feel like the victim of an eight-legged plot.

A loud crash and screams brought my attention back to the matter at hand. I unleashed my Colt and pushed open the front door.

"Where is it? Tell me!" I heard a shrill female voice ask.

"I don't have it." The response came from a throat that was being badly constricted. I followed the grunting churning sounds of a wrestling match into the kitchen. It was an absolute mess. Food was everywhere. Flour, broken jars of preserves and milk littered the floor. In the centre of it all, Rose Eng and Valerie Sutherland were locked in combat.

"What the hell…" was the best I could manage. I put the Colt away and grabbed each of them by an arm. "All right you two, up!"

In a moment they were standing opposite one another. With me between them. It was easy.

"Look at my kitchen!" Mrs. Sutherland screamed at Rose.

"It's nothing compared to what I'm going to do to you!"

The two of them seemed to go crazy at the same moment. Before I knew what had happened, I was in the middle of a donnybrook. I was kicked, punched, elbowed, kneed and clawed. I gave as good as I got. With the exception of the scratching. But for all of it, I couldn't seem to get out from the middle. It wasn't until Van fired his pistol that things slowed.

I was out of breath and hurting when I got up. That was twice in as many days that I'd been beaten up. Once by men, once by women. I resolved to stay away from herds of animals for the next little while.

"A pretty mess you've become since I saw you last," Van joked at me.

"I slipped."

"You filthy…" Mrs. Sutherland sputtered and hissed at Rose.

"Now ladies," I intervened. "Let's all go into the parlour and discuss this like civilized people, shall we?"

I led. The women followed, with Van bringing up the rear. We had to set most of the furniture right before we could sit.

"First of all," I started, winded from all my recent exertions. "Have you anything to drink? I mean real drinks."

"Yes," the bloodied homeowner replied.

"Please go and get it."

"I'll help her," Rose stood, her fists clenched. A cruel smile played itself across her lips.

"I don't think so, Rose. Sit down."

"What makes you so big?" she shouted.

"Hell, he is big, lady," Van said pointing at me.

"How'd you find out about her and Hall?" I asked Rose.

"A little bird told me."

"A little bird? Named Nosey Parker maybe?

"How'd you know?"

"How'd he know? That's what I want to know."

"He asked me a bunch of questions. Said he was working on a story."

Valerie Sutherland came back into the room with glasses and a bottle of Bushmills.

"Irish whisky. Perfect," Van said.

We all had a drink. The two women glowered at one another over their glasses. In my experience, hostility between men ended quickly once the fight was over. With women it never seemed to end.

"Who'd like to start?" I asked.

Neither of them said a word. Van and I waited. It didn't take long.

"Everett Hall was mine! He was going to take me away from all…this!" Valerie Sutherland gestured at the house around us then burst into tears.

"If he'd been that interested, he wouldn't even have looked at me, would he?" Blood was beginning to ooze from a small cut above Rose's right eye.

We were all covered with flour and other baking ingredients. The foundation of Valerie Sutherland's pie business.

"Someone fed Everett Hall a poisoned pie," I said. The Sutherland woman stopped crying and looked up. "Apple pie. Isn't that what you were baking when I came to see you the first time?"

"You killed him?" Rose surprised us all by swinging her arm. Instead of throwing the glass she smashed it against Van's gun hand.

"Ouch!" he yelled. His automatic hit the floor with a thud.

In the second it took me to swing the .45 around and take aim, Mrs. Sutherland grabbed the decanter and slammed it against my forearm. My arm went completely dead. My hand couldn't tell it was holding a gun.

The two women clashed in the centre of the room. Rose landed a hard right on the widow's jaw. As she went down she kicked Rose's feet out. My first love fell in an unceremonious heap whacking her head as she went down.

The two of them got back up at the same time. As Rose stood, she reached into her boot and pulled out seven inches of razor sharp steel. A filleting knife.

CHAPTER NINETEEN

"Is this what you detectives call a break?" Van asked. The pie and the filleting knife in the same room. Blind luck. It was about time.

"Drop it, Rose," I said leveling the .45. I hoped she couldn't tell that I had no feeling below my elbow. She dropped the knife. It landed tip down in the floor.

"Van, get your gun." As I said it, my dead hand finally let go of the .45. It fell to the floor. Rose was quick but Van was quicker.

Valerie Sutherland collapsed on the floor in a heap.

"He took everything," she sobbed. "Everything my Robby left me."

Rose gave a contemptuous sniff. "He took me for a ride too. What he stole was my heart."

An hour later, Van and I were sitting quietly in my study. There was a fire in the grate. We each had whisky and a cigar. It had been a long couple of days and I was tired.

"Why didn't you turn them in?" he asked.

"I have a plan."

Van had taken Rose to her father's house. I'd stayed with the widow Sutherland to help with the clean-up. Unfamiliar as I was with the tools of housework, I had made more of a mess out of things. She finally sent me on my way. I declined the offer of an apple pie.

"What plan?" Van asked. "You've already got the murderesses."

"Murderesses? Are you sure that's a word? Isn't it murdererettes or something like that? Besides, don't forget Hall was also sapped and shot."

"How'd he get into the river?"

"You're right. We mustn't forget he drowned. So if we assume Rose Eng and Valerie Sutherland each had a hand in the murder…"

"Then there are two, maybe three more out there," Van finished for me. "And since neither Rose nor Mrs. Sutherland has the money…"

"One of the others has."

We were interrupted by a knock at the front door. It was Ken Carr. Dressed in evening wear from top hat to patent pumps. There was a car on the road. I could hardly see it for the snow and wind. Van and I had barely escaped a February blizzard.

"I was on my way from dinner with the mayor," he explained as I invited him into the front hall. He removed fawn kid gloves to reveal perfectly manicured hands. The hat and coat I stowed carefully in the front closet.

"Join us for a drink?"

"Us?"

"I have a house guest."

"Oh, if this isn't a convenient time, I can meet with you in the morning."

"Not at all."

I introduced him to Van. "He's from Balaclava," I said, pouring drinks.

"'Half a league, half a league / Half a league onward / All in the valley of Death / Rode the six hundred.'" Ken Carr surprised us with a quote from Tennyson's Charge of the Light Brigade celebrating a battle at another Balaclava.

I handed the drinks over, impressed by the impromptu recital.

"What do you hear from your government about war?" Van asked.

"President Harding has withdrawn our troops from the Rhineland. We will not be involved in whatever occupation or confrontation occurs there."

"We both fought in the Great War. Is there going to be another?"

"The French will occupy the Ruhr Valley until they get their payment of coal and timber."

"There'll be trouble then?"

"The National Socialist Party held its first public congress last week. It wants to repeal the Treaty of Versailles. The Party has a lot of support."

"I can't imagine this turning into war," I said. "Can you?"

"The war shouldn't have been a war," Carr said with a snort.

"I'll drink to that," Van said holding up his glass. We joined him.

"How's your investigation coming?" Carr asked. I filled him in on the events of the past few days. "So the two women don't have the money?"

"No."

“Who are they?”

“I can’t tell you that.”

“I don’t have any jurisdiction here, but it’d be helpful for me to know. I have to cable my embassy a couple of times every day.”

“Are you planning to lay charges against the people involved in the murder?”

“Everett Hall was one of our citizens.”

“You don’t need their names. Neither of them has the money.”

“Who has?”

“One of the other murderers.”

“The guy they found today didn’t have it.”

“Guy? What guy?”

“Of course.” He slapped a hand to his head. “You were in Balaclava all day. There’s been another murder.”

CHAPTER TWENTY

The cops arrived bright and early. I knew they would. Ken Carr had filled me in on the details. The body belonged to the hotel gunman we had chased into the roundhouse. He'd been shot in the chest with a large calibre rifle. The slug they dug out of him was a .303, the same bullet my Lee Enfield and about a dozen other rifles used. The body had been been found in Mudtown with my card in the overcoat pocket.

I was waiting by the door with a cup of coffee and my jacket on. Lori was still in bed and Van had long since departed. I'd asked him to find Tom Carson. I needed to know why the man Carr and I had chased down wasn't in jail.

"Charlie the Carp. And Rennet. You know you guys represent two completely different food groups?"

"Ha ha, funny guy," Carp said.

"You still got that Lee Enfield?" Rennet interrupted his partner.

"Sure. It's right here in the hallway."

They both tensed. Rennet's hand was inside a pocket of his overcoat.

"It's not loaded," I said.

Carp slid by me and into the front hallway. He grabbed the Lee from where I'd left it and sniffed the barrel.

"It's been fired."

"I think you better come downtown with us D.B. You got some questions to answer." I set my coffee cup down and pulled a hat on. Carp motioned me to walk in front of them.

"Lock the door behind you," I said. He did what I asked and followed me down the front walk. I looked but there was no car at the curb. No horses. The storm had stopped for the moment. A wall of grey surrounded the city. It promised more snow before the day was over.

"How'd you guys get here?" I asked.

"Walked," Rennet said with a smile. "It's a beautiful day."

"For you maybe."

"Shut up and walk," Carp growled. The snow was a foot deep and the going was slow. We walked down 8th Street towards the police office.

The question in my mind had nothing to do with my predicament. It had to do with the attack on Miss Armstrong and me. Apparently I'd been mistaken in assuming it was the Costellos. The man I'd followed from Everett Hall's hotel room had been one of the attackers. Who were the other two?

"Hands up!" a nasal voice barked. It sounded like a Costello with a broken nose.

Three masked men had come up behind us from the path below the 8th Street bridge. Rennet and Fish had their hands in the air before I could move. They were patted down and disarmed. Two guns disappeared into the deep pockets of the ancient Hudson's Bay parka Doug was wearing. Then we were forced at gunpoint to take the path down to the riverbank and onto the ice.

The lead man stopped directly under the bridge. He turned in a rush and slugged me in the gut. I went down like a bag of spuds.

"We came to finish delivering that warning."

"You don't sound very menacing with that whine," I said when my breath returned. I guessed it was Dave whose nose I'd smacked in. He made up in meanness what he lacked in brains.

"Yeah, and this time there aren't going to be any interruptions," Don said from the other side of him. He slapped a big leather billy into the palm of his left hand. Over his shoulder and down the river I could see Doug the runt holding a gun on Carp and Rennet.

"Learn him something, Donny," Dave shouted from behind his gun and mask.

I kept my eyes on the circling Costello. I feinted to the right to draw his swing. As it passed by without hitting me I cut over and caught him in the face with my elbow. It was a good hit and he went down hard on the ice.

Dave couldn't shoot for fear of hitting his brother so he came for me. I stepped on Don's wrist and grabbed the billy from him with a great yank. Don screamed. I turned and swung as Dave reached me. His gun clunked me a good one on the side of the head, but not before I nailed him on the ear. He dropped his gun and in an instant I had it too. Doug had spied the trouble his brothers were having and slip-walked up the river as quickly as he could. Rennet and Carp were in hot pursuit. They soon overtook him and in a brilliant demonstration of police bravado the two of them jumped him from behind and retrieved their weapons.

"Better get him up. We're going," I said to Dave.

"Get up!" he shouted, and gave his brother a kick in the kidneys.

The other man moaned and got to his knees.

"Help him," I said, expecting a fight. But he didn't. Without another word he bent over and helped his brother up. The two of them stood there, unsteady until Dave got Don's arm around his shoulder. We started marching through the snow, towards the police station.

"Why'd those two guys have guns?" Don finally asked.

"They're cops, you dolt," I said.

"Oh," was the dull response. "Didn't recognize 'em as such."

"Where's my gun?" I asked.

"Huh?"

"My gun. The one you took from the drawer in my office."

"Watch your mouth. We ain't got yer gun and we ain't burglars. We're teachers. Came to teach you a lesson about minding your own business."

CHAPTER TWENTY ONE

Snake Foster looked at me from the other side of his desk. Carp and Rennet had taken the Costellos downstairs to the lock-up I had so recently occupied. It was a good sign that I hadn't gone there with them. The chief wanted me in his office instead.

"They attacked Miss Armstrong and me. On our way to Balaclava."

"And you thought it was the Costellos?"

"Yes."

"Can Miss Armstrong verify that?"

"Sure. Just call out to Bill Van Wyck's general store."

"Storm knocked out all the telephone lines."

"She's the only witness. Except for the other two attackers."

"I doubt they'll show up to defend you."

"What are you going to do with me?"

"Can't put you in the lock-up with the Costellos."

"They don't like me much right now. Once Carp and Rennet get through with them, I think you'll find those are the boys who have been stealing coal. Your officers still favour rolling 'em up in mattresses and kicking the daylights out of them?"

"I'll have to ask," he said with a smirk. "How are you going to find Everett Hall's money?"

"Look for his murderer."

"Ah. Between you and me, we've been told not to look too hard."

"What?"

"Some of our politicians are feeling a little oversensitive about the whole situation. They don't care who killed him. They just want the money back, and to leave well enough alone."

"The city willing to pay the same ten per cent finder's fee that the private shareholders are offering?"

"You'll have to ask the mayor and council about that."

"How much time have I got?"

"Carp and Rennet'd like to throw you in the can right now. You've been implicated in both an assassination attempt and a murder in the past twenty-four hours. I oughta let them lock you up. Be the smart thing to do. If the press hears about it..."

"Don't worry about the press." I thought of Nosey Parker. "It's on our side."

He tugged at his lower lip with a thumb and forefinger and looked out onto the market square. "I could give you until tomorrow noon to prove your alibi."

"Thanks chief."

"Good luck."

★★★

Van was waiting for me in the City Hall lobby. "Let's go in." I led the way to the clerk's department where Miss Ballantyne was watching us warily. I could see it would be some time before I was not an assassin in the eyes of Owen Sounders. If ever.

"Mr. Murphy," she said with false cheerfulness. "Good to see you again. How may I help?"

"Who told you I was looking for my coat the other night?"

"I'm afraid I don't..."

"Please think. It could be important."

She frowned and bit her lower lip. A real picture of concentration.

"No, I'm sorry," she said with an apologetic smile. "I just don't remember."

★★★

We were waiting to cross the street to my office when Nosey Parker came out of City Hall.

"Just the guy I want to see. What did you say to Rose Eng last night? She tried to murder Valerie Sutherland."

He pulled the ever present note book from an inside pocket and wrote something down. "Too busy to work on it now. You won't believe what I'm onto," he said. He was fairly quivering with excitement.

"Tell me," I said. "By the way, this is Bill Van Wyck. He's helping me out on this one. But you're not really seeing either of us here. Are you?"

"Who? What? Someone say something?" he pretended not to see us.

"So what gives? I'm freezing here."

"Get anything from the Ballantyne frail?"

"Frail? Learn that from Black Mask?" I asked.

"Funny. Well?"

"No. Now tell me something new."

"I can't. Not yet. I have to talk to one more person, then I'll know for sure."

"Know what?" I asked.

"It's my scoop. For tomorrow's paper."

"I thought we had a deal."

He paused to think it over. Owen Sound was a small town and it was best not to upset sources. Otherwise the word would get around and doors would begin to close, especially for a journalist. Nosey knew the score.

"I'll come to your place by midnight. Tell you before the paper hits the streets."

Parker hurried off. Van and I crossed the street to my office. The snow had started to fall again. The first half foot was barely tromped down on the sidewalks.

"How's it going D.B.?" MacLean stuck his head out the front door of the marketeria.

"No money yet. A couple of suspects though."

"Suspects? Who?"

"Can't say. I'm just looking for the money."

"I didn't really want to know anyway," he lied. "Did you hear about the chariot?"

"No. What?"

"Covered in gold and precious jewels. Soon they're going to bring Tut Ankh Amen out."

"What do you want to bet he's covered in gold and precious stones?" Van asked the portly shopkeeper.

MacLean guffawed and let the door swing shut. A moment later he popped his head out and said, "By the way, the other investors have agreed to pay you 10 per cent…"

"Oh, oh," I said before he could finish. "Titanic Dick."

"What?" Van laughed.

I gestured to the man walking up the street towards us. "Titanic Dick."

"It's his name," MacLean said from behind us.

Van laughed even harder.

The ice cutter stopped in front of us on the sidewalk.

"Hi, D.B.," he said. "I got something to tell you."

"Talk."

"Not here. Somewhere private."

MacLean had gone back into his shop. The street door to my office was unlocked. I led the way upstairs with Dick behind me and Van behind him.

I had the keys in my hand but the office door was unlocked too. I pushed it open and went in. Dick stopped in the doorway.

"Well, well," Uncle Hank said from behind my desk. "If it ain't iceberg Dick."

Van pushed Dick into the room and closed the door. I only had two chairs. The one behind my desk and one client chair. The pieces of the one that had broken under MacLean were piled in the corner.

"What are you doing here?" I asked.

"I see," Hank started. "You can come to my workplace, but I can't come to yours. The way I heard it, you wanted anyone that seen anything to come down here."

"Did you see something?"

"No. And nobody else did either." He gave Dick a meaning-filled glare.

"You're speaking for everyone now?" I asked.

"Him too," Hank gestured violently towards Dick. "He's got nothing to say."

Before I could speak or move Dick was out the door. Van gave me an inquisitive look. I shook my head. We'd catch up with him later. I wanted Van to stay. Otherwise I might be appearing before Police Magistrate Creasor.

"You get down to the river before anyone in the morning. You must have seen something."

Hank stood and came around the desk. I was younger, bigger and stronger. But Hank still scared a part of me.

"You stay away from my river." He poked my chest with his index finger to illustrate every word. I'd always hated when he'd used that finger to emphasize points he made during many boyhood lectures. It was making me angry again.

"I'll go anywhere I want. You can't stop me."

"You think you're pretty big, don't you?" His voice carried the acid tone of a deadly serious insult. "Well, you're nothing but a coward. A coward who killed my brother."

He brushed past and slammed the door shut as he went out. I didn't move.

"Who on earth was that?" Van asked. He hung his coat and hat on the rack. I did the same. Then I crossed to the desk and sat. I was having quite a day.

"My uncle."

"What'd you do to him?"

"His ice crew is on the river near the mill dam. One of them might have seen something."

"He owns an ice house?" Van asked.

"That's been bothering me since you asked who else might want to kill Hall."

"An ice house owner might."

"If he thought Hall really was going to make electric iceboxes."

CHAPTER TWENTY TWO

I felt as though I'd been punched in the gut. All along I'd known there was a connection with the ice crew but I hadn't seriously considered Uncle Hank being involved. Van had asked who else stood to lose from the Hall deal. That's when I'd begun to suspect. Hank was first at the river every morning. He had both opportunity and motive. I felt sick. Drowning had been the final cause of Hall's death. If charges were brought against them, Rose and Valerie would face attempted murder. For my uncle, the charge would be murder.

"What now?" Van asked.

"We have to find the money."

"How?"

"Find the other killers. Find out who framed me. Find out who the guy I shot was."

"Easy."

"Yeah."

"You gonna go to the ice house?"

"Tonight. After dinner."

"You want me to go instead?"

"Desperately. But no. This has been coming a long time. I have to face it." There was a knock at the office door. Ken Carr walked in. In the hallway behind him I saw the dog curled on a floormat. I appeared to be gaining his confidence. But I didn't need a dog.

"Come in," I said.

"Just stopping for a second. Hello, Van." Van nodded as Carr pushed the door shut.

"I'm on my way to the Rotary Club," he said. "They've asked me to speak at their weekly luncheon meeting."

"Hope you like roast beef," I said. I'd been to my share of Rotary luncheons.

"Sure. What's happening?"

"Nothing with me. But Nosey Parker says he's got the whole thing sewn up. It'll be in the papers tomorrow."

"He's that annoying reporter. The one who kept trying to get my picture?"

"Yup."

"That's interesting," Carr said. "Any leads on the money?"

"Not yet."

"Is there anything I can help you with?"

"This body that's turned up with a slug from my gun in it is a problem. Can you double check whether Hall ever had a partner? Through your government sources?"

"As I said before, I don't think he did. But I'll send a cable as soon as I leave here."

"How soon will you hear?"

"Late today. Where can I find you?"

"I'll be down at the ice house. One of the owners may be involved. Why don't we meet at The Manjuris later?"

"Fine," he said. "My daughter has taken quite a liking to that place. May as well see what all the excitement is about."

"You'll need it after the Rotary."

Van and I walked downtown together and split up at the corner of 2nd Avenue East and 8th Street. He was on his way to see Oddball, to ask the High Constable to travel to Balaclava to pick up my alibi. I'd also asked him to snoop around and see what he could find out about the body from Mudtown. The corpse was that of the gunman I had encountered in Hall's hotel room, so he was clearly linked to the case I was working on. It didn't matter now why he hadn't been in jail. It was more important to know who his accomplices were.

While Van headed across 8th Street, I walked down 2nd to Oak Hall Men's and Boys' Wear where my friend William Johnson was the manager. We'd known each other forever. Along with the Razor. The three of us had been great pals since we were kids. Once Billy had tried to balance on the top rail of the 10th Street bridge across the Sydenham River. When the fire brigade fished him out, the Chief called him Silly. Over the years it had been shortened to Sil.

"Hello!" I shouted as I pushed through the door.

All six feet of Sil popped up from behind a rack of clothing. He had sandy brown hair, spectacles and an immaculate suit of clothes.

"D.B.!" he welcomed me with a wave.

I followed him into the back room. The wood furnace was there making it warmer than the rest of the store. By opening time the entire building would be warm. I filled Sil in on the events of the last few days.

"Your uncle?" He clapped a hand to his head as I finished talking. "I don't believe it."

"A woman named Valerie Sutherland is involved. Rose Eng too."

"Rose? Oh, my. Have you seen her lately?"

Sil had been there for the beginning, middle and end of my relationship with Rose Eng.

"I saw her last night," I said and filled him in on the circumstances.

"What about the cops? The charges against you?"

"The cops have been told not to look too deeply into the Hall killing. The Chief won't mind if I find the killers. I think he's been telling Tom Carson to feed me information all along."

"Can I help?" Sil asked.

"I'm still missing a couple of killers," I answered. Sil had a lot of connections and heard a lot of downtown gossip. "How about checking your sources? Has anyone been acting out of character, spending a lot, stuff like that? Maybe you can turn something up."

"I'll call you in the morning."

CHAPTER TWENTY THREE

The dog trotted beside me all the way to Murphy's Ice Works. I pushed through the door into the dim interior. The building was half full. It was also half empty. The rest of the ice would come from the bay later in the week. The crews were set to move out to the deeper water, the paper had said, thanks to the cold snap we'd been having.

"Hank? Marty!" It was past eight, and I knew one or both of them would be there. Drinking coffee by the pot bellied stove in the office was my guess.

"Hello!" I called into the pile of ice once more.

"What do you want, gumshoe?" Hank growled from behind me.

"Hello, Hank," I started. I could feel the anger coming. It felt dangerous. "I came to hear it."

"Hear what, Danny-Boy?"

"Your confession."

"Confessions are for church."

"I came to hear about Everett Hall."

"Hall?" For a moment he seemed uncertain. Then angry. "You think I was in league with that devil?"

"I think you killed him." His fists crunched into hard little balls. He made a sound low in his throat then dropped his stance.

"Hank," I sighed. "Can't you come clean? Does it always have to come to blows?"

"Afraid, are you? You should be. You've never beaten me, not once since you were a snot nose. You're still one. A snot nose." It didn't matter whether he was right or not. His words reached inside and slapped the little boy I'd been across the face. I wanted to kick the hell out of him.

"Sticks and stones, Hank. Sticks and stones."

"The truth hurts, doesn't it D.B.?"

"It's not the truth that hurts, Hank. It's the lie."

"The lie? I never even met Hall."

"I did not kill Dad."

Hank charged straight at me and threw an overhand punch at my head. I feinted left. He followed and caught the brunt of my right in the side. I tried to sidestep but lost my footing. His head was buried in my gut when we landed. We both were covered in sawdust when we got up. I held my fists out in front of me, in the guard position. We circled one another.

"You killed him as sure as if you'd put a gun to his head. He had to close the shop when you left. No son. No shop. My brother died of a broken heart."

"He died of a heart attack. No one was sorrier than I was, Hank. No one."

"He was my brother!" the older man cried in rage and pain.

"He was my father," I bellowed back at him.

"Hank?" I heard Uncle Marty call from the direction of the office.

"Over here," I called back.

"Tell me now," I said. "Before Marty gets here."

"Tell you what?" Marty asked warily. This was the confrontation that had been simmering for years. I could tell he didn't want it to go any farther.

"This snot-nose thinks I killed Everett Hall." A look of genuine shock crossed Uncle Marty's face.

"How can you say something like that about Hank?" he cried.

"Motive and opportunity. He had 'em both."

"Like what?" Hank yelled. He was heating up again. Now that there was an audience.

"Everett Hall was going to build electric iceboxes. It would have put you out of business."

"They ain't practical for the home. Too big. Everyone says so," Uncle Hank countered.

"Hall's body was at the mill dam. Pretty convenient to where the crew is working now. You're the first to arrive in the morning. Lots of time to shove Hall into the river and clean up the blood before anyone else gets there for work."

"Everyone knew Hall was on the grift," Marty said. "It could have been anyone who killed him. Why pick Hank?"

"A few people had a hand in it," I said. "In the end Hall drowned. That's what killed him."

Hank came at me again. This time I was ready. I aimed a swift kick at his knee and sent him to the ground with a howl of pain. He came up a whole lot madder than he went down.

His fists were clenched so tight that his shoulders trembled. His face was crimson and there was a bit of froth on his lips as he stepped towards me again.

"I didn't kill Hall," he growled, "but I'm going to kill you!"

"Hank, no!" Marty jumped between us and tried to stop his brother. The two of them struggled with increasing intensity until Hank started to kidney punch Marty. I decided to intervene and tried to get between the two of them.

"Hank, Hank, stop! Stop!" Marty cried. I got them apart and put all of my two hundred pounds into a left-right combination to Hank's jaw. He stumbled backwards. I followed and gave it to him again. The rage was on me and I was ready to let it go.

"D.B., stop!" Marty was yelling at me. "Stop, stop you'll kill him. You'll kill him." He grabbed my arm and stopped a blow. "It was me. All along. Me. I did it. I killed Everett Hall!"

My arm hung in mid air, Marty hanging onto it. Too winded to ask a question, I just stared at him, unsure I'd heard him right.

"You, Marty?" Hank whispered. He had turned a sickly grayish-green colour. His skin looked waxy. Both hands clutched at the left side of his chest.

"Oh…oh my…" Hank stumbled towards me but fell flat on his face before he arrived. Marty rushed to his brother's side and put a hand against his neck. Hank's breathing was ragged.

"A doctor. Quick, Danny. Get a doctor."

CHAPTER TWENTY FOUR

"It looks as though he'll make it," Doc Soames said to Marty and me later in the hospital waiting room.

"What was it, Doc?" I asked. "Heart?"

"Yep. He's lucky you were both there." Marty and I exchanged a glance.

"Maybe not," I said.

"Were you having another one of those Irish brawls?" he asked. "I thought those stopped with your dad."

"It was nothing," Marty dismissed it before Doc could get too interested.

"We thought he was going to die," I said.

"Hank Murphy will never die," Doc said, smiling as he walked off. "He's too stubborn." I pulled my pocket watch out. It was nearly eleven. Lori would be wondering where I was.

"Let's sit down and talk," I suggested.

"I'm too tired," Marty sighed. "All I want to do is sleep."

He sank back on one of the hospital chairs and closed his eyes. He looked awful. Older. Deflated somehow. Not the way I expected a killer would look.

"I have to meet someone, anyway," I said. "But first I have to ask. Do you have the money?"

"It had nothing to do with the money."

It was a brisk walk from the Owen Sound General and Marine Hospital to The Manjuris. The storm had let up for the moment. The sky was clear, a million stars and half a moon lighting my way. The snow underfoot squeaked as I walked. It was cold, the kind of cold that makes your nostrils stick together when you inhale too quickly.

This case was getting out of hand. There had been too many complications and I wasn't feeling any closer to finding the money Hall had thimblerigged. I hoped Van had been able to learn something about the mystery corpse. Aside from the fact it had a hole in it from my gun.

Marty's involvement in Hall's death was making me feel queasy. My instinct was to protect my uncle. Hank and I were the only ones who knew the truth. Hank wouldn't tell. Would I? I wasn't sure. All along I'd been telling everyone I was just after the money. But now I was slowly finding out who each of the murderers were. There were two assailants left. I felt sure one of them would have the money. The question was, who?

The Manjuris was crowded and smoky when I went up. Ken Carr was sitting with Eddie at the preferred table. Each was smoking a real Cuban cigar, not an Owen Sound Cuban. A blue pall hung over the table.

I dropped into an extra chair, accepting the cigar Carr offered. Eddie poured a drink while I worked.

"How did you make out at the ice house?" Carr asked once I was settled. "Was the owner one of the people we were looking for?"

"The ice house?" Eddie started. "That's your…"

Carr looked from me to Eddie. "We can speak freely in front of Eddie," I said. "He can be trusted."

Carr relaxed. "What does the ice house have to do with you?" he asked.

"My uncles own it. One of them was involved in Hall's death."

Eddie let a low smoky whistle out. I gave them a summary of my evening. At the end Eddie squeezed my arm.

"Jeez Danny, I'm sorry," he said. "He'll be okay," I said. "I just hope we don't have to charge him." I said this while looking directly at Carr.

"As I said earlier," he began, "my government is willing to employ a certain degree of lenience. This has been confirmed by the cable I received back tonight. Hall was wanted, and would certainly have faced prison if he had been returned to my country, costing the government even more. If the cash is returned and the damage Hall has done is repaired, then we would be prepared to forget about the whole thing. With the co-operation of Canadian authorities. As for your question about accomplices, D.B., none are known. Hall worked alone."

"Too bad," I said. "I would have liked the guy I shot to be an accomplice. He's dead. I thought the money might have been wherever he was staying. It would have made a nice tidy ending."

"You could pin the murder on him, too. Save your uncle," Eddie said.

"Endings are rarely tidy," Carr said. "Have you had any luck with his identity?"

"Van was working on that. I haven't seen him yet."

"Daddy!"

Nadine Carr was bouncing towards us. On her way, she turned every head in the room. Carr stood and offered his cheek to her perfect lips. He got a giggle along with it. Eddie pulled another chair to the table and pushed it in for her.

"You know everyone darling?" Carr asked as Eddie poured.

"Yes, of course." She pulled her evening gloves off one finger at a time, then reached into her bag. Her hand emerged holding a Turkish cigarette. Eddie quickly offered a light. Before the bag closed I saw the pearl handle of a small gun. I'd heard Americans preferred to be well armed.

"Thank you, Mr. Razor," she said with a languid smile. "How can you stand living in this dreary little town? I would absolutely die."

"There's been lots of excitement lately," I said.

"Oh yes. And how is your little investigation going?"

"Darling," Carr jumped in. "You must remember we represent our country. You wouldn't want to give these gentlemen a bad impression, would you?"

"Of course not, Daddy," she smiled sweetly. "It's just that this place is so…so…hick. I want to go back to Toronto."

"As soon as Mr. Murphy finishes his investigation we can return. I'm sure it won't be much longer, will it?" Before I could answer the door to the bar slammed open. Van crossed the room in a hurry.

"What is it?" I asked.

"Someone knocked off Nosey Parker," Van said breathlessly.

CHAPTER TWENTY FIVE

It was almost midnight. The newspaper office was swarming with cops. Snake Foster was at the front door talking to Carp. "If you're sniffin' around for work, there ain't any," the fat detective sneered in my direction.

"Watch it, fat boy. It hasn't been a good day."

"You're the one who should watch it," he moved in my direction. "We still ain't heard from the skirt you said was in Balaclava. I could haul you in right now. In fact, maybe I will."

"Easy now, Charlie," the Chief grabbed him by the arm. "Why don't you go down and see how the boys are doin'. I'll handle this." For a moment it looked like he wasn't going to go. Then he did, but not before a parting shot. "I don't get some proof by tomorrow, you're gonna be in the slammer."

"Doesn't like you much, does he?" the Police Chief asked after his man had gone. "C'mon in." Van and I stepped into the vestibule with him. It was slightly warmer.

"This is an associate of mine. Bill Van Wyck."

"Have you learned anything?" the chief asked after they'd shaken hands. "A lot seems to be happening."

"I've got a few leads. No money though."

"Find out who killed Hall?"

"No." I hated to lie, but the whole game had changed with my uncle's involvement. If Carr was serious about his government's forgiving attitude there was no way I would let the names of any of the suspects become public. In the court of public opinion being a suspect was the same thing as being guilty.

"Why are you here?" the Chief asked.

"Parker told me he'd figured it all out. Said there was going to be a story in tomorrow's edition."

"He won't be writing anything anymore. He was shot in the pressroom."

"Anyone see anything?" I asked.

"No one saw, no one heard," was the terse response from the Chief.

"How did the gunman get in?"

"Parker must have let him in. The doors are locked after regular business hours."

"Why would he let his murderer in?" Van asked. "That seems pretty stupid."

"Unless it was someone he knew," I said, looking over at Van. "Remember he said he had one person left to talk to?"

"Did he now?" the Chief queried with interest.

"Mind if I have a look around?"

"Don't touch anything," Foster said, allowing us past, "and stay out of Carp's way."

"You mean Detective Fish don't you?"

"Sure," he smiled. "That's what I said. Remember. Noon tomorrow."

"Oddball Scott is going out there to get her. He'll have Miss Armstrong here on time."

The pressroom of *The Daily Sun-Times* was at the back of the building, away from the business offices. It was quiet. The presses didn't start running until around four in the morning.

Parker was in the farthest corner of the room near the loading dock. He was face up, eyes open, a crushed Roi-tan still in his mouth. A stream of blood led away from the body towards the doors. Doc Soames was leaning over him.

"Yep. He's dead," the old fellow said, standing up.

"How'd he die, Doc?" I asked.

"Don't you ever go home to that little wife of yours?"

"Haven't had much of a chance this week."

"I don't know how she stands it. This one," he gestured with the toe of his boot, "died of a gunshot wound to the head."

"What kind of gun?"

"A .32 calibre is my guess. Won't know more until I get him opened up."

"Thanks Doc. Let's go out front," I said to Van.

"The .32 seems to be a popular weapon in Owen Sound these days," Van said as we walked upstairs towards the business offices of *The Daily Sun-Times*.

"It does," I agreed, leading him into Parker's office which was more untidy than it had been during my visit the day before. At least then there had still been some semblance of order.

"It's been tossed," I said to Van.

"Someone looking for the story?"

"He was going to print it in tomorrow's edition."

"Do you think he got it written?"

"I guess it depends. If he expected the person who killed him to deliver the last piece of the puzzle, then I'd say probably not."

"Think it was one of Hall's killers?"

"I doubt it. The suspects we've found so far all had both motive and opportunity to kill Hall. Not Parker."

"We haven't found all of the killers yet."

"True. But if they're anything like the others, Hall was their primary target."

"Unless the person with the money was afraid Parker would reveal his or her identity."

"No." I wasn't convinced. There were too many other things going on, including my mystery assailants. I still wasn't sure what role they played in all of this. "I think there are some players in the game we don't know about yet. I need to ask the Doc something."

★★★

A couple of cops were loading Parker's body onto a stretcher. A janitor stood nearby with a bucket and mop. The Doc was washing his hands in a big work sink off to one side of the room.

"Doc?"

"Yes?"

"I need to know something else about Everett Hall."

"If I can."

"When you did the autopsy, could you tell the order of his injuries?"

"Huh?"

"Was he shot first? Sapped? What?"

"The pie was well digested so he was almost surely poisoned first."

"Was there enough to kill him?"

"No. It was an amateur attempt. There was just enough to make him sick. The stab wound had lots of bruising and blood, so it was next. Again, an amateur attempt. It missed all his vital organs. The bullet hole had started to bruise, but there was hardly any blood."

"So he was stabbed and then shot?"

"Yes," Doc said. "The blow to the head was last. There was no bruising at all, so he must have gone into the drink immediately."

"He drowned?"

"He drowned. I was able to squeeze water out of his lung tissue."

"That's the way that Russian monk got it."

"Rasputin?" Doc asked. "Hall didn't get quite the same treatment. Aside from the holes and a few gallons of water, his corpse was intact."

"What?" I asked.

Doc motioned Van and I closer. "Rasputin lost his willie," he said in a whisper just loud enough for the three of us.

"Go on!" Van said in disbelief

"No. It's been preserved in a silver box inside some bank vault." We left then, pondering Rasputin's mummified member on the walk back to the house.

★★★

"Is this what your life is like all the time?" Van asked once we were inside.

"No. In fact I usually spend a lot of time at The Manjuris playing pool and wishing I had work. I'm looking forward to getting back to that."

"I guess you'll be able to if you find the money."

"That's still a pretty big if."

"Two more killers out there. One of them must have it."

"Unless Hall got rid of it first."

After I showed Van to his room I went straight to bed. I was dead tired and my muscles were stiff from all the abuse I'd suffered. I stripped off my clothes and climbed in next to Lori. My side of the bed was cold so I snuggled close and curled an arm around her.

"Mmm," she said in a sleepy voice. "Do I know you? Do you live here?"

"Just trying to bring home the bacon."

"Goody. Sil was trying to get you tonight. Said it was urgent. You're to call first thing."

CHAPTER TWENTY SIX

I was out of the house and on my way to the hospital before seven. I had a lot of ground to cover and I wanted to start with my uncles. I had to find out what Marty had been confessing when Hank had his heart attack. They didn't have the money. Marty wouldn't lie about that.

The waiting room was empty when I arrived. Surprising. I assumed Marty would sleep there. I walked down the hall to the nurse's station. A woman with a severe face who was wearing about an acre of starched white answered my inquiry.

"Both of your uncles are in the same room," she said consulting the big book on the desk in front of her.

"I thought Marty might stay the night. He's pretty worried about Hank."

"Indeed." She gave me a strange look. "Room 112."

The person who had done the layout in the General and Marine had been more masochist than mathematician. Instead of being in numerical order, the rooms seemed to be numbered randomly. I had to double back twice before I found 112.

The door was open so I went right in. Doc Soames was there. But he wasn't looking at Hank. It was Marty he was leaning over.

"What the…" The sentence died in my mouth when I got a look at Marty. Someone had worked him over pretty well.

"It's all pretty superficial," Doc said. "I don't know what it is about you Murphys. Next thing we'll be wheeling in a bed for you Danny. Maybe that wife of yours too. Oh well, I guess I got to practice my stitching on someone."

"It don't hurt so much," Marty said, attempting a smile.

"What happened?"

"I went down to the ice house last night after it looked like Hank was gonna be okay. I just wanted to close 'er up good an' proper. When we rushed outta there we didn't even lock the doors."

"It's February, Marty. Who's going to steal ice in February?"

"That ain't the point. It's our place and it needs to be locked up."

"Still doesn't explain how you got beat up."

"After I locked up I went on over to the house to fetch some things for Hank. Y'know, slippers, whisky, robe and such. On the way I thought someone was following, but I wasn't sure. When I come out of the house is when they set on me."

"How many of them?"

"Two. Big one and a little one. All dressed in black and with their faces covered. Tried to get my bag away from me. I fought 'em."

"Over slippers and a bathrobe?"

"They was stealin' something of mine. I had to fight 'em."

"Atta boy, Marty," Doc said. "Too many of these young punks think they can just take what they want from citizens like you and me. Now if you gentlemen will excuse me, I've got rounds to make."

"Sure Doc. Say, how's Hank?" I had looked his way several times while Marty told his story. His breathing was still ragged and his closed eyelids were almost translucent.

Doc motioned me to follow him out into the hallway.

"It's going to be a slow recovery. He'll never work again."

"That'll kill him. Hank doesn't have anything except Marty and that business."

"That may be. The condition his heart is in, it would be suicide for him to go back."

"Uh…oh, okay. Thanks."

He continued down the hall. I went back into the room and sat beside Uncle Marty's bed.

"I need to know what happened. Between you and Hall."

Marty closed his eyes wearily. His face was covered with bruises. Stitches had been used to close a cut above his eye and another on his lower lip.

"I was scared."

"Of Hall?"

"Of what he said he was going to do."

"The electric iceboxes." Marty opened his eyes. A tear spilled out of one.

"What's going to happen to me?"

I looked at him for a long moment.

"I know what should happen to you. Jail, you silly old bugger. What were you thinking?"

"About Hank an' me, what do you think? We got nothing, Danny. Nothing but Murphy's Ice Works."

"I know."

"You told me you was looking for the money. Not the killer. The money."

"Do you have it?"

"No."

"Who does?"

"I don't know."

"That's too bad. Y'know, I haven't found one person who's seen the money."

"He kept it in a leather club bag."

"What?" This was news to me.

Marty looked embarrassed. "I followed him around a bit. Just to see what he was up to. He had this leather bag. Carried it with him when he collected the share money from around town."

"How'd you come to have a hand in killing him? Were you all in on it together?"

"All? All who? Whaddaya mean?"

"Just tell me what happened."

"I rode Bob Hooper down to the mill dam the night before Hall was found."

"You still got that old horse? I thought he went to the glue factory a long time ago."

"He's got a few miles left in him," Marty yawned. "I'm really tired, D.B."

"Give me the short version and I'll get out of here."

"I was riding along near the mill. A little fella all dressed in black came out of nowhere and spooked old Bob. He bolted and ran into some other fella leaning up against a tree who slid right into the water. At the last second I seen it was Hall."

"Bob bumped into him? Is that how Hall got hit on the head?"

Marty looked puzzled. "Hit on the head? No, Bob caught him on the shoulder."

"Did Hall say anything? Yell? React in any way?"

"That was the funny thing. He didn't make a peep. Not one."

"I'll bet he was unconscious.

"What?"

"He was propped up against that tree," I explained. "Listen, get some rest. I'll see you later. If Hank wakes up tell him I was here to see him, okay?"

"Sure. Listen, could you go around to the ice house and check things out? After all that's happened, I'm a little worried."

From the hospital I walked down 13th Street A West. A pleasant, domestic street just waking up. The air smelled of woodsmoke, bacon and coffee. My stomach grumbled.

Kids carrying massive packs of books headed to school on both sides of the street. An occasional horse and cutter passed with a jingle, most on their way towards the centre of town. I cut down 1st Avenue to check the ice house as Uncle Marty had requested. I looked up the bay and caught sight of low clouds rolling down the ice to ruin the day. Snow was in the forecast.

I was halfway through the alleyway between the ice house and the tannery when I heard the sound of an automatic being charged. I turned and found myself looking straight down the barrel of a Webley & Scott .455.

My gun.

CHAPTER TWENTY SEVEN

It was the pair I'd mistaken for the Costellos. Both had guns, dark clothing and masks. One of them was large, about my size. He was holding my weapon. The other was slight and held the most popular pistol in Owen Sound. A .32 automatic.

"The mystery muggers strike again."

Neither spoke. The big one closed the space between us and shoved the muzzle of the Webley & Scott into my gut. If his trigger finger got itchy there'd be nothing left of my spine. I didn't move.

He didn't disarm me, correctly guessing I wasn't going to reach for my pistol in present circumstances. Instead he patted down my pockets looking for something.

"Any harder for you guys to rob people as a duo instead of a trio?" I asked.

My quip didn't get the desired response. It didn't get any response. The one searching me didn't find what he was looking for. He turned to the other and shook his head. Slim made an impatient departure gesture and pushed past me. I turned slightly to try and keep them both in my view. Too late I heard the swish of fabric and saw the downward swing of an arm. The frozen ground hit me in the face and everything went black.

"You're lucky they didn't kill you," a voice said. I wasn't clear on what was being said, who was saying it or whether it was even real. I seemed to be sitting up, then I wasn't. Then I just wasn't there at all.

The next time I came to I knew exactly where I was. On the floor of the office of Murphy's Ice Works. A fire was going in the stove. It was warm and I was covered in blankets. Van was sitting in a chair looking down at me.

"Welcome back," he said.

I tried to sit up but couldn't. An anvil of pain was holding me down.

"Easy," Van said. "After the hit you took you're lucky to be here at all."

"That bad?" I croaked through dry lips.

"Not too bad. If you'd spent much more time out of doors I could have packed you in sawdust."

"What happened?"

"I went to the hospital but just missed you. Your uncle said you were coming back to lock up. But when I got here the doors were already locked. I looked around and found you unconscious in the alley. Nice egg behind your ear all ready to hatch. That dog was sitting next to you. He might have saved your life. Don't know where he got to. Wouldn't come in."

I reached back and felt the lump on my head. My hand came away bloody. I wiped it on my jacket.

"Hate to tell you, but this thing has already hatched. I need a drink. There's some in the desk."

Van crossed the room and pulled the bottom drawer open. He took the whisky back to the stove, where he poured me a coffee topped with liquor. He also handed me a bag of ice.

"I got the Doc over here to take a look at you."

"Oh yeah?"

"He says you should stay off your head for a few days."

"Easy for you to joke."

"I'm glad it's not me. That's all."

I finished the drink and held out the mug for another. I was feeling better already. As long as I didn't move.

"I think I figured out who sapped Hall," I said when Van brought the second coffee. There was less booze in it. It was early and I had work to do. I told him about my unknown assailants reappearing.

"Who are they?" he asked when I finished.

"Don't know."

"Y'know, something just occurred to me."

"What's that?"

"You've been attacked every time you've left a suspect. They're after the money." I sat up. Slowly. The pain in my head bloomed. Then settled down to a throb in pace with my heart. I'd have to try not to get excited.

"I think you're right."

"The telephone lines are back up so I phoned the store. Oddball and Miss Armstrong are on their way back to town."

"Great." I stood. For a second I wavered and thought I might go down again. Then the world steadied itself and my horizon became more or less level.

"Where to?" Van drained his coffee and stood.

"Downtown. We've gotta go see Sil."

★★★

It was still too early for Oak Hall Men's and Boys' Wear to be open. But Sil was the manager. He'd been there for some time when we arrived.

"Christ in a sidecar!" he said when he saw me. "What happened to you?"

"Why don't you let us in first. Back by the stove where it's warm." I was still cold to the bone. All I really wanted to do was go home to bed. That's the kind of week I'd been having. But things were moving so fast I was afraid that if I did take it easy the money and the case would slip through my fingers.

Sil opened the door wider and let us through.

"Hi, Van," he said as we walked into the store.

"Another dump of snow coming today," Van said in response.

"Go on," Sil stared back out the door for a moment.

"For sure," I answered. "You can see the clouds stacking up over the bay."

It smelled of mothballs and wood smoke. The air was still cool. Sil had probably stoked the wood furnace when he came in. It would take a while for the shop to warm.

"C'mon back," Sil said winding his way through racks and shelves of shirts and ties. When he pushed the swinging door on the stockroom open I felt a gust of warm air. My head was beginning to pound again. I was looking forward to sitting down.

There was coffee on the top of the little pot bellied stove. I gladly accepted a cup.

"So what happened to you?" Sil asked.

"He got sapped with a very large billy," Van said.

"Ouch. Let's see." He crossed to where I was sitting and pulled my hat off. At the first touch I flinched pretty badly. Then the pain settled down a little.

"It's still oozing. You got a coupla stitches in there already by the look of it."

"Van called the Doc over to fix me up." Between us, Van and I filled Sil in on the morning's events.

"They have your gun? I thought the Costellos took it when they broke into your office."

"I thought so too. It looks like someone else was in the office before the Costellos."

"Who?" I asked

"Beats me," Sil replied.

"We were hoping you could tell us." Van helped himself to more coffee.

"No one I know has heard anything. You might have more luck with Eddie," Sil suggested.

"That's too bad," Van responded.

"I didn't say I don't know anything." Sil said. The smile on his face was so wide I could hear it.

"What'd you find out?" I asked. "Is the mayor in on it? An alderman?"

"You're in the right building. Someone in the City Clerk's department was involved with Everett Hall. A woman. She gave her notice yesterday. Catherine Ballantyne."

CHAPTER TWENTY EIGHT

Things were beginning to make sense. Catherine Ballantyne had been the last one to handle my overcoat before the .22 dropped out of it. She'd asked about the money the first time we met. And she'd known about Valerie Sutherland.

City Hall was less than half a block from Oak Hall Men's and Boys' Wear. We went straight over. The officious Mr. Williams was working the counter himself.

"Yes, sir? May I be of help?"

"I'm looking for Miss Ballantyne."

"Then sir, you are too late. She is no longer employed here."

"I heard that. Where can I find her?"

"That sir, is not my business. All I can say is, Miss Ballantyne is no longer employed here." I grabbed a handful of jacket, shirt and tie and hoisted him over to my side of the counter.

"Listen shorty, I've had about enough of you. I have information about Miss Ballantyne. She was mixed up in this Everett Hall business. She may have been involved in his death."

"Yes, but..." he started to say.

"A big pile is about to hit the fan, my diminutive friend. You can be in front of the fan or out of the way. The choice is yours."

"Er, out of the way. Please. She's at the Station Hotel."

"Anything else?"

"She said she was leaving today. By train. To Toronto I think."

"What's going on here?" Ken Carr's voice came from the lobby door.

I replaced Williams behind the counter and let go of his shirt front.

"Good morning, Mr. Carr," I said. I crossed the room and followed him into the lobby. "I was liberating some information."

"I was coming to see His Worship the Mayor. My government is interested in discussing the cross lake traffic. It seems a lot of bootleg whisky passes through this port."

"No more than anywhere else."

"We shall see."

"I think I've finally found our pigeon. And she's feathering her nest with our money."

"Excellent. Did I mention I'd received another cable?

"No."

"My government is prepared to offer a reward for the quick settlement of this matter."

"Reward?" Van asked.

"A substantial reward."

"Hear that D.B.?"

"I heard him." My headache was coming back. It was time to start moving again.

★★★

The Manjuris had barely opened when we got there. Eddie was sitting at a felt covered poker table drinking coffee and reading the newspaper. It was light on local content, with nothing by Nosey Parker.

"Morning boys," he said from behind the broadsheet. "Help yourselves to coffee."

The only other person in the place was Red. Wherever Eddie went, Red went too. I sat down and poured from the carafe on the table in front of him.

"Are those what I think they are?" Van asked pointing to a nearby plate.

"Of course," Eddie folded his paper. "Croissants. Just like we got in France."

"Gee, croissants. I always preferred lard sandwiches," I joked. "Like the ones we got in England."

"We'd have been hungry if it hadn't been for the Grey Rooms," Eddie agreed. "Ever go to 'em Van?"

"Sure. Once or twice. But I wasn't over there very long." The Grey Rooms were a haven for Grey County boys in London during the war. They were started by Mrs. Eaton from Owen Sound, with the help of two ladies from Holland Township, Mrs. Boulter, and Mrs. Ball. Later Mrs. Howey joined them. The ladies provided down home comfort for boys in the service. There was a light luncheon every day, and tea at four-thirty sharp. Casualty lists were posted as well, so we could keep tabs on friends and family. The Grey Rooms had made a big difference for lots of us away from home for the first time. And they didn't serve lard sandwiches.

Van and I helped ourselves to the spread Eddie had laid out. Lots of butter and jostaberry jelly.

"I'm going to need some help," I said between bites.

"When?" Eddie asked.

"Soon as we're done here."

"What's the deal?"

I told him about Catherine Ballantyne. And the attacks after I interviewed each suspect.

"So you need protection? Me and Red can come."

"I don't want to put you out."

"Not at all," Eddie smiled. "We got some new artillery that needs testing."

"Great."

The Station Hotel is on 1st Avenue East at the corner of 12th. Right across from the train station. Not one of Owen Sound's more reputable establishments. A few days earlier I might have been surprised at Catherine Ballantyne's choice of dwelling. Now I knew she was a dangerous woman. Probably desperate too. Eddie and Red were along to protect us from her, as well as the masked bandits I'd run into a couple of times. If I was right, Miss Ballantyne had the money. Fifty-one thousand dollars, give or take a few. I had no doubt we'd be seeing our masked friends again.

We walked up the broad steps at the northwest corner of the building. I pulled the big front doors open and we went in. The lobby wasn't much although it was slightly warmer than outside. Men and women sat at tables, some playing rummy, others reading pulps. A few were on overstuffed sofas listening to a player piano that had heard better days. There was smoke in the air but it was tobacco, not coal. A film of grease seemed to congeal in my hair, on my skin and throughout my clothes.

I crossed to the desk and spoke through a small opening in the centre of a smudged glass window.

"What room is Catherine Ballantyne in?" I asked the fat sweating man in the cubicle. He had a small coal brazier and was much warmer than the inhabitants of the lobby.

"Can't tell ya."

"Not even when it's the King who wants to know?" I asked shoving a fin in his direction.

"Room 204. Top of the stairs go left." He passed me a key. "Don't break the door."

It smelled worse upstairs. Body odor, disinfectant and cheap perfume. The hallway was dim, and from behind the doors came sounds of love, hate and war. It was the kind of place where people lived and died. No one much cared which you chose.

I stopped in front of Room 204. Eddie and Red each staked out an end of the hallway. They had new Thompson submachine guns. Model M1921, the same one the New York City Police Force was using. On automatic it fired about 300 rounds a minute. Eddie had his set on automatic. And he was using a type C magazine containing one hundred rounds, the largest available.

"Where'd you get that?" I'd asked him.

"A friend of mine. He's in the business across the border."

For Eddie, 'across the border' meant somewhere in the middle of Lake Huron. Much of his business was done there, far from the reach of police and the Coast Guard. He was the major supplier to Michigan of Montreal whisky.

Van was on one side of the door and I was on the other. I put an ear to it but couldn't hear anything. I knocked and stepped back. I thought I heard a rustle but nothing else happened.

I tried the knob but it was locked. I slid the five dollar key into its hole and turned. I put the key back into my pocket and shifted my .45 to my right hand. I nodded to Van. He was ready.

CHAPTER TWENTY NINE

The door opened with the metallic sigh of rusted hinges. I knew without looking the room was empty. I walked in, my gun leveled and headed to the left. Van went right.

It was a wide room with a three-sided bay window looking out over the train station and harbour. One of the windows was open and February was rushing in. I was nearly there when the gunshots sounded. The first round caught the arm of my jacket but missed me. The next two rounds were aimed at Van. One hit the wall beside him. I didn't see what stopped the other one.

My Colt boomed like a cannon in the small room. I heard pounding feet in the hallway, and shouts. Van and Red burst into the room guns a-blazing. I hit the floor. At its best, the Thompson could empty a one hundred round drum magazine in twenty seconds. There wasn't much left of the room when Eddie and Red finished.

"She's not even here!" I shouted at the two of them. The air was filled with dust and smoke. Van lay on the bed. I ran to the window for a quick look, just in time to see Miss Ballantyne jumping off the fire escape ladder. She was carrying a leather club bag in one hand, a pistol in the other.

I drew a bead on her but she ducked behind a wagon and I lost sight of her.

"Are you okay?" I asked Van, crossing to the bed.

"It's only a flesh wound."

I stopped and took a look. A small calibre slug had passed through the big muscle at the top of his shoulder. The hole was tiny and there wasn't much blood.

"You're lucky she's using a parlour pistol," I said. "I'll get Red to take you over to see the Doc."

"Sure, go. Catch her. She have the money?"

"She had a club bag."

"Hurry up then. Don't let her get away."

"Red get Doc. I'm going with D.B.," Eddie said.

At the bottom of the stairs we crossed the small lobby without concealing our weapons. We got few stares. Most of the residents either didn't notice or didn't care. I suspected the latter.

Outside a squall had descended. The snow was so thick I could hardly see the train station across the street. It was going to be difficult to find Catherine Ballantyne.

"She's leaving on the Toronto train."

"That's almost an hour from now."

"It's a place to start."

"Okay. Let's go."

The Toronto train was on the tracks in front of the station, half a dozen cars long including the locomotive and coal car. Up front I could see the fireman stoking the boiler. Smoke rose from the stack, but it would take almost an hour for the big engine to build up enough steam to move. I could see the conductor loading the pot bellied stove at the front of one of the coaches. If he kept at it, he'd have it warm by the time the passengers arrived. The platform was empty. There was no sign of Miss Ballantyne.

"Where do you think she went?" Eddie asked. He'd removed the stock from the Thompson so he could hide it inside the skirt of his overcoat. I tucked the .45 into my coat pocket but kept a hand on it.

"That train is her only way out in this weather. She's got to be nearby."

"Down by the water?"

"Yeah, maybe. Let's go and have a look." We walked to the end of the train and crossed the tracks behind it. The squall raged on. We were forty feet from the harbour where I knew for a fact there were dozens of ships wintering. But we couldn't see a single one, the snow was so thick. Catherine Ballantyne was waiting for us down there. I was sure of it.

"She's got a bag full of money and a gun. She's desperate."

"She'll try and kill us so she can make that train," Eddie said.

"Watch your back." Boats sitting up on the shore gradually emerged. It was twilight in the narrow alleyways between them. Treacherous.

"How far does this line of boats go?" Eddie asked in a low voice.

"I can't remember."

"Me neither," he replied.

"I'll go first. You turn around, and we'll go through back to back. Put the Thompson on semi-automatic." Eddie yanked the drum magazine off the gun and tucked it into a deep pocket. Out of another pocket he pulled a twenty-round stick magazine and snapped it into place. I reached into my boot for the .32. The .45 stayed in my right hand.

I stepped in between the first two boats and waited for Eddie to get into position behind me. When our backs touched I started to walk forward. Instantly I slipped and nearly broke my leg. The pathway between the boats was solid ice, caused by the drips from melting snow. There was no way I could carry two guns. I'd need at least one hand to steady myself. I dumped the .32 in a pocket and kept moving.

We came up against the hull of a boat. A T-junction. I looked one way and then the other, but the murk was impenetrable. I turned right. We followed that hull to the next intersection and turned left, west, back towards the water.

As I came around the corner I sensed movement in the wall of white which obscured my view. I stopped abruptly but Eddie kept going. He knocked forward hard enough that I lost my balance on the ice and went down in a heap. The .45 flew out of my hand and clattered under a boat.

Eddie fell on top of me. As he landed the Thompson roared, chopping a hole in the hull of the boat beside us.

"I thought I told you to put that on semi-automatic!" I shouted at him.

"Move and you're dead," Catherine Ballantyne growled from under the same boat. If I hadn't fallen I wouldn't have seen her.

She was sitting on top of the club bag. A .22 target pistol was pointed straight at us. I didn't have a full sense of the danger we were in until I saw her smile.

CHAPTER THIRTY

"There are two of us," I said.

"Together you barely add up to one." She slid across the ice, still on top of the club bag. A grim smile remained on her face, the gun was still pointed our way. She'd already shot Van. It was starting to look bad for Eddie and me.

"This skirt is enjoying herself," Eddie said.

"She's a killer alright."

"Enough of the small talk. If either of you make a move for your guns, I will shoot." She barely resembled the courteous city employee I'd met just days before. Her face was distorted with greed. Viciousness gleamed in her eyes and informed her every movement.

"Curtains, boys." She spat out the words.

"You'll never get away with it," I said.

"Who's gonna stop me, gumshoe?" The muzzle of her gun was aimed at the centre of my chest.

There was a sudden movement in the snow beside her and then the dog had her gun hand firmly clamped in his jaws.

"Aaaiiieee!" Miss Ballantyne screamed and dropped the gun. The dog let her go, picked the gun up in his mouth and with a wag of his tail brought it over and dropped it in front of me.

We were all too stunned to do anything. The dog had saved my life and retrieved the gun. It was bizarre. I snapped out of it when Miss Ballantyne attempted to scramble back under the boat, club bag clutched tightly in her hand.

The dog was back at her in a flash. Growling, fangs bared in a wicked smile. The woman stopped moving. Eddie and I stood up.

"That's some good little dog you've got yourself there, D.B." Eddie said.

"He's not my dog," I said.

"Well don't tell him that. He seems to like you."

I walked to Miss Ballantyne and reached for the bag. It was a struggle to get it. I ended up dragging her out from under the boat. When I finally got the bag and opened it I could see why she'd fought so hard. There was a jumble of cash inside, piled, bundled, and loose.

I whistled and held it out to Eddie. "Get a load of this."

"How many people'd you kill to earn this, doll?" Eddie asked the woman from the City Clerk's office.

"I earned it," she said. "Every penny. It's mine."

"How do you figure?" I asked.

"Everett loved me. Just me."

"Oh? What about Valerie Sutherland and Rose Eng? And who knows how many other women in how many other towns?" Tears began to roll down her face and her shoulders began to shake. I thought she was upset. But only for a moment.

"If I get half a chance, I'll kill you. Both of you!" She spat at me and raised her fists. The dog renewed his growling. She stopped moving. At least she was afraid of something. Not Eddie and me, that was for sure.

I retrieved my .45 from under the boat, then gestured to Miss Ballantyne. "C'mon Miss. Let's go."

We marched Miss Ballantyne through the storm back to the train station. As we walked onto the platform, Ken Carr arrived. He had a gun in his hand. A .45 not dissimilar to mine. Only mine was safely tucked in the holster under my arm again.

"D.B., Eddie. Van said you needed help. I got here as quickly as I could."

"Thanks," I said. "We bagged her."

I was still concerned. The whole point of having four men had been to protect the money. If the masked attackers caught me again, it would be the final attack. Because this time I did have the money. And I didn't want to lose it. Or my life.

"Is she the one?" Carr asked.

"Yup," I said. "She had the dough." I quickly explained the attacks and when they had occurred.

"So you think you're a marked man because of the money?" Carr asked.

"Exactly."

"No one is looking for me. Why don't I take it?"

I thought about it. Then decided against asking Eddie to take Miss Ballantyne in alone. If she had accomplices Eddie wouldn't stand a chance. Ken Carr was armed and no one would expect him to have the money.

"I'll take it back to City Hall," Carr said. "The mayor is in his office. I'll wait for you there."

I shoved the bag into his hand. "Go inside and get another bag. This one is pretty well known."

Carr hurried off. The platform was growing busier as train time approached. Miss Ballantyne walked with her eyes down, looking at nothing. My mood was significantly improved. The lump behind my ear wasn't even bothering me. Inside the hour I'd have my pay, and I'd finally be able to get the rest I so richly deserved.

Miss Ballantyne didn't say a word as Eddie and I walked her the five blocks to the Grey County Courthouse. The dog ran circles around us, nipping at our heels. He barked occasionally to keep us moving in the right direction. The jail was right next door to the courthouse. By the time we got there Eddie had the Thompson rigged up inside his jacket again so it couldn't be seen. The local police might not take kindly to his having it even though they had nothing to fear from it. Eddie was a friend to the police. Well, more of a benefactor. He contributed heavily to the Officers' Relief Fund for the Underprivileged.

"Need me to come to City Hall with you?" Eddie asked as we walked in the front door of the jail. We hadn't seen a trace of my masked assailants.

"No." I was hoping they would pay me without asking any questions. Questions about who had killed Everett Hall.

"You could pin the whole thing on her," Eddie gestured at Miss Ballantyne. She pretended not to listen, but she'd stiffened at the suggestion.

"We'll see how co-operative she is," I said. There was some paperwork to be done. Eddie left me to do it. When I finished, the matron, who doubled as the jail cook, came and took Miss Ballantyne away. As she left she turned and looked back at me.

"I'll never forget you, D.B. Murphy. And when I get out you better watch it. I'll kill you if I can." She said it calmly and with no inflection. A chill ran down my spine.

"You won't be the first to try," I said as the door closed on her. "You won't even be the next." I stepped out the front door and walked across the stone porch to the County Courthouse next door.

"Time's up, boyo," a voice said. I turned. Des Rennet was coming at me with a pair of bracelets in his hand. Charlie the Carp was beside him, pistol drawn. They'd been waiting for me.

"Jeez fellas, you scared me. I guess by now you heard I've got it all sewn up." I was shooting in the dark. My noon deadline had only barely passed and my next destination was Oddball's office.

"Whaddaya mean, wrapped up?" Fish asked.

"I found the money. Just as it was about to fly south for the winter."

"Isn't that special," Rennet said. "Just in time. 'Cause you ain't got no witness yet, and we're takin' ya in."

"I was just heading over to Oddball's office to see if he's back with her yet."

"Too late," the Carp sneered. I looked from one to the other. They were serious. I turned to let Rennet put the cuffs on me. At the same moment the cutter I had rented for Miss Armstrong rolled past the jail into the parking lot in front of the courthouse. Before Rennet could move I bolted down the steps and across the yard separating jail and court.

"Hey, stop." Carp gave a futile yell as they followed me down the stairs. I was fairly confident he wouldn't shoot. The snow was deep in the yard but I couldn't waste time going around. I had to get to Miss Armstrong. Otherwise Carp and Rennet would haul me in out of spite. It would mean an appearance in police court in the morning before I could clear my name. I found the idea of another night in the clink rather unappealing.

"Hey! Oddball!" I called. Hitching the horses to the rail he looked up in surprise.

"D.B. In a hurry or something?"

"Didn't Van tell you to get back here with her by noon? Hello, Miss Armstrong."

"Mr. Murphy," she smiled at me with lips blue from cold.

"Sure sure, he told me," Oddball said. "We would have been too, if not for that squall."

"These goons," I said, pointing to Carp and Rennet who had caught up to me, "want to haul me in. Please Miss Armstrong, could you tell them about the attack?"

"Not a word until she warms up. We've been in the open for three hours." It was unlike Oddball to consider another person's welfare. I was taken aback. So were Rennet and Carp.

We followed the pair inside. The county police office was warm, a fire burning quite nicely in the wood stove in the corner. There was no one else around and the coffee wasn't too old. Oddball poured us all a cup and we sat on wooden office chairs in a circle around the fire.

"Now, Miss Armstrong," Rennet began. "Tell us about this so-called attack."

She told it exactly the way it happened, much to their chagrin. I could see by their faces they'd really been hoping to toss me into the can, at least for one more night.

"We'll need an official deposition," Carp said at the end. "And until we get it Murphy here'll have to cool his heels in the basement at headquarters."

"Nonsense," Oddball jumped up. "I heard it all and I'm as good as a deposition. You don't need to haul him in at all, Carp."

"What'd you call me?" Detective Fish jumped up his face going crimson. No one ever called him Carp to his face.

"Carp. Carp. Carp. That's what I called you. Now sit down, Fish. You're in my office, not your own." Oddball addressed me. "Some people are so sensitive. How many years have I been called Oddball?"

"Pretty much since the accident," I responded with a smile. "Before that we called you Bullet Head."

"Har, har. You boys get lost," he said to Carp and Rennet. "I wanna talk to D.B. and Miss Armstrong."

The two detectives began to protest but Oddball showed them out.

"I'll bring Miss Armstrong over to Police Magistrate Creasor's office to make a formal statement. You tell the Chief."

Both men sent ugly looks in my direction. I'd have to watch my step around them in the future. Though given the size of the reward I was due, that future might include retirement. I was bored with being shot at and beaten up. When the door closed Oddball turned to me.

"So how's it been going?" I filled the two of them in on the latest developments, right up to my delivery of Miss Ballantyne to the jail.

"That's great," Oddball said looking under my chair and around the floor near me. "Where's the money? Let's see it."

"Ken Carr has it. I'm going over to city hall to meet him now."

"Ken Carr?" Miss Armstrong asked. "The man from the train?"

"The American Deputy Vice Consul from Toronto. Came up with his daughter."

"Yes, I remember you were telling me when all that shooting started," she said. "But I rode the train from Toronto. They boarded at a place twenty minutes from here."

CHAPTER THIRTY ONE

"What?" I couldn't believe what I'd just heard.

"Ken Carr got on the train in Chatsworth. And if she's his daughter, I'm his wife," Miss Armstrong repeated.

"You must be mistaken." I desperately wanted her to be.

"I don't think so. The way the two of them were acting you couldn't help but notice. Not after you've been bored out of your mind on a train for hours."

"The way they were acting?"

Oddball was shaking his head. "Beats me how these city folk figure they're totally anonymous when they come to the country. This is the one place everyone notices them."

"*Scheiss Dreck*!" I shouted, reverting to language I'd learned overseas. "Gotta go. Oddball, you stay here. I might need you."

I left the office at a dead run. The snow was still coming down and visibility was bad. It didn't matter to me. I ran straight along the middle of the road. Down 3rd Avenue East to 10th Street and then down to 2nd to the centre of the city. I ran all the way to the telegraph office. Out of breath, it was all I could do to get the question out.

"How…how…how many cables has Ken Carr sent to the American Embassy in Toronto?"

"Ken Carr? You mean that American feller I seen in the paper? None," the operator said in surprise.

"Where has he been sending them?"

"He hasn't sent any at all. None."

"None?"

"Not a one."

"Thanks." I pounded back out the front door and up 2nd Avenue to City Hall. I was really out of wind by the time I got there. Little Mr. Williams was still on the front desk when I arrived.

"Not you. Not again," he cringed away from me when I came in the front door.

"Relax, little man. I'm here for the mayor."

"He isn't here."

"What?" I stopped short of His Worship's door.

"The mayor is not here."

"Has Ken Carr been here?"

"No."

"How long have you been here?"

"All day."

I rushed out the front door dodging shoppers and business people as I sprinted up the street towards the King George Hotel, a block east on 8th Street. There was an occasional 'hey' or 'look out' as I surprised people. Grown men didn't usually run down the sidewalks in Owen Sound. Except maybe on Veterans Day. Never in the winter, when the going tended to be tough.

I was halfway up the block when I turned around and ran back to the City Hotel. In the stable I yelled to the Lugan, "Saddle him up. Quick." Seeing the look on my face, the usual sarcasm died in his mouth. He was all motion and purpose.

"A long trip?"

"Yes."

"Food for both of you?"

"Right. And I need a long gun."

"Cops still got the Enfield?"

"Yes. You got a gun I can use?"

He was leading Scotty out of his stall at this point. The horse came straight over and nuzzled my hand for a treat.

"I got a gun. All cleaned and oiled."

"I'll be back in five minutes."

My legs were getting tired and I was sweating heavily inside my jacket. I rushed into the lobby of Owen Sound's more elegant hotel. The man at the front desk was Samuel Johnson. Sil's brother.

"Sam. Ken Carr and his daughter Nadine. What room?"

"Was seven and eight. Not any more. They checked out. Said they were catching the train."

Back to square one. "Thanks Sam," I threw the words over my shoulder as I headed out. I ran straight back to the stables. The Lugan had Scotty ready to go.

"Thanks," I said. I gave Scotty a kick and then immediately reined him. "Say, could you go over to my house and tell Lori I might not be home tonight, but that everything is okay?"

"Sure."

"You know where it is?"

"Over by the library?"

"Yes. Thanks." Then I got Scotty moving and we made some real time. We easily passed the few cars that were on the main street. Scotty really enjoyed himself. It reinforced his superiority complex.

At the C.P.R. station I didn't even bother to tie him up. Just dove off when we stopped and hit the platform at a dead run. Straight to the ticket wicket.

"Hey, Uncle Jerry." He looked up from his work with a smile.

"Danny. I don't see you for months then suddenly it's twice in one week."

"No time to chat. Did Ken Carr and his daughter get on the train?"

"Yup."

"When did it leave?" He consulted a pocket watch on a long gold chain. He'd worn it as long as I could remember.

"Twenty-one minutes ago," he said. I was moving so fast the words barely caught me.

CHAPTER THIRTY TWO

An hour of hard riding put Scotty and me in Chatsworth. It was still snowing heavily. We were a long way behind the train. Ken and Nadine Carr could be anywhere.

The C.P.R. station was typical in design. There was a siding lined with boxcars running parallel to the main track. Across the tracks, opposite the station, a water tower and windmill leaned into the wind. The buildings were painted brick red, with a sign above the platform that read Chatsworth.

I tied Scotty to the hitching rail and went in. It was warm. The smells of woodsmoke, Old Chum pipe tobacco and wet wool and leather assailed my nostrils. It took my eyes a moment to adjust to the dim interior. When they did, a group of good old boys appeared, sitting around a fireplace in the centre of the room. Most were smoking straight-stemmed pipes and drinking from tin cups. One of the younger fellows was chewing and using the spittoon with some frequency. I wished I had time to join them long enough to warm myself up.

I walked right to the agent's desk. "Did a man and woman get off the train that just came through?"

He looked at me over a pair of horn rimmed glasses. "It is not railway policy to divulge such information to just anyone."

"I'm not just anyone." I flipped a card onto the desk in front of him. He picked it up and examined it carefully.

"So you're a private cop. What of it?"

I pulled the emergency ten out of my wallet and slid it across the desk. The money disappeared before he even finished looking to see whether anyone noticed the bribe. No one had. It was a good thing I was working for more than my daily rates. Otherwise I'd be going broke with all the bribes I was paying.

"Ken and Nadine Carr. Seen 'em?"

"Hey Frenchie," he called in the general direction of the stove. "Anyone get off that train?"

"Sure. A couple. They rented some horses and headed south." By now the stoveside crew was listening intently to the conversation.

"Their names were Ken and Nadine Carr," I said. "Anyone know them?"

"They're from Arnott," one of the men said.

"Did you see them get off the train?"

"Nawp. I jes' got here. But I come from Arnott. Ken and Nadine Carr live there."

"Thanks," I said, turning back to the ticket agent. "When the high constable gets here tell him I've gone down to Arnott."

At one time the Toronto-Sydenham Road had ended at Arnott. Early settlers had been forced to use sideroads which were nothing more than rutted paths through the bush. Eventually the Toronto-Sydenham Road had been extended to Chatsworth where it joined the Garafraxa Road from Durham. The combined road took travelers north to the Port of Owen Sound.

Travelling southeast from Chatsworth it was another twenty minutes to Arnott, the next siding down the C.P.R. line before Holland Centre. The train didn't actually stop in Arnott. It slowed long enough to snag the mailbag off a tall pole, or to toss out a bag for the local post office. The post office itself was inside the Arnott General Store. That's where we headed. I tied Scotty up outside, stomped the snow off my boots onto the front steps, and went in.

Another circle of men sitting around another stove smoking more pipes. This time I was even more tempted to stay. A hard ride atop Scotty had done nothing to help my catalogue of injuries. I was cold and I hurt all over. I took my coat off and hung it with the others on hooks near the stove which felt warm enough to be glowing. I picked a tin cup off a shelf behind the stovepipe and poured myself a coffee from the pot on top.

At the dry goods counter the shopkeeper was measuring flour from a large bag into smaller ones. Jars of pickled eggs, sweet pickles, jerky and sausages lined the counter. The coffee was good.

"Haven't seen you around here before," the shopkeeper smiled.

"You may see me again. This coffee is good. Know everyone around here, do ya?"

"Sooner or later I see most of the local folks."

"Then you're just the man I need to talk to."

"Where you from?"

"Owen Sound."

He dropped his measuring scoop into the big bag of flour. "You rode down here today from Owen Sound?"

"Yes."

"Hey, Lester," he called to the group of men by the fire. Three of the dozen or so men looked our way. "Not you Lester. You either Lester. I mean Lester."

I heard no difference in his enunciation of the names, but two of the men went back to the muttered conversation. A fat man in greasy coveralls continued looking our way.

"This fella rode all the way here from Owen Sound." Lester guffawed and the story spread around the room. Soon they were all laughing.

"What's so funny?" I asked when things got a little quieter.

"Mister," one of the Lesters said. "No one visits Arnott ever. Most especially not in winter." This sent them into further paroxysms of laughter.

"I'm looking for Ken and Nadine Carr."

The mood in the room changed in a blink. Suspicious, the storekeeper asked, "What do you want them for?"

A man with a wooden leg got up from the fire and left in a hurry.

"I followed them from Owen Sound to Chatsworth. Someone told me they live around here."

The group was silent. The storekeeper regarded me through eyes that had narrowed down to slits.

"Like I said. What do you want them for?"

I heard voices outside and the sound of three feet and a peg leg pounding up the wooden front steps of the store. The door burst open. A portly grey haired man stood in the doorway, wiping his hands on a towel.

"I'm Ken Carr. What I want to know is, who are you?"

The man with the wooden leg followed him through the door. Carrying a shotgun.

CHAPTER THIRTY THREE

You could have heard a pin drop. The man who had called himself Ken Carr took the gun and addressed his partner.

"Pat him down Peg Leg." The second man ran his hands over me. It was no surprise when he found the .45. Nor was it a surprise he missed the .32 in my boot. Not many thought to look there.

"Did you say Peg Leg?" I asked. "Peg Leg Murray? The barn builder?" He looked at me as though I'd asked him to perform an indecent act.

"How'd ya know that?"

"Everyone knows about Peg Leg Murray the one-legged barn builder. You build the best barns in Grey County." He beamed.

"All that's fine and good," Ken Carr said, "but who the hell are you?"

"If you'll reach into my coat pocket my identification is there."

"Careful, Peg Leg," Ken said from behind him. "It could be a trick."

"Mister," I said, "I won't be playing any tricks as long as you've got that ten gauge pointed at my belly." There was more nervous laughter.

"My name is D.B. Murphy. I'm a private cop from Owen Sound. Anyone been up to the city this week?" There were no takers. It was the middle of winter. There were still chores to be done. No one wanted to travel in the kind of weather I'd been forced to ride in.

"No one. Well I'm going to give you my theory," I addressed my remarks in the direction of Carr but spoke loudly enough for all to hear. "I would guess you have a relative, probably a daughter, named Nadine. Her identification and yours were stolen sometime during the past week." A collective gasp was followed by the buzz of muted conversation.

"I'll tell you how I knew that." I gave them the short version of events in Owen Sound. Some of them had heard of Everett Hall. Some had even heard of his death. All of them had heard of Ken and Nadine Carr, members of the Carr family who had lived in Arnott all their lives. Only one fellow knew of the pair I was looking for. There was much general guffawing about the role that Ken Carr played in the whole affair.

"They're staying in a place north of the tower," Peg Leg said. "I only know because of the big wind we had in January. Old man Cruickshank had me go up there and fix up the barn a bit."

"The tower?"

"Half a mile northeast of here. The highest hill around. Tower on it stands one hundred and forty-seven feet high. On a clear day you can see Georgian Bay at Collingwood and Owen Sound."

"Who told you that Peg?" another man shouted. The rest of them laughed.

"Climbed up and seen it myself," he replied.

"On a wooden leg?"

"Naw, it's dead weight. I left it at the bottom."

The room broke up in laughter. Most of the men went back to the fire, picking up conversations or starting new ones.

"What's the tower for?" I asked.

"Something to do with the army," someone said.

"Is not," another man interjected.

"It's got something to do with some kind of surveying."

"So, when I see it…?"

"Cruickshank place is just the other side of it."

"The county constable is on his way down here from Chatsworth," I said.

"The county constable?" Several heads perked up. I'd wager there was more than one blind pig producing moonshine in Arnott.

"This isn't about the Temperance Act. Don't worry. You'll like him," I said to Peg. "He's an amputee too."

"What's he got? Wooden leg like me? Wooden arm? What?"

"You know, that's a good question. Why don't you ask him?" He gave me a strange look then handed back my Colt.

"Thanks," I downed the cold coffee that remained in my cup. "I think I'm going to need it."

The storm was letting up as Scotty and I pounded up the third concession of Holland Township. The dog had been sitting beside Scotty when I came out. Now it was scouting ahead of us, checking the way.

I'm not sure if it was the cold or Ken Carr's betrayal, but I was tired of the whole investigation. I just wanted it to be over. I was cranky. Angry with myself for believing Carr. Now the case was about more than money. It was personal.

I unslung the long gun the Lugan had sent along. It was a Ross .303. I knew because I'd seen one like it in The Hudson's Bay mailorder catalogue. I hoped they performed better than the Ross rifles the infantry had been stuck with during the war. Made for gentlemen's sport, not the dirty work of war, those Rosses could get jammed by the smallest grain of sand.

The Lugan's was a target shooting model. Six shots in the clip. It was accurate up to twelve hundred yards. If you could see that far.

Scotty and I crossed the county road and continued north down a long hill and up the other side. I could see the tower at the top. The dog had found something interesting to sniff and dropped behind.

We crested the hill and stopped. The tower was across a field just at the edge of a bush. It was a hundred or so yards away. Thirty yards from me was the pair I was seeking. They came to a very sudden and surprised stop in the middle of the road when they spotted me coming towards them.

CHAPTER THIRTY FOUR

I threw the Ross to my shoulder. The thimbleriggers turned tail and rode straight across the field towards the tower. I fired off a round. In my hurry I missed them both by a country mile which was good, since that was my plan. With the second shot I took more time. I sighted carefully and let my breath out slowly. At the bottom of my exhalation I squeezed the trigger and put a bullet right over the head of Carr's horse. The animal screamed and threw Carr. He was up in a flash and running, a black duffel clutched in his left hand, a gun in his right.

I quickly looked around but there was no sign of Nadine coming back to pick him up. She headed straight past the tower and over the brow of the hill into the woods. I'd track her down when I was finished with him.

Carr, or whoever he was, went straight to the tower and started climbing.

When I got close enough I saw the whole thing was constructed of wood. Each corner was made of pine logs with the bark stripped off. Wooden crosspieces nailed across the outside passed for steps. At the bottom of the tower the uprights were easily thirty feet apart, narrowing as they went up. Fifteen feet from the top there was a platform. A second smaller platform was ten feet higher. A five-foot rail surrounded it, creating an open air observation deck high above the field.

I dismounted and strode to the corner Carr was climbing. He was more than halfway up and moving fast. I wondered if I should just wait for him to come down. It's not like there was anywhere for him to go. I wasn't crazy about heights either. Then I thought how easy it would be for him to shoot me once he got to the first platform and looked down. I had to move fast if I wanted to catch him.

I dropped the .303. There was no way I could carry it and climb. I pulled my pistol out. I could manage it. I was younger and moved up the ladder more quickly than Carr. So I wasn't far behind him when he got to the top. As I expected, he laid down on the first platform and looked out over the edge. I was only twenty feet away and fired two quick rounds with the Colt. His head ducked back in. I climbed the last few rungs and stopped just below the platform. There was no way to determine whether he'd gone up. My gut told me he had.

I peeked over the edge at a vacant plank floor, pulled myself up, and gained the illusion of ground which made me feel a lot better. Until the shooting started.

I heard the roar of Carr's gun and saw the sky through a hole that appeared simultaneously in the ceiling. My stomach dropped as I recognized the sound of the gun. It was a Webley and Scott .455. That could only mean one thing. Ken Carr had stolen my gun. And if that was true, then he had also been the one who had followed me and assaulted me, and was partners with the man I had killed.

Another roar and the hole in the ceiling was much closer. He was walking in a straight line towards the tower leg I'd climbed. I took aim with the .45 and fired two rounds at the place where I guessed he'd be standing. He yelled then muttered some curses and fired two more shots down at me.

"What's your real name?" I fired two more shots and changed my position.

On one side of my platform there was a ladder leading up through a hole in the platform above. In a roundabout way I had to get there. Without getting my head blown off.

His next two shots blew holes through both platforms. In the exact spot I'd been sitting. "Sucker," he said in a low voice.

I crept to the foot of the ladder.

"I'm gonna take that money." I pumped two rounds through the opening, then quickly moved to the leg which I guessed would be behind his position.

Sharp reports indicated three more rounds. Carr was standing at the opening firing wildly in all directions. He still expected me to be near the stairs. I had the element of surprise.

"Peek-a-boo," I shouted at his back. He wheeled, but didn't get the Webley high enough to fire.

"Uh-uh," I said, warning with my .45 not to bother trying. He stopped mid motion.

"Drop it and back away." Sweating despite the cold Carr seemed to consider the situation for a moment, weighing the odds. He decided against a gunfight and dropped the pistol. I was glad. He had more bullets left than I did.

I pulled myself onto the platform and stood to face him.

"Well, you sure fooled me."

"It wasn't just you. I fooled everyone."

"Doesn't it ever bother you? Lying and stealing?"

"No, it's easy," he said. "People want to believe they can have something for nothing."

"When you're really selling them nothing for something. Now they want to kill you. Look what happened to your partner. What was his name?"

"Everett Hall."

"Sure. Like your name is Ken Carr. I just met Ken Carr in Arnott. You aren't him."

"True."

"There's something I've been wondering."

"What?"

"You held me up three times," I began. His look of surprise confirmed that he didn't know I'd figured it out. "Why did you attack Miss Armstrong and I when we were on our way to Balaclava? You must have known we didn't have the money."

"To get you moving. I wanted my money but I didn't want to wait around in Owen Sound forever."

"Why didn't you hold me up when we had the money? At the train station."

"You had company. I couldn't be sure of succeeding. Besides, having you hand it to me was a lot more satisfying." I could have punched him in the mouth. I didn't. He knew he'd gotten to me. The smirk was a dead giveaway.

"You know," I started, "when I got into this it really was just for the money. I didn't care about Everett Hall or his killers. Now I've got you and the money. And I can see you're the kind of guy who needs to be put away."

"Me? But you've only been employed to retrieve the money. Suppose I give it to you? What then?"

"The difference between me and the other suckers is they can't do anything about you. I can."

"Then I shall have to dispose of you too."

"Just like Nosey Parker."

"It wasn't me who killed Parker," he said with an evil smile. "I was at The Manjuris with you."

"Who killed him?"

"Who killed Nosey Parker? What an interesting question."

"With an interesting answer, I'm sure. Cough it up."

"Shall I tell him?" he asked, looking past me, "or will you?"

I'm fast, but not that fast.

"Drop it dick," Nadine Carr ordered, "or I'll kill you just like I killed Nosey." She was standing at the corner of the platform, having pulled the same trick on me that I had pulled on her partner. I let the .45 drop to the floor. Carr smiled and planted a right cross on my chin. It wasn't much of a punch but I went down on one knee for effect anyway. It took me awfully close to the edge. The woman climbed onto the platform. She picked up my gun and pocketed hers.

"Thanks baby," Carr said. "That was a tight spot I was in."

"Ten years ago you'd have never gotten into trouble like this." She was angry and he knew it.

"Baby, listen…"

"You listen," she said. "This whole job has been one botch after another. First Ernie almost blows it. I had to take care of him."

"Who is Ernie?" I asked. I was having trouble keeping all the names straight.

"Hall," she spat at me.

"It was you? You're Uncle Marty's man in black?"

"That fool on the horse was your uncle? He did me a favour, shoving Ernie into the river like that."

"You gave Ernie the works?" Carr said disbelievingly. "After all the years the three of us have been on the road together?"

"I didn't hear you complaining much when our shares got bigger. Then gumshoe here saved me the trouble by blasting Walter on the way to Leith. Seems to me you're the only thing standing between me and all that money. Why don't you do something right for a change and toss the bag over here?"

"You're double-crossing me? Why you two timing…" He held the bag of money in front of himself and backed away from her. He was perilously close to the edge.

"C'mon Jimmy," she said moving towards him. "Gimme the dough." I didn't think she cared much whether Jimmy went over the side or not. It was the money she wanted. My chance came as she got close to me. I slid a leg out and nearly tripped her. But not quite. It didn't matter because when she stumbled she pulled the trigger. The .45 calibre slug tore straight through the bag and into Jimmy's chest. Soundlessly he went over the edge.

CHAPTER THIRTY FIVE

In all the excitement I'd managed to get the .32 out of my boot. It was the reason I had gone to my knees in the first place. I held it in my right hand, which was out of her sight.

"Any last words?" she asked.

"You're some kind of businesswoman."

"Is that it? Aren't you going to beg me or something?"

"Listen, sister, I've been in tighter spots than this."

"Have you?"

"I'm not even worried yet."

"Didn't you see what I did to Jimmy?"

"I saw."

"Well?"

"You're out of bullets." The slide on the automatic was back, indicating an empty clip.

"What?"

"You used the last bullet in that gun when you aired out your friend. That's why the slide is back. Go ahead. Pull the trigger."

She tried and confirmed what I'd said. The .455 was at her feet. The .32 she'd been carrying was in a pocket.

By then my gun was in view. There wasn't a move she could make.

"Keep your hands where I can see them," I said, getting to my feet. "So you killed Hall?"

She smiled and batted her eyes at me. I had the drop on her, so she was turning on the charm. "Jimmy was a gentleman. He couldn't kill anyone."

"He just tried to kill me."

"He was keeping you busy until I could double back."

I stepped towards her and reached out to grab her wrist. She took a step back and stumbled towards the hole. Time slowed to a standstill. Too late, I noticed her hand inside her coat pocket. There was the pop of a small calibre weapon and a smoking hole opened in the fabric. The impact was instantaneous. My right arm went dead and I dropped my gun. She disappeared. I felt rather than heard her impact. I looked down at my jacket. There was a small hole and some blood.

Using my left hand I opened my jacket, undid my shirt and tried to get a look at the wound. My undershirt had soaked up a lot of blood. I couldn't see the hole. There was no way I was going to take my jacket off.

There was an awful scream from below. I bent down and picked up all the guns one by one, then went over to the top of the ladder. Nadine was lying on the platform beneath me, one leg grotesquely twisted beneath her body.

"Help me," she whined piteously then seemed to pass out. My arm was still numb. It was probably a good thing.

I took the ladder slowly, hanging onto gun and rung with just one hand. I decided to take a look at her leg while she was out. I put the gun in my pocket and turned her onto her side. Shattered below the knee. I didn't know what to do.

"Help me." The words were whispered, barely conscious.

"I'll have to climb down and get help."

"No. Don't leave me. Cold…" She did another fade. There was no way I could leave her. The snow had started again. Exposed on the tower platform she wouldn't last long.

The feeling was coming back into my right am. The shoulder was bad but my hand was working. Using the butt of my gun as a hammer I pried two rungs off the ladder. I grabbed her leg with both hands and slowly brought it around closer to where it was supposed to be. I lashed the pieces of wood on either side of her leg using pieces of lining torn from the inside of her coat.

Piggyback was the only way I could think to get down. When she came around again I got her up on my back, her arms around my neck. Her leg hung free below me as we climbed down one of the legs. My right wasn't much use, but some was better than none at all. Hand over hand we descended, one painful rung at a time. They were slippery with ice and snow.

Twenty or so feet down we found Carr hanging upside down from one of the supports that held the tower together. He was definitely dead.

"Where's the money? Can you see the money?" Her voice was anxious, whining. "I'll split it with you. Fifty-fifty. That's thirty thousand each."

"Thirty?"

"Oh yes. Ernie was busy while he was in Owen Sound."

"Where did he find the time?"

"Every word out of his mouth was a game. He never stopped. Can you see the money yet?"

"It's down there."

The bag had fallen to the next set of support beams. It looked as though it had caught and torn in the area of the bullet hole. A cash squall had hit the field below.

"No! No! Hurry," the woman screamed in my ear. "We have to hurry. The money! It's blowing away."

"Neither one of us is in the right kind of shape for chasing after it." I slipped on a rung. Her grip tightened. I managed to hold on but not before bashing my shin a good one.

We were about twenty feet from the ground. Scotty, the dog and her horse were all within view, milling around. I continued, eager to get my feet on the ground. I was starting to feel really bad. Lightheaded and weak. Like I was going to pass out. My load was getting heavier and her grip was getting tighter. Maybe she'd passed out. I was having trouble breathing.

"Loo…loosen your grip!" I wheezed through the pinhole opening in my throat.

There was no response. Ten feet to go and darkness was creeping in at the edges of my vision. My legs were rubbery and once I nearly lost it completely. I stumbled down the last few rungs and fell to my knees on the ground. Behind me the girl screamed. Her grip didn't loosen.

It was dusk in my head and stars were beginning to come out. I tried to flail her off but it was too late. I had nothing left. I tipped over and landed on my side. Far away I heard the sound of a growl. Followed by a scream.

CHAPTER THIRTY SIX

My face was being licked. I was still on the ground. My shoulder was a mass of hot fire and pain. I opened my eyes. The dog wagged his tail furiously and nuzzled my face.

"Lucky for me you were here."

There was movement in the periphery of my vision. The dog was off, snarling and yipping. He sounded vicious. Turning my head I saw the woman. She was about ten feet away, trying to crawl to the horses. Her broken leg dragged uselessly across behind her. The dog positioned himself between her and the horse, his teeth bared. A low growl sounded deep in his chest.

"I wouldn't try it if I were you."

"D. B.! Hey D.B.!" Oddball was somewhere nearby. I didn't think I had the energy to put a new clip in the .45. I pulled the Webley out of my pocket and boomed a round into the air.

In less than a minute he rode up to us with his gun drawn.

"You're a little late," I said.

"Jeez, D.B. you're a mess."

"So is she. Broken leg. Put the cuffs on her. I'll explain while we ride back."

He walked over to the woman. The dog returned to my side.

"See that flea-bitten mutt is still hangin' around you," Oddball said as he put the bracelets on her.

"Lucky."

"Huh?"

"His name is Lucky."

"Thought he wasn't your dog."

"I was wrong."

"She can't ride," he said, gesturing at the woman. "I'll have to build a travois."

"A what?"

"You know. A stretcher type affair."

"I know what a travois is. You just surprise me sometimes."

"Here's something to occupy your time." He handed me a bottle of whisky and the Ross rifle from my saddle. "Keep an eye on her."

While he wandered off I used my teeth to pull the cork stopper out of the bottle. I spit it to the ground and poured a generous amount of the burning liquid down my throat. It quenched my thirst. Made me feel much warmer. The pain receded.

I gave Lucky a scratch between the ears. He liked it.

Oddball came back with two long poles of slippery elm. He pulled a spare parka off the back of his saddle and turned the sleeves inside out. Then he buttoned the jacket and slid the poles through the arms. Oddball loaded the woman onto the contraption, and cuffed her to the poles. Then he helped me onto Scotty and we started back.

The next few hours are pretty hazy. I remember being back at the General Store in Arnott. On a stretcher in the back of a logging sledge. Buried in blankets. The cold stars. The bright hospital. Wheeling into the surgery. Doc Soames peering at me over his mask. Darkness.

★★★

"It's lucky they could fit another bed in," Uncle Marty's voice was saying. I opened my eyes. Hank was in the bed across from me. He was staring.

"He's awake," he said to someone beside me. I looked over. Uncle Marty smiled and waved from his bed.

"Am I in hell?"

They both laughed. It sounded like the best thing I'd ever heard.

The noise drew the attention of those in the hall. There was a tap at the door and Lori came in.

"Hey, hi! You're awake." She crossed the room and kissed me on the lips. It was the best kiss I'd ever had.

"How long have I been here?"

"Two days."

"Am I in bad shape?"

"No. You just needed sleep."

"Doc says the bullet missed everything," Marty said. "Right Hank?"

"Right," was the gruff response from the other side of the room.

"How long am I going to be in here?"

"At least a week," Lori said with a mischievous wink.

There was another knock at the door.

"He awake?" Tom Carson had arrived.

"Not if it's Rennet. Or Carp."

"You sure got things wrapped up nicely," Tom said pulling a chair up at the end of the bed.

"How do you mean?"

"You cracked that thimblerig open right good and proper."

"Where's the woman?"

"Just down the hall."

"I'd keep an eye on her if I were you."

"A constable and one of the matrons from the jail are with her. She was quite a customer."

"Brother, you said a mouthful."

"She sounds cold-blooded," Lori said to Carson.

"She's singin' like a bluebird now. Says all four of them have been around since Veterans Day. Midge McCoul, that's her real name. She and this Jimmy Lane were waiting for Hall to call them to Owen Sound to close out the scheme. Get this, they really were coming to town as the American Deputy Vice Consul and his daughter. On their way up on the train they learned Hall was dead. They came anyway, and changed their story to make it seem like they'd come because an American had been killed."

"They didn't have American identification." I pointed out.

"They didn't think anyone would check to see if they really were from the consulate. Of course, no one did."

"What does that say about Owen Sounders? Are we really so gullible?"

"Nosey Parker put it in the paper. Everyone assumed it was true. Until Parker checked it himself and learned the truth. But he didn't live long enough to tell anyone," Tom replied.

"Hall had American identification."

"Ernie Jacobs was his real name. We found a dozen or so stolen identities in the bag that had the money in it."

"How is Van?" I asked.

"Okay," Lori said. "In fact, he's staying at the house for a couple of days until he can ride."

"How did Carr get my gun?" I asked Carson.

"Remember the guy you shot out by Leith? He was their partner. Walter."

"I know, but why did Carr help me chase Walter when I saw him in Hall's hotel room?"

"They'd just learned Hall was dead. They get off the train and their other partner is being chased. Carr joined in to see if there was an angle he could use. There was," Tom said.

"She tell you all this?"

"She doesn't want to hang."

"She will. I saw her shoot one partner just after she admitted killing the other. And what about the others who were involved?"

Marty and Hank had been waiting for this.

"Others?" Tom asked. "What do you mean?"

"Everett Hall and his many causes of death."

"Everett Hall never died. He lives in Port Huron, Michigan. Ernie Jacobs died. None of the other injuries to his body were fatal, and there's no way to prove beyond a doubt who caused them. He drowned. Case closed. No one will miss him."

I raised my eyebrows. It hurt. Marty and Hank were beaming at one another across the room like a couple of idiots.

"Where were Midge McCoul and Jimmy Lane going when I caught up with them north of Arnott?"

"They didn't expect you to catch up so quickly, so they'd stopped to pick up their things. They were heading over to Chesley to catch a C.N. train. To throw off pursuers."

"How much of the money flew away?"

"If it goes to seed, there'll be cash crops all over Holland Township."

"What about my pay?"

"Council voted on it. Agreed unanimously to give you Everett Hall's car."

A car? What would I tell Scotty?

"Great," I said. "I've always wanted a McLaughlin Buick. But what about money?"

"The Costello boys confessed everything."

"The coal yards paid up," Lori added.

"What about the rest? The ten per cent of Hall's take?"

"I'm sure some of it will turn up," Tom said. "In the spring."

With that he left, and it was just the four of us in the room again. "Well there you go boys, in the clear."

Thanks to you Danny," Uncle Marty said. "Isn't that right Hank?" Hank didn't answer right away. The silence stretched out and became uncomfortable. Finally he cleared his throat.

"Thanks," he said. "I'm sorry."

"Me too," I said.

It was a start. We had a whole week to turn it into something more. A whole lifetime.

"Well, well, well," Doc Soames said, coming into the room. "And how is everyone today?"

Moving from one bed to another, Doc checked out his patients. I was last, but the stethoscope didn't seem any warmer.

"You're lucky," he said. "The bullet missed your lung."

"I heard."

"You might want to try a less hazardous occupation. You're gonna be fine." He finished his examination and dragged the sheet back over me. As almost an afterthought he pulled a thermometer out and shook it down. Then he bent over and placed it in Lori's mouth.

"What's this?" I asked.

"Didn't you know she hasn't been feeling well?"

"Sure. She said it was nothing serious."

Doc laughed and checked her pulse. "It's not. Though, there are folks who might consider five Murphys in one room a serious problem."

Math had never been my strong subject.

"That's right," Lori smiled, as the truth finally hit me. "Daddy."

THE END